Praise for
The Kingdoms of Thorn and Bone

The Blood Knight

"[A] sophisticated and intelligent high fantasy epic."
—*Publishers Weekly*

"Enthralling." —*Locus*

"Well-written magical duels ante up the action in this formidable precursor to the final volume of the series."
—*Cinescape*

The Charnel Prince

"There is adventure and intrigue, swordplay and dark sorcery aplenty." —*Realms of Fantasy*

"Keyes's world is rich, detailed, and always believable; the twisty plot is delightful and frightening in turns." —*Locus*

"Strong world building and superior storytelling."
—*Library Journal*

The Briar King

"A wonderful tale . . . It crackles with suspense and excitement from start to finish."
—TERRY BROOKS, *New York Times* bestselling author
of the Shannara series

"A graceful, artful tale from a master storyteller . . . [The novel] starts off with a bang, spinning a snare of terse imagery and compelling characters that grips tightly and never lets up."
—ELIZABETH HAYDON, bestselling author
of *Prophecy: Child of Earth*

"Epic high fantasy . . . Keyes mixes cultures, religions, institutions, and languages with rare skill."
—*Publishers Weekly* (starred review)

By Greg Keyes

The Chosen of the Changeling
THE WATERBORN
THE BLACKGOD

The Age of Unreason
NEWTON'S CANNON
A CALCULUS OF ANGELS
EMPIRE OF UNREASON
THE SHADOWS OF GOD

The Psi Corps Trilogy
BABYLON 5: DARK GENESIS
BABYLON 5: DEADLY RELATIONS
BABYLON 5: FINAL RECKONING

Star Wars®: The New Jedi Order
EDGE OF VICTORY I: CONQUEST
EDGE OF VICTORY II: REBIRTH
THE FINAL PROPHECY

The Kingdoms of Thorn and Bone
THE BRIAR KING
THE CHARNEL PRINCE
THE BLOOD KNIGHT
THE BORN QUEEN

The BLOOD KNIGHT

BOOK THREE OF THE KINGDOMS OF THORN AND BONE

GREG KEYES

BALLANTINE BOOKS · NEW YORK

The Blood Knight is a work of fiction. Names, characters, places, and incidents are the products of the author's imagination or are used fictitiously. Any resemblance to actual events, locales, or persons, living or dead, is entirely coincidental.

2007 Del Rey Books Mass Market Edition

Copyright © 2006 by J. Gregory Keyes
Excerpt from *The Born Queen* copyright © 2007 by J. Gregory Keyes

Published in the United States by Del Rey Books, an imprint of The Random House Publishing Group, a division of Random House, Inc., New York.

DEL REY is a registered trademark and the Del Rey colophon is a trademark of Random House, Inc.

This book contains an excerpt from the forthcoming book *The Born Queen* by Greg Keyes. This excerpt has been set for this edition only and may not reflect the final content of the forthcoming edition.

Originally published in hardcover in the United States by Del Rey Books, an imprint of The Random House Publishing Group, a division of Random House, Inc., in 2006.

Map illustration by Kirk Caldwell

ISBN 978-0-345-44072-3

Printed in the United States of America

www.delreybooks.com

OPM   9   8   7   6   5   4   3

For my son,

John Edward Arch Keyes

Welcome, Archer

PROLOGUE

✢

IN THE CHAMBER
OF THE WAURM

SMILING, Robert Dare offered Muriele a rose.

"Keep it," she suggested. "Perhaps it will improve your smell."

Robert sighed, stroking the small black beard that sharpened his naturally fine features. Then he retracted both hand and flower, allowing them to rest on his breast, fixing his dark gaze on Muriele.

He looked far older than the twenty winters he had spent in the world, and for the barest instant she felt a distant sympathy for this man who had murdered her husband and daughters, for what he had become.

Whatever that was, however, it wasn't human, and her sympathy was dragged off by a tide of revulsion.

"As charming as ever, my dear," Robert said evenly.

His gaze shifted slightly to the other woman who stood with them in the room as if he were a cat trying to keep track of two mice. "And how does the beautiful Lady Berrye fare today?"

Alis Berrye—Muriele's maid and protector—favored Robert with a cordial smile. "I am very well, Your Highness."

"Yes, I can see that," Robert said. He stepped near and lifted his right hand to stroke Alis' russet locks. The girl didn't flinch, except perhaps around the eyes. Indeed, she held very still. Muriele imagined she might react thus to an adder poised to strike.

"In fact, you have quite the bloom on your cheeks," he went on. "It's no wonder my dear deceased brother was so taken with you. So young—so full of health and vigor, so smooth and firm. No, age hasn't begun even to breathe on you yet, Alis."

That bait was meant for Muriele, but she would not rise to it. Yes, Alis had been one of her husband's mistresses—the youngest, as far as she knew—but since his death she had proved herself a useful and loyal friend. A strange thing, but there it was.

The girl lowered her azure eyes demurely but did not answer.

"Robert," Muriele said, interrupting the silence, "I am your prisoner and therefore at your mercy, but I hope I've made it plain that I am *not* afraid of you. You are a kinslaughterer, an usurper, and something far worse for which I have no name. I deem you will not be surprised when I say I do not enjoy your company.

"So if you could please get on with whatever degradation you have planned for me, I would much appreciate it."

Robert's smile froze on his face. Then he shrugged and dropped the flower to the floor.

"The rose is not from me, anyhow," he explained. "Have it as you will. Please take a seat."

His diffident wave indicated several chairs surrounding a thick oaken table. The furniture rested on carved talons, in keeping with the monstrous theme of the room, a little-used chamber hidden deep in the windowless interior of the castle known as the Waurmsal.

Two large tapestries hung on the walls. One depicted a knight wearing antique chain mail and a conical helm, wielding an improbably broad and lengthy sword against a waurm with scales picked in gold, silver, and bronze threads. Its snakelike body coiled around the borders of the weaving, flowing toward the center where the knight stood, and there lifted deadly claws and gaped a mouth filled with iron teeth dripping venom. So well crafted was the textile that at any moment it seemed as if the great serpent would slither out of it and onto the floor.

The second tapestry seemed much older. Its colors were faded, and in places the fiber appeared worn through. It was woven in a simpler, less realistic style and portrayed a man standing beside a dead waurm. The figure was so austerely imagined that she could not be certain it portrayed the same knight, whether he wore armor or merely a jerkin of odd design. The weapon he held was much more modest, more a knife than a sword. He had one hand lifted to his mouth.

"You've been in here before?" Robert asked as she reluctantly took a seat.

"Once," she said. "Long ago. William received a lord from Skhadiza here."

"When I discovered this chamber—I suppose I was about nine—I found it all dusty," he said, "scarcely fit to sit in—and yet so charming."

"Utterly," Muriele said drily, regarding a grotesque reliquary that stood against one wall. It was mostly wooden, carved somewhat in the form of a man with arms held outstretched. In each clawed hand he held a gold-plated human skull. Instead of a Mannish face, he had a snake's head with ram's horns, and his legs were very short, ending in birdlike claws. His belly was a glass-doored cabinet behind which she could make out a narrow, slightly curved cone of ivory about the length of her arm.

"That wasn't here before," she said.

"No," Robert agreed. "I bought that from a Sefry merchant a few years ago. That, my dear, is the tooth of a waurm."

He said it like a little boy who had found something interesting and expected to be rewarded with special attention.

When none came, he rolled his eyes and rang a little bell. A maidservant appeared, bearing a tray. She was a young woman with dark hair and a single pox mark on her face. Her eyes had dark circles beneath them, and her lips were pressed together so tightly as to be pallid.

She set goblets of wine before each of them, left, and then returned with a platter of sweets: candied pears, butter biscuits, brandied cakes, sweet cheese fritters in honey and—Muriele's favorite—maiden moons, saccharine turnovers filled with almond paste.

"Please, please," Robert said, taking a drink of his wine and gesturing broadly at the treats.

Muriele regarded her wine for a moment, then took a sip. Robert had no particular reason to poison her at the moment, and if ever he did, there wasn't anything she could do about it. Everything she ate and drank in her prison tower came ultimately through him.

The drink was surprising, not wine at all but something with a honey taste.

"There," Robert said, setting his goblet on the table. "Lady Berrye, is it to your liking?"

"It's very sweet," she allowed.

"A gift," Robert said. "It is an extraordinarily fine mead from Haurnrohsen—a present from Berimund of Hansa."

"Berimund is very generous lately," Muriele remarked.

"And he has a high regard for you," Robert said.

"Obviously," she replied, unwilling to curb her sarcasm.

Robert drank again, then took the cup in both hands, turning it slowly between his palms. "I noticed you enjoying the tapestries," he said, peering down into his mead. "Do you know the man depicted here?"

"I do not."

"Hairugast Waurmslauht, the first of the house of Reiksbaurg. Some called him the blodrauhtin, or Blood Knight, because they say that after slaying the monster, he drank the waurm's blood and mingled it with his own. He thus partook of its strengths, as did his every descendant. And for that reason the Reiksbaurgs have remained strong."

"They weren't so strong when your grandfather drove them out of Crotheny," Muriele noted.

Robert wagged a finger at her. "But they were strong when they took the throne away from *your* Lierish ancestors."

"That was a long time ago."

Again he shrugged. "Hansa is mightier now than it was then. It's all a great dance, Muriele, a red duchess pavane.

The emperor of Crotheny was Lierish, then Hansan; now he's of Virgenyan descent. But wherever his blood comes from, he *is* the emperor of Crotheny. The throne remains."

"What are you suggesting, Robert?"

He leaned onto his elbows and regarded her with an almost comically serious expression.

"We stand on the brink of chaos, Muriele. Monsters from our darkest Black Marys roam freely across our countryside, terrorizing our villages. Nations gird for war, and our throne, seeming weak, presents a target few can ignore. The Church sees heresy everywhere and hangs whole villages—which seems hardly productive to me, but they are, after all, among our few allies."

"Nevertheless, you are *not* going to give the throne over to Marcomir of Hansa," Muriele asserted confidently. "You've worked too hard to steal it for yourself."

"Yes, that would be silly, wouldn't it?" he agreed. "No. But I shall do what kings often do to secure their power. I shall marry.

"And so, dear sister-in-law, shall you," he added.

"I've made myself quite clear," Muriele replied. "Murder me if you want, but I will not marry you."

He shrugged and shrugged again, as if trying to shake something off his back. "No, indeed," he said wryly. "I can see that you won't do that. The knife you thrust into my heart was a distinct clue that you didn't take kindly to my proposal."

"How fortunate for you it no longer beats, your heart."

He leaned back and closed his eyes. "Must you always quibble about such things?" he said. "Who is alive, who is dead? You think you are better off merely because you have a beating heart. How pretentious of you.

"And—if I must say it—how ungenerous."

"You are entirely mad," Muriele opined.

Robert grinned and opened his eyes again.

"That, at least, is a familiar complaint. But please allow me to return to my original point, won't you. In fact, I wasn't renewing my own proposition—one stabbing from you is quite enough for me. No, you shall marry Berimund Fram Reiksbaurg, the heir to the throne of Hansa. And I shall marry his sister Alfswan. Between us, we will secure *my* throne."

Muriele laughed bitterly.

"I think not, Robert," she said. "I've rejected Berimund's offer once already."

"Not really," Robert pointed out. "Actually, your son Charles rejected that proposal because, after all, he was king at the time and the prerogative fell solely to him. Of course, Charles is a half-wit, and you were entirely in control of his actions.

"But he isn't king any longer," Robert continued. "I am. And as per *my* prerogative, I have given your hand to Berimund. The wedding will take place in a month's time."

The air seemed denser suddenly—almost like water. Muriele fought the urge to lift her head above the floodline.

Robert could do this thing. He *would* do it, and there was absolutely nothing she could do about that.

"It will never happen," she finally managed, hoping she still sounded defiant.

"Well, we shall see," Robert responded cheerfully. Then he turned. "Lady Berrye, is something the matter?"

Muriele followed Robert's gaze and noticed that Alis did look suddenly pale. Her eyes—no, her pupils—seemed very large.

"It's nothing," Alis averred.

"I forgot to ask," Robert said, turning his wrist to include them both. "Have you had a chance to reflect upon the musical performance we were subjected to last wihnaht? The lustspell presented by our dear Cavaor Ackenzal?"

Muriele forced a smile.

"How that must nag at you—to have yourself revealed for what you are, in front of the entire kingdom, and be helpless to stop it. I daresay Leovigild Ackenzal is a genius."

"I see," Robert mused. "Then you are of the opinion that the villain of the piece was supposed to represent me?"

"You *know* he did, and so does everyone who saw it. How

did Ackenzal manage it? I wonder. Certainly you and the praifec must have kept close watch on him, monitored his script, his score, his rehearsals—and yet *still* he showed you for fools."

"Well," Robert said, "I think the praifec was even more troubled by the performance than I was. In fact, he felt it necessary to question Fralet Ackenzal very closely. Very closely indeed, along with many of the performers."

"That was foolish," Alis said softly, rubbing her forehead.

"Did you say something, Lady Berrye?"

"Yes, Highness. I said the praifec was foolish to torture the composer—and you were foolish to let him. You must know that you need the support of the landwaerden to hold this city against attack. Leovigild Ackenzal was their darling, all the more so after the performance of his wonderful music."

"Hmm," Robert mused. "Lady Berrye, that is a most considered opinion. Such political acumen from someone whom I've long believed to be a simple whore."

"One can be very simple, indeed," Alis said, "and still understand things you do not."

"Well, I suppose that's true," Robert admitted. "In any event, there are ways to regain the trust of the landwaerden, should that be needed. But with Hansa and the holy Church on my side, I don't think the landwaerden will present much of a problem. I need only keep them quiet for another month or so, yes?"

"The Church?" Muriele asked.

"Indeed. The praifec has written to the Fratrex Prismo in z'Irbina, and the fratrex has kindly agreed to send a few troops to help us keep the peace and to prosecute the resacaratum until this throne is secure."

"First Hansa, now the Church. You would give our country to every enemy we have if it would buy you time on the throne. You truly are despicable."

"I didn't realize that you considered the Church our enemy," Robert said blandly. "Praifec Hespero might find fault with that. In fact, he might discover the need to question *you*."

There was the sudden sound of shattering glass.

"Lady Berrye," Robert said, "you've dropped your goblet."

Alis turned unfocused eyes in his direction.

"Saints damn you," she rasped. She tried to stand, but her legs seemed too weak to support her.

Sudden terror stroked through Muriele like a sword. She reached out for Alis. "What have you done to her, Robert?"

Robert fondled his beard.

"I gave her to you as your maid because I thought it would annoy you. But to the contrary, you two actually seem to have cultivated a friendship. It also seems that our dear Alis seduced information from one of your guards and has perhaps done so on other occasions.

"I believe I not only misunderstood Lady Berrye but underestimated her. And so I wonder what other things she might be capable of accomplishing. Doubtless you told her of the secret passages that riddle this castle, if she did not already know of them. Perhaps she has some scheme to spirit you away from me."

He smiled more broadly.

"If so, then she will take her plot with her to Eslen-of-Shadows."

Muriele knelt at Alis' side now, taking her hand. The girl's skin already had a bluish cast, and her arms had begun to convulse. Her fingers were like ice.

"Alis!" Muriele gasped.

"Gallowswort," Alis managed, her voice so faint, Muriele had to lean close. "Knew . . ." She shook, and black spittle came from her mouth. She murmured a few words Muriele did not understand, and Muriele felt a slight heat on her skin. The hairs stood up on her arm.

"Keep safe," Alis hissed. *"Soinmié. Soinmié, Fienden."*

Her breath became more ragged until she seemed to be hiccupping rather than breathing. Then, with a sudden, soundless scream, that stopped, too.

Muriele peered up at Robert, her hatred so strong that she couldn't think of any words that would not belittle it.

"I think I'll put her in the Dare crypt," Robert mused. "Should William's soul ever find its way there, he will be pleased."

He rose then. "The seamstress will come around tomorrow to fit you for your wedding gown," he said pleasantly. "It has been a pleasure visiting with you, Muriele. Good afternoon."

He left her there with Alis, whose flesh was already cold.

PART I

✦

THE WATERS BENEATH THE WORLD

On the stony west shore of Roin Ieniesse, Fren MeqLier met Saint Jeroin the Mariner, and in Saint Jeroin's ship they passed over the western waves through sleet and fog until they came to a bleak shore and a dark forest.

"That is the Wood Beyond the World," Saint Jeroin told him. "Take care that when you step from the boat, your boot does not strike the water. If you but touch the waves, you will forget everything you have ever known."
—FROM Frenn Rey-eise: A Tale of Saint Frenn Told
     on Skern, SACRITOR ROGER BISHOP

The Dark Lady took Alzarez by the hand and pointed at the river.

"Drink from that," she said, "and you will be like the dead, without memory or sin."

Then she pointed to a bubbling spring.

"Drink there, and you will know more than any mortal."

Alzarez looked at both.

"But the river feeds the spring," he observed.
"Of course," the Dark Lady replied.
—FROM *"SA ALZAREZASFILL,"* A HERILANZER
　　FOLKTALE

Ne piberos daz'uturo.
Don't drink the water.
—FROM A VITELLIAN FUNERARY INSCRIPTION

CHAPTER ONE

✛

LOST

Here's my wish;
A man with blood-red lips
With snow-white skin
With blue-black hair
Like a raven's wing.
That's my wish.

ANNE DARE murmured the words to the song, a favorite of hers from when she was younger.

She noticed that her fingers were trembling, and for a moment she felt as if they weren't attached to her but were instead strange worms clinging to her hands.

With blood-red lips . . .

Anne had seen blood before, plenty of it. But never like this, never with such a striking hue, so brilliant against the snow. It was as if she were viewing the true color for the first time rather than the pale counterfeit she had known her whole life.

At the edges it was watered pink, but at its source, where it pulsed into the cold whiteness, it was a thing of utter beauty.

With snow-white skin
With blue-black hair . . .

The man had flesh gone gray and straw-colored hair, nothing like the imagined lover of the song. As she watched, his fingers unclenched from the dagger he'd been holding, and he let go the cares of the world. His eyes went round with wonder as they saw something she could not, beyond the lands of fate. Then he sighed a final steaming breath into the snow.

Somewhere—very far away, it seemed—she heard a hoarse cry and the sound of clashing steel, followed by silence. She detected no motion through the dark trunks of the trees except the continuing light fall of snow.

Something chuffed nearby.

In a daze, Anne turned to find a dappled gray horse regarding her curiously. It looked familiar, and she gasped faintly as she recalled it charging toward her. The snow told that it had stamped all around her, but one trail of hoofprints led in from over a hill, the direction from which it must have come. Part of the way, the prints were accompanied by pink speckles.

The horse had blood in its mane, as well.

She stood shakily, feeling pain in her thigh, shin, and ribs. She turned on her feet to take in the whole of her surroundings, searching for a sign that there was anyone else nearby. But there were only the dead man, the horse, and trees stripped to bark by winter's winds.

Finally she glanced down at herself. She wore a soft red doeskin robe lined with black ermine and beneath that a heavy riding habit. She remembered she'd gotten them back in Dunmrogh.

She remembered the fight there, too, and the death of her first love and first betrayer, Roderick.

She pushed her hand under the hood and felt the curls of her copper hair. It was growing back but was still short from the shearing she'd had in Tero Gallé what seemed like an age ago. So she was missing hours or days, not ninedays, months, or years. But she had still misplaced time, and that frightened her.

She remembered leaving Dunmrogh with her maid Austra, a freewoman named Winna, and thirty-eight men whose company included her Vitellian friend Cazio and her guardian Sir Neil MeqVren. They'd just won a battle, and most were wounded, including Anne herself.

But there had been no time for leisurely recovery. Her father was dead, and her mother the prisoner of an usurper. She'd set out determined somehow to free her mother and reclaim her father's throne. She remembered feeling very certain about the whole thing.

What she didn't know, couldn't remember, was where those friends were and why she wasn't with them. Or, for that matter, who the dead man was, lying at her feet. His throat had been cut; that much was plain enough—it gaped like a second mouth. But how had it happened? Was he friend or foe?

Since she didn't recognize him, she reckoned he was most likely the latter.

She sagged against a tree and closed her eyes, studying the dark pool in her mind, diving into it like a kingfisher.

She'd been riding beside Cazio, and he'd been practicing the king's tongue . . .

"Esno es caldo," Cazio said, catching a snowflake in his hand, eyes wide with wonder.

"Snow is cold," Anne corrected, then saw the set of his lips and realized he'd mispronounced the sentence on purpose.

Cazio was tall and slim, with sharp, foxy features and dark eyes, and when his mouth quirked like that, he was all devil.

"What is *esno* in Vitellian?" she demanded.

"A metal the color of your hair," he said in such a way that she suddenly wondered what his lips would taste like. *Honey? Olive oil?* He'd kissed her before, but she couldn't remember . . .

What a stupid thought.

"*Esno es caldo* is Vitellian for 'copper is hot,' right?" she translated, trying to hide her annoyance. By the way Cazio was grinning now, she knew she certainly was missing something.

"Yes, that's true," Cazio drawled, "if taken literally. But it's a sort of pun. If I were talking to my friend Acameno and said *'fero es caldo,'* it would mean 'iron is hot,' but iron can also mean a sword, and a sword can mean a man's very personal armament, you see, and would be a compliment to his manhood. He would assume I meant *his* iron. And so copper, the softer, prettier metal can also represent—"

"Yes, well," Anne quickly cut in, "that will be enough Vitellian colloquialism for now. After all, you wanted to work on your king's tongue, didn't you?"

He nodded. "Yes, but it's funny to me, that's all, that your word for 'cold' is my word for 'hot.'"

"Yes, and it's even funnier that your word for 'free' is 'lover,'" she countered sarcastically, "considering that one cannot have the second and be the first."

As soon as she saw the look on his face, though, she wished she hadn't spoken.

Cazio immediately raised an interested eyebrow. "*Now* we're onto a topic I approve of," he said. "But, eh—'lover'? *Ne commrenno.* What is 'lover' in the king's tongue?"

"The same as Vitellian *Carilo,*" she replied reluctantly.

"No," Austra said. Anne jumped guiltily, for she had almost forgotten that her maid was riding with them. She glanced over at the younger woman.

"No?"

Austra shook her head. "*Carilo* is what a father calls his daughter—a dear one, a little sweetheart. The word you're looking for is *erenterra.*"

"Ah, I see," Cazio said. He reached over and took Austra's hand and kissed it. "*Erenterra.* Yes, I am approving of this conversation even more with each revelation."

Austra blushed and took her hand back, brushing gilden curls back up into the black hood of her weather cloak.

Cazio turned back toward Anne.

"So, if 'lover' is *erenterra,*" he said, "I must disagree with you."

"Perhaps a *man* can have a lover and remain free," Anne said. "A woman may not."

"Nonsense," Cazio said. "So long as her—eh, *lover*—is not also her husband, she can be as free as she likes." He smiled even more broadly. "Besides, not all servitude is unpleasant."

"You've slipped back into Vitellian again," Anne said, lacking entirely Cazio's affection for the subject. She was sorry to have brought it up. "Let's return to the topic of snow. Tell me more about it—in the king's tongue."

"New thing for me," he said, his voice going instantly from glib near-music to clumsy, lumbering prose as he switched languages. "Not have in Avella. Very, eh, *fullovonder*."

"Wonderful," she corrected as Austra giggled.

In fact, the snow didn't seem wonderful to Anne at all—it seemed a nuisance. But Cazio sounded sincere, and despite herself, it made her smile to watch as he grinned at the white flakes. He was nineteen, two years older than she, but still more boy than man.

And yet she could see a man in him now and then, just on the verge of escaping.

Despite the uncomfortable turn of the conversation, for a moment Anne felt content. She was safe, with friends, and though the world had gone mad, she at least knew her footing now. Forty-some men weren't enough to free her mother and take back Crotheny, but soon they would reach the estates of her aunt Elyoner, who had *some* soldiers, and perhaps she would know where Anne could acquire more.

After that—well, she would build her army as she went. She knew nothing of what an army needed, and at times—especially at night—that gripped her heart too tightly for sleep. But at the moment she somehow felt as if it would all work out.

Suddenly something moved at the corner of her vision, but when she looked, it wasn't there . . .

Leaning against the tree, Anne exhaled frost and noticed that the light was fading.

Where was Cazio? Where was everyone else?

Where was she?

The last she remembered. They'd just struck north from the Old King's Road, through the forest of Chevroché toward Loiyes, a place where she'd once gone riding with her aunt Lesbeth many years ago.

Her bodyguard Neil MeqVren had been riding only a few paces away. Austra had dropped back to talk to Stephen, the young man from Virgenya. The holter, Aspar White, had been scouting ahead, and the thirty horsemen who had attached themselves to her at Dunmrogh had been ranged protectively about her.

Then Cazio's expression had changed, and he had reached for his sword. The light had seemed to brighten to yellow.

Was this still Chevroché? Had hours passed?

Days?

She could not remember.

Should she wait to be found, or was there no one left to search for her? Could an enemy have snatched her away from her guardians without killing them all?

With a sinking heart, she realized how unlikely that was. Sir Neil certainly would die before allowing her to be taken, and the same was true of Cazio.

Trembling still, she realized that the only clue she had to her current situation was the dead man.

Reluctantly, she trudged back through the snow to the place where he lay. Gazing down on him through the dimming light, she searched for details she might have missed before.

He wasn't a young man, but she couldn't say how old he was, either—forty, perhaps. He wore dark gray wool breeches stained at the crotch with what had to be his own urine. His buskins were plain, black, worn nearly through. His shirt was wool, too, but beneath it bulked a steel breastplate. That was worn and dented, recently oiled. Besides the knife, he had a short, wide-bladed sword in an oiled leather sheath. It was affixed to a belt with a tarnished brass buckle. He wore no visible sign that proclaimed his allegiance.

Trying not to look at his face or bloody throat, she pushed

and patted her hands through his clothes, searching for anything that might be hidden.

On his right wrist she noticed an odd marking, burned or dyed into the skin. It was black and depicted what appeared to be a crescent moon.

She gingerly touched the marking, and a mild vertigo reeled through her.

She tasted salt and smelled iron and felt as if she had plunged her hand up to the elbow into something wet and warm. With a shock she realized that though his heart no longer beat, there was still quick in the man, albeit leaking rapidly away. How long would it take for all of him to be dead? Had his soul left him yet?

They hadn't taught her much about souls at the Coven Saint Cer, though she had learned something about the body. She had sat through and aided in several dissections and remembered—she thought—most of the organs and their primary humors. The soul had no single seat, but the organ that gave it communication was the one encased in the skull.

Remembering the coven, she felt inexplicably calmer, more reassuringly detached. Experimentally, she reached up and touched the corpse's brow.

A tingle crept up her fingers, passing through her arm and across her chest. As it moved on up her neck to her head, she felt suddenly drowsy.

Her body became distant and pillowy, and she heard a soft gasp escape from her lips. The world hummed with music that would not quite resolve itself into melody.

Her head swayed back, then down again, and with what seemed great effort she parted her eyelids.

Things were different, but it was difficult to say just how. The light was strange, and all seemed unreal, but the trees and the snow remained as they had been.

As her gaze sharpened, she saw dark water bubbling forth from the dead man's lips. It cascaded down his chest and meandered through the snow a few kingsyards until it met a larger stream.

Her vision suddenly lengthened, and she saw a hundred such streamlets. Then a thousand, tens of thousands of black rills, all melting into larger streams and rivers and finally merging with a water as wide and dark as a sea. As she watched, the last of that man flowed away, and like leaves on a stream there passed the image of a little girl with black hair . . .

The smell of beer . . .

The taste of bacon . . .

A woman's face more demon than human, terrifying, but the terror itself was already nearly forgotten . . .

Then he was gone. The liquid from his lips slowed to a trickle and ended. But from the living world the dark waters continued to flow.

It was then that Anne noticed that something was watching her; she felt its gaze through the trees. Inchoate fear turned in her, and suddenly, more than anything, she didn't want to see what it was. The image of the demon-woman in the dying man's eyes freshened, the face so terrible that he hadn't been able to really *see* it.

Was it Mefitis, saint of the dead, come for him? Come for Anne, too?

Or was it an estriga, one of the witches Vitellians believed devoured the souls of the damned? Or something beyond imagining?

Whatever it was, it grew nearer.

Gathering the courage in her core, Anne forced her head to turn—

—and swallowed a scream. There was no clear image, only a series of numbing impressions. Vast horns, stretching to scratch the sky, a body that spread out through the trees . . .

The black waters of a moment before were fastened to the thing like leeches, and though it tore at them with a hundred claws, each tendril that fell away was replaced by another, if not two.

She had seen this thing before, in a field of black roses, in a forest of thorns.

The Briar King.

He had no face, only dreams in motion. At first she saw nothing she recognized, a miasma of colors that had scent and taste and palpable feel. But now she could not look away, though her terror was only growing.

She felt as if a million poisoned needles quilled her flesh. She could not scream.

And Anne was suddenly very certain of two things . . .

She jerked awake and found her face pressed into the pool of blood on the man's chest. His body was very cold now, and so was she.

She rose, gagging, and stumbled away from the corpse, but her limbs were numb. She shook her head, clearing the last of the Black Mary. She vaguely knew she ought to take the horse and follow the hoofprints that had brought her here back to their source, but it seemed like too much trouble. Anyway, it was snowing harder now, and soon the tracks would be filled.

She folded herself into a crevice in the roots of a huge tree and, as warmth slowly returned, gathered her strength for what needed to be done.

CHAPTER TWO

THE OGRE'S TRAIL

AN ARROW skipped off Neil MeqVren's helm as he churned his way over the snowbank, the hoarse battle cry of his fathers ringing through the trees. His shield turned aside another death-tipped shaft. And another.

Only a few kingsyards away, four archers continued to

hold their ground behind the shields of six swordsmen. Together, the men formed a small fortress well situated to rain death on the only course Neil had any desire to follow—the track of the horsemen bearing Anne.

He decided to charge right at them, as suicidal as that might be. Anything else only delayed the inevitable.

Neil concentrated as he ran, feeling clumsy in his ill-fitting armor, longing for the beautiful set of lord's plate Sir Fail had once given him, the armor that now rested at the bottom of the harbor of z'Espino, hundreds of leagues away.

The world seemed slow at times like this, and wondrous detailed. Geese trumpeted, distant and overhead. He smelled the resin of broken pine. One of the shieldmen had bright green eyes behind the burnished noseguard of his helm and a downy auburn mustache. His cheeks were red with the cold. His face was clenched in a determination that Neil had seen more than once behind the war board. On another day this young man might drink wine with his friends, dance with a girl, sing a song known only in the tiny hamlet of his birth.

On another day. But today he was ready to die if need be and take whoever he might with him to greet the ferry of Saint Jeroin.

And on the faces of his companions there was the same look.

Neil stumbled, saw a bow bend and the tip of an arrow come down, felt the line drawn through the air to his eye. He knew his shield had dropped too low, that he would never bring it back up in time.

Suddenly the archer dropped his weapon and reached awkwardly for the shaft that had appeared in his own forehead.

Neil couldn't afford the time to turn and see who had saved his life. Instead, he crouched deeper behind his shield, measuring the last few yards, and then—howling again—flung himself at the shield wall, battering boss to boss with the green-eyed boy.

The fellow did what he ought to do and gave ground so that his fellow shieldmen could move up and put Neil inside the line, surrounding him.

But they didn't know what Neil carried. The feysword he'd taken from the pieces of a man who could not die lashed through the air, leaving in its soughwake the faint scent of lightning. It cleaved the lifted shield that hovered before him, through the metal cap and skull beneath, through an emerald eye, exiting finally below the ear before twisting to shear through the ribs of the next closest man.

Along with his battle rage, Neil felt a sort of sick anger. There was nothing chivalrous about the use of such a weapon. To fight against overwhelming odds was one thing. To claim victory by shinecraft was another.

But duty and honor didn't always go together, he had learned. And in this case, it was duty that swung the sword he had named Draug.

The simple fact was, feysword or not, this wasn't a fight he was likely to win.

Someone grappled with him at his knees, coming at him from behind, and Neil cut down and back, only to find another armored body in the way. Draug bit deeply, but the pommel of a broadsword smacked hard into Neil's helm, and he toppled into the snow. Another man wrapped around his arm, and he couldn't swing the sword anymore.

The world flared entirely red as he struggled, waiting for the dagger that would inevitably work around his gorget or through his visor. He was suddenly and strangely reminded of sinking into the waves back in z'Espino, dragged down by his armor, his helplessness mingling with relief that his trials were finally over.

Except that this time there was no relief. Anne was out there, in danger, and he would burn the last tinder of his strength to prevent her coming to harm. To more harm. If she wasn't already dead.

So he struck with the only weapon he had left, his head, butting it into the nearest panting face, and was rewarded with the cartilage crunch of a breaking nose. That was the fellow pinning his left arm, which he brought up now with all the strength of his battle rage, punching into the fellow's throat. That sent him back.

Then something slammed into his helm with all the weight of the world, and black snow fell from a white sky.

When his head cleared, Neil found someone kneeling over him. He levered himself up with a snarl, and the man leapt back, gabbling in a foreign tongue. To his surprise, Neil found that his limbs were free.

As the red haze parted, he realized that the man kneeling over him had been the Vitellian, Cazio. The swordsman was standing at a respectful distance now, his odd light weapon held in a relaxed ward.

"Hush, knight," a nearby voice said. "You're with friends now."

Neil pushed himself up and turned to regard a man of early middle years with a sun-browned face and close-cropped dark hair plentiful with silver. Another shake of his head and he recognized Aspar White, the king's holter. Just beyond were the younger Stephen Darige and the honey-haired Winna Rufoote, both crouching and alert in the bloodied snow.

"Best keep your head down," Aspar said. "There's another nest of archers out that way." He gestured with his chin.

"I thought you were all dead," Neil said.

"Yah," Aspar said. "We thought you were, too."

"Anne is where?" Cazio demanded in his heavy Vitellian accent.

"You didn't see?" Neil asked accusingly. "You were riding right next to her."

"Yes," Cazio said, concentrating on trying to get his words right. "Austra riding a little behind, with Stephen. Arrows started, yes, and then, ah, *eponiros* come up road with, ah, long *haso*—"

"The lancers, yes," Neil said. Archers had appeared all along their flanks, and then a wedge of horsemen, charging down the road. The cavalry from Dunmrogh hadn't had time to form up well but had met them, anyway.

Neil had killed three of the riders personally but had found himself pushed farther and farther away from Anne. When he'd returned to the scene, he'd discovered nothing but the dead and no sign whatever of the heir to the throne of Crotheny.

"Was trick," Cazio said. "Came, ah, *aurseto,* struck me here." He indicated his head, which was sticky with blood.

"I don't know that word," Neil said.

"Aurseto," Cazio repeated. "Like, ah, water, air—"

"Invisible," Stephen interrupted. The novice priest turned to Cazio. *"Uno viro aurseto?"*

"Yes," Cazio said, nodding vigorously. "Like cloud, color of snow, on *epo,* same—"

"A horse and rider the color of the snow?" Neil asked incredulously.

"Yes," Cazio confirmed. "Guarding Anne, I hear noise behind me—"

"And he hit you in the back of the head."

"Yes," Cazio said, his face falling.

"I don't believe you," Neil snapped. He hadn't entirely approved of this fellow since he had helped persuade Anne to leave Neil to his death back in Vitellio. True, Cazio had saved Anne's life on several occasions, but his motives seemed to be mostly salacious. Neil knew for a fact that such motives were untrustworthy and subject to violent change. He was a braggart, too, and though he was an effective enough street brawler—phenomenal, in fact—he hadn't the slightest sense of war discipline.

More than all that, Neil had learned to his chagrin that few people in the world were what they seemed.

Something dangerous glinted in Cazio's eyes, and he stood straighter, then put his palm on the hilt of his sword. Neil took a deep breath and dropped his hand toward Draug.

"Believe him," Aspar grunted.

"Asp? You?" Winna said.

"Werlic. There were three of 'em, at least. Why do you think I didn't make it back to warn you about the ambush? They aren't invisible, not exactly, but it's as the lad said. They're like smoke, and you can see through 'em. If you know where to look, you can tell they're there, but if you don't, they can give you quite a surprise.

"The other thing is, if you kill 'em, they come solid again, them and their mounts, even if the mounts aren't scratched. Near as I can tell—their trick aside—they're just men."

Stephen frowned. "That reminds me of— I read about a faneway once . . ." He scratched his jaw, his brow furrowed in concentration.

"More churchmen," Aspar grunted. "Just what we need."

Cazio was still tense, focused on Neil, hand on the hilt of his weapon.

"Apologies," Neil told the swordsman. "*Persnimo*. I am overwrought and jumped to conclusions."

Cazio relaxed a bit and nodded.

"Holter White," Neil asked, "do these invisible men leave tracks?"

"Yah."

"Then let's kill those fellows over there and find our queen."

Their attackers had left more than two groups of defenders in their path, that became clear.

Another few hundred pereci from where they found the knight, they ran into another bunch, though these were fewer in number. They didn't last long, but Aspar warned them to expect more up ahead.

Cazio was reminded of the nursery tale about a boy, lost in the forest, who came upon a grand triva. The triva turned out to be the home of a three-headed ogre who caught the boy and planned to eat him. Instead, the ogre's daughter took a liking to him and helped him escape.

Together they fled, pursued by the father, who was faster and soon caught up to them. The girl had her own tricks, though. She threw a comb behind them, and it became a hedge through which the ogre was forced to tear. She flung down a wineskin, which became a river . . .

"What are you thinking about?"

Cazio realized with a start that the priest was only a few paces away. Stephen spoke Vitellian, and though he sounded very old-fashioned, it was a relief to be able to talk without so much *thinking.*

"Combs and hedges, wineskins and rivers," he said mysteriously.

Stephen quirked a smile. "So we're the ogre?"

Cazio blinked. He'd *thought* he was being mysterious.

"You think too quickly," he commented wryly.

"I walked the faneway of Saint Decmanus," Stephen replied. "I can't help it—the saint blessed me." He stopped and smiled. "I'll bet your version of the story is different from the one I know. Does the boy's brother kill the ogre in the end?"

"No, he leads it to a church, and the attish sacritor slays it by ringing the clock three times."

"Oh, now that's very interesting," Stephen said, and he seemed to mean it.

"If you insist," Cazio granted. "In any event, yes, we're all turned around. It's the ogre we're pursuing, and he's the one leaving obstacles. But I wonder why.

"Up until now they've been trying to *kill* Anne. The knights who pursued us never made any effort to capture her alive. But if these *melcheos* had wanted to kill her, they could have done it easily, when they caught me napping." He gingerly touched the wound on his head.

"At least you saw him for a second," Stephen said. "I didn't even catch a glimpse of the one who took Austra. Really, it's not your fault."

"Of *course* it is," Cazio insisted, waving away the absolution. "I was with her—and I'll get her back. And if they've harmed her, I'll kill every last one of the *purcapercators.*

"But that still doesn't answer my question. Why didn't they just murder her?"

"There could be any number of reasons," Stephen said.

"The priests back in Dunmrogh wanted her blood for a ritual sacrifice—"

"Yes, but that was only because they needed a woman of noble birth, and the one they had was killed. Besides, we stopped that business."

"It might not be the same business. We prevented the enemy once, but there are many more cursed faneways in this forest, and I'm willing to bet that there are more renegades trying to awaken them. Each faneway is particular, with its own gift—or curse. Maybe they need the blood of a princess again."

"The men in Dunmrogh were mostly churchmen and knights from Hansa. I've seen neither in this group we're facing now."

Stephen shrugged. "But we've fought foes like this before, before we met you. There were monks involved then, too, and men without any identifiable standard or nation. Even Sefry."

"Then the enemy isn't the Church?"

"We don't know *who* the enemy is, ultimately," Stephen admitted. "The Hanzish knights and churchmen at Dunmrogh had the same dark goals as the men Aspar and Winna and I fought before—not far from here, in fact. We think they're all taking their commands from the praifec in Crotheny, Marché Hespero. But for all we know, he's taking *his* orders from someone else altogether."

"What do they all want?"

Stephen chuckled bitterly. "As far as we can tell, to waken a very ancient and potent evil."

"Why?"

"For power, I suppose. I can't genuinely say. But these men attacking us now? I don't know what they want. You're right; they seem different. Maybe they're in the employ of the usurper."

"Anne's uncle?" Cazio thought that was who Stephen meant. In truth, the whole situation was a bit confusing.

"Right," Stephen confirmed. "He might still have reason to want her kept alive."

"Well, I hope so," Cazio said.

"You have feelings for her?" Stephen asked.

"I am her protector," Cazio said, a little irritated by the question.

"No more than that?"

"No. No more."

"Because it seems as if—"

"Nothing." Cazio asserted. "I befriended her before I knew who she was. And besides, this is none of your business."

"No, I suppose it isn't," Stephen said. "Look, I'm sure she and her maid—"

"Austra."

Stephen's eyebrow lifted, and he quirked an annoying little smile. "Austra," he repeated. "We'll find them, Cazio. You see that man up there?"

"Aspar? The woodsman?"

"Yes. He can follow any trail; I can personally guarantee it."

Cazio noted that light flakes were falling from the sky again.

"Even in this?" he asked.

"In anything," Stephen said.

Cazio nodded. "Good."

They rode along in silence for a moment.

"How did you meet the princess?" Stephen asked.

Cazio felt a smile stretch his lips. "I am from Avella, you know? It's a town in the Tero Mefio. My father was a nobleman, but he was killed in a duel and didn't leave me much. Just a house in Avella and z'Acatto."

"The old man we left in Dunmrogh?"

"Yes. My swordmaster."

"You must miss him."

"He's a drunken, overbearing, arrogant— Yes, I miss him. I wish he were here now." He shook his head. "But Anne— z'Acatto and I went to visit a friend in the country—the countess Orchaevia—to take some air. As it happened, her triva and estates were near the Coven Saint Cer.

"I was walking that way one day and found the princess, ah, in her bath." He turned quickly to Stephen. "You must understand, I had no idea who she was."

Stephen's look sharpened abruptly. "Did you *do* anything?"

"Nothing, I *swear.*" His smile broadened as he remembered. "Well, I perhaps flirted a bit," he admitted. "I mean, in a barren countryside to find an exotic girl, already unclothed—it certainly seemed like a sign from Lady Erenda."

"Did you actually *see* her unclothed body?"

"Ah, well, just a bit of it."

Stephen sighed heavily and shook his head. "And here I was beginning to like you, swordsman."

"I told you, I had no idea."

"I probably would have done the same thing. But the fact that you didn't *know* who she was, well, it doesn't matter. Cazio, you saw a princess of the blood in the flesh, a princess who, if we succeed in our quest, will become the queen of Crotheny. Don't you understand what that means? Didn't she *tell* you?"

"Tell me *what*?"

"Any man who looks upon a princess of the blood—any man save her consecrated husband—must suffer blinding or death. The law is more than a thousand years old."

"*What?* You're joking."

But Stephen was frowning. "My friend," he said, "I have never been more serious."

"But Anne never said anything."

"I'm sure she wouldn't. She probably imagines that she can beg leniency for you, but the law is very specific, and even as queen, the matter would be out of her hands; it would be enforced by the Comven."

"But this is *absurd,*" Cazio protested. "I saw nothing but her shoulders, and perhaps the smallest glimpse of—

"I did not *know*!"

"No one else knows this," Stephen said. "If you were to slip off . . ."

"Now you're being even more ridiculous," Cazio said,

feeling his hackles rise. "I've braved death for Anne and Austra many times over. I've sworn to protect them, and no man of honor would back away from such a promise just because he feared some ridiculous punishment. Especially now, when she's in the clutches of—"

He stopped and stared closely at Stephen.

"There is no such law, is there?" he demanded.

"Oh, there is," Stephen said, controlling himself with obvious effort. "As I said, it's a thousand years old. It hasn't been enforced in more than five hundred, though. No, I think you're safe, old fellow."

Cazio glared at Stephen. "If you weren't a priest . . ."

"But I'm not," Stephen said. "I was a novice, and I did walk the faneway of Saint Decmanus. But I had a sort of falling-out with the Church."

"With the Church itself? You think the entire Church is evil?"

Stephen clucked his tongue for a moment. "I don't know. I'm starting to fear so."

"But you mentioned this praifec . . ."

"Hespero. Yes, Aspar, Winna, and I were sent on a mission by Praifec Hespero, but not the mission we ended on. What we discovered is that the corruption runs very deep in the Church, perhaps all the way back to z'Irbina and the Fratrex Prismo."

"That's impossible," Cazio asserted.

"Why impossible?" Stephen said. "The men and women of the Church are just that, men and women, as easily corrupted by power and wealth as anyone else."

"But the lords and ladies—"

"In the king's tongue we call them saints," Stephen said.

"Whatever you call them, they would never allow so deep a stain on their Church."

Stephen smiled, and Cazio found it a very unsettling smile.

"There are many saints," he said. "And they are not all pure." He suddenly looked distracted. "A moment," he murmured.

"What?"

"I hear something," he said. "More men up ahead. And something else."

"Your saint-blessed ears, yes? Before, when they ambushed us, why didn't you hear *that*?"

Stephen shrugged. "I really don't know. Maybe whatever saint-gift or dwemor it was that made the kidnappers invisible dulled my hearing, but you'll have to excuse me. I need to tell Aspar . . . and Neil."

"Yes," Cazio said. "I'll keep my sword ready."

"Yes. Please do."

Cazio watched Stephen trot his horse, Angel, up toward the rest, and, feeling somewhat glum, drew Caspator and rubbed his thumb along the deep notch that marred the strong part of the blade, a notch made by the same glittering witch-sword now carried by Sir Neil.

That notch was Caspator's death wound. There was no repairing such damage without reforging the entire blade, and with a new blade it wouldn't really be Caspator anymore but a different weapon. But even having a new blade forged wasn't so likely in these northern climes, where everyone favored overgrown butcher's cleavers to the rapier, the soul of dessrata. Dessrata was impossible without the right weapon, and where was he to find another sword that would serve, short of going back to Vitellio?

He really did miss z'Acatto. Not for the first time, he wished he'd returned to Vitellio with his old swordmaster.

He'd begun the expedition in high hopes for adventure. Harrowing as it had been at times, he'd seen more wonders since leaving Vitellio than in all his life until that time. But it had been just the four of them: Anne, Austra, z'Acatto, and himself.

Now Anne had a knight with a magic sword, a woodsman who could drill an arrow through a pigeon at six miles, and a priest who could hear twelve leagues in every direction. Winna didn't have any arcane abilities that he could see, but he wouldn't be entirely surprised if she suddenly began calling the animals, imploring them to fight at their side.

And what was he? A fellow who'd let the queen and her maid be kidnapped from beneath his very nose, who couldn't even speak the language of the kingdom, and who would be dead useless once his sword inevitably snapped.

The strangest thing was that that didn't bother him so much. Well, it did, but not the way it would have a year before. He *did* feel inadequate, but that in itself wasn't the problem. It wasn't his pride that hurt; it was the fact that he couldn't serve Anne the way he should.

It was that Austra was in the hands of someone evil.

He'd been trying to distract himself with selfish thoughts to keep himself from dwelling on the really soul-crushing possibility—that his friends were already dead.

Up ahead he noticed Stephen beckoning him with one hand and holding a finger to his lips with another. He spurred his horse forward, wondering what this fight would be like.

As it turned out, there was mixed news. The men Stephen had heard were allies—four of the knights from Dunmrogh—crouched behind a cairn of stones at the top of the nearest hill. They were hunkered there because the next ridge over was held by their enemies.

"This was very well planned," Neil said to Aspar. "A main assault to distract us, sorcelled horsemen to take the girls, and a series of rear guards to slow us down while they escaped. But why not brave it all on a single assault?"

Aspar shrugged. "Maybe they've heard tell of us and think we're stronger than we are. More likely you're wrong. Could be their plans didn't go as well as it seemed. I think they *did* mean to kill us all in a single assault, and if you think about it, they came pretty close. We had near forty men when we left Dunmrogh. Now there are nine of us left, but they don't know that. What with the snow and us separating, they're as confused as we are.

"For all we know, we outnumber *them* now. That could be the last three of 'em there, over on that ridge, and the girls might be with 'em. No way to tell, now that it's getting dark."

"There are six of them," Stephen said, "and I do hear a girl, though I can't swear she's one of ours."

"It must be," Neil said.

"Werlic," Aspar agreed. "So we'll just have to go and get 'em." His eyes traced lazily through the trees, down into the small valley, up to the opposing ridge.

"Aspar . . ." Stephen murmured.

"Yah?"

"There's something—something else. But I can't tell you what it is."

"With the men?"

Stephen shook his head. "No. It might be very far away."

"Then we'll grab the first branch before reaching for the next," Aspar said. "But if you make out anything more clearly—"

"I'll let you know," Stephen promised.

Neil was still studying the terrain. "They'll have plenty of clear shots at us before we can get to them," he noted.

"Yah," Aspar said. "That would be a good reason not to charge them through the valley."

"Is there another way?"

"Plenty of other ways. They've got the highest ground, but this ridge joins theirs up to our left."

"You know this place?"

Aspar frowned. "No. But that brooh down there's pretty small; see? And I can smell the springhead. And if you look at the light through the trees—well, it's high ground up there, trust me. The only thing is, if we all go that way, they might bolt.

"If they follow the ridge down, it'll take 'em to the marshes on the Warlock, and we'll get them there. But if they go north, down the ridge, they'll find themselves breaking out of the woods onto prairie, and there they'll have a choice of crossing the river and taking the Mey Ghorn plain or heading east.

"Either way, we'll have to catch them again, if we can. Right now we *know* where they are."

"But why are they waiting there?" Neil asked.

"I reckon they're lost," Aspar said. "They can't see the open ground from where they are. If they ride a hundred kingsyards, though, they will. Then we've got trouble."

"What do you propose? Have someone sneak around on the high ground?"

"Yah," Aspar said.

"And I suppose that person would be you."

For answer, the holter suddenly bent his bow and let fly a shaft. A sharp cry of consternation echoed from across the dale.

"Ney," the holter said. "I'm needed here to convince 'em that we're still on this ridge. You and Cazio go. When Stephen hears you near, we'll make our run down the valley and back up the other side. You just be sure and keep them busy."

Neil thought about it for a moment, then nodded. "That's worth trying," he said.

"Can you keep it quiet?"

"In the forest? I'll leave my armor. But still . . ."

"I've no sense that they're woodsmen," Aspar said. "We'll try to keep things lively here."

Neil glanced over at Cazio. "Stephen," he said, "could you explain to Cazio what we just said?"

Stephen did, and when he was done, the swordsman grinned and nodded. Neil stripped down to his quilted gambeson, took up Draug, and a few moments later they were skirting the ridge east, wincing at the sound of each broken twig, hoping Aspar was right about everything.

They needn't have worried. The ridge turned, just as the holter had predicted, forming a sort of cul-de-sac below. The hill dipped again as it curved, then began rising toward the high point where their enemies waited.

Now and then Neil heard shouted exchanges between Aspar, Winna, Stephen, and the men ahead of them. That was a relief, because it provided a further guide.

Neil found himself holding his breath. Annoyed, he forced himself to breathe evenly. He had attacked in stealth before; in the strands and high meadows of the isles he had fought many a night battle, positioning himself for surprise. But the islands were sand and stone, moss and heather. Moving with the easy silence of Aspar White through these treacherous hills and trees was well beyond his abilities.

He glanced at Cazio and found the Vitellian stepping with the same exaggerated care.

The shouting up ahead was growing nearer now. Crouching lower, Neil reached for his sword.

Aspar turned when he heard Stephen gasp.

"What?"

"All around us," Stephen said. "Moving from every direction."

"More of them? An ambush?"

"No, no," Stephen said. "They're quieter than they were before, much quieter, almost like wind in the trees. His power is growing, and theirs is, too."

"Slinders," Winna gasped.

"Slinders," Stephen said.

"Sceat," Aspar grunted.

Cazio stopped when he caught a glimpse of color through the autumn-shorn trees. The understory was thick and brambly with wild blueberry, harlot creeper, and cruxflower vine.

To his right he saw that Neil MeqVren also had paused.

The brush was both a boon and a problem. The archers among their enemies would have difficulty finding a target until they were nearly in the clearing. However, it would slow Cazio and the knight as they made their approach.

Wrong. Suddenly Sir Neil was charging, whirling that eerie butchering blade of his in front of him like a gardener's bill, and the underbrush was no more resistant to it than was flesh or armor.

Wishing he could have known a little more about the plan, he fell in immediately behind Neil, excitement winding in him like the cord of a ballista arming.

The instant Neil burst into the clearing, Cazio dodged

around him, neatly stepping into the path of a black-feathered shaft. It skinned along his belly, leaving a deep score of pain. He couldn't tell if he'd been eviscerated or merely scratched, and he didn't really have time to check, since a piggish brute with a broadsword came snuffling quickly toward him.

Cazio put Caspator out in a line; the rapier was easily twice the length of the hacking weapon his opponent carried. The fellow was bright enough to understand that and beat fiercely at the narrow blade to move it out of his path. He wasn't smart enough to stop charging, though, apparently confident that his wild attack on the blade would succeed.

But with a deft flick of his wrist, Cazio avoided the searching weapon without withdrawing his line so that the man obligingly ran straight onto the tip of his weapon.

"Ca dola da," Cazio began, customarily explaining to his foe what deftness of dessrata had just wounded him. He didn't finish, though, because—impaled or not—the pig aimed a ferocious cut at Cazio's head. He avoided it only by ducking, which sent a fresh sear of pain along his wounded belly.

The blade missed him, but the momentum of the swing carried the man's sword arm into Cazio's shoulder. Cazio caught the arm with his left hand and held it as he twisted Caspator free from the man's lungs. For an instant sea-green eyes filled Cazio's world, and with a shudder he understood that what he saw there wasn't hatred, or anger, or even a seething battle rage but horror and desperation.

"Don't . . ." the man gasped.

Cazio pushed him away, feeling sick. There was no 'don't.' The man was already dead; he just wasn't able to accept it yet.

What was he doing here? Cazio had been a duelist since he was twelve, but he had rarely fought to kill. It simply hadn't been necessary.

But now it is, he thought grimly as he drew-cut a crouching archer's string, thus preventing the man from shooting him in the face. He followed that with a violently swung boot that caught the fellow beneath the chin and lifted him toward a bed of briars and bushes.

He was just turning to meet another attacker when the forest exploded.

He had a sudden sense of darkness, the scent of unbathed bodies, and something else: a smell like the sweet alcohol perfume of grapes rotting on the vine, the odor of black dirt. Then it seemed a hundred limbs were clutching at him, clenching him, and he was borne down into chaos.

CHAPTER THREE

COUNTRY KNOWN AND STRANGE

ANNE'S MOUNT snuffled in fear as they approached yet another wall of black thorns wound so thickly through the trees as to deny entrance to anything larger than a vole.

"Hush," Anne said, patting the beast's neck. It flinched and shied from her touch.

"Be nice." Anne sighed. "I'll give you a name, all right? What's a good name?"

Mercenjoy, a little voice in her seemed to titter, and for an instant she felt so dizzy, she feared she might fall off.

"No, then, not Mercenjoy," she said, more to herself than to the horse. That was the name of the Dark Knight's mount in the phay stories, she remembered, and it meant "Murder-Steed."

"You belonged to a bad man," she said as reassuringly as possible, "but you aren't a bad horse. Let's see, I think I'll call you Prespine, for the saint of the labyrinth. She found her way out of *her* maze—now you'll help me find our way out of this one."

Even as she said it, Anne remembered a day that now seemed long ago, a day when her cares had been relatively simple ones and she'd been at her sister's birthday party. There had been a labyrinth there, grown of flowers and vines, but in a moment she'd found herself in another maze, in a strange place with no shadows, and since then nothing had been simple.

Anne hadn't wanted to get up, to catch the horse and ride. She'd wanted to stay huddled in the roots of the tree until someone came to help her or until it didn't matter anymore.

But fear had driven her up—fear that if she stayed in one place for long, something worse than death would catch up with her.

She shuddered as a change in the wind brought a stench from the black briars, a smell that reminded her of spiders, though she couldn't recall ever having actually smelled a spider. The strange growth was somehow like spiders, too. The vines and leaves glistened with the promise of venom.

She turned Prespine, following the thorns but keeping a respectable distance from them. Far off to her left, she thought she heard a sort of howling for a time, but as quickly as it began, it was gone.

The sun passed noon, then continued on toward its night home in the wood beyond the world. Anne imagined that the country where the sun slept couldn't be any stranger or more terrible than this place. The thorns seemed almost to be guiding her, *herding* her toward some destination she almost certainly did not desire to visit.

As the sky darkened, she also began to feel something behind her, and she knew she had been right back at the tree. Something *was* coming for her. It began as small as an insect, but it grew, with its many eyes fastened greedily on her back.

When she turned, however, no matter how quickly, it was gone.

She'd played this game as a child, as most children do. She and Austra had pretended the dread Scaos was after them, a monster so terrible that they could not look at it without being turned to stone. Alone, she had imagined a ghost walking behind her, sometimes at the corner of her vision but never there when she turned to confront it. Sometimes it frightened her, sometimes it delighted her, and usually both. Fear that one had under control had a certain delicate flavor.

This fear was not under her control. It did not taste good at all.

And it only grew more substantial. The unseen fingers clutched ever closer to her shoulder, and when she spun about, there was something, like the stain the bright sun leaves beneath the eyelids. The air seemed to clot thickly around her, the trees to bend wearily earthward.

Something had followed her back. But back from where? Where was that place of dark waters?

She had journeyed beyond the world before, or at least beyond her part of it. Most often she had been to the place of the Faiths, which was sometimes a forest, sometimes a glen, sometimes a highland meadow. Once she had taken Austra there with her to escape some murderous knights.

The place she had gone with the dying man was different. Had it been the land of the dead or only the borderlands? She remembered that the land of the dead was supposed to have *two* rivers—though she couldn't remember why—but here there had been more than two; there had been thousands.

And the Briar King. He had been shackled by those waters, or at least they were *trying* to bind him. What did that mean? And who was *he*?

He had communicated something to her, not with words, but his desire had been clear nonetheless. How did he even know who she was?

The face of the demon-woman flashed through her memory, and terror tremored freshly through her. Was *that* who followed her? She remembered the Faiths telling her that the law of death had been broken, whatever that meant. Had she committed some crime against the saints and brought death after her?

Red-gold sun suddenly spilled like a waterfall through the upper branches, and with terrible relief she suddenly realized that the briars had ended. Not much farther ahead the trees thinned to nothing as well, giving way to a sweeping, endless field of yellowed grass. With a mixed shout of fear and triumph, she spurred Prespine out into the open and felt the creeping presence behind her diminish, slinking back into the thorn shadows where it was comfortable.

Tears sprang in Anne's eyes as her hood fell away and the wind raked through her breviated hair. The sun was just above the horizon, an orange eye half-lidded by clouds bruised upon a golden west. The glorious color faded into a vesperine heaven so dark blue, she almost imagined that it was water, that she could swim up into and hide in its depths with its odd bright fish and be safe far above the world.

The clouds were mostly gone, the snow had stopped, and everything seemed better. But until the forest was a thinning line behind her, Anne kept Prespine at a run. Then she brought her to a walk and patted the mare's neck, feeling the great pulse beating there, nearly in time with her own.

It was still cold; indeed, it felt colder than when the snow had been falling.

Where was she? Anne swept her gaze about the unfamiliar landscape, trying to conjure up some sort of bearings. She never had paid much attention to the maps her tutors had shown her when she was younger. She'd been regretting that for several months now.

The sunset marked the west, of course. The plain sloped gradually down from the forest, so she could see for some distance. In the east, the dusk glimmered on a broad river across which, far away, she could see the black line of more trees. The river curved north and vanished into the horizon.

Nearer, she happily made out the spire of what must be a bell tower. The landscape in that direction seemed pimpled with tiny hills, which after a moment she realized must be haystacks.

She paused for a long moment, watching the distant signs of civilization, her feelings clouding a bit. A town meant people, and people meant food, shelter, warmth, companionship. It could also mean danger; the man who had attacked her—he *must* have attacked her—had come from somewhere. This was the first place she had seen that might explain him.

And where were Austra and the rest? Behind her, in front of her—or dead?

She took a deep breath, trying to release the tension in her shoulders.

She had been talking to Cazio, and everything had been fine. Then she had been alone with a dying man. The most logical assumption was that somehow he had abducted her, but why couldn't she remember how it had happened?

Even trying to think about it brought a sudden panic that threatened to cloud all other thoughts from her mind.

She pushed that away and concentrated on the present. If her friends were alive, they were searching for her. If they were not, then she was alone.

Could she survive a night on the plain by herself? Maybe, maybe not. It depended on how cold it got. Prespine's saddlebags contained a bit of bread and dried meat but nothing more. She had watched Cazio and z'Acatto start fires, but she hadn't seen anything that resembled a tinderbox in the dead man's possessions.

Reluctantly, she made her decision and prodded the mare toward the town. She needed to know where she was, at the very least. Had she made it to Loiyes? If so, the village ahead ought to be under the governance of her aunt. If she wasn't in Loiyes, she needed to get there. She was more certain of that now than ever, for she had seen it in the face of the Briar King.

She realized that she knew something else.

Stephen Darige at least was alive. She knew this because the Briar King knew it. And there was something Stephen was supposed to do.

* * *

Not much farther along she came across a rutted clay road wide enough for wains; cut down into the landscape as it was, it had hidden itself from her earlier view. From where she met it the road wound off through cultivated fields. She noticed bits of green peeking through the snow, leading Anne to wonder what sorts of crops the farmers grew in winter or whether they were just weeds.

The haystacks she had seen as tiny at a distance were here prodigiously tall. Gaunt scarecrows in tattered rags stared empty-eyed from heads of gourd or shriveled black pumpkin.

The woodsmoke and its comforting aroma draped across the cold earth, and before long she came to a house, albeit a small one, with white clay walls and a steeply pitched thatch roof. A shed attached to the side seemed to serve as the barn; a cow watched her from beneath its eaves with dull curiosity. She could just make out a man in dirty tunic and leggings, pulling hay down from a loft with a wooden-tined pitchfork.

"Pardon me," she called tentatively. "Can you tell me what that town ahead is named?"

The man glanced back at her, his tired eyes suddenly rounding a bit.

"Ah, edeu," he said. "She ez anaméd *Sevoyne,* milady."

Anne was taken aback by his accent, which was a bit difficult to decipher.

"Sevoyne?" she said. "That's in Loiyes?"

"Edeu, milady. Loiyes ez here. Whereother should she beeth, to beg theen perdon?"

Anne let the question go as rhetorical. "And can you tell me where Glenchest is from here?" she pursued.

"Glenchest?" His brow furrowed. "She most to four leagues, creed-I, 'long the road most to way. You are working for the duchess there, lady?"

"That's where I'm going," Anne said, "I'm just a little lost."

"Never-I've been thet faer along," the fellow said. "But they tell ez net s'hard to find to 'er."

"Thanks, then," Anne said. "Thanks for that."

"Velhoman, and good road ahead, lady," the man said.

As Anne rode on, she heard a woman's voice behind her. The man answered, and this time the language was one she did not know, though it carried the same peculiar cadence as his very odd king's tongue.

So this was Loiyes, in the heartland of Crotheny. How was it, then, that the peasants here didn't speak the king's tongue first?

And how was it that she hadn't known as much? She had been to Loiyes before, to Glenchest. The people in the town in Glenchest spoke perfectly good king's tongue. According to the man, this was less than a day's ride from there.

She had spent so much time traveling in foreign lands. The thought of a homecoming—of reaching a place where people spoke the language she had grown up with and everything was familiar—was something she had been longing for for months.

Now here she was, only to discover that the country of her birth was stranger than she had ever known.

It made her feel a little sick.

By the time Anne reached Sevoyne, the appearing stars were vanishing behind a new ceiling of cloud rolling in from the east, bringing for Anne a return of the claustrophobia she'd experienced in the forest. Her silent pursuer was near again, emboldened by the deep shadows.

She passed the town horz, the one spot where things were allowed to grow absolutely wild, albeit caged by an ancient stone wall. For the first time Anne recognized that contradiction, and she felt it sharply, another familiar stone in her world that had turned over to reveal the crawling things festering beneath.

The horz represented wild, untamed nature. The saints of the horz were Selfan of the Pines, Rieyene of the Birds, Fessa of the Flowers, Flenz of the Vines: the wild saints. How must the wild saints feel about being bound when once the whole world must have been theirs? She remembered the horz back in Tero Gallé, where she had entered the other world. She'd had a sense of diseased anger there, of frustration become madness.

For a moment the stone walls seemed to become a hedge of black thorns, and the image of the antlered figure returned to her.

He was wild, and, like everything truly wild, he was terrifying. The thorns were trying to bind him, weren't they? The way the walls of the horz bound wildness. But who sent the thorns?

And had she thought of that herself, or had *he* left it in her head? How had she made that connection?

On the east she couldn't remember what had happened to her. On the west her mind found strange conclusions. Had she lost control of her thoughts entirely? Was she mad?

"Detoi, meyez," someone said, interrupting her ponderings. *"Quey veretoi adeyre en se zevie?"*

Anne tensed and tried to focus through the dark. To her surprise, what had seemed to be a mere shadow suddenly clarified as a man of middle years wearing livery she recognized: the sunspray, spear, and leaping fish of the dukes of Loiyes.

"Do you speak the king's tongue, sir?" she asked.

"I do," the man replied. "And I apologize for my impertinence. I could not see in the dark that you are a lady."

Anne understood the peasant's reaction now. Her king's tongue and the accent she spoke it with gave her away immediately as a noble of Eslen, or one of the nobles' close servants, at least. Her clothes, however dirty, surely confirmed it. That could be good or bad.

No, not good or bad. She was alone, without protectors. It was most probably bad.

"Whom do I have the honor of addressing, sir?"

"Mechoil MeLemved," he replied. "Captain of the guard of Sevoyne. Are you lost, lady?"

"I'm on my way to Glenchest."

"Alone? And in these times?"

"I had companions. We were separated."

"Well, come in from the cold, lady. The *coirmthez*—I'm

sorry, the inn—will have a room for you. Perhaps your companions are already waiting for you."

Anne's hopes slumped further. The captain seemed too unsurprised, too ready to accommodate her.

"I should warn you, Captain MeLemved," she said, "that attempts have been made to deceive me into harm before, and my patience is very short with that sort of thing."

"I don't understand, Princess," the captain said. "What harm could I mean you?"

She felt her face freeze.

"None, I'm sure," she said.

She kicked Prespine into motion, wheeling to turn around. As she did so, she discovered there was someone behind her, and even as she perceived that, she noticed something in her peripheral vision just before it slapped her hard across the side of the head.

She gasped as everything spun in four or five directions, and then strong fingers pinched into her arms, dragging her from her mount. She squirmed, kicked, and screamed, but her cries were stifled quickly by something shoved into her mouth, followed immediately by a smell of grain as a sack was pulled over her head. Anger flared, and she reached to the place in her where sickness dwelled, sickness she could give to others.

What she found instead was a terror so vivid that her only escape from it was another retreat into darkness.

She woke sputtering, her nose burning, her throat closed. An acrid alcoholic stench suffused everything, but that seemed strangely distant.

Her eyes peeled open, and she saw through a glassy vertigo that she was in a small room lit by several candles. Someone was holding her hair back, and though she felt her roots pulling, it didn't hurt that much.

"Awake now, eh?" a man's voice growled. "Well, drink, then."

The hard lip of a bottle was pressed against her lips, and something wet poured into her mouth. She spit it out, confused, recognizing how she felt, remembering that something had happened but not sure what. There had been a woman, a terrible woman, a demon, and she had fled her, just as she had before . . .

"Swallow it," the man snarled.

That was when Anne realized she was drunk.

She had been drunk a few times before with Austra. Mostly it had been pleasant, but on a few occasions she had been very sick.

How much had they made her drink while she was asleep? *Enough.* Horribly, she almost giggled.

The man held her nose and poured more of the stuff down her throat. It was like wine but oceans harsher and stronger. It went down this time, fire snaking through her throat and arriving in a belly already warmed to burning. She felt a sudden nausea, but then that cleared away. Her head was pulsing pleasantly, and things around her seemed to be happening much too quickly.

The man stepped to where she could see him. He wasn't very old, maybe a few years older than she. He had curly brown hair, lighter at the ends, and hazel eyes. He wasn't handsome, but he wasn't ugly, either.

"There," he said. "Look, there's no reason for you to make this hard."

Anne felt her eyes bug, and tears suddenly stung them. "Going to *kill* me," she said, her words slurring. She wanted to say something much more complicated, but it wouldn't come out.

"No, I'm not," he said.

"Yes, you are."

He frowned at her without speaking for a few moments.

"Why—why am I drunk?" she asked.

"So you don't try to escape. I know you're a shinecrafter. They say brandy makes it harder for you to use your arts."

"I'm not a shinecrafter," she snapped. Then, all restraint gone, she began shouting. "What do you *want* with me?"

"Me? Nothing. I'm just waiting for the rest. How did you get away, anyway? What were you doing alone?"

"My friends are coming," she said. "Believe me. And when they get here, you'll be sorry."

"I'm already sorry," the man said. "They left me here just in case, but I never thought I would have to deal with *you*."

"Well, I—" But as soon as she started the thought, she lost it.

It was getting harder to think at all, in fact, and her earlier fear that she was losing her mind resurfaced as something of a private joke. Her lips felt huge and rubbery, and her tongue the size of her head.

"You gave me a lot to shr—drink."

"Yes, I did."

"When I fall asleep, you're going to kill me." She felt a tear collect in the corner of her eye and start down her cheek.

"No, that's stupid. I would have killed you already, wouldn't I? No, you're wanted alive."

"Why?"

"How should I know? I just work for my reytoirs. The others—"

"Aren't coming back," Anne said.

"What?"

"They're all dead. Don't you see that? All of your friends are dead." She laughed, not quite sure why.

"You saw them?" he asked uneasily.

Anne nodded the lie. It felt as if she were wiggling a huge kettle at the top of a narrow pole. "*She* killed them," she said.

"She who?"

"The one you see in your nightmares," she said tauntingly. "The one who creeps on you in the dark. She's *coming* for me. You'll be here when she finds me, and you'll be sorry."

The light was dimming. The candles were still lit but seemed to have faded somehow. The darkness wrapped around her like a comforter. Everything was spinning, and it seemed far too much trouble to talk.

"Coming . . ." she murmured, trying to keep a sense of urgency.

She didn't fall asleep exactly, but her eyes closed, and her head seemed full of strange trumpets and unnatural lights.

She drifted in and out of scenes. She was in z'Espino, dressed like a maid, scrubbing laundry, and two women with large heads were making fun of her in a language she didn't recognize.

She was on her own horse, Faster, riding so hard that she felt like vomiting.

She was in the house of her dead ancestors, the house of marble in Eslen-of-Shadows with Roderick, and he was kissing her on the bare flesh of her knee, moving up her thigh. She reached down to stroke his hair, and when he looked up at her, his eyes were maggoty holes.

She shrieked, and her eyes fluttered open to watery, half-focused reality. She was still in the little room. Someone's head was pressed against her chest, and she realized with dull outrage that her bodice was open and someone was *licking* her. She was still in the chair, but his body was between her legs, which she could see were bare of stockings. He had hiked her skirts up all the way to her hips.

"No . . ." she murmured, pushing at him. "No."

"Be still," he hissed. "I told you this wouldn't be so bad."

"No!" Anne managed to scream.

"No one can hear you," he said. "Calm down. I know how to do this."

"No!"

But he ignored her, not understanding that she wasn't yelling at him anymore.

She was yelling at *her* as she rose up from the shadows, her terrible teeth showing in a malicious grin.

CHAPTER FOUR

A NEW MUSIC

LEOFF CLUNG to his Black Marys. No matter how terrible they were, he knew waking would be worse.

And sometimes, in the miasma of darkness and embodied pain, among the distorted faces mouthing threats made all the more terrible by their unintelligibility, amid the worm-dripping corpses and flight across plains that gripped up to his knees like congealed blood, something pleasant shone through, like a clear vein of sunlight in a dark cloud.

This time, as usual, it was music—the cool, sweet chiming of a hammarharp drifting through his agonized dreams like a saint's breath.

Still he clenched; music had returned to him before, always beginning sweetly but then bending into dread modes that sent him plunging ever deeper into horror, until he put his hands to his ears and begged the holy saints to make it stop.

Yet it stayed sweet this time, if clumsy and amateurish.

Groaning, he pushed at the sticky womb of dream until he tore through to wakefulness.

He thought for a moment he had merely moved to another dream. He lay not on the cold, stinking stone he had become accustomed to but on a soft pallet, his head nested on a pillow. The stench of his own urine was replaced by the faint odor of juniper.

And most of all—most of all, the hammarharp was real, as was the man who sat on its bench, poking awkwardly at the keyboard.

"Prince Robert," Leoff managed to croak. To his own ear his voice sounded stripped down, as if all the screaming he had done had shredded the cords of his throat.

The man on the stool turned and clapped his hands, apparently delighted, but the hard gems of his eyes reflected the candlelight and nothing more.

"Cavaor Leoff," he said. "How nice of you to join me. Look, I've brought you a present." He flourished his hands at the hammarharp. "It's a good one, I'm told," he went on. "From Virgenya."

Leoff felt an odd, detached vibration in his limbs. He didn't see any guards. He was alone with the prince, this man who had condemned him to the mercies of the praifec and his torturers.

He searched his surroundings further. He was in a room a good deal larger than the cell he had occupied when last sleep and delirium had claimed him. Besides the narrow wooden cot on which he lay and the hammarharp, there was another chair, a washbasin and pitcher of water, and—and here he had to rub his eyes—a bookshelf full of tomes and scrifti.

"Come, come," the prince said. "You must try the instrument. Please, I insist."

"Your Highness—"

"I *insist*," Robert said firmly.

Painfully, Leoff swung his legs down to the floor, feeling one or two of the blisters on his feet burst as he put weight on them. That was such a minor pain, he didn't even really wince.

The prince—no, he had made himself king now, hadn't he? The *usurper* was alone. Queen Muriele was dead; everyone he cared about was dead.

He was worse than dead.

He stepped toward Robert, feeling his knee jar oddly. He would never run again, would he? Never trot across the grass on a spring day, never play with his children—likely never *have* children, come to that.

He took another step. He was almost close enough now.

"Please," Robert said wearily, rising from the stool and gripping Leoff's shoulders with cold, hard fingers. "What do you suppose you will do? Throttle me? With these?" He grabbed Leoff's fingers, and such a shock of pain exploded through Leoff that it tore a gasp from his aching lungs.

Once it would have been enough to make him scream. Now tears started in his eyes as he looked down to where the king's hand gripped his.

He still didn't recognize them, his hands. Once the fingers had been gently tapered, lean and supple, perfect for fingering the croth or tripping on keys. Now they were swollen and twisted in terribly unnatural ways; the praifec's men had broken them methodically between all the joints.

They hadn't stopped there, though; they had crushed the bones of each hand as well, and shattered the wrists that supported them. If they had cut his hands completely off, it would have been kinder. But they hadn't. They had left them to hang there, a reminder of other things he would never, ever do again.

He looked again at the hammarharp, at its lovely red-and-black keys, and his shoulders began to tremble. The trickle of tears turned to a flood.

"There," Robert said. "That's right. Let it out. Let it out."

"I-I did not think you could hurt me more," Leoff managed, gritting his teeth, ashamed but almost, finally, beyond shame.

The king stroked the composer's hair as if he were a child. "Listen, my friend," he said. "I am at fault for this, but my crime was that of neglect. I did not supervise the praifec closely enough. I had no idea of the cruelty he was visiting upon you."

Leoff almost laughed. "You will forgive me if I am skeptical," he said.

The usurper's fingers pinched his ear and twisted a bit. "And you will address me as 'Your Majesty,' " Robert said softly.

Leoff snorted. "What will you do if I don't? Kill me? You have already taken all I have."

"You think so?" Robert murmured. He released Leoff's ear and withdrew. "I have not taken everything, I promise you. But let that pass. I regret what has happened to you. My personal physician will attend you from here on out."

"No physician can heal this," Leoff said, holding up his maimed hands.

"Perhaps not," Robert conceded. "Perhaps you will never again play yourself. But as I understand it, the music you create—compose—is done within your head."

"It cannot come out of my head without my fingers, however," Leoff snarled.

"Or the fingers of another," Robert said.

"What—"

But at that moment, the king gestured and the door opened, and there, in the lamplight, stood a soldier in dark armor. His hand rested on the shoulder of a little girl whose eyes were covered by a cloth.

"Mery?" he gasped.

"Cavaor Leoff?" she squealed. She tried to start forward, but the soldier pulled her back, and the door closed.

"Mery," Leoff repeated, lumbering toward the door, but Robert caught him by the shoulder again.

"You see?" Robert said softly.

"They told me she was dead!" Leoff gasped. "Executed!"

"The praifec was trying to break your heretic soul," Robert said. "Much of what his men told you is untrue."

"But—"

"Hush," Robert said. "I have been charitable. I can be more so. But you must agree to help me."

"Help you how?"

Robert smiled a ghastly little smile. "Shall we discuss it over a meal? You look half-starved."

For what seemed an eternity, Leoff's meals had consisted of either nothing or some nameless mush that under the best of circumstances was more or less without taste and under the worst reeked of putrefying offal.

Now he found himself staring at a trencher of black bread

that had been heaped with roast pork, leeks braised in must, redbutter cheese, boiled eggs sliced and sprinkled with green sauce, and cream fritters. Each scent was a lovely melody, wafting together into a rhapsodic whole. His goblet was filled with a red wine so sharp and fruity, he could smell it without bending toward it.

He looked at his useless hands, then back at the meal. Did the king expect him to lower his face into the food like a hog?

Probably. And he knew that in a few more moments he would.

Instead, a girl in black-and-gray livery entered, knelt by his side, and began offering him morsels of the repast. He tried to take it with some measure of grace, but after the first explosion of flavor in his mouth, he gulped unashamedly.

Robert sat across the table from him and watched him without apparent amusement.

"That was clever," he said after a time, "your lustspell, your singing play. The praifec greatly underestimated you and the power you wield through your music. I can't tell you how angry I felt, sitting helplessly as the thing unfolded, unable to stand, speak, or bring it to a halt. You put a gag in the mouth of a king, Cavaor, and you tied his hands behind his back. I don't suppose you expected to escape without some punishment."

Leoff laughed bitterly. "I hardly think that now," he said, then lifted his head defiantly. "But I do not accept you as king."

Robert smiled. "Yes, I quite gathered that by the content of the play. I am not entirely a buffoon, you see."

"I never took you for one," Leoff replied. *Vicious and murderous, yes, stupid, no,* he finished silently.

The usurper nodded as if he had heard the unvoiced thought. Then he waved his hand. "Well, it is done, isn't it? And I will be candid; your composition was not without effect. Your choice of subject matter, your casting of a landwaerden girl in the major role—well, it certainly won over the landwaerden, and not to me, as I had hoped." He leaned forward. "You see, there are those who think of me as you do, as an usurper. I had hoped to unite my kingdom to stand against the evil that bears on us from all sides, and to do that I really needed the landwaerden and their militias. Your actions have rendered their allegiance more ambiguous than ever. You've even managed somehow to create sympathy for a queen no one liked."

"It was my honor to do so." Then he understood. "Queen Muriele is not dead, is she?"

Robert nodded affirmation, then pointed a finger at Leoff. "You still don't understand," he said. "You talk like a dead man, speaking with the bravery of the condemned. But you can live and compose. You can have your friends back. Wouldn't you like to see little Mery grow up, oversee the progress of your protégé?

"And what about the lovely Areana? Surely she has a bright future ahead, perhaps even at your side . . ."

Leoff listed to his feet. "You *dare* not threaten them!"

"No? What would prevent me?"

"Areana is the daughter of a landwaerden. If you are trying to win their allegiance—"

"If I give up hope of doing so, if I cannot unite by conciliation, I will have to do so through force and fear," Robert snapped. "Besides, I am sometimes prone to, shall we say, black humors. My humors were particularly black after the performance of your little farce."

"What are you saying?"

"Areana was taken into custody soon after you were. I quickly realized the error in that, but as king I must be careful about admitting my mistakes, you see. I must work at things from where I am."

Leoff's head swirled.

At one point in his torture he had been told that the entire cast that had performed his singing play had been arrested and publicly hanged and that Mery had been quietly poisoned in the night. That was when he had broken and "confessed" that he had practiced "heretical shinecraft" most foul.

Now he found that they were alive, which brought joy beyond measure. But the threat to their lives was renewed.

"You're most clever yourself," he told the king. "You know I will not risk losing them again."

"Why should you? Your allegiance to Muriele is senseless. She has no mandate to rule, and certainly not the talents. Despite my faults, I am the best the Dare family has to offer. Hansa will declare war on us any day unless I can appease them. Monsters threaten all of our borders and appear in the midst of our towns. Whatever you think of me, Crotheny is better united behind one leader, and that will be me or no one, because there is no one else."

"What would you have me do?"

"Undo what you have done, of course. Write another lust-spell to win them over for me. I have provided you with hammarharp and every book of music the kingdom has to offer. I will make Mery and Areana available to you as helpmates, to make up for the unfortunate state of your hands. I will, of course, have to supervise your work more carefully than did the praifec, and we will hire the musicians who will perform the work."

"The praifec has branded me heretic before the world. How can any work of mine be performed now?"

"You will be offered as proof of divine forgiveness and intercession, my friend. Where before you took your inspiration from the darkness, now you will take it from the light."

"But that is a lie," Leoff said.

"No," Robert replied drily. "That is politics."

Leoff hesitated slightly. "And the praifec will go along with this?"

"The praifec has his hands full," Robert told him. "The empire, it seems, is a veritable hornet's nest of heretics. You are lucky, Cavaor Leovigild. The gallows make a constant music of their own these days."

Leoff nodded. "I hardly need you to repeat your threat, Your Majesty. I quite understood it the first time."

"So it's 'Your Majesty' again. I take it, then, that we're getting somewhere."

"I am at your mercy," Leoff said. "I wonder if you have a subject for your commission."

The king shook his head. "No, I haven't. But I've seen your library, and it is stocked with popular tales of the region. I trust you will find some inspiration there."

Leoff gathered his strength of will.

"One thing," he said. "I will need helpmates, I grant you. But please show mercy and send Mery back to her mother and Areana back to her family."

Robert stifled a yawn. "You were told they were dead, and you believed it. I could tell you I had sent them home, but how could you know it was true? In any case, I would rather you not convince yourself that you have made them safe. It might inspire you to some new foolish behavior. No, I would prefer you had their company, to steady you in your purpose."

With that he rose, and Leoff knew the conversation had ended.

Shivering suddenly, he started toward his cot, anxious to close his eyes and lose himself once more in dreams. Instead he remembered Mery when he'd first met her, hiding in his music room, listening to him play and afraid that if her presence were known, he would send her out.

Instead of retreating to sleep, he turned his path and trudged wearily to the books the king had provided him, then began to read their titles.

CHAPTER FIVE

THE DEMON

THE MAN SCREAMED as the demon-woman plunged her clawed fingers into his chest, through the hard bone and tight skin to the soft, wet stuff beneath.

Anne tasted iron on her tongue as the spinning slowed, stilled, and centered. Her fear suddenly gone, she looked into the face of the monster.

"Do you know me?" the demon roared in a voice that burred through flesh and bone. "Do you know who I am?"

Light flashed behind Anne's eyes. The earth seemed to tilt, and she was suddenly on horseback.

She was riding with Cazio once more. She remembered Austra gasping behind her and then a terrific stir.

Something struck her to the ground, and then a hard arm wrapped about her, lifting her forcefully into a saddle. She remembered the acrid smell of her abductor's sweat, the gasp of his breath in her ear. The knife to her throat. She could only see his hand, which had a long white scar that ran from his wrist to the lowest knuckle of his little finger.

"Ride," someone said. "We'll deal with these."

She remembered staring dully over the head of the horse, watching the rise and fall of the snowy forest floor, the trees blurring by like the columns of an endless hall.

"You sit still, Princess," the man commanded. His voice was low and warm, not unpleasant at all. His accent was educated, slightly alien but unplaceable. "Sit still, give me no trouble, and things will go better for you."

"You know who I am," Anne said.

"Well, we knew it was one or the other of you. I reckon you just cleared it up, but we'll be taking you to someone who knows your face to be sure. No matter, since we've got both."

Austra, Anne thought. *They've got you, too.* That meant her friend might still be alive.

"My friends will come for me."

"Your companions are probably dead by now," the man said, his voice shaking with the galloping of the horse. "If they aren't, they'll find it difficult to follow us. But that needn't concern you, Princess. I wasn't sent to kill you, or you would be dead by now. Do you understand?"

"No," Anne said.

"There are those who would kill you," the man replied. "That you know, yes?"

"I most certainly know that."

"Then believe me when I tell you that their masters are not mine. I am charged with your safety, not with your destruction."

"I don't *feel* safe," Anne said. "Who sent you? My uncle, the usurper?"

"I doubt that Prince Robert cares much for your welfare. We suspect he is in league with those who murdered your sisters."

"Who is *we*?"

"I can't tell you that."

"I don't understand. You say you don't want me dead. You imply you wish to preserve me from harm, yet you've taken me from my most loyal protectors and my friends. So I know you can't wish me well."

The man didn't reply, but he tightened his grip.

"I see," Anne said. "You have some need of me, but not one that I would approve of. Perhaps you intend to sacrifice me to the dark saints."

"No," the man said. "That is not our aim at all."

"Then enlighten me. I am at your mercy."

"Indeed you are. Remember that. And believe me when I

say that I will not kill you unless I have to." The knife came away from her throat. "Please don't struggle or try to escape. You might manage to fall off the horse; if you don't break your neck, I'll easily recapture you. Listen and you will know your friends aren't following."

"What's your name?" Anne asked.

Again a pause. "You can call me Ernald."

"But it isn't your name."

She felt him shrug behind her.

"Ernald, where are we going?"

"To meet someone. After that, I cannot say for certain."

"I see." She thought for a moment. "You say I won't be killed. What of Austra, now that you're certain she isn't me?"

"She . . . she won't be harmed."

But Anne heard the lie in his voice.

Taking a deep breath, she snapped her head back and felt it crush into the man's face. He yelped, and Anne flung herself from the mare.

She landed badly, and pain coursed up her leg, which already was aching from an unhealed arrow wound. Gasping, she struggled to her feet and tried to get her bearings. She made out their trail and began hobbling back along it, shouting.

"Cazio! Sir Neil! Help me!"

She glanced back over her shoulder, almost feeling him there . . .

. . . but saw no one, only the horse. Why would he be hiding?

She quickened her pace, but the pain nearly paralyzed her. She went down on one knee, then doggedly fought her way back up.

Something moved in front of her, but she couldn't see just what. It was like a brief shadow across water.

"Help!" she shouted again.

A palm snapped against the side of her head then, and as she fell, she saw a snowy blur. Then her arm was twisted hard behind her, and she was being forced back toward the horse. She gasped, wondering where Ernald had come from. Behind her? But she had looked for him.

Wherever he had gone, he was here now.

"Do not try that again, Princess," he said. "I have no desire to hurt you, but I *will* do it if I must."

"Let me go," Anne demanded.

The knife was suddenly pricking into her neck again.

"Mount back up."

"Not until you promise not to kill Austra."

"I told you, she won't be harmed."

"Yes, but you were lying."

"Mount, or I'll cut your ear off."

"My leg is hurt. You'll have to lift me up."

He laughed harshly. The knife came away, and he grasped her suddenly by the waist and threw her over the saddle, then pushed her injured leg over. She screamed, and bright speckles gyred before her eyes. By the time she could think again, he was sitting behind her, the knife again at her throat.

"I see now that being nice will get me nowhere," he said, kicking the horse into motion.

Anne gasped for breath. It felt as if the pain had broken something loose in her, and the entire world was rushing up like a whirlwind or a hurricane from the sea. She shivered and felt the hairs on her neck stand on end.

"Let me go," she said, her heart thundering in her chest. "Let me go."

"Hush."

"Let me go."

This time he cuffed her with the hilt of the knife.

"Let me go!"

The words ripped out of her, and the man screamed.

Anne felt the knife in her hand suddenly, gripped in white knuckles, and with terrible desperation she drove it into his throat. In the same instant she felt a strange pain in her own throat and the sensation of something sliding under her tongue. She saw his eyes go wide and black and in those dark mirrors there was the image of a demon coming up from beneath.

Screaming, she wrenched the knife through his windpipe, noticing even as she did so that her hands were empty, that it wasn't she who was holding the knife at all. And she understood just enough to flee, to run into the gaping darkness where her rage came from, to close her eyes and stop her ears to his gurgling . . .

The light dimmed, and she found herself back in her chair, facing the other man, the one who had been trying to rape her. The demon was there, stooping over him just as she had come down upon Ernald.

"Oh, no," she murmured, staring up into the terrible face. "Oh, saints, no."

She woke on a small mattress, unbound, with her clothes returned to a reasonable state of propriety. Her head throbbed, and she recognized the beginnings of a hangover.

Her captor sat on the floor a few kingsyards away, weeping quietly. Of the demon there was no sign.

Anne started to rise, but a sudden wave of nausea forced her back down. That wasn't enough, however, and she had to struggle to her hands and knees to vomit.

"I'll get you some water," she heard the man say.

"No," she growled. "I won't drink anything else you give me."

"As you wish, Your Highness."

She felt the surprise dimly through her sickness and confusion.

"I'm sorry," he added, and began crying again.

Anne groaned. She was missing time again. The demon hadn't killed this man as it had killed Ernald, but it had done something.

"Listen to me," she said. "What's your name?"

He looked confused.

"Your name?"

"Wist," he murmured. "Wist. They call me Wist."

"You saw her, didn't you, Wist? She was here?"

"Yes, Your Highness."

"What did she look like?"

His eyes tried to bug from his head, and he gasped, clutching at his chest.

"I can't remember," he said. "It was the worst thing I ever saw. I can't—I can't see that again."

"Did she untie me?"

"No, I did."

"Why?"

"Because I'm supposed to," he whimpered. "I'm supposed to help you."

"Did *she* tell you that?"

"She didn't say anything," he said. "Not that I can remember. That is, there were words, but I couldn't make them out, except that they *hurt,* and they still hurt unless I do what I'm supposed to do."

"And what else are you supposed to do?" she asked suspiciously.

"Help you," he said again.

"Help me what?"

He raised his hands helplessly. "Whatever you want."

"Really," she said. "Give me your knife, then."

He clambered to his feet and presented her the weapon, hilt first. She reached for it, expecting him to withdraw it, but instead she grasped the smooth wooden handle.

She gagged, bent double, and began to vomit again.

When she was done, her head hurt as if struck from the inside by a hammer. Her chest felt ripped in two, and her vision was blurry. Her erstwhile captor was still whimpering before her, holding out the knife.

She arranged her clothes again and stood, finding the pain in her leg only slightly dulled.

"I'll take that water now," she said.

He brought her water and bread, and she had a bit of both. After that she felt better, calmer.

"Wist, where are we?" she asked.

"In the cellar of the beer hall," he said.

"In Sevoyne?"

"Yes, in Sevoyne."

"And who knows I'm here?"

"Myself and the captain of the guard. No one else."

"But others are coming, and they will know where to find us," she pushed on.

"Yes," he admitted.

"Yes, *Majesty*," she corrected gently. That simple act helped her find her center.

"Yes, Majesty."

"There. And who is coming?"

"Penby and his lot were supposed to waylay you in the woods. They should be back by now, but I don't—I don't know where they are. Did you kill them?"

"Yes," she lied. *One of them is dead, at least.* "Is anyone else meeting them here?"

He cowered a bit more. "I shouldn't."

"Answer me."

"Someone is supposed to meet them, yes. I don't know a name."

"When?"

"Soon. I don't know, but soon. Penby said by this afternoon."

"Well, then we had better go now," Anne said, picking up the knife.

His features contorted. "I . . . Yes. I'm supposed to do that."

Anne looked him in the eye as hard as she could. She didn't understand what was going on here. Was the demon, terrible as she was, an *ally*? Certainly she had killed one of Anne's enemies and seemed to have . . . *done* something to this one. But if whatever had followed her back from the land of the dead was friendly, why did she fear it so?

And there was still the possibility that this was some sort of a trick Wist was playing on her, though she couldn't see the point of such a ruse.

"They didn't tell me who you were," he began, but stopped.

"If you had known who I was, would you have tried to rape me?" she asked, anger flaring suddenly.

"No, *saints* no," he said.

"That doesn't make it better, you know," she said. "It still makes you a worm."

He just nodded at that.

For a moment she wanted to reach into him with her power, the way she had reached into Roderick back in Dunmrogh, the way she had reached into the men at Khrwbh Khrwkh. To hurt him, maybe kill him.

But she rejected that. She needed him right now. But if it turned out to be some strange trick, she wouldn't have any mercy.

"Very well," she said. "Help me, Wist, and you may earn my protection. Go against me again and not even the saints can preserve you."

"How can I serve you, Princess?"

"How do you think? I want to leave here. If the captain of the guard sees us, tell him the plans have changed and you're supposed to take me someplace else."

"And where will we go?"

"I'll tell you that once we're out of town. Now, bring me my weather cloak."

"It's upstairs. I'll go fetch it."

"No. We'll go get it together."

Nodding, Wist produced a brass key and fitted it into the lock on the door. It creaked open, revealing a narrow stair. He took a candle and started up. Anne followed to where the last stair ran apparently into the ceiling. Wist pushed, and the ceiling lifted into another dark room.

"It's a storehouse," he whispered. "Hang on."

He went over to a wooden crate and reached in. Anne tensed, but what he came out with was nothing other than her cloak. Never taking her eyes off him, she settled it on her shoulders.

"I have to blow out the candle now," he said, "else someone will see the light when I open the outer door."

"Do it, then," Anne said, tensing again.

He brought the candle near his face. In the yellow glow his features looked young and innocent, not the way the face of a rapist ought to look at all. He pursed his lips and blew, and darkness fell. It crawled on Anne's skin like centipedes as she strained her eyes and ears, her hand on the hilt of Wist's knife.

She heard a faint creak, then saw a widening sliver of not so black.

"This way," Wist whispered.

She perceived his silhouette now.

"You go first," she said, feeling for the door and catching its edge.

"Mind the step," he whispered. She saw the shadow of his head drop a bit.

She felt for the ground with her foot and found it. Then she stepped into the street.

It was bitterly cold outside. No moon or stars looked down; the only lights were lamps and candles still burning here or there. What time was it? She certainly didn't know. She didn't even know how long she had been in this place.

The alcohol was still in her. Rage and panic had cut through it, and now she was starting to feel achy and sick, though the stupid feeling remained. The boldness it had brought was starting to fade, leaving a dull fear.

The shadow that was Wist moved suddenly, and she felt his hand close on her arm. Her other hand tightened on the knife.

"Quiet, Majesty," he said. "Someone is coming."

She heard what he meant: the clopping of horses' hooves.

Wist pulled her against the side of another building, and then slowly they backed along it as the sound grew nearer.

Anne couldn't see anything, but she felt suddenly as if something were being pressed against her eyes. It wasn't light but a presence, a weight that seemed to draw everything toward it.

Wist's grip on her arm was now the most comforting thing in the world.

She heard someone dismount and felt feet strike the earth like sledgehammers. She heard a brief whispering she couldn't make out, and then the door creaked, sounding very near.

She backed away more quickly, aching to simply turn her back and run. But Wist wouldn't let her. He was trembling, and his breath seemed incredibly loud, as did her own.

The door clapped shut, and she felt the presence fade.

Now Wist tugged more urgently on her arm, and they did turn their backs. Her eyes began to adjust to the darkness, and she began to discern vague shapes. They made their way into what looked to be the village center, a broad square surrounded by the looming shadows of multistoried buildings.

"We have to hurry," he said. "It won't be long till they find us gone."

"Who was that?" she asked.

"I don't know," he said. "I would tell you if I knew. Someone important, the one who hired us, I think. I've never met him."

"Then how do you know—"

"I don't know!" he hissed desperately. "They said he would come. They didn't know what he would look like, but they said he would feel, ah, heavy. I didn't know what that meant until now. But you see?"

"Yes, I know what you mean," she said. "I felt it, too." She gripped his arm. "You could have called out to him. Why didn't you?"

"No, I couldn't," he said miserably. "I wanted to, but I couldn't. Now, where are we going?"

"Can you find Glenchest?"

"Glenchest? Auy, that's just down the road."

"How far on foot?"

"We could be there by midday."

"Let's go, then."

"He's likely to search that way."

"Nevertheless."

In the gray of dawn Wist looked tired, worn beyond his years. His clothes were dirty, and so was he, and it was a pervasive sort of filth. She believed he could be scrubbed for a year and somehow still be unclean.

He seemed dangerous again, too, though in a subdued way, like a vicious dog that had been beaten into lying still for a time. He kept glancing at her in a manner that suggested he was wondering exactly what he was doing and why.

She wondered the same thing.

The landscape was rather drab. Farmsteads and fields crowded to the road, but beyond them were flat plains with little relief or sights of interest.

She wondered again if any of her friends were alive, if the road to Glenchest was the right course, whether she ought to go back toward where she had been abducted. But if they were dead, there was nothing she could do. If they were fighting for their lives, she couldn't do much about that, either, not with only one very untrustworthy companion.

No, she needed to reach Aunt Elyoner and the knights she commanded.

Assuming they still existed or were at Glenchest. What if they already had gone to Eslen to fight the usurper? Or worse, what if Elyoner had thrown in with Robert? Anne didn't think that was likely, but then, she didn't really know what was going on.

In truth, she had always rather liked her uncle Robert. It seemed strange that he had taken the throne while her mother and brother yet lived, but that was the news that had come to Dunmrogh.

Perhaps Robert knew something she didn't.

She sighed and tried to push that thought away.

"Keep still," Wist said suddenly. Anne noticed that he had a knife in his hand now and that he was near enough to use it on her without any trouble. He was glancing around. They had passed into a small grove of trees full of lowing cattle, and visibility wasn't good.

But Anne felt and heard the horses coming. A lot of them.

CHAPTER SIX

THE SLINDERS

"SLINDERS," Stephen said.

Aspar had his gaze fixed across the valley, watching for one of their newly arrived opponents to show themselves.

"Coming from the east," Stephen clarified. "Moving quickly—and, for them, quietly."

Aspar strained his hearing to catch what Stephen's ears had heard. After a moment he had it, a sound like a low, hard wind sweeping through the forest, the sound of so many feet that he couldn't discriminate the individual steps, and with it, a faint humming in the ground.

"Sceat."

"Slinder" was the name the Oostish had given the servants of the Briar King. Once they had been human, but the ones Aspar had seen did not seem to have retained much Mannish about them.

They wore little or no clothing and ran howling like beasts. He had seen them tear men limb from limb and eat the raw, bloody flesh, watched them throw themselves on spears and pull their dying bodies up the shafts to reach their enemies. They couldn't be talked to, much less reasoned with.

And they were *close* already. How could he not have heard them? How had Stephen not, with his saint-sharpened senses? The boy seemed to be losing his knack.

He glanced quickly around. The nearest trees were mostly slender and straight-boled, but some fifty kingsyards away he saw a broad-shouldered ironoak reaching toward the sky.

"To that tree," he commanded. "Now."

"But Neil and Cazio—"

"There's nothing we can do for them," Aspar snapped. "We can't reach them in time."

"We can warn them," Winna said.

"They're already over there," Stephen said. "See?"

He pointed. Across the narrow valley, bodies were pouring over the rim and down the steep slope. It looked as if a flood were carrying an entire village of people down a gorge, except that there was no water.

"Mother of Saint Tarn," one of the Dunmrogh soldiers gasped. "What—"

"Run!" Aspar barked.

They ran. Aspar's muscles ached to bolt him ahead, but he had to let Winna and Stephen start climbing first. He heard the forest floor churning behind him and was reminded of a cloud of locusts that once had whirred through the northern uplands for days, chewing away every green thing.

They were halfway to the oak when Aspar caught a motion in the corner of his eye. He shifted his head to look.

At first glance the thing was all limbs, like a huge spider, but familiarity quickly brought it into focus. The monster had only four long limbs, not eight, and they ended in what resembled clawed human hands. The torso was thick, muscular, and short compared to its legs but more or less human in its cut if one ignored the scales and the thick black hairs.

The face had little of humanity about it; its yellow carbuncle eyes were set above two slits where a nose might be, and its cavernous, black-toothed mouth owed more to the frog or snake than to man. It was loping toward them on all fours.

"Utin," Aspar gasped under his breath. He'd met one before and killed it, but it had taken a miracle.

He had one miracle left, but looking past the shoulder of the thing, he saw that he needed two, for another identical creature was running scarcely thirty kingsyards behind it.

Aspar raised his bow, fired, and made one of the luckiest shots in his life; he hit the foremost monster in its right eye, sending it tumbling to the ground. Even as Aspar continued his flight to the tree, however, the thing rolled back to its feet and came on. The other, almost caught up now, seemed to grin at Aspar.

Then the slinders were there, pouring from between the trees. The utins wailed their peculiar high-pitched screams as wild-eyed men and women leapt upon them, first in twos, then in threes, then by the dozens.

The slinders and utins were not friendly, it seemed. Or perhaps they disagreed on who should eat Aspar White.

They finally reached the oak, and Aspar made a cradle of his hands to vault Winna to the lowest branches.

"Climb," he shouted. "Keep going until you can't climb anymore."

Stephen went up next, but before he had a firm foothold, Aspar was forced to meet the fastest of their attackers.

The slinder was a big man with lean muscles and bristling black hair. His face was so feral, Aspar was reminded of the legends of the wairwulf and wondered if this was where they had come from. Every other silly phay story seemed to be coming true. If ever there was a man who had become a wolf, this was it.

Like all of its kind, the slinder attacked without regard for its own life, snarling and reaching bloody, broken nails toward Aspar. The holter cut with the ax in his left hand as a feint. The slinder ignored the false attack and came on, allowing the ax to slice through its cheek. Aspar rammed his dirk in just below the lowest rib and quickly pumped the blade, shearing into the lung and up toward the heart even as the man-beast rammed into him, smashing him into the tree.

That hurt, but it saved him from being knocked to the ground. He shoved the dying slinder away from him just in time to meet the next two. They hit him together, and as he lifted his ax arm to fend them off, one sank its teeth into his forearm. Bellowing, Aspar stabbed into its groin and felt hot blood spurt on his hand. He cut again, opening the belly. The slinder let go of his arm, and he buried his ax in the throat of the second.

Hundreds more were only steps away.

The ax was stuck, so he left it, leaping for the lowest branch and catching it with blood-slicked fingers. He fought to keep the dirk, but when one of the slinders grasped his ankle, he let it drop to secure his tenuous hold, trying to wrap both arms around the huge bough.

An arrow whirred down from above, and then another, and his antagonist's grip loosened. Aspar swung his legs up, then levered himself quickly onto the limb.

A quick glance down showed the slinders crashing into the tree trunk like waves breaking against a rock. Their bodies began to form a pile, enabling the newer arrivals to drag themselves up.

"Sceat," Aspar breathed. He wanted to vomit.

He fought it down and looked above him. Winna was about five kingsyards higher than the rest, with her bow out, shooting into the press. Stephen and the two soldiers were at about the same height.

"Keep climbing!" Aspar shouted. "Up that way. The narrower the branches, the fewer can come after us at a time."

He kicked at the head of the nearest slinder, a rangy woman with matted red hair. She snarled and slipped from the branch, landing amid her squirming comrades.

The utins, he noticed, were still alive. There were three of them now that he could see, thrashing in the slinder horde. Aspar was reminded of a pack of dogs taking down a lion. Blood sprayed all around the slinders as they fell, dismembered and opened from sternum to crotch by the vicious claws and teeth of the monsters, but they were winning by sheer numbers. Even as he watched, one of the utins went down, hamstrung, and within seconds the slinders were dark crimson with its oily blood.

There would be plenty of slinders left when the utins were dead. Aspar gave up the vague hope that their enemies might cancel one another out.

Winna, Stephen, and the two Hornladhers had done as Aspar directed, and now he followed them until at last they reached a perch above a long, nearly vertical ascent. Aspar took his bow back off his shoulder and waited for the creatures to follow.

"They're different," he muttered under his breath, sighting down a shaft and impaling the first one to reach the base of the branch.

"Different how?" Stephen shouted down from above.

Aspar's neck hairs pricked up—now Stephen's uncanny senses seemed to be fine.

"They're leaner, stronger," he said. "The old ones are gone."

"I only saw the dead ones at the fane by the naubagm," Winna said, "but I don't remember them being tattooed like that, either."

Aspar nodded. "Yah. That's what I couldn't put my finger on. That's new, too."

"The mountain tribes tattoo," Ehawk said.

"Yah," Aspar agreed. "But the slinders we saw before came from a mixture of tribes and villages." He shot the next climber in the eye. "These all have the same tattoos."

They did. Each had a ram-headed snake wound around one forearm and a greffyn on the biceps of the same arm.

"Maybe they're all from the same tribe," Ehawk offered.

"Do you know any tribe with that tattoo?"

"No."

"Neither do I."

"The ram-headed serpent and the greffyn are both symbols associated with the Briar King," Stephen said. "We've been assuming that the Briar King drove these people mad somehow, took away their human intelligence. But what if . . ."

"What?" Winna said. "You think they *chose* this? They can't even speak!"

"I'll need you to start passing down arrows soon," Aspar said, shooting again. "I've only six left. The rest are on Ogre."

"The horses!" Winna exclaimed.

"They can take care of themselves," Aspar said. "Or they can't. Nothing we can do about it."

"But Ogre—"

"Yah." He thrust away the pain. Ogre and Angel had been with him a long time.

But everything died eventually.

Slinders continued to arrive from the forest, with no end of them in sight. So many teemed below, he couldn't see the forest floor for a hundred kingsyards.

"What do we do when we run out of arrows?" Winna asked.

"I'll kick 'em down," Aspar said.

"I thought you were on friendly terms with the Briar King and his friends," Stephen said. "Last time they let you live."

"Last time I had the king at the tip of an arrow," Aspar said. "The one the Church gave us."

"You still have it?"

"Yah. But unless the king himself shows his face, I don't reckon to use it until it's the only one I have left."

It also occurred to him that the Sefry woman Leshya had been with him then. Maybe that had been the difference; Leshya's true allegiance was—had always been—something of a mystery.

"That won't be too long," Winna said.

Aspar nodded and cast his gaze about. Maybe they could get to another tree, one with a straighter, higher bole, then cut the branch that got them there.

He was looking for such an escape route when he heard the singing. It was a weird rising and falling melody that caught at something in his bones. He was sure he had heard the song before, could almost imagine its singer, but the true memory eluded him.

The source of *this* song was visible, however.

"Saints," Stephen said, for he had seen it, too.

The singing came from a short, bandy-legged man and a slender, pale-skinned girl whose green eyes blazed even at this distance, which was about fifty kingsyards. The girl looked to be only about ten or eleven, the youngest slinder Aspar had ever seen. She held a snake in each hand—from this distance they looked to be rattling vipers—and the man held a crooked staff with a single drooping pinecone attached to it.

Both had the tattoos. Otherwise, they were as naked as the day they were born. They directed their song upward, but it took only an instant to understand that they weren't singing to the sky.

Ironoaks, the very ancient ones, had boughs so huge and heavy that they often sagged to the ground. The one Aspar and his companions were perched in wasn't that old; only two branches were low enough even to jump up and grab. But as the holter watched, the tips of the farthest branches quivered earthward, then began to bend, as if they were the fingers of a giant reaching down to pick something from the ground.

"Raver," Aspar swore.

Ignoring the next slinder clambering up the tree, he took aim at the singing man and sent his shaft flying. His aim was true, but another slinder somehow danced in the way of the arrow, taking the point in the shoulder. The same happened with his next shot.

"This is bad," Stephen said.

The whole tree shuddered now as the thicker boughs began straining toward the pair. The slinders around them were beginning to leap at the descending branches, and though the branches weren't low enough to catch yet, they soon would be. Then the entire tree would swarm with them.

Aspar looked up at the men-at-arms. "You two," he said. "Start cutting branches. Anything that leads here. Move out to where they're thinner so they'll be easier to cut."

"This is our doom," one of the men said. "Our lord was evil, and now we pay the price of serving him."

"You don't serve him now," Winna snapped. "You serve Anne, the rightful queen of Crotheny. Gather your manhood and do as Aspar says. Or give me your sword and let *me* do it."

"I heard what she did," the man replied, tracing the sign

against evil on his forehead. "This woman you call queen. Killed men without touching them, using shinecraft. It's all done. The world is ending."

Stephen, who was nearest the man, reached his hand out. "Give me your sword," he said. "Give it to me now."

"Give it, Ional," the other soldier snapped. He looked at Stephen. "I'm not ready to die. I'll go up this way. You'll take the other?"

"Yes," Stephen agreed.

Aspar gave Stephen and the Hornladher a quick glance as they moved out farther. If they could isolate the main branch they were on, they might have a chance.

Winna was looking at him, though, and he felt something sink down through his guts. Winna was the best and the most unexpected thing that had come into his life in a long time. She was young, yes, so young that sometimes she seemed as if she might be from a different country across some distant sea. But most of the time she seemed to know him, know him in a way that was unlikely—and sometimes was more unsettling than comfortable. He'd been alone for a long time.

The past few days she hadn't talked to him much, not since she'd found him keeping watch by the wounded Leshya. In that, at least, she didn't know him as well as she might. What he felt for Leshya wasn't love or even lust. It was something else, something even he had a hard time naming. But it resembled, he imagined, kinship. The Sefry woman was like him in a way that Winna could never be.

But maybe Winna *did* understand that. Maybe that was the problem.

It's all moot if the slinders get us, he reckoned, and he nearly chuckled. It sounded like one of those sayings. *As well stretch your neck for the Raver as marry. A good day is the one you live through. It's all moot if the slinders come . . .*

Sceat, he was starting to think like Stephen.

He shot another slinder.

Three arrows left.

* * *

It wasn't as easy cutting through branches as Stephen might have wished or imagined. The sword had an edge, but it wasn't that sharp, and he'd never really done much wood chopping, so he wasn't certain about the best way to go about the task.

A glance showed him that the outer branches were nearly low enough for the slinders to reach; that meant he had to hurry.

He reared back for a more powerful swing and nearly fell. He was straddling a limb, clutching it with his inner thighs the way one did a horse. But like a horse, the branch refused to be still, and it seemed a dizzying long way to the ground.

He renewed his balance and made a more modest cut, feeling the living wood shiver under the blow and watching a smallish chip fly. Maybe if he cut straight, then at an angle . . .

He did, and that worked better.

He couldn't stop paying attention to the slinder song. There was a language there; he felt the cadence, the flow of meaning. But he couldn't understand it, not a single word, and given his saint-blessed memory and knowledge of languages, that was astonishing. In his mind he compared it to everything from Old Vadhiian to what little he knew of the language of Hadam, but nothing fit. Nevertheless, he felt as if the meaning was incredibly close, resting on his nose, too near to his eyes to quite see.

Aspar thought the slinders had changed. What did that mean?

"Slinder" was an Oostish word that just meant "eater" or "devouring one." But what were they really? The short answer was that they had once been people who lived near or in the King's Forest, before the Briar King awoke. Since his awakening, entire tribes had abandoned their villages to follow the king, whatever he was.

There were legends of such things, of course. There was a detail in the *Tale of Galas,* the only remaining text from the ancient vanished kingdom of Tirz Eqqon. The great bull of the Ferigolz had been stolen by Vhomar giants, and Galas had been sent to retrieve it. In his quest he had met a giant named Koerwidz who had a magic cauldron, a drink from which transformed men into beasts of various kinds.

Saint Fufluns was said to possess a pipe whose music filled men with madness and turned them cannibal. Grim, the Raver—the dark and terrible Ingorn spirit that Aspar swore by—also was said to inspire battle madness in his worshippers, making birsirks of them.

The limb gave way with a snap, hung for a moment by its bark, then fell. The portion Stephen was on sprang up like the arm of a catapult, and he suddenly found himself airborne and feeling stupid.

On the Sundry Follies of the Thinks-Too-Much, he began, a new essay he'd just decided to write in his head. He reckoned he had time for another line or so as he flailed wildly for purchase. His thigh hit a branch, and he scrabbled for it, losing the sword, of course, in the process and not securing a hold, either.

Looking up, he saw Winna's face far above, tiny but beautiful. Did she know he loved her? He was sorry he hadn't told her even though it might mean the end of their friendship—and of his friendship with Aspar.

His hand caught a branch, and fire seemed to shoot up his arm, but he held it, nevertheless. Gasping, he glanced down. The slinders were there, leaping for him, missing his dangling feet by a yard or so.

The chief virtue of the Thinks-Too-Much is that it isn't likely to reproduce its kind, for its lack of attention to matters at hand oft leads to an untimely demise. Its only virtue is its love of friends and sorrow that it could not help them more.

He saw that the sorcelled tree limbs had reached the ground, and the man-beasts were swarming up into the branches. He looked up in time to see a leering face just before another body grappled his and pulled him into the salivating mob below.

"I'm sorry, Aspar!" he managed to shout before he was smothered in greedy hands.

CHAPTER SEVEN

VENGEANCE

LEOFF GAGGED at the pain as his fingers were stretched toward what had once been a natural angle for them,"The device is my own invention," the leic explained proudly. "I've had great success with it."

Leoff blinked through his tears and peered at the thing. It was essentially a gauntlet of supple leather with small metal hooks at the end of each finger. His hand had been inserted into the glove and placed on a metal plate with various holes drilled for the hooks to catch in. The doctor had stretched his fingers out in the directions they ought to lie and fixed them there with the hooks.

Then—the most painful part—a second plate was fitted above his hand and tightened down with screws. The tendons of his arm ran with fire, and he wondered if this was just a more subtle form of torture devised by the usurper and his physicians.

"Let's go back to the heat and the herbs." Leoff winced. "That part felt good."

"That was just to loosen things up," the leic explained, "and to invoke the healing humors. *This* is the important part. Your hands were mending all wrong, but fortunately they had not been allowed to progress for too long. We must now guide them into the proper shape; after that, I can build rigid splints that will hold them in place until the true healing can occur."

"This comes up often, then?" Leoff gasped as the fellow further tightened the screws. His palm was still far from flat, but already he could feel multiplied tiny snaps within his bruised flesh. "Hands done up like this."

"Not like this," the leic admitted. "I've never worked on hands damaged quite in this way. But hands crushed by blow from mace or sword are common enough. Before I was leic to His Majesty, I was physician to the court of the Greft of Ofthen. He held tournaments every month, you see, and he had five sons and thirteen nephews of jousting age."

"So you've only recently come to Eslen?" Leoff asked, glad for the distraction.

"I came about a year ago, though at the time I was attendant to the leic who served His Majesty King William. After the king's death, I served Her Majesty the queen briefly before becoming attendant to King Robert's physician."

"I am recently come here as well," Leoff said.

The physician tightened the screws.

"I know who you are, of course. You gained a reputation rather quickly, I should say." He smiled thinly. "You might have exercised a bit more prudence."

"I might have," Leoff assented. "But then we wouldn't have the fun of seeing exactly how effective your device will be."

"I will not deceive you," the leic said. "Your hands can be made better, but they cannot be made as new."

"I never imagined they could be." Leoff sighed, blinking away tears of pain as another half-healed bone snapped and went groaning into a new position.

The next day he clumsily pawed through one of the books the usurper had supplied him, using hands encased in rigid gloves of iron and heavy leather, as the physician had promised. They were splayed out, fully stretched, and looked altogether too much like the comically exaggerated hands of a puppet. He couldn't decide whether he appeared droll or horrible as he tried to turn the pages with his cumbersome mittens.

He soon forgot that, however, as he was lost in puzzlement.

The book was an older one, printed in antique Almannish characters. It was entitled *Luthes sa Felthan ya sa Birmen*—"Songs of Field and Birm"—and those were the only intelligible words in the book. The rest of it was inked in characters Leoff had never seen before. They resembled the alphabet he knew in some regards, but he couldn't be certain of any single letter.

There were some pages with odd poetic-looking configurations that also seemed somewhat familiar, but all in all it appeared that the book's cover and its contents did not go together. Even the paper inside didn't seem to match; it looked much older than the binding.

He'd found an intriguing page of diagrams that didn't make any more sense than the text, when he heard someone rattling at the door again. He sighed, steeling himself for yet another round with the prince or his doctor.

But it was neither, and Leoff felt a rush of pure joy as a young girl walked in through the portal, which promptly slammed and locked behind her.

"Mery!" he cried.

She hesitated a moment, then rushed into his arms. He lifted her, his ridiculous hands crossing behind her back.

"Urf!" Mery grunted as he squeezed.

"It's so good to see you," he said as he set her down.

"Mother said you were probably awfully dead," Mery said, looking terribly serious. "I so hoped she was wrong."

He reached to tousle her hair, but her eyes grew wide at the sight of his claws.

"Ah," he said, clapping them together. "This is nothing. Something to make my hands feel better. How is your mother, then, the Lady Gramme?" he asked.

"I don't know, really," Mery replied. "I haven't seen her for days."

He knelt, feeling things pop and pull in his legs.

"Where are they keeping *you*, Mery?"

She shrugged, staring at his hands but never directly into his face. "They put a blindfold on me." She brightened a bit. "But it's seventy-eight steps. My steps, anyway."

He smiled at her cleverness. "I hope your room is nicer than this."

She looked around. "It is. I have a window, at least."

A window. Were they no longer in the dungeons?

"Did you go up or down stairs to get here?" he asked.

"Yes, down, twenty." She had never stopped staring at his hands. "What happened to them?" she asked, pointing.

"I hurt them," he said softly.

"I'm sorry," Mery said. "I wish I could make them better." Her frown deepened. "You can't play the hammarharp like that, can you?"

He felt a sudden clotting in his throat. "No," he said, "I can't. But you can play for me. Would you mind doing that?"

"No," she said. "Though you know I'm not very good."

He peered into her eyes and placed his hands gently on her shoulders. "I never told you this before," he said, "not in so many words. But you have it in you to be a great musician. Perhaps the best."

Mery blinked. "Me?"

"Don't let it go to your head."

"My head is too large for my shoulders, anyhow, Mother says." She frowned. "Do you suppose I could ever compose, as you do? That would be the very best thing."

Leoff rose, blinking a bit in surprise. "A female composer? I've never heard of that. But I see no reason . . ." He trailed off.

How would such a creature be treated, a woman composer? Would she reap commissions? Would it bring gold to her pocket?

Probably not. Nor would it increase her chances of a good marriage; in fact, it probably would decrease them.

"Well, let's talk about that when the time comes, eh? For

now, why don't you play me something—anything you
want, something for fun—and then we'll have a lesson,
yes?"

She nodded happily and took her seat at the instrument,
placing her tiny fingers on the yellow-and-red keys. She hit
one experimentally and held it down, giving it a delicate
tremble with her finger. The note sang so sweetly in the
stone room that Leoff thought his heart would flow like
warm wax.

Mery gave a little cough and began to play.

She began plainly enough with what he recognized as a
Lierish nursery tune, a simple melody played quite naturally
in etrama, the mode known also as the Lamp of Night, lilting, plaintive, soothing. Mery fingered the melody with the
right hand, and with the left she added a very simple accompaniment of sustained triads. It was altogether charming,
and his astonishment grew as he realized that he hadn't
taught her this—it had to be her own arrangement. He
waited to see how it would continue.

As he suspected, the last chord hung unsustained, drawing
him into the next phrase, and now the humming chords became a moving set of counterpoints. The harmonies were
flawless, sentimental but not overly so. It was a mother,
holding her infant close, singing a song she'd sung a hundred times before. Leoff could almost feel the blanket
against his skin, the hand stroking his head, the slight breeze
blowing into the nursery from the night meadow beyond.

The final chord was again unsustained, and very odd. The
harmonies suddenly loosened, opened up, as if the melody
had flown out the window, leaving infant and mother behind.
Leoff realized that the mode had changed from the gentle
second mode to the haunting seventh, sefta, but even for that
mode the accompaniment was strange. And it got stranger,
as Leoff realized that Mery had moved from lullaby to
dream and now—quite quickly—to nightmare.

The bass line was a Black Mary crawling under his bed,
the tune had shifted to some nearly forgotten middle line,
and the high notes were all spiders and the scent of burning

hair. Mery's face was perfectly blank with concentration, white and smooth as only a child's could be, unmarred by the march of years, the stamp of terror and worry, disappointment and hatred. But it wasn't her face he was hearing now but rather something that had come out of her soul and that clearly was *not* unmarred.

Before he knew it, the melody had suddenly broken: fragmented, searching to put itself back together but unable to, as if it had forgotten itself. The hush-a-bye had become a whervel in three-time, calling up images of a mad masked ball in which the faces beneath were more terrible than the masks—monsters disguised as people disguised as monsters.

Then, slowly, beneath the madness, the melody came back together and strengthened, but now it was in the low end of the scale, played with the left hand. It gathered the rest of the notes to itself and calmed them down until the counterpoint was nearly hymnlike, then simple triads again. Mery had brought them back to the nursery, back to where it was safe, but the voice had changed. It was no longer a mother singing but a father, and this time, at last, the final chord resolved.

Leoff found himself blinking tears when it was over. Technically, it would be surprising from a student of many years, but Mery had studied with him only for a couple of months. Yet the sheer intuitive power of it—the soul it hinted at—was nothing short of astonishing.

"The saints are working here," he murmured.

During his torture, he'd almost stopped believing in the saints, or at least stopped believing that they cared about him at all. With a few strokes of her hands, Mery had changed all that.

"You didn't like it?" she asked timidly.

"I loved it, Mery," he breathed. He fought to keep his voice from trembling. "It's—can you play it like that again? Just like that?"

She frowned. "I think so. That's the first time I've played it. But it's in my head."

"Yes," Leoff said. "I know what you mean. That's how it

is with me. But I've never met— Can you start again, Mery?"

She nodded, put her hands to the keyboard, and played it again note for note.

"You must learn to write your music down," he said. "Would you like to learn that?"

"Yes," the girl said.

"Very good. You'll have to do it yourself. My hands are . . ." He held them up helplessly.

"What happened to them?" Mery asked again.

"Some bad men did it," he admitted. "But they aren't here anymore."

"I should like to see the men who did that," Mery said. "I should like to see them die."

"Don't talk like that," he said softly. "There's no sense in hatred, Mery. There's no sense in it at all, and it only hurts you."

"I wouldn't mind being hurt if I could hurt them," Mery insisted.

"Perhaps," Leoff told her. "But I would mind. Now, let's learn to write, shall we? What's the name of this song?"

She looked suddenly shy.

"It's for you," she said. " 'Leoff's Song.' "

Leoff stirred from sleep, thinking he had heard something but not certain what it was. He sat up and rubbed at his eyes, then winced as he was reminded that even so simple a task had become complicated and somewhat dangerous.

Still, he felt better than he had for some time. The visit from Mery had helped him more than he cared to admit to himself, certainly more than he would ever admit to his captors. If this was some new form of torture—to show him Mery again and then take her away—his tormentors would fail. Whatever the usurper had said to him, whatever he had said back, he knew his days were numbered.

Even if he never saw the girl again, his life was already better than it would have been.

"You're wrong, you know," a voice whispered.

Leoff had begun to lie back down on his simple bed. Now he froze in the act, uncertain whether he had really heard the voice. It had been very faint and raspy. Could it be his ears, turning the movement of a guard in the corridor beyond into an indictment of his thoughts?

"Who's there?" he asked quietly.

"Hatred is well worth the effort," the voice continued, much more clearly this time. "In fact, hatred is the only wood some furnaces will burn."

Leoff couldn't tell where the voice was coming from. Not from inside the room and not from the door. Then *where*?

He got up, clumsily lighting a candle and searching the walls as he stumbled about.

"Who speaks to me?" he asked.

"Hatred," the reply came. "Lo Husuro. I have become eternal, I think."

"Where are you?"

"It is always night," the voice replied. "And once it was quiet. But now I hear so much beauty. Tell me what the little girl looks like."

Leoff's eyes settled to one corner of the room. Finally he understood and felt stupid for not guessing earlier. There was only one opening in the room besides the door, and that was a small vent about the length of a kingsfoot on each side, too small for even an infant to crawl through—but not too small for a voice.

"You're a prisoner, too?"

"Prisoner?" the voice murmured. "Yes, yes, that is one way to say it. I am prevented, that is, prevented from the thing that means the most to me."

"And what is that?" Leoff asked.

"Revenge." The voice was softer than ever, but now that Leoff was closer to the vent, it was very clear. "In my language we call it *Lo Videicha*. It is more than a word in my language—it is an entire philosophy. Tell me about the girl."

"Her name is Mery. She is seven years of age. She has nut-brown hair and bright blue eyes. She was wearing a dark green gown today."

"She is your daughter? Your niece?"

"No. She is my student."

"But you love her," the voice insisted.

"That is not your business," Leoff said.

"Yes," the man replied. "That would be a knife to give me, yes, if I were your enemy. But I think we are not enemies."

"Who are you?"

"No, that is too familiar, don't you see? Because it is a very long answer and is all in my heart."

"How long have you been here?"

A harsh laugh followed, a small silence, then a confession. "I do not know," he admitted. "Much of what I remember is suspect. So much pain, and without moon or sun or stars to keep the world below me. I have drifted very far, but the music brings me back. Do you have a lute, perhaps, or a chithara?"

"There is a lute in my cell, yes," Leoff replied.

"Could you play something for me, then? Something to remind me of orange groves and water trickling from a clay pipe?"

"I can't play anything," Leoff said. "My hands have been destroyed."

"Of course," Hatred said. "That is your soul, your music, that is. So they struck at that. They missed, I think."

"They missed," Leoff agreed.

"They give you the instruments to taunt you. But why do they let the girl see you, do you think? Why do they give you a way to make music?"

"The prince wants me to do something," Leoff replied. "He wants me to compose for him."

"Will you?"

Leoff stepped back from the hole in the floor, suddenly suspicious. The voice could be anyone: Prince Robert, one of his agents, anyone. The usurper certainly knew how he had tricked Praifec Hespero. He wasn't going to let such a thing happen again, was he?

"The wrongs done me were done by others," he said finally. "The prince has commissioned music from me, and I will write it as best I can."

There was a pause, then a dark chuckle from the other. "I see. You are a man of intelligence. Smart. I must think of a way to win your confidence, I think."

"Why do you want my confidence?" Leoff asked.

"There is a song, a very old song from my country," the fellow said. "I can try to make it into your language if you like."

"If it pleases you."

There was a bit of a pause, then the man began. The sound was jarring, and Leoff understood immediately what he was hearing: the voice of a man who had forgotten how to sing.

The words came haltingly but plain.

The seed in winter lies dreaming
Of the tree it will grow into

The Cat-Furred Worm
Longs for the butterfly it will become

The Tadpole twitches its tail
But desires tomorrow's legs

I am hatred
But dream of being vengeance

After the last line he chuckled. "We will speak again, *Leffo*," he said. "For I am your *malasono*."

"I don't know that word," Leoff said.

"I don't know if your language has such a word," the man said. "It is a conscience, the sort that leads you to do evil things to evil people. It is the spirit of *Lo Videicha*."

"I have no word for that concept," Leoff confirmed. "Nor do I wish one."

But in the darkness, later, as his fingers longed for the hammarharp, he began to wonder.

Sighing, unable to sleep, he took up the strange book he'd been studying earlier and puzzled at it again. He fell asleep on it, and when he woke, something had fit together, and in a burst of epiphany he suddenly understood how he might be able to slay Prince Robert. He didn't know whether to laugh or cry.

But he would certainly do it, if he got the chance.

CHAPTER EIGHT

A HARD CHOICE

ASPAR TURNED at Winna's scream, just in time to watch as Stephen was pulled from the branch.

It seemed familiar somehow, and it happened slowly enough for Aspar to understand why. It was like a Sefry puppet play, a miniature of the world, unreal. At this distance Stephen's face was no more expressive than that of a marionette carved of wood, and when he looked up at Aspar one last time, there was nothing there, only the dark spaces of his eyes, the round circle of his mouth.

Then he was gone.

Then another figure plunged through the frame, caricatured by distance as Stephen, a knife gleaming in his hand as he swung purposefully from the branch into the grove of raised arms and their five-petaled blooms.

Ehawk.

From somewhere near Aspar heard a raw scream of rage. Part of him wondered vaguely who it was, and it was only later, when he felt the soreness of his throat, that he realized it had been his own.

He started forward on his branch, but there was nothing he could do. Winna shrieked again, a sound that somewhat resembled the boy's name. Aspar watched, his heart frozen, as Stephen's face appeared once, streaked with blood, and then went back down in the mass.

Ehawk he didn't see again. He aimed the bow, wondering what target to hit, what miracle shot could save his friends.

But the cold lump in his chest knew the truth: They were already dead.

Fury welled up in him. He shot, anyway, wanting to kill another of them, wishing he had enough arrows to slaughter them all. He didn't care what they had been before the world went mad. Farmers, hunters, fathers, brothers, sisters—he didn't care.

He looked at Winna, saw the tear-brimmed eyes, the utter helplessness that was mirror to his own. Her gaze pleaded for him to do something.

His survival instinct made him turn to use his last few arrows on those slinders who still would be climbing up after them, but to his surprise he realized that they were gone. As he watched, the last of their attackers leapt from the tree, and like a wave retreating after it runs up a shingle, the mass of grotesque bodies flowed away into the twilight.

In but a few heartbeats, there was only the hushed sound of them retreating through the forest.

Aspar continued to crouch, staring after them. He felt incredibly tired, old, and lost.

"It's snowing again," Winna said sometime later.

Aspar acknowledged the truth of that with a little shrug.

"Aspar."

"Yah." He sighed. "Come on."

He stood on his perch and helped her down. She wrapped her arms around him, and they clutched there for a few moments. He was aware of the two men-at-arms watching them, but for the moment he didn't care. The warmth and the smell of her felt good. He remembered the first time she had kissed him, the confusion and the exhilaration, and he wanted to go back to that moment, back before things had become so confusing.

Before Stephen and Ehawk had died.

"Hello!" a voice called up from below.

Looking past Winna's curling snow-damped locks, Aspar saw the knight Neil MeqVren. The Vitellian swordsman was standing with him and the girl Austra. An oblique black anger stirred. These three and the men-at-arms—they were almost strangers. Why should they be allowed to live when Stephen was torn limb from limb?

Sceat on it. There were things to be done.

"Let me go," Aspar muttered gruffly, pulling at Winna's arms. "I need to talk to them."

"Aspar, that was Stephen and Ehawk."

"Yah. I need to talk to these men."

She let him go, and, avoiding her eyes, he helped her the rest of the way down the tree, jumping to avoid the bodies piled up on the spreading roots, wary that one or more of them might still be alive. But none moved.

"You're all all right?" he asked Neil.

The knight nodded. "Only by the mercy of the saints. Those things had no interest in us."

"What do you mean?" Winna demanded.

Neil lifted his hands. "We were just attacking Austra's captors when they came pouring out from the woods. I cut three or four of them down before I realized they were just trying to run around us. We sheltered against a tree to keep from getting trampled. When they were passed, we fought Austra's kidnappers. I'm afraid we had to kill them all."

Austra nodded as if in agreement but seemed too shaken to speak, clinging tightly to Cazio.

"They ran past you," Aspar repeated, trying to understand. "Then they were after us?"

"No," Winna said thoughtfully. "Not us. They were after Stephen. And as soon as they got him, they left. Ehawk . . ." Her eyes widened with hope. "Aspar, what if they're still alive? We didn't actually see—"

"Yah," he said, turning it this way and that in his head. After all, they had thought Stephen dead once before, and then they actually had had his body.

Winna was *right*.

"Well, we have to go after him, then," Winna said.

"A moment, please," Neil said, still studying the land-scape of bodies. "There's a lot here I don't understand. These things that attacked us—these are the slinders you described to the queen on our first day of riding?"

"That they are," Aspar admitted, impatience beginning to grow in him.

"And these serve the Briar King?"

"Same answer," Aspar replied.

"And what is *that*?" Neil pointed to the half-chewed carcass of an utin.

Aspar looked at the thing, thinking that Stephen would probably like to see it dissected like this so he could study it.

Instead of skin, the utin was covered in horny plates, not unlike the scuts of a tortoise. From the joints of those plates, black hairs bristled. In Aspar's experience, that natural armor was good enough to turn arrows, dirks, and axes, but somehow the slinders had pried some of the horn up and dug into the flesh, exposing the wet organs within the thickly boned rib cage. The creature's eyes had been clawed out, the bottom jaw broken and half torn off. A human arm, severed at the shoulder, was jammed in its throat.

"We call it an utin," Aspar said. "We fought one before."

"But these were killed by the slinders."

"Yah."

"From what you've been saying, then, of all of us, the slinders only attacked the utins and Frete Stephen."

"That's what it looks like," Aspar agreed brusquely. "That's what we've been saying."

"But you think they took Stephen alive?"

For answer, Aspar spun on his heel and paced to where he had last seen his friend, where the oak's unnaturally twisted branches still touched the earth. The others followed him.

"I've seen the slinders kill," he said. "They either eat the dead on the spot or leave them torn to pieces. There's no sign of that here, so they took Stephen and Ehawk with them."

"But why would they take just those two?" Neil persisted. "What would they want with them in particular?"

"Why does it matter?" Winna challenged angrily. "We have to go get them back."

Neil blushed, but he lifted his shoulders higher and tilted his chin up.

"Because," he said, "I understand what it's like to lose comrades. I know right well the conflict of two loyalties. But you are pledged to serve Her Majesty. If your friends are dead, they are dead, and nothing can be done about it. If they are alive, then they were spared for some reason also beyond your control. I implore—"

"Neil MeqVren," Winna said, her voice cold now with fury. "You were there, at Cal Azroth, when the Briar King appeared. We all fought together there, and we all fought again at Dunmrogh. If it weren't for Stephen, we would *all* be dead, and Her Majesty, too. You cannot be so unfeeling."

Neil sighed. "Meme Winna," he said, "I've no wish to hurt or offend you. But without any other bond, all of us— besides Cazio, here—we all are subjects of the throne of Crotheny. Our first allegiance is there. And if that were not so, remember that we all took an oath before leaving Dunmrogh to serve Anne, the rightful heir to that throne, and see her on it or die.

"Stephen and Ehawk took that oath, too." His voice raised a bit. "And we have *lost* her. Someone has taken her from us, and we—her supposed protectors—are much reduced in number. Now you propose to divide us further, meme. Please remember your promise and help me find Anne. For the saints, we don't even know Stephen and Ehawk are alive."

"We don't know *she* is, either," Aspar countered.

"You're the royal holter," Neil protested.

Aspar shook his head. "As a matter of fact, I'm not. I was removed from that position. I'm supposed to answer to the praifec, and *he* charged me to kill the Briar King. Them that just took Stephen are the Briar King's servants, and I reckon they'll lead me to 'im."

"That same praifec was behind the murders and shinecraft at Dunmrogh and likely was in league with the assassins at Cal Azroth," Neil pointed out. "He is the enemy of your rightful ruler, and thus you owe no allegiance to him at all."

"Don't know it for sure," Aspar grunted. "Besides, if I'm the holter, like you say, well, this forest falls in my jurisdiction, and I ought to find out what all of this is about.

"Either way, it's my choice to make."

"I *know* it's your choice to make," Neil said. "But I'm the only one here who can speak for Anne, and I'm begging you to consider my argument."

Aspar met the knight's earnest gaze, then glanced at Winna. He wasn't sure what he was going to say but was spared voicing it by the sound of something else coming through the forest.

"Hear that?" he asked Neil.

"I hear *something,*" the knight replied, hand straying to the hilt of his sword.

"Riders, a lot of 'em," Aspar growled. "I'd say this matter can wait until we see what new insult has come looking for us."

CHAPTER NINE

REBIRTH

THE DEAD whispered her awake.

Her first breath was agony, as if her lungs had been blown of glass and then shattered by the intake. Her muscles tried to crawl off her bones. She would have screamed, but her mouth and throat were cloyed with congealed bile and mucus.

Her head was hammering against stone, and there was

nothing she could do about it but watch the sparks that formed in her eyes. Then her entire body bent backward as if she were a bow being pulled by a saint, and the arrows exploded wetly from her mouth, again, again, until finally everything unclenched and she lay quietly, unhurried breaths rasping in and out of her as the pain gradually washed away from her, leaving exhaustion behind.

She felt as if she were sinking into something soft.

Saints, forgive me, she silently prayed. *I did not want to. I had to.*

That was only half-true, but she was too tired to explain it to them.

The saints didn't seem to be listening, anyhow, though the dead were still whispering. She thought she had understood them not that long ago, comprehended the strange tenses of their verbs. Now they flitted at the edge of her understanding, all but one, and that one was trying to lick into her ear like a lover's tongue.

She didn't want to hear it, didn't want to listen, for the very simple fear that if she did, her soul would return to oblivion.

But the voice wasn't going to be denied by anything as simple as fear.

No, by the damned ones, it burred. *You can hear me. You will hear me.*

"Who are you?" She relented. "Please . . ."

"My name?" The voice gathered strength immediately, and she felt a hand press against the side of her face. It was very cold.

"It was Erren, I think. Erren. And who are you? You are familiar."

She realized then that she had forgotten her own name.

"I don't remember," she said. "But I remember you. The queen's assassin."

"Yes," the voice said triumphantly. "Yes, that's me. And I know you now. Alis. Alis Berrye." Something like a chuckle followed that. "By the saints. I missed you, didn't know what you were. How did I miss you?"

Alis! I am Alis! she thought in desperate relief.

"I did not want to be found," Alis said. "But I always feared that you would catch me. Indeed, I was terrified of you."

The hand stroked against her neck.

"Coven-trained, yes." The dead woman sighed. "But not by any proper coven of the Church, were you? Halaruni?"

"We call ourselves the Veren," Alis answered.

"Ah, yes, of course," Erren said. "Veren. The mark of the crescent moon. I know something of you. And now you are my queen's protector."

"I am, lady."

"How did you accomplish this escape from death? Your heart was slowed to beating only once a day, your breath stilled. Your blood stank of gallowswort, but now it is clean."

"If he had *not* used gallowswort—if he had used lauvleth or merwaurt or hemlock—I *would* be dead," Alis replied.

"You might die, anyway," Erren replied. "Even now you are very near. A thing as insubstantial as I cannot do much, but you are so very close to us, I think I might manage it . . ."

"Then she would have no one to aid her," Alis said.

"Tell me quickly why you did not die. I know of no faneway, no shinecraft that will stop the work of gallowswort."

"Our ways are different," Alis said. "And the law of death *has* been broken. The markland between the quick and the dead is much wider than it was; the passage both ways less certain. Gallowswort is more sure than most poisons, because it acts not only on the body but also on the soul. There is a very old story in our order about a woman who let herself be taken by death and yet returned. It was the last time the law of death was broken, during the time of the Black Jester.

"I felt I might be able to accomplish the same thing, and knew the sacaums necessary to try. And I had no choice, really. The poison was already in me." She paused. "You should not kill me, Sor Erren."

"Does my queen understand the aim of your order?"

"My order is dead. All of them but me," Alis replied. "I am no longer bound by their mission."

"Then she doesn't."

"Of course not," Alis said. "How could I tell her? She needs to trust me."

"At this moment," the shade of Erren murmured, "it is *I* who must trust you."

"I might have killed her many times," Alis said. "Yet I have not."

"You wait for the daughter, perhaps."

"No," Alis said, desperately now. "You do not understand the Veren so well as you think if you suggest that we might harm Anne."

"Perhaps you wish to control her, though," Erren said. "Control the true queen."

"That is nearer the truth, at least as far as the coven was concerned," Alis admitted. "But I was not of the inner circle. I never fully understood the goals of the Veren, and now I do not care."

"You say the sisters are all dead. What of the brothers?"

Alis felt her heart trip. "You know of them?"

"Not before now. I guessed. The Order of Saint Cer has its male counterpart. The Veren must as well. But do you understand how dangerous it is if only the males remain? If only their voices are raised in council?"

"No," Alis said, "I don't. I wish only to serve Muriele, to bring her to safety, to help her preserve her country."

"Is this true?"

Alis felt something pinch someplace inside her. It didn't hurt, but she felt suddenly very faint, and her pulse beat weirdly, as if trying to escape her body.

"I swear to you it is true," she gasped. "I swear it on the saint we swear by."

"Name her."

"Virgenya."

After a pause, the pressure eased a bit but did not vanish.

"It's so hard to hang on," Erren said. "We forget, the dead."

"You seem to remember quite a lot," Alis observed, recovering her composure.

"I cling to what I must. I do not remember my parents or being a little girl. I do not recall if I ever loved a man or a woman. I cannot imagine the shape of my living face. But I remember my duty.

"I remember that. And I remember *her*. Can you protect her? Will you?"

"Yes," Alis said weakly. "I swear it."

"And what if the men of the Veren remain and come to you? What then? What if they come to you and ask you to do harm to her or her daughter?"

"I am *the queen's* now," Alis insisted. "Hers, not theirs."

"I find that difficult to believe."

"You were coven-trained. If the Church had asked you to kill Muriele, would you have done it?"

Erren's laughter was soft and without humor. "I *was* asked," she said.

The hairs pricked up on Alis' neck. "Who?" she asked. "Who gave you that order? Hespero?"

"Hespero?" Her voice seemed more distant. "I do not remember that name. Perhaps he is not important. No, I don't remember who sent the word. But it must have been someone very highly placed, or I would never have considered it."

"You *considered* it?" Alis asked, shocked.

"I think that I did."

"Then there must have been a reason," Alis said.

"Not reason enough to do it."

"What is happening, Erren? The world is coming apart. The law of death is broken. Who is my enemy?"

"I died, Alis," the shade said. "If I had known these things, if I had known what to watch for, do you imagine I would be dead?"

"Oh."

"Your enemies are her enemies. That is all you need to know. It makes it simple."

"Simple," Alis agreed, though she knew it could not be simple.

"You will live," Erren said. "Everyone thinks you are dead. What will you do?"

"Anne is alive," Alis said.

"Anne?"

"Muriele's youngest daughter."

"Ah, yes. I told her that."

"She lives, and so does Fail de Liery and many others loyal to the queen. Robert fears that an army will gather behind Anne, and not without reason."

"An army," Erren mused. "The daughter leading an army. I wonder how that will work out."

"I think I can help," Alis said. "The queen is watched too closely, and she is kept in the Wolfcoat Tower, far from any of the hidden passages. I think her only hope for freedom is if Anne prevails, but that must happen soon, before Hansa and the Church can become involved."

"How will you help, then? By murdering Robert?"

"I've thought of that, of course," Alis said. "But I'm not certain he *can* be killed. He has also returned from death, Lady Erren, but he was wholly dead. He does not bleed like a man. I know not how to kill what he has become."

"I may have once known such things," Erren said. "No longer. What, then?"

"There is a man the usurper has imprisoned. If I can free him in Anne's name, I believe even the most reluctant landwaerden will rally to her cause. It should tip the balance."

"The passages, then."

"It will be a risk," Alis said. "Prince Robert is alone among men in that he knows of the passages and can remember them. But—"

"But he thinks you are dead," Erren said. "I understand. It is a weapon you can use only once, really."

"Exactly," Alis replied.

"Have a care," Erren said. "There are things in the dungeons of Eslen that should have died a very long time ago. Do not think them impotent."

"I will help her, Erren," Alis said.

"You will," Erren agreed.

"I cannot replace you, I know. But I will do my best."

"My best wasn't good enough. Be better."

A chill passed through Alis, and the voice was gone.

Her head was suddenly filled with the stench of putrefying flesh, and as her senses returned, she could feel ribs digging into her back. The hand on her cheek was still there. She touched it; it was wet and slimy and mostly bone.

Robert had lied to Muriele. He'd put her in the Dare crypt, all right, but not in William's tomb; she was in the same sarcophagus as Erren.

On top of her. His little joke or a coincidence?

Maybe his mistake.

She lay there a long moment, shivering, garnering her strength, and then pushed at the stone above her. It was heavy, too heavy, but she searched deep, found more resolve, and shoved enough to make it budge a bit. She rested, then pushed it again. This time a sliver appeared in the darkness.

She relaxed, letting fresh air flow in to strengthen her. Bracing hands and feet, she shoved with all the might her slight frame would allow.

The lid scraped another fingersbreadth open.

She heard a distant bell and realized it was ringing the noon hour. The world of the quick, of sunlight and sweet air, was suddenly real to her again. She redoubled her efforts, but she was very, very weak.

It was six bells later—Vespers—before she managed to unseat the lid and crawl off the rotting body of her predecessor.

A little light was coming through from the atrium, but Alis did not look back at her host, nor did she at present have the energy to replace the lid. She could only hope that no one had reason to come here before she had managed to regain it or find help.

Feeling as frail and light as a broomstraw, Alis Berrye made her way out of the crypt into Eslen-of-Shadows, the dark sister to the living city on the hill high above it. Looking up at Eslen's spire and walls, for a moment she felt more daunted and alone than she ever had before. The task she had chosen—that she had promised a ghost she would carry out—seemed altogether beyond her.

Then, with a wry laugh, she remembered that not only had she survived one of the deadliest toxins in the world, but she had vanished from beneath the very eye of the usurper Robert Dare. Thinking himself careful, he had made himself careless.

She would make that mistake into a dagger with which she would strike at his heart and loose whatever strange blood rotted in it.

PART II

✢

THE VENOM IN THE ROOTS

Fram tid du tid ya yer du yer
Taelned sind thae manns daghs

Mith barns, razens, ja rengs gaeve
Bagmlic is gemaunth sik

Sa bagm wolthegh mith luths niwat
Sa aeter in sin rots

From tide to tide and year to year
A man's days are counted

Wealthy in children, homes, and rings
He feels strong, like a tree

A tree proud in limbs may not feel
The venom in its roots
—*OLD ALMANNISH SAYING*

CHAPTER ONE

AMONG THEM

STEPHEN WASN'T SURE how long he fought against the slinders, but he knew he had no strength left in him. His muscles were limp bands wracked by occasional painful spasms. Even his bones seemed to ache.

Oddly, after he stopped struggling, the hands gripping him became strangely gentle, as if he were like the stray cat he once had removed from his father's solar. When the cat struggled, it had to be held tightly, even a bit roughly, but once it calmed down, he could afford to loosen his hold, stroke it, let it know that he'd never intended it any harm.

"They haven't eaten us," he heard a voice observe.

It was only then that he realized that one of the hands clutching him belonged to Ehawk. He remembered the Watau boy's face in the first moments of confusion, when he'd been dragged roughly across the forest floor. Now he was being carried faceup, cradled in interlocked arms and held at the wrists by eight of the slinders. Ehawk was being carried similarly, but his right hand had latched firmly onto Stephen's.

"No, they haven't," Stephen agreed. He raised his voice. "Can't any of you speak?"

None of his bearers answered.

"Maybe they're going to cook us first," Ehawk said.

"Maybe. If so, they've changed their habits since Aspar saw them last. He said they ate their prey alive and raw."

"Yah. That's what I saw when they killed Sir Oneu. This bunch, they're different. This is all different."

"Did you see what happened to Aspar and the rest?" Stephen asked.

"I think all the slinders attacking the tree came with us," Ehawk said. "They didn't keep after the others."

"But why would they only want the two of us?" Stephen wondered.

"They didn't," Ehawk said. "They only wanted you. It was only after I grabbed on to you that they started carrying me along, as well."

Then why would they want me? Stephen wondered. *What could the Briar King want with me?*

He tried to turn more toward Ehawk, but their conversation seemed to have upset the slinders, and one of them struck Ehawk's wrist so hard that the boy gasped and let go. They began carrying the lad away from Stephen.

"Ehawk!" Stephen shouted, trying to summon the energy to fight again. "You leave him alone, you hear me? Or by the saints . . . Ehawk!"

But fighting just made his bearers tighten their grip again, and Ehawk didn't answer. Eventually Stephen's voice grew hoarse, and he sank glumly into his own thoughts.

He'd made many odd journeys in the past year, and though this wasn't the strangest of them, it certainly earned a place in his *Observations Quaint & Curious*.

He'd never traveled anywhere looking mostly up, for instance. Without the occasional glance at the ground, lacking the feel of his feet against it or the mass of a horse between his thighs, he felt disconnected, like a zephyr wafting along. The passing branches and dark gray sky were his landscape, and when it began to snow, the entire universe constricted to a tunnel of gyring flakes. Then he was no longer wind but white smoke drifting through the world.

Finally, when night took all sight from him, he felt like a wave borne along by the deep. He dozed, possibly, and when his perception sharpened again, there was a hollowness to the clatter of their passage, as if the sea that swept him along had poured down a crevice and become an underground river.

A faintly orange sky appeared. At first he thought it was already sunrise, but then he realized the clouds weren't clouds at all but a ceiling of irregular stone, and the light born of a huge fire was punching great fists of flame toward the cavern roof. The cave itself was large enough that the light faded before striking any limits except the immediate roof and floor.

Crowded about the great hollow were countless slinders, stretched asleep or sitting awake, walking or standing, staring seemingly into nothing. So thick were their numbers that it hardly seemed as if there was a floor at all. Besides the omnipresent astringent smoke, the air was filthy with the stink of ammonia, the sour musk of sweat, and the sweet pungent rot of human feces. He'd believed the sewers of Ralegh stank as much of human waste as any place could, but he was here proved wrong. The damp, clammy air seemed to coat his skin with the stench so thoroughly, he reckoned it would take days of bathing to feel clean again.

Without warning, the slinders carrying Stephen suddenly set him unceremoniously on his feet. His weakened knees collapsed, and he fell where they dropped him.

Propping himself up, he looked around but saw no sign of Ehawk. Had they eaten the boy, after all? Had they killed him? Or merely ejected him from the procession, ignoring him as they had Aspar, Winna, and the knights?

The aroma of food suddenly broke through the smell of the slinders and struck him like a physical blow. He couldn't quite identify the scent, but it was like meat. When he understood what it probably was, his stomach knotted, and if he had had a meal to vomit, he certainly would have. Had Ehawk been right? Had the slinders refined their culinary tastes? Was he to be braised, roasted, or boiled?

Whatever their ultimate intentions, at the moment the slinders appeared to be ignoring him, so he studied the scene around him, trying to arrange sense from it.

At first he had seen only the huge flame in the center of the chamber and an undifferentiated mass of bodies, but now he noticed dozens of smaller fires, with slinders grouped about them as if in clans or cadres. Most of the hearths bore kettles, the sort of copper or black iron kettles he might find at any farmstead or small village. A few of the slinders actually were tending the pots; that struck him somehow as the strangest thing he had seen yet. How could they be so senseless yet still be capable of domestic tasks?

Using his hands, he managed to climb unsteadily to his feet, and then he turned, trying to remember which way they had come from. He found himself looking squarely into a pair of vivid blue eyes.

Startled, he stepped back, and the face came into perspective. It belonged to a man, probably around thirty years of age. His face was streaked with red pigment and his body was as naked and tattooed as the others, but his eyes seemed—sane.

Stephen recognized him as the magician who had been calling down the branches.

He held a bowl in his hands, which he proffered to Stephen.

Stephen examined it; it was full of some sort of stew. It smelled good.

"No," he said softly.

"It isn't manflesh," the man said in king's tongue with an up-country Oostish burr. "It's venison."

"You can talk?" Stephen asked.

The man nodded. "Sometimes," he said, "when the madness lifts. Eat. I'm sure you have questions for me."

"What's your name?"

The man's brow knotted. "It seems like a long time since I had a name that mattered," he said. "I'm a dreodh. Just call me Dreodh."

"What is a dreodh?"

"Ah, a leader, a sort of priest. We were the ones who believed, who kept the old ways."

"Oh," Stephen said. "I understand now. Vadhiian *dhravhydh* meant a kind of spirit of the forest. Middle Lierish *dreufied* was a word for a sort of wild man who lived in the woods, a pagan creature."

"I am not so learned in the ways our name has been misused," Dreodh said, "but I know what I am. What we are. We keep the ways of the Briar King. For that, our name has been maligned by others."

"The Briar King is your god?"

"God? Saint? These are words. They are of no value. But we waited for him, and we were proved right," he said bitterly.

"You don't sound glad of that," Stephen noted.

Dreodh shrugged. "The world is what it is. We do what needs being done. Eat, and we can talk some more."

"What happened to my friend?"

"I know of no friend. You were the object of their quest, no other."

"He was with us."

"If it will ease your mind, I will search for him. Now eat."

Stephen poked at the stew. It smelled like venison, but then, how did human meat smell? He seemed to remember that it was supposed to be something like pork. And what if it was human?

If he ate it, would he become like the slinders?

He set the bowl down, trying to ignore the pain in his belly. It wasn't worth the risk on any level he could think of. A man could go a long time without food. He was sure of it.

Dreodh returned, looked at the bowl, and shook his head. He left again, returned with a small leather purse, and tossed it to Stephen. Opening it, Stephen found some dried and slightly molded cheese and hard, stale bread.

"Will you trust that?" Dreodh asked.

"I don't want to," Stephen replied.

He did, though, scraping off the mold and devouring the ripe stuff in a few hard bolts.

"The ones that brought you, they don't remember your friend," Dreodh told him as he ate. "You must understand, when the calling is on us, we don't perceive things the way you do. We don't remember."

"The calling?"

"The calling of the Briar King."

"Do you think they killed him?"

Dreodh shook his head. "This calling was simply to locate you and bring you here, not to kill or feed."

Stephen decided to let the particulars of that go for a moment. He had a more pressing question.

"You say that the slinders came after me. Why?"

Dreodh shrugged. "I am not certain. You have the stink of the sedhmhari about you, and so our instincts tell us that you should be destroyed. But the lord of the forest thinks otherwise, and we can but obey."

"Sedhmhari—I know that word. The Sefry use it to refer to monsters like greffyns and utins."

"Just so. You might add to your list the black briars that devour the forest. All the creatures of evil."

"But the Briar King is not sedhmhari?"

To Stephen's surprise, Dreodh looked shocked. "Of course not," he said. "He is their greatest enemy."

Stephen nodded. "And he speaks to you?"

"Not as you understand it," Dreodh said. "He is the dream we all share. He feels things, we feel them. Needs. Desires. Hatreds. Pain. Like any living thing, if we feel a thirst, we try to quench it. He put a thirst for you in us, and so we found you. I do not know why, but I know where I am to take you."

"Where?"

"Tomorrow," he said, waving the question away with the back of his hand.

"May I walk, or must I be carried again?"

"You may walk. If you struggle, you will be carried."

Stephen nodded. "Where are we?"

Dreodh gestured. "Under the earth, as you can see. An old rewn abandoned by the Halafolk."

"Really?" That raised interest in him. Aspar had told him of the Halafolk rewns, the secret caverns where most of the strange race called Sefry dwelled.

The Sefry most people knew of were the traders, the entertainers, those who traveled about on the face of the earth.

But those were the minority. The rest had lived in recondite caverns in the King's Forest until just recently. Then they had left the homes they had lived in for countless millennia, fleeing the coming of the Briar King.

Aspar and Winna had entered one such abandoned rewn. Now, it seemed, he was in another.

"Where is their town?"

"Not far from here, what remains of it. We have begun to raze it."

"Why?"

"All the works of man and Sefry, throughout the King's Forest, will be destroyed."

"Again, why?"

"Because they should not be here," Dreodh said. "Because men and Sefry broke the sacred law."

"The Briar King's law."

"Yes."

Stephen shook his head. "I don't understand. These people—you—you must have been villagers, tribesmen at one time. Living in the King's Forest or near it."

"Yes," Dreodh said softly. "That was our sin. Now we pay for it."

"By what sorcery does he compel you? Not everyone comes under his spell. *I've* seen the Briar King, and I didn't become a slinder."

"Of course not. You do not drink from the cauldron. You do not swear the oaths."

Stephen felt his throat go dry as once again the world seemed to leave him, spin around a few times, and return distorted.

"Let me understand this," he said, trying to keep his voice from revealing his outrage. "You *chose* this? All of these people serve the Briar King of their own volition?"

"I don't know what choice is anymore," Dreodh said.

"Well, let me be plain," Stephen said. "By 'chose,' I mean the act of consciously making a decision. By 'chose,' I mean, did you scratch your chin one day and say, 'By my beard! I believe I'll run naked like a beast, eat the flesh of my neighbors, and live underground in caves'? By 'chose,' I mean could you have, let's say, *not* done this?"

Dreodh lowered his head and nodded.

"Then why?" Stephen exploded. "Why, by the *saints,* would you *choose* to become base animals?"

"There is nothing base about the animals," Dreodh said. "They are sacred. The trees are sacred. It is the saints who are corruption."

Stephen started to protest, but Dreodh waved him off. "There were those of us who always kept to the old ways— *his* ways. We made the ancient sacrifices. But what we remembered, we did not remember truly. Our understanding wasn't complete. We believed that because we honored him, we would be spared when he returned. But the Briar King knows nothing of honor, or truth, or deceit, or any human virtue. His understanding is the understanding of the hunter and the hunted, the earth and the rotting, the seed and springtime. Only one agreement was ever made with him by our race, and we broke it. And so now we must serve him."

"*Must* you?" Stephen said. "But you just said you had a choice."

"And this is what we have chosen. You would have done the same, had you been one of us."

"No." Stephen sneered. "I rather think not."

Dreodh stood abruptly. "Follow me. I will show you a thing."

Stephen followed, stepping gingerly around the slinders. In sleep, they seemed normal men and women save for their general state of undress. He reflected that until now he rarely had glimpsed the nakedness of a woman. Once, when he was twelve, he and some friends had watched through a crack in a wall while a girl changed her frock. More recently, he'd accidentally caught a glimpse of Winna as she was bathing. Both times the sight seemed to have seared through his eyes, straight through his belly to where his lust dwelled.

Other times the act of merely imagining what a woman might look like beneath her clothes was a powerful distraction.

Now he saw scores of women, some quite beautiful, all as naked as the saints had made them, and he felt nothing but a general sort of revulsion.

They waded through a shallow stream and were soon out of the light.

"Keep your hand on my shoulder," Dreodh instructed.

Stephen did so, following him through the darkness. Though the saints had blessed his senses, he could not see without *any* light. He could almost hear the shape of the cavern by the echo from their footfalls, however, and he made a conscious effort to remember the turnings and how many steps came before each.

Presently, a pale new light shone ahead, and they reached the stony shores of an underground lake where a small boat waited for them, tied at a polished limestone quay. Dreodh gestured him in, and in moments they had started across the obsidian waters.

The illumination came from dancing motes like fireflies, and in their tiny lamps the shadow of a city took shape, dreamlike and delicate. Here a spire suddenly glinted like a trace of rainbow; there the hollow eyes of windows gazed out like watchful giants.

"You're going to destroy *that*?" Stephen breathed. "But it's so beautiful."

Dreodh didn't reply. Stephen noticed that a few of the floating lights had begun drifting toward them.

"Witchlights," Dreodh explained. "They are not dangerous."

"Aspar told me about these," Stephen said, reaching toward one of them. They were like little glowing wisps of smoke, flames with no substance or heat.

More arrived, escorting them to the farther shore.

Stephen already heard a hushed chatter beyond. Human voices or Sefry, he could not say, but they were high in pitch.

When he saw their low forms on the bank, illumined faintly by the ephemeral lights, Stephen suddenly understood. "Children," he breathed.

"*Our* children," Dreodh clarified.

They came ashore, and a few of the youngsters wandered up to them. Stephen recognized one as the other singer back at the tree, the girl. She leveled her gaze at Dreodh.

"Why have you brought him here?" she asked.

"He has been called. I am to take him to the Revesturi."

"Still," she said, sounding extraordinarily adult, "why bring him here?"

"I wanted him to see the jungen."

"Well, here we are," the girl said.

"Ehawk said he never saw any signs of children in the abandoned villages," Stephen said. "Now I think I understand. He's holding your children hostage, isn't he? If you don't serve the Briar King as slinders, your children are forfeit."

"They serve the Briar King," the girl said, "because we *told* them to."

CHAPTER TWO

✢

CONVERSATION WITH THE DUCHESS

THE WET SLOG of hooves through snow grew nearer, accompanied by snatches of conversation. The language sounded like the king's tongue, but sounds in the forest were deceptive.

For that and many other reasons, Neil was sick of this forest. The island of Skern, where he'd been born, was a place of mountains and sea, but one could walk the length and breadth of it, from the highest, rockiest asher to the lowest gleinn, and never see more than three scraggly bushes in any one place.

These trees blinded and deafened him; they made him misjudge distance.

More than that, Neil was convinced, forests were places of death where rot was always around and the oldest, sickest things in the world seemed to dwell. Give him the clean, open sea or wind-scrubbed heath, and thank Saint Loy.

But the forest is where I am, he thought, *and by the sound of it, it's where I'll die.*

He crouched a bit deeper in the brush. His company's horses were scattered, if not eaten by the slinders, and on foot against horsemen none of them stood a chance, with the probable exception of Aspar White. But Neil couldn't imagine the holter leaving Winna to her fate.

So if this was a new foe—or more of the old—they would stay concealed or die.

Then, as the frontriders of the company came into view, Neil saw a flash of short red hair and the face of Anne Dare. The riders with her bore a standard familiar to him: the crest of Loiyes.

Relief flooded through him. He was sheathing his sword and preparing to step out to greet them, when a thought occurred and held him back. What if their attackers had been *sent* from Loiyes? What if the fickle Elyoner had joined her brother, the usurper?

But Anne did not seem a captive; she sat confidently on her horse, the hood of her weather cloak thrown back, her expression searching but not fearful. When she and her new companions saw the carnage, they reined to a stop.

"What has happened here?" he heard Anne ask.

"I cannot say, Majesty," a male voice replied. "But you should not look upon such unseemly butchery."

That was followed by a feminine laugh that was not Anne's but that Neil nevertheless recognized immediately.

Neil sighed and rose from concealment. His joy at finding Anne alive and apparently unharmed did not entirely put his new suspicion to rest, but there was no point he could see to hiding anymore.

"Your Majesty," he called. "It's myself, Neil MeqVren."

All heads turned toward him, and he heard bows creak.

"No," Anne said, her voice commanding. "This is my man. Sir Neil, you are well?"

"I am, Majesty."

"And the rest?" She smiled uncertainly, then lifted a hand. *"Tio video,* Cazio."

Neil followed her gaze and saw that Cazio also had stepped from cover. He shouted something at Anne in Vitellian that sounded as Neil felt: relieved and overjoyed.

"What about Austra?" Anne called then. "Have you seen Austra?"

But Austra was already running toward Anne, and forgetting all dignity, the heir to the throne of Crotheny leapt from her horse and met her friend in a fierce embrace. Instantly they were both weeping and talking very quickly, but Neil could not hear what they were saying, nor did he try.

"Sir Neil," purred the voice that went with the familiar laugh. "What excellent fortune to see you again."

Neil followed that throaty music to the lady who produced it. Indigo eyes teased him, and her small mouth bowed in a mischievous smile. For an instant he was taken to another day, a day when his soul hadn't seemed quite so heavy and some of the boy in him was still alive.

"Duchess," he said, bowing. "It's a pleasure to see you, as well, and in good health."

"My health is passing fair," she sniffed. "I daresay this ride in the cold is doing nothing to improve it." But her smile broadened. "So many heroes of Cal Azroth here," she said. "Aspar White and Winna Rufoote, I believe."

"Your ladyship," the two chorused.

"Are we in danger here, Sir Neil?" Anne asked, looking up from Austra's shoulder. Again, Neil was struck by the command in her, something he had not seen in the young woman just a few months before.

"I know of no immediate threat, milady, but I consider this forest unsafe," he answered. "Most of the men who accompanied us from Dunmrogh have gone beyond the wood in the west. What you see here is all I know who remain alive."

"Where is Frete Stephen?"

Neil glanced at Aspar.

"He was taken by the slinders," the holter said stiffly. "He and Ehawk."

Anne gazed off into the forest as if searching for the two men, then returned her gaze to the holter.

"Do *you* believe that they are dead?" she asked.

"No, I don't."

"Neither do I," Anne said. "Holter White, a word with you in private, if you don't mind."

Neil watched in mild frustration as his charge and the holter stepped away from the rest. He found it difficult not to watch them, and so he turned his attention back to the duchess.

"Glenchest is well?" he asked.

"Glenchest is as beautiful as ever," she replied.

"And untouched by the present conflict?"

"Untouched, no. Nothing is untouched by my brother's rash actions. But I do not think he has ever considered me a threat."

"Should he?" Neil asked.

The duchess smiled sweetly. "Some publish that I am a threat to virtue," she replied. "And I *do* hope that I am the enemy of boredom and ennui, wherever I find them. But my brother knows I have not the faintest design on the throne and all the ridiculous tedium that goes with it. I am content merely to be left to my own amusements."

"Then you don't favor one claimant over another?"

The duchess put one hand up to stifle a yawn. "I had forgotten, Sir Neil, that being beautiful and young does not prevent you from being—at times—something of a bore."

"My apologies, Highness," Neil said, recognizing full well that she hadn't answered his question. That might be a good sign; the duchess was very clearly in control of the situation. She could afford to let him know her intentions even if he wouldn't like them.

Glancing over, he saw that Anne's conversation with the holter had ended, and Aspar White was now approaching.

"Duchess," Aspar said, affecting a rather crude bow.

"Holter. How are you and your young creature?"

"Well enough, y'r grace. And you?"

"I have a bit of an appetite," she murmured, "for wild game. I don't suppose there's any convenient, is there?"

"Ah—" Aspar said.

"I generally prefer something tender and milk-fed," she added, "or at least not long off the teat. But sometimes one wants something that's been well seasoned, don't you think?"

"I don't—with the slinders and all, most game has—ah, your grace—"

"Aunt Elyoner," Anne said, "leave the poor man be. There's no use to torture him that way. He has to go now. He's just trying to make his farewells."

"Is that true?" Neil asked the holter. "Then you convinced her?"

Clearly relieved to take the conversation in a different direction, Aspar scratched his jaw and returned his regard to Neil.

"Well, no, not exactly," he said. "Her Highness thinks it best if Winna and I go after Stephen."

"I wish I'd had a word or two in that," Neil said flatly.

The holter's expression darkened, but Anne broke in before he could reply.

"He didn't convince me of anything, Sir Neil," Anne said. "I've my own reasons for sending him after Frete Stephen." So saying, she went back to her mount.

Neil straightened, feeling suddenly out of his depth again. Queen Muriele had often put him at a disadvantage by not telling him enough. Now, it seemed, Anne was to be the same sort of mistress.

"I'm sorry," he told Aspar. "I've not known you long, but I do know you better than that. I'm not fighting on the terrain I favor, Aspar White. It makes me edgy."

"I understand," Aspar said. "But you're more suited to this sort of thing than I am. I know nothing of courts, or coups, or fighting with armies. I'm of no use to you when it comes to putting her on the throne. Grim, I don't even understand everything that's going on out here in the forest, but I *do* know that it's my place. Her Majesty canns that, too, I reckon."

Neil nodded and took his arm. "You're a good man, holter. It was a pleasure to fight at your side. I hope to see you again."

"Yah," Aspar said.

"Nere deaf leyent teuf leme," he told the holter in his native tongue. "May the saints not weaken your hand."

"And you keep your eyes open," Aspar returned.

The slinders' lack of interest in eating them apparently extended to their mounts, as well, because while they were talking, Ogre quietly led the other horses to the gathering.

Aspar stroked Ogre's muzzle while the duchess's men resupplied them, an expression curiously akin to relief on his face. When that was done, he and Winna mounted up. Leading Stephen's horse, Angel, they departed along the somewhat obvious trail, leaving Neil feeling more unprotected than ever.

As soon as the holter was on his way, the balance of the party started toward Glenchest.

Neil listened in mounting horror as Anne explained what had happened to her: her abduction, her escape, and her second capture in Sevoyne.

"After Wist helped me escape," she concluded, "we set off on the road to Glenchest, but we ran into Aunt Elyoner straightaway."

"That certainly was fortunate," Neil said. "The Faiths must have been watching over you."

"Don't give the Faiths more than their due." Elyoner, who was riding well within earshot, joined the discussion. "Loiyes is *my* province, and I grew up in this country. There are few places where I have no eyes or ears.

"I had received reports of the men who attacked you. They rode in from the east, pretending to be a company of soldiers detached from service to my cousin Artwair. I also had a report of a girl with red hair and a highborn accent who entered Sevoyne and then mysteriously vanished. I decided that was worth my personal attention."

She yawned.

"Besides, I've had a frightful time entertaining myself lately. No one interesting has come to see me in an age, and I'm not particularly taken with the present court in Eslen." She tilted her head thoughtfully. "Although I'm told there was a rather interesting musical performance there during Yule."

"You have current news from the court?" Neil asked eagerly, hoping she had more useful information, as well.

"Silly thing," Elyoner replied. "Of *course* I do."

Neil waited, but that seemed to be all the duchess was intending to offer.

"It's a long ride to Glenchest, Aunt Elyoner," Anne said finally. "You *could* fill him in."

"But dear, I've just gone through all of that with you," Elyoner complained. "You don't want me to gain a reputation for repeating myself, do you?"

"I could stand to hear it again myself," Anne replied. "I'm far more awake now."

"More sober, you mean."

"Yes, about that," Neil said. "This Wist fellow. What became of him?"

"We beheaded him, of course," the duchess said gaily.

"Oh," Neil replied. "You questioned him first, I hope?"

"Why would I want to do that?" the duchess asked.

"She's joking with you again, Sir Neil," Anne said. "He's just there, under guard—you see?"

Neil looked back and saw a sullen-looking fellow sitting on a dun mare, closely attended by soldiers.

"Ah," Neil said.

"And now, shall I bore you with the state of the court?" Elyoner asked.

"Please do, metreine."

She sighed.

"Well, black is the color, they say. Ostensibly because the court is in mourning, but it's odd that it wasn't actually observed until Prince Robert reappeared, and him being one of the ones they were mourning for! No, really, I think it's because the prince wears black. Although I suppose I ought to call him the emperor now."

" 'Usurper' will do," Anne said.

"And Queen Muriele?" Neil asked, trying to keep his voice from straining, afraid to know the answer. "How is my lady? Have you any news of the queen?"

"Muriele?" Elyoner said. "Why, she's locked in a tower, like that onion girl in the phay story."

Neil felt his heart slow. "But she lives?"

Elyoner patted his arm. "My reports are a few days old, but no execution has been carried out, nor has one been scheduled. That would be a bad move on Robert's part. No, I'm certain he has other intentions."

"How did this happen, exactly? How did the queen lose her grip?"

"Well, how did she *not*?" Elyoner said. "With the emperor murdered, Muriele had few allies she could count on. Charles was on the throne, of course, but while Charles is a sweet lad, the entire kingdom knows that he is, well, saint-touched."

Neil nodded. The true heir to the throne possessed the form of a man but the mind of a child.

"That left Muriele as the power behind the king. But there were plenty of others who wanted to fill that role: Praifec

Hespero, any number of nobles from the Comven, princes from Hansa, Liery, and Virgenya. Then there was Lady Gramme, who has her own claimant to the crown."

"My half brother," Anne muttered.

"Illegitimate but nevertheless of Dare blood," Elyoner replied. "In any event, Muriele might have kept Charles on the throne, but she made more than a few mistakes. She replaced her bodyguard with warriors from Liery, under the command of her uncle, who is a baron there."

"I know Sir Fail," Neil said. "He is my benefactor."

"Almost a father, I'm told," Elyoner said. "You'll want to know that he, too, is alive—and safe."

Neil felt more of his muscles loosen. "Thank you," he said. He missed Sir Fail more than he could ever say. He had never felt the need for the old man's advice as much as he had these last few months.

"Anyway," Elyoner went on, "that was seen as a sign that she had decided to hand the throne over to her Lierish relatives across the sea. Then her men attacked a ball at the mansion of Lady Gramme. Those who had gathered there were mostly landwaerden, not nobles, but—"

"Landwaerden?" Neil asked.

The duchess blinked at him. "Yes? What about them?"

"I've, ah, no idea who they are."

"Ah, my duckling," Elyoner said. "Noble lines rule, you know: the king the country, the archgrefts the greffys, the dukes and duchesses the dukedoms, and so on. That's how it is in most countries, and most places in Crotheny.

"But in the province of Newland, where Eslen is, things are a bit different. It's below the level of the sea, you know. The malends that pump the water out must always be functioning; the dikes must be kept in good repair. For centuries the crown has granted land to those who showed themselves able to keep things running smoothly. Those people are the landwaerden. Many of them are wealthier than the nobility, they command troops, and they usually enjoy the loyalty of the people who live on and work their land. They are, in short, a power to be reckoned with, but they have been treated with indifference by the court for more than a century. Lady Gramme was courting them, trying to convince them to back her claim to the throne, so Muriele drew their anger when she attacked Gramme's party.

"And then my poor dead brother Robert made his appearance—not so dead as was commonly thought. By that time Muriele had no clear friends save her Lierish guard; the nobles all supported Robert instead of Charles, and so did the Church. The only other living heir was Anne, and none of us knew where she was. Muriele was quite secretive about where she had sent her. I think Fastia knew."

Her features softened, and Neil guessed that he had let something show in his face.

"I'm sorry, my dear," Elyoner said, her sympathy sounding, for once, quite genuine. "I should not have mentioned her."

"Why is that?" Anne asked abruptly.

Suddenly uncomfortable, Neil glanced away, trying to sort out something to say from the chaos of his thoughts.

"I shouldn't have brought it up," Elyoner said. "No more talk of those who have passed for the moment."

"No, never mind. I think I see," Anne said. Her tone was flat, but whether she was angry, Neil couldn't tell.

"In any event," the duchess went on, "Muriele understood the situation well enough to send Charles away with Sir Fail and her Lierish guard, and the Craftsmen, too, who despite her treatment of them still appear to be loyal. Sir Fail took Charles to Liery, where he is for the moment safe."

"And what of the Craftsmen?" Neil asked.

Elyoner's right eyebrow went up. "Why, look around you, Sir Neil."

Neil did so. He had noticed vaguely familiar faces among Elyoner's men from the start but reckoned it was because he had met her guard. Now he realized that some of them, indeed, were men he had first seen in Eslen.

"They don't wear their livery," he remarked.

"They are outlawed," Elyoner said. "It seemed premature for them to make themselves targets until they had something to fight and someone to lead them."

Neil nodded. He had traveled without standard himself, in Vitellio.

"The queen left herself defenseless, then."

"Exactly. She must have known she hadn't a chance of successfully fighting the coup, so she sent her men away to where they would do the most good: outside the walls. Anyway, that's when Robert put her in the tower. He pulls her out and parades her around now and then to show that she is still alive."

"If the queen is become so unpopular, why should he care whether the people know that?"

Elyoner smiled faintly. "Because a most peculiar thing occurred. The performance of some sort of musical stage-play—I mentioned it earlier.

"Somehow it swayed many of the landwaerden back toward Muriele and her children. In part because a daughter of one of the landwaerden families was involved and was arrested by Robert on the charge of treason. She was also condemned by the praifec, for heresy and shinecraft, along with the composer of the piece, a man who was already a popular hero of Newland. Robert is apt, I'm afraid, to act more from rage than from reason at times. Now he finds the landwaerden do not really care for him, after all."

"Then we have a chance," Neil said. "How many troops do these landwaerden control?"

"Their combined militias number near eight thousand, I'm told," Elyoner said. "Robert can muster perhaps twelve thousand from the nobles who remain loyal to him. The nobles in the east and along the forest are too busy fighting slinders—and stranger things—to spare troops to help either Robert or those who oppose him."

"What about Hornladh and the Midenlands?"

"I think Anne might be able to raise a host to match that which defends Eslen," Elyoner said. "We shall hear more of that directly."

"Well," Neil mused. "Then we *can* make a fight of it."

"Only if you do it very soon," Elyoner replied.

"Why is that?"

"Because Muriele is to marry the heir of Hansa, Prince Berimund. It's all been announced. Once that union takes place, Hansa will be able to send troops without courting the prejudice of the Church. Indeed, Robert has already agreed to let z'Irbina station fifty knights of the Church—and their guards—in Eslen to support any ruling that comes down from Fratrex Prismo. They are on the march as we speak. You cannot fight Robert, Hansa, *and* the Church."

"And you, Duchess? What part will you play in all of this?" Neil asked. "You seem awfully keen on the small details of this conflict for someone who shan't take sides."

Elyoner chuckled. It was an odd sound, both childlike and world-weary.

"I never said I hadn't taken sides, my dove," she replied. "It's just I find the question of my allegiance tedious, like the rest of this business. War does not suit me well. As I said earlier, I mostly want to be left alone, to do as I please. My brother assures me that this can be the case so long as I follow his instructions."

Now, at last, Neil began to hear the warning bell ringing in his head.

"And those instructions were . . . ?" he asked.

"They were rather specific," she said. "If Anne comes across my stoop, I am to make certain that she vanishes, immediately and permanently, along with anyone who accompanies her."

CHAPTER THREE

✦

CHILDREN OF MADNESS

STEPHEN GLANCED at Dreodh, but the man didn't challenge the girl's assertion.

"You *told* your parents to become slinders?" Stephen asked, trying to find some way the pronouncement made sense. "Why would you do that?"

Stephen studied the girl for some sign that she was something else, perhaps an old soul transposed to a young body or a creature that resembled a human being only so much as a hummingbird resembled a bee.

All he saw, however, was that odd, long moment that suspended between child and woman. The children, unlike the adults, were not naked; the girl wore a simple yellow shift that hung on her like a narrow bell. A bit of faded embroidery at the cuffs showed that someone—mother, grandmother, sister, perhaps even the girl herself—had tried to pretty it up at some point.

She was slim, but her hands, head, and cowskin-slippered feet looked too large. Her nose was a small dipping slope—a girl's nose still—but her cheekbones were beginning to lift her face into a woman's. In the pale light, her eyes appeared hazel. Her brown hair was lighter on the crown and at the ends. And he could easily imagine her in a meadow, wearing a necklace of clover, playing Rickety Rock Bridge or Queen o' the Grove. He could see her twirling so that the hem of her dress puffed out like a ball gown.

"The forest is ill," the girl said. "The sickness is spreading. If the forest dies, so does the world. Our parents broke the ancient law and helped bring this sickness upon the trees. We've asked them to set things right."

"When you blew the horn, you summoned the Briar King to his work in the world," Dreodh explained. "But his way has been prepared for generations. Twelve years ago, we dreothen sang the elder rites and made the seven sacrifices. Twelve years—the heartbeat of an oak—that's how long it has taken for the earth to give him up at last.

"And in that twelve years, every child born on the ground hallowed of the forest was born of wombs stroked by hemlock and oak, ash and mistletoe. Born *his*. When he awoke, *they* awoke."

"We knew what we had to do, all of us at once," the girl took up. "We left our homes, our towns and villages. Those who were too young to walk, we carried. And when our parents came after us, we told them how things would be. Some resisted; they wouldn't drink the mead or eat the flesh. But most did as we asked. They are his army now, his host to sweep the forest clean of the corruption that invades it."

"Mead?" Stephen asked. "Is that what's in the cauldrons? It's mead that robs them of their senses?"

"Mead is a convenient word," Dreodh said, "but it's not the get of honey. It is Oascef, the Water of Life, it is Oasciaodh, the Water of Poetry. And it does not rob us of our senses—it restores them. It returns us to the forest and to health."

"My mistake," Stephen said. "The slinders that brought me here seemed rather . . . insane. This Oascef isn't made from a mushroom that resembles a man's member, by any chance?"

"What you call madness is divine," the girl replied, ignoring his question. "Him in us. There is no fear or doubt, no pain or desire. In such a state we can hear his words and know his will. And only he can save this world from the fever that crawls up from its roots."

"I'm at a loss, then," Stephen said. "You say you have *chosen* to become what you are, that the unspeakable acts you commit are justified because the world is ill. Very well, then: What is this illness? What are you fighting, exactly?"

Dreodh smiled. "Now you've begun to ask the right questions. Now you begin to understand why *he* called for you and commanded that you be brought to us."

"No, I do not," Stephen said. "I'm afraid I don't understand at all."

Dreodh paused, then nodded sympathetically. "Nor are we the ones to explain it to you. But we will take you to the one who will. Tomorrow."

"And until then?"

Dreodh shrugged. "This is what remains of the Halafolk settlement. It will be destroyed in time, but if you wish to explore it, feel free. Sleep where you want; we will find you when the time comes."

"May I have a torch or—"

"The witchlights will accompany you," Dreodh said. "And the houses have their own illumination."

Stephen walked through the dark, narrow streets, trying to sort out his priorities, but found himself captivated by the city itself. The street was bounded on both sides by buildings two, three, sometimes four stories tall. They were fantastically slender, many joined side to side, others separated by narrow alleys. Although built of stone, they had a gossamer quality, and where the witchlights drifted close, they gleamed like polished onyx.

The first few structures were occupied by more of the children. He could hear laughter, song, and the soft lisps of them sleeping. If he extended his senses, he could make out the murmur of at least a thousand of them, if not more. A few of the very young ones were crying, but other than that he heard nothing that he would characterize as fear, anguish, or despair.

He couldn't be certain how much of what the girl and Dreodh had told him was true, but one thing seemed certain: These children were not captives, at least not captives of anything they feared.

He pushed farther into the ancient city, seeking solitude. He knew he should be looking for a way out, but it seemed unlikely that his captors would let him wander freely if there was any chance of escape. Besides, at the moment he was too curious to really *want* to escape.

If Dreodh was telling the truth, Aspar and Winna were safe enough, at least from the slinders. If he was lying, his friends were almost certainly dead already. He didn't—wouldn't—believe that or even think too much about it until he had some evidence of it. But the chance to find out more of what was going on, what the Briar King wanted—well, that was what they were all looking for, wasn't it?

What good would he have been trying to help a princess regain her throne? He wasn't a warrior or a strategist. He was, he mused, a scholar with an interest in the past and in languages common and obscure. *Surely I can do more good here than marching to Eslen.*

Following his curiosity, he tried one of the doors. It was wooden and not too old. The Halafolk, he reasoned, must have traded constantly with their aboveground neighbors. They had to eat, after all, and while subterranean lakes might produce *some* fish and some sort of crops might be grown without sunlight, surely most of their sustenance had come from the surface.

Stephen wondered briefly how that trade had been accomplished while keeping the location of the rewns secret, but the answer was so obvious, he felt stupid for the three heartbeats he had wondered at it.

The Sefry. Those who traveled above, in the caravans—they were the suppliers.

The door pushed easily inward, revealing an apartment of stone. The place smelled faintly peppery. The hard floor was softened by a carpet woven of what appeared to be wool. Could sheep live underground? He doubted it. The pattern was vaguely familiar, a little like the colorfully abstract swirls painted on Sefry tents and wagons. Four cushions formed a loose ring around a low round table. In one corner a loom waited patiently for a weaver. Had the carpet been woven on it? Nearby wicker baskets overflowed with skeins of yarn and wooden tools he didn't recognize.

The room seemed rather lived in, as if the Halafolk hadn't taken much with them when they left. Perhaps they hadn't.

Where had they gone? Had they fled the Briar King or the mysterious illness of which the Dreodh spoke?

Not long after they had met, Aspar had said something about the forest "feeling sick" to him. Aspar had lived his whole life in the pulse of the woodlands, so he should know.

Then they had encountered the greffyn, a beast so poisonous that its mere footprint could kill, and soon afterward the black thorns that sprang up in the footprints of the Briar King and grew to smother every living thing they crept over. Then even more monsters from Black Marys had appeared: utins, the nicwer—sedhmhari, Dreodh had called them. The best translation Stephen could make of that was "sedos demon."

Did the monsters, like human priests, walk the faneways and gain gifts from them?

Something about the utins in particular troubled him. He had almost been killed by one, but by now he had been almost killed by several things. No, there was something more . . .

Then he realized what was bothering him.

The utin that had attacked him was the *only* one he had ever encountered, yet for some reason he was thinking of them in the plural. There had been only one greffyn, though Aspar had seen another after slaying the first. But no one he knew had seen more than one of these new monsters at a time.

So why was he thinking "utins" instead of "utin"?

He closed his eyes, calling upon the memory Saint Decmanus had given him, thinking back to the moment when the slinders had first attacked. In the chaos, there had been something else . . .

There. He could see it clearly now, as if some meticulous artist had painted the scene for him. He was glancing over his shoulder as he pushed Winna up into the tree. There was Aspar, turning with his knife in hand. Beyond were the slinders, breaking from the forest. But what was Aspar looking at?

Not the slinders . . .

It had been at the corner of Stephen's vision; he saw only its limbs and part of its head, but there was no mistaking it. There had been an utin back there, just ahead of the slinders. Perhaps more than one.

Then what had happened to them? Had the slinders killed them, or were they working *with* the slinders?

The latter didn't seem likely. The greffyn, the first utin, the nicwer they had encountered in the river at Whitraff, the black thorns—

The black thorns grew in the Briar King's footsteps, yet they clung to him viciously, as if they sought to cover him, drag him down into the earth. According to Aspar, he once *had* been imprisoned by them, in a valley hidden in the Mountains of the Hare.

Slinders had attacked and killed the men performing human sacrifices on the sedos mounds throughout the forest, and those men seemed allied to the greffyn; they were the only creatures who could stand to be near it without becoming deathly sick.

No, he silently corrected. The renegade monks weren't the only ones immune to the greffyn's poison. He himself had caught the greffyn's gaze and had suffered no ill effect. Aspar, too, seemed to have at least a raised tolerance, since the Briar King had healed him from the monster's touch. So what did that mean?

Was it because he had walked a faneway? Were all ordained priests immune to sedhmhari?

It is the saints who are corruption, Dreodh had claimed.

If the slinders were the army of the Briar King, the monsters they had met were a part of some army, too: the army of the Briar King's foe. But who could that be?

The most natural answer was the Church. He knew that the corrupt monks had friends as high as the praifec of Crotheny, Marché Hespero. Their influence might well go higher.

But even if Fratrex Prismo himself was involved, did that mean he was the master of the greffyn? Or was he just another monster, serving an even greater power?

He thought back through all the lore he had read concerning the Briar King, trying to remember who his adversaries were supposed to be, but few sources had mentioned enemies of any sort. The king was from the time before the saints, before humanity, perhaps even before the Skasloi who had enslaved the Mannish and Sefry races in ancient times. He appeared as a harbinger of the end of times.

If the king had any enemies, it would have to be, as Dreodh had seemed to suggest, the saints themselves.

And that brought him back to the Church, didn't it?

Well, he'd been promised answers tomorrow. He wasn't naïve enough to imagine that all his questions would be answered, but if he learned anything more than he knew, that would be *something*.

He pressed on through the Halafolk house and, finding nothing to hold his attention, left it and ambled farther into the doomed city, crossing slender stone arches over quiet canals, all sketched half-visible in the witchlight. The distant chatter of children had been augmented by an atonal chanting farther away, probably coming from the first chamber he'd been brought to.

Were the slinders preparing for another sortie aboveground, drinking their mead and working up their bloodlust?

The street angled down, and he followed it, vaguely hoping to discover some sort of scriftorium, a cache of Sefry writings. Their race was ancient and had been among the first to be enslaved by the Skasloi. They might well have recorded things the other peoples had forgotten.

As he wondered just what a Sefry scriftorium might look like, it occurred to Stephen that he had never seen Sefry writing of any sort or ever heard of a separate Sefry language. They tended to speak the local tongue wherever they lived. They had a sort of cant of their own but rarely used it. Aspar once had spoken some for Stephen, and Stephen had discerned words from some fifteen different languages but not a single word that seemed uniquely Sefry.

The assumption was that they had been enslaved so far back in the past that they had lost whatever language they might once have had, speaking instead the pidgin that the Skasloi had devised for their slaves. So hateful was that language that they had abandoned it as soon as the masters were all dead, adopting instead the tongues of their human companions.

It seemed entirely plausible. He'd read in several sources that the native language of the Skasloi could not be spoken by a human throat and tongue, so they had devised an idiom that could be used by both themselves and their slaves. Human slaves must have all spoken that language, but many had retained their own speech to use among themselves.

Yet almost no word of that slave tongue was retained in any modern dialect. Virgenya Dare and her followers had put every Skasloi creation to the torch and forbade the speech of slavery. They never taught it to their children, and so it died.

"Skaslos" might be the only word of their language that remained, Stephen mused, and even that exhibited the singular form "-os" and the plural "-oi" inherent to elder Cavari, a human language.

Perhaps even the *name* of that demon race had been forgotten.

He paused, finding himself at a canal wider than those he had crossed before, and his skin prickled as he had an unholy thought.

What if the Skasloi *hadn't* all died? What if they, like the greffyns, utins, and nicwers, had merely gone somewhere else for a very long nap? What if this illness, this enemy, was the most ancient enemy of all?

Hours later he took that unsettling thought to sleep with him, resting on a mattress spiced with the Sefry scent.

He awoke to a sharp poke in his ribs and found the girl staring down at him.

"What's your name?" he murmured.

"Starqin," she replied. "Starqin Walsdootr."

"Starqin, do you understand that your parents are dying?"

"My parents are dead," she said softly. "Killed in the east, fighting a greffyn."

"Yet you feel no sorrow."

Her lips pursed.

"You don't understand," she said at last. "They had no choice. *I* had no choice. Now, come along, please."

He followed her back to the boat he'd arrived on. She motioned for him to get in.

"Just the two of us?" he asked. "Where's Dreodh?"

"Preparing our people to fight," she said.

"Fight what?"

She shrugged. "Something is coming," she replied. "Something very bad."

"Aren't you afraid I might try to overpower you and escape?"

"Why would you do that?" Starqin asked. In the faint light her eyes seemed as black and liquid as tar. Her face and hair, in contrast, made her seem ghostlike.

"Maybe because I don't like being held captive."

Starqin settled next to the tiller. "Would you row?" she asked.

Stephen took his seat and placed his hands on the oars. They felt cool and light.

"You'll want to talk to him, the one we're going to see," Starqin said. "And I don't think you'll murder me."

Stephen pulled on the oars, and the boat glided almost soundlessly away from the stone quay.

"It's interesting to hear you talk about murder," Stephen said. "The slinders don't just attack greffyns, you know. They kill people, too."

"Yah," Starqin said, almost absently. "So have you."

"Evil people."

She laughed at that, and Stephen felt suddenly stupid, as if he had been lecturing a sacritor on holy writ. But after a moment she grew more serious.

"Don't call them slinders," she said. "It demeans their sacrifice."

"What do you call them?" he asked.

"Wothen," she said. "We call ourselves the wothen."

"That just means 'mad,' doesn't it?"

"Divinely mad, actually, or inspired. We are a storm blowing the forest clean."

"Will you really help the Briar King destroy the world?"

"If it's the only way to save it."

"Does that really make sense to you?"

"Yes."

"How do you know he's right, the Briar King? How do you know he isn't lying to you?"

"He isn't," she said. "And you know it, too."

She steered them along the dark waters, and soon they were in a tunnel so low-roofed that Stephen had to duck his head to keep from striking it. The sound of the oars chuckled off into the distance and back to them.

"Where were you from, Starqin?" Stephen wondered aloud. "What town?"

"Colbaely in the Greffy of Holtmarh."

A little chill went up his spine. "I have a friend from there," he said. "Winna Rufoote."

Starqin nodded. "Winna was nice. She used to play the holly pole with us and give us the barley rusk after her father made beer. She was too old, though. Not one of us."

"She had a father—"

"He owned the Sow's Teat."

"Is he a wothen?"

She shook her head. "He left when we started burning the town."

"You burned your own town?"

She nodded. "It had to be done. It wasn't supposed to be there."

"Because the Briar King said so."

"Because it wasn't supposed to be. We children always knew that. We had to convince the adults. Some weren't convinced, but they left. Fralet Rufoote was one of them."

They continued on in silence; Stephen wasn't sure what else to say, and in the absence of questions, Starqin didn't seem inclined to pursue conversation.

The ceiling rose again until it vanished from the faint glow of the witchlights. After a time, another illumination arose, a distant, slanting shaft of radiance that turned out to be sunlight descending through a hole high up in the roof of the cavern.

Starqin brought the craft to rest at another stone quay.

"There are steps carved in the stone," she said. "They lead up to the exit."

"You're not going with me?"

"I have other things to do."

Stephen regarded the girl's eyes, now jade in the sunfall from above.

"This can't be right," he told her. "All of this death, all of this killing—it can't be right."

Her features shifted briefly through something he didn't understand, but it was a glimmer of a silvery fish in a deep pool. Then the water was again empty and calm.

"Life is always coming and going," she said, "if you watch. Always something being born, always something dying. In the spring more is being born; in late autumn more is dying. Death is more natural than life. The bones of the world are death."

Stephen's throat tightened. "Children shouldn't talk like that," he said.

"Children know these things," she said. "It's only adults that teach us that a flower is more beautiful than a rotting dog. *He* just helped us keep what we were born knowing, what every beast that doesn't know how to lie to itself understands in its marrow."

Stephen's sorrow and sympathy suddenly twisted, and for an instant he was so angry at the girl, he wanted to strangle her. In the midst of his doubts and uncertainty the sheer *satisfaction* of that absolute feeling was so wonderful and terrible that it left him gasping, and when it passed, as it did seconds later, he was actually shaking.

Starquin hadn't missed it.

"Besides," she said softly, "you have whole seasons of death in you."

"What do you mean?"

But she just pushed off and did not answer, and soon the skiff was lost from view.

Stephen began to climb.

* * *

The stone steps switched their way back and forth up the stone wall until at last they brought him to a small landing. The cave opening was quite small, and beyond it he could see little more than a screen of cane. A narrow path led through the stiff vegetation, however, and he picked his way along it until suddenly the hillside opened up.

He found himself gazing down upon pasture, and beyond that the orderly rows of apple trees. Across the little valley, above the trees, a stone building rose. He gasped involuntarily as emotions rushed up to him like old acquaintances: anticipation, boyish excitement, pain, disillusionment, rank terror.

Anger.

It was the monastery d'Ef, where he first had learned how corrupt the Church of his childhood had become, where he had met and been tortured by Desmond Spendlove. Where he had been forced to decipher the scrifti that had perhaps doomed the world.

"Wilhuman, werliha. Wilhuman hemz," a voice scratched behind him.

"Welcome, traitor. Welcome home."

CHAPTER FOUR

✛

THE TALE OF ROSE

"YOU'RE SUPPOSED to kill me?" Anne asked, fixing Elyoner with her gaze.

The duchess of Loiyes smiled lazily back at her.

Anne could almost feel Neil MeqVren tightening next to her, like the string of a lute.

She waited until I sent Aspar away, she thought. *Not that he and Winna would have made a difference against this many . . .*

She lifted a hand to rub her forehead but let it drop. It would only make her look weak.

Too much had happened, and far too quickly. She'd still been blurry with alcohol when she'd met Elyoner and her men on the road. And then the relief of seeing a familiar face—the face of family, even—had been so intense that she hadn't allowed herself to entertain the most obvious thoughts.

That Elyoner had sent her attackers.

Elyoner Dare had always been a mystery to Anne, albeit a pleasant one. She was Anne's father's sister, older than Lesbeth and Robert, but she had always seemed much younger than Anne's father. Anne guessed her to be around thirty.

Family trips to Glenchest had always been a treat; there was even a sense among the children that the adults were having more fun than they were, though it wasn't until much later that she had begun to understand what *sort* of fun it was.

That impression had grown as Anne got older. Elyoner always appeared to do pretty much as she pleased. Though she had a husband somewhere, he was never really in evidence, and Elyoner was well known for taking young and highly temporary lovers. Muriele—Anne's mother—had always seemed to disapprove of Elyoner, which for Anne was another thing that recommended her aunt. Though a great gossip, she had never seemed in the least political, or even particularly aware of what went on beyond the who-was-sleeping-with-whom.

Now Anne was suddenly, acutely conscious that she did not really know her aunt at all.

"Kill you and bury the body where it will not be found," Elyoner amplified. "Those were the instructions. In return, Robert tells me my life at Glenchest will go on much as it always has." She sighed wistfully. "Such a comforting thought."

"But you aren't," Anne said. "You aren't going to have me killed . . . are you?"

Elyoner's cerulean eyes focused sharply on her.

"No," she said. "No, of course not. My brother doesn't know me quite as well as he thinks he does, which is a bit disheartening." Her face grew more serious, and she leveled an accusing finger at Anne. "But you should never have trusted me, for I *might* have," she said. "Consider that if your dear uncle Robert has ordered your murder, no other relative of yours is trustworthy, with the likely exception of your mother. Taking your side makes my life very difficult and could in fact end it. That's not an easy choice to make, even for you, my sweet."

"But you made it."

Elyoner nodded. "After what happened to Fastia and Elseny, practically in my very own parlor—no, not you, too. I loved William above all my siblings. I could never betray his last daughter that way."

"Do you think Uncle Robert has gone mad?" Anne asked.

"I think he was born mad," Elyoner said. "It happens with twins, you know. Lesbeth got everything that was good from their parents' union, and Robert was left with the dregs." Her gaze cut aside to Sir Neil.

"You may relax now, sweet knight," she said. "To repeat myself in plain words, I'm here to help Anne, not to harm her. If I wanted her dead, I should have accomplished that long before finding you and then used your grief to make you my lover. Or some other wicked and delightful thing."

"You always speak such comforting words," Neil replied.

Anne thought that the familiar response seemed to confirm what Elyoner had implied earlier, that Sir Neil and her sister Fastia had had some sort of affair.

On the surface that seemed impossible. Fastia had been ludicrously dutiful, and so was Neil. One would think they would have reinforced those qualities in each other rather than abrogating them. But Anne was quickly learning that nothing about the heart was simple or, rather, that it was *very* simple, but the consequences were baroque.

In any event, she didn't have time to consider what her sister had or hadn't done with this young knight. She had other priorities.

"Now that you mention her, has there been any word at all from Lesbeth?" Anne asked.

"No," Elyoner replied. "The rumor is that she was betrayed by her betrothed, Prince Cheiso of Safnia, that he gave her over to some ally of Hansa so they could blackmail William. That was the reason your father went to the headland of Aenah: to negotiate her release.

"I suppose only Robert knows what really happened there."

"Then you think Uncle Robert had something to do with my father's death?"

"Of course," Elyoner said.

"And Lesbeth? What do you think really happened to her?"

"I do not—" Elyoner's voice caught for an instant. "I would not imagine that she still lives."

Anne took a few breaths to try to absorb that.

The snow had begun again, and she hated it. She felt as if a bone had broken in her someplace. A small one, but one that would never quite heal.

"You really think Uncle Robert would kill his own twin sister?" she finally posed. "He loved her more than he loved anyone. He *doted* on her. He was silly about it."

"Nothing can bring down bloody murder more readily than true love," Elyoner said. "As I said, Robert was never made of the finest stuff."

Anne opened her mouth to reply but found she had nothing to say. The snow came a bit harder, numbing her nose with cold and wet.

Where have I been? she wondered. *Where was all of this when I was growing up?*

But she knew the answer to that. She'd been racing horses to spite the guards, stealing wine and drinking it in the west tower, sneaking off to play kiss-and-feel with Roderick in Eslen-of-Shadows.

Fastia had tried to tell her. And her mother. To prepare her for all of this.

Mother.

She suddenly remembered her mother's face, sad and stern, the night she'd sent her off to the Coven Saint Cer. Anne had told her she hated her . . .

Her cheeks were wet now. Quite without knowing it, she had begun crying.

Realizing that only made matters worse, and great sobs began to choke up from her belly. She felt exposed, like the time all her hair had been shorn from her head, like the time as a little girl she'd been caught naked out in the hall.

How could *she* be queen? How could she even have imagined it? She didn't understand *anything*, couldn't control anything—not even her own tears. All she had learned in the last year was that the world was huge and cruel and beyond her comprehension. The rest of it—the illusion of destiny and power, the determination that had seemed real only a few days ago—now seemed stupid, a pose everyone could see through but she.

A hand fell on her thigh, and she started at the warmth of it.

It was Austra, her own eyes brimming. The other riders had cleared a bit of a space, probably so they could pretend they didn't see her pain. Neil rode just behind her, but out of whispering earshot. Cazio was up with Elyoner.

"I'm so glad you're alive," Anne told her friend. "I tried not to think about it, to keep my mind on other things, but if you were dead . . ."

"You'd go on; that's what you'd do," Austra said. "Because you have to."

"Do I?" Anne asked, hearing the rancor in her voice, knowing it was petty and not caring.

"Yes. If only you could have seen what I saw from the forest, back in Dunmrogh. When you stepped out, bold as a bull, and told those murderers who you were—if you had seen that, you would know what you were meant to do."

"Have the saints touched you?" Anne asked softly. "Can you hear my thoughts?"

Austra shook her head. "I'll never know anyone better than I know you, Anne. I never know exactly what you're thinking, but usually I can see the general way the wind is blowing."

"Did *you* know all this? About Robert?"

Austra hesitated.

"Please," Anne said.

"There are things we never talked about," Austra said reluctantly. "You always pretended I was just like a sister, and that was nice, but I could never forget the truth, never *allow* myself to forget the truth."

"That you are a servant," Anne said.

"Yes." Austra nodded. "I know you love me, but even you've come to face the facts of the matter."

Anne nodded. "Yes," she admitted.

"In Eslen, in the castle, servants have their own world. It's right next to yours—below it, around it—but it's separate. Servants know a lot about your world, Anne, because they have to survive in it, but you don't know much about theirs."

"Don't forget, I've worked as a servant, too," Anne said. "In the house of Filialofia."

Austra smiled and tried not to appear condescending.

"For just under twice nineday," her maid qualified. "But see here, did you learn anything in that time that the lady of the house did not know?"

Anne thought about that for a moment. "I learned that her husband philandered with the housemaids, but I think she knew that, almost expected it," she said. "But what she *didn't* know was that he was also involved with her friend dat Ospellina."

"And you discovered that by observation."

"Yes."

"And the other servants—did they talk to you?"

"Not much."

"Right. Because you were new, you were a foreigner. They didn't trust you."

"I'll grant you that," Anne said.

"And yet the lord and lady of the house didn't make that distinction, I'll wager. To them you were a servant, and when you were doing your job as you were supposed to, you were invisible, as much a part of the house as the banisters or the windows. They only noticed you—"

"When I did something wrong," Anne said. She was starting to understand.

How many servants were there in Eslen. Hundreds? Thousands? Around all the time but scarcely existing so far as the nobles were concerned.

"Go on," Anne said. "Tell me something about the servants in Eslen. Something small."

Austra shrugged. "Did you know that the stablejack, the one we called Gimlet, was the son of Demile, the seamstress?"

"No."

"Do you remember who I'm talking about?"

"Gimlet? Of course." *I just never wondered who his mother was.*

"But he isn't the son of Armier, Demile's husband. His real father is Cullen, from the kitchen staff. And because Cullen's wife, Helen, was so angry over that, Gimlet—his real name is Amleth, by the way—was never allowed a position within the castle, because Helen's mother is the Boar, old lady Golskuft—"

"—the mistress of the household servants."

Austra nodded. "Who in turn is the illegitimate daughter of the late Lord Raethvess and a landwaerd girl."

"So you're telling me that the servants do more sleeping about than they do work?"

"When a turtle takes a breath in a pond, you only see the tip of his nose. And all you know of the servants in Eslen is what they allow you to see. Most of their lives—their interests, passions, connections—are kept from you."

"Yet you seem to know quite a lot."

"Only enough to understand what I *don't* know," Austra said. "Because I was so close to you, because I was treated with the appearance of gentle birth, I was not well trusted—or well liked."

"And what has all of this to do with my uncle Robert?"

"The servants have very dark rumors of him. The say that

when he was a boy, he was exceedingly cruel, and unnatural."

"Unnatural?"

"One of the housemaids, when she was a girl—she said Prince Robert made her wear Lesbeth's gown and demanded that she answer to that name. And then he—"

"Stop," Anne said. "I think I can imagine."

"I think you can't," Austra said. "They did *that,* yes, but his desires were perverse in more than one way. And then there is the story of Rose."

"Rose?"

"That one they are very quiet about. Rose was the daughter of Emme Starte, who was in the laundry. Robert and Lesbeth made a playmate out of her, dressed her in fine clothes, took her on walks, rides, and picnics. Treated her as if she were gentle."

"As you were treated," Anne said, feeling something twinge in her breast.

"Yes."

"How old were they?"

"Ten years old. And here's the thing, Anne—the thing they say, but it's so hard to believe."

"I think I would believe anything at this moment," Anne said. She felt blunted, a knife used too often to cut bone.

Austra lowered her voice further. "They say that when they were young, Lesbeth was like Robert: cruel and jealous."

"Lesbeth? Lesbeth is the sweetest, most gentle woman I have ever known."

"And so she became, they say, after Rose vanished."

"Vanished?"

"Never to be seen again. No one knows what happened. But Lesbeth cried for days on end, and Robert seemed more agitated than usual. And after that, Robert and Lesbeth were not seen together as much. Lesbeth was like a new person, seeking always to do good, to live like a saint."

"I don't understand. Are you saying that Robert and Lesbeth killed Rose?"

"As I said, no one knows. Her family prayed, and wept, and made petition. Soon after, her mother and closest relatives were lent to the household of the Greft of Brogswell, a hundred leagues away, and there they remain."

"That's *horrible*. I can't—are you saying that my father never made any investigation of this?"

"I doubt very much it ever reached the ears of your father. It was settled within the world of the servants. If the rumor had gotten to your family, it might as easily have come to the attention of your father's political enemies. In that case, any servant who knew anything might have vanished quite as suddenly—and without explanation—as Rose.

"So the Boar put it out that Rose had gone to work with her sister in Virgenya and made sure there was a record of her request to do so. Rose's remaining family was quietly moved off lest in their grief they should begin talking to the wrong people."

Anne closed her eyes and felt a face there, pushed against the shutters of her lids, a pretty face with green eyes and an upturned nose.

"I *remember* her," she gasped. "They called her *Cousin* Rose. It was that time on Tom Woth, the Feilteme celebration. I couldn't have been more than six winters."

"I was five, so you were six," Austra confirmed.

"You really think they killed her?" Anne murmured.

Austra nodded.

"I think she's dead. It may have been an accident or a game that went too far. Robert has a lot of games, they say."

"And now he's on the throne. *My father's throne.* And he has my mother locked up in a tower."

"I-I've gathered that," Austra said. "I'm sure he hasn't hurt her."

"He's ordered my death," Anne replied. "There's no knowing what he'll do to Mother. That's what I must concentrate on, Austra. Not whether I can be a queen or not but on freeing my mother and putting Robert where he can do no more harm. Just that, for now."

"That sounds sensible."

Anne breathed deeply and felt a bit of weight lift from her shoulders.

They were back out of the forest now and coming down to the road. Anne could see Sevoyne in the distance, and she wondered if this time she would actually go past it.

"Anne!" Someone shouted from behind. "*Casnara,* ah, *rediatura!*"

She glanced back and saw Cazio, boxed closely on all sides by Craftsmen.

"What is it, Cazio?" she replied in Vitellian.

"Could you please instruct these men that I am one of your very valued companions? If indeed I am?"

"Of course," Anne said. She switched to the king's tongue. "This man is one of my bodyguards," she told the Craftsmen. "He may approach me whenever he wishes."

"Your pardon, Highness," one of the knights said, a pleasant-looking young man with auburn hair and something vaguely gooselike about him. "But we may take nothing for granted."

She nodded. "What is your name, sir knight?"

"If it please you, Majesty, my name is Jemme Bishop."

"A good Virgenyan name," Anne said. "I thank you very much for your protection. Despite his demeanor, this man has my trust."

"As you say, Majesty," the fellow replied. The horses gave a little ground, allowing Cazio to ride up.

"We've a retinue again," he said, glancing back at the knights. "I wonder if this one will survive longer than the last."

"Let us hope so," Anne said. "I'm sorry we haven't spoken until now. Things are becoming more and more complicated, and I'm sure it must seem even more so to you."

"My day improved considerably when I discovered that you were still alive," Cazio said. He rubbed his head ruefully. "I was a poor guardian to you—to the both of you. I have apologized to Austra, and now I apologize to you."

"You risked your life for us, Cazio," Anne said.

"Anyone can risk his life," Cazio replied. "A man with no

skill and no wits could die for you. I had hoped I was better than that. If I had died preventing you from being taken, that would have been one thing. But to be left, humiliated, in the wake of your kidnap—"

"—is a matter of personal pride," Anne finished. "Don't be foolish, Cazio. I am alive, as you see. We were all caught sleeping: Aspar, Sir Neil, Frete Stephen, myself. You were in good company."

"It won't happen again," Cazio said adamantly.

"If that pleases you," Anne replied.

Cazio nodded. "This lady, she is related to you?"

"Elyoner? Yes, she's my aunt, my father's sister."

"And she is trustworthy?"

"I have chosen to trust her. If you see evidence that I should not, however, please bring it to my attention."

Cazio nodded. "Where are we going?" he asked.

"Glenchest, her residence," Anne replied.

"And what will we do there?"

"We will plan to go to war, I suppose," Anne replied.

"Ah. Well, you will let me know when I can be of aid, then, yes?"

"Yes."

"Anne!" Elyoner's voice wafted forward. "Be a dear and send that Vitellian fellow back. I've begun to find this ride exceedingly boring."

"His king's tongue is rather poor," Anne answered.

"Fatio Vitelliono," she replied sweetly. *"Benos, mi della."*

"She speaks my language," Cazio said happily.

"Yes," Anne replied. "So it seems. And I'm sure she wants to practice with you."

He glanced back. "Should I?" he asked.

"Yes," Anne replied. "But be cautious; my aunt can be dangerous to a man of virtue."

Cazio smiled and replaced his broad-brimmed hat. "If I meet such a man, then," he said, "I shall be sure to warn him."

He turned and rode back.

Austra watched him go with a rather disconcerted look on her face.

"Austra," Anne said. "The men who abducted you—did they say anything?"

"They thought I was you," Austra said, "or thought I might be."

Anne nodded. "I had the same impression, that their description of me wasn't very good. Did they mention anyone by name?" Anne asked. "Anyone at all?"

"Not that I remember."

"Did they touch you?"

"Of course. They tied me up, put me on horseback—"

"That's not what I meant," Anne said.

"Not—oh. No, nothing like that. I mean they talked about it, threatened me with it even, trying to get me to say whether I was you or not. But they didn't actually do anything." Her eyes suddenly widened. "Anne, did they—were you—?"

Anne jerked her head back toward Wist. "He tried. Something happened."

"Let Sir Neil kill him," Austra gritted. "Or tell Cazio and let him challenge him to a duel."

"No. He failed, and I still may have use for him," Anne said. She studied the reins in her hands. "Something happened, Austra. The man who kidnapped me, he died."

"Did you—did you kill him, the way you killed those horrible men in the grove?"

"I killed the men in the grove by wishing them dead," Anne said. "There was power there, beneath me, like a well of water I could drop my bucket into. I felt their insides, and I twisted them. It was the same as when I blinded the knight back in Vitellio or when I made Erieso sick—just, well, *more*.

"But this was different. The man who abducted me was killed by a demon. I saw her."

"Her?"

Anne shrugged. "I went to some other place. I think she followed me back. She stopped Wist from raping me."

"Maybe she isn't a demon, then," Austra said. "Maybe she's more of a guardian angel."

"You didn't see her, Austra. She was terrible. I don't even know who I can ask about these things."

"Well, Frete Stephen seemed to know a lot," Austra said, her voice sounding sorrowful. "But I suppose he's—"

"He's fine," Anne said. "And needed elsewhere."

"Really? How do you know that?"

Anne thought about the Briar King and the things she had seen in his eyes.

"I don't want to talk anymore about this," she said. "Later. Later."

"Very well," Austra said in a mollifying voice. "Later."

Anne took a deep breath. "You just said you know me better than anyone. I think that's true. And so I need you to watch me, Austra. Pay attention to me. And if ever you think I've lost my mind, you must tell me."

Austra laughed a little nervously. "I'll try," she said.

"I've kept things from you before," Anne said. "I need—I need someone to talk to again. Someone I can trust, who won't tell my secrets to another living soul."

"I would never betray your promise."

"Even to Cazio?"

Austra was silent for a moment. "Does it show?" she asked.

"That you love him? Of course."

"I'm sorry."

Anne rolled her eyes. "Austra, I have friendly affections toward Cazio. He has saved our lives several times, which can be most endearing. But I do not love him."

"Even if you did," Austra said defensively, "he would be below your station."

"That's not at issue, Austra," Anne said. "I do not love him. I do not care if you do so long as I can trust you not to tell him anything I ask you to hold in confidence."

"My first allegiance is, has always been, and will always be to you, Anne," Austra said.

"I believe that," Anne said, gripping her friend's hand. "I just needed to hear it again."

In the westering light, they reached Glenchest.

It looked just as Anne remembered it, all spires, gardens, and glass, like a castle spun by the phay from spider silk. As a child she had thought it was a magical place. Now she wondered how, or if, it could be defended. It didn't look like the sort of place that could stand a siege.

At the gate there were ten men on horseback, wearing black surcoats. The leader, a tall, gaunt man with hair cropped right to his skull and a narrow beard, rode up to meet them.

"Oh, dear," Elyoner whispered. "Sooner than I would have hoped."

"Duchess," the man said, bowing in the saddle. "I was just about to ride out in search of you. My lord will not be pleased at your behavior. You were to await me in your mansion."

"My brother has rarely been pleased with my behavior," Elyoner said. "But in this case, he may not be so displeased. Duke Ernst, may I introduce my niece, Anne Dare? She seems to have been misplaced, and everyone has been scrambling about to find her, and look—I have.

"And as I understand it, she has come to take your master's crown."

CHAPTER FIVE

IN THE TREES

"ARE Y' GOING to tell me what that was all about?" Winna asked as their horses took them over a low ridge and out of sight of the princess—or queen, or whatever she was—and her newfound entourage of knights.

"Yah," Aspar said.

After a few more minutes of silence Winna drew Tumble's reins and brought the brindle mare to a halt.

"Well?"

"You mean *now*?"

"Yes, *now*. How did you convince Her Majesty to release you to follow Stephen?"

"Well, there was no need for convincing, as it happened. She wanted me to go after Stephen."

"That was nice of her."

He shook his head. "No, it was weird. She seemed to know he'd been taken. She said he'd need our help, that we had a task to perform, and that our going with Stephen was as important as her reclaimin' the throne. Maybe more so."

"Did she say why?"

"She didn't *know* why, exactly. She said she'd had a vision of the Briar King, and he put it in her head that Stephen was important, somehow. And in danger."

"That doesn't make an ale cup of sense," Winna said. "The slinders came and got him, and they're the creatures of the Briar King. So why should he be in danger? And if His Mossy Majesty wanted us to come along, why didn't he just have us kidnapped, too?"

"You're asking the wrong fellow," Aspar said. "I don't even believe in visions. I'm just happy she let us go. Although . . ."

"What?"

"You saw the utins, yah?"

"Utins?" She paled. "Like that thing that—" She stumbled off.

"Yah. Three of 'em, at least. The slinders killed 'em. Maybe they were after Stephen, too. Maybe that's why the king sent the slinders: to *protect* him."

"I thought you didn't believe in visions."

"I'm just talking," Aspar said. "I'm just happy to be on the trail."

"What else did Her Majesty say?"

"That's it—follow Stephen. Find him, protect him, help him. She said to let my own judgment be my guide. Said I was her deputy in the region, whatever that means."

"Really? Her deputy?"

"You know what that means?"

"It's Virgenyan. Means you carry the same authority she does—that she'll vouch for you. I don't suppose she gave you any way of proving your authority."

Aspar laughed. "Like what? A sealed letter, a ring, or a scepter? The girl was chased halfway around the world, and from what I understand, most of that time she only had the clothes on her back. I reckon it'll be sorted out later, if it needs sorting out.

"Anyway, at the moment, I maunt having her authority doesn't mean too much, yah? They may be callin' her a queen, but she's not one yet."

"Werlic," Winna murmured under her breath. "There's that way of looking at it."

They rode on in silence for a few moments. Aspar wasn't certain what to say; every time he glanced at her, Winna appeared more troubled.

"Stephen and Ehawk'll be all right," he assured her. "We'll find 'em. We've come through worse than this, the four of us."

"Yah," she said despondently.

He scratched his face. "Yah. They're fine."

She nodded but didn't reply.

"Meantime, it's nice. I mean, we haven't been alone together in a while."

She looked up at him sharply.

"What's that supposed to mean?" she snapped.

"I . . . , ah, don't know." He felt his tumble, all right, but didn't know what he had tripped over.

She opened her mouth, closed it, then started again. "It's not the time now. When we find Stephen."

"Time for what?" Aspar asked.

"Nothing."

"Winna—"

"You've been cold as a post for twice a nineday," she erupted, "and all of a sudden you're trying to sweeten up your talk?"

"It's kind of hard to make luvrood when so many people are around," Aspar grunted.

"It's not like I was expecting posies and poesy," Winna said. "Just a squeeze of the hand and a whisper in my ear now and then. We might have died, without . . ." She dipped her head and clamped her lips shut.

"I have to think you knew what you were getting into when you—" He stopped, unsure of what he was going to say next.

"Threw myself at you?" she finished. "Yah. I never meant to do that. When I saw you at the Taff, I thought you were dead. I thought you had died never knowing how I felt. And when you were alive again, and we were away from everything—from my father, from the Sow's Teat, from Colbaely altogether—I just didn't care anymore, about consequences, about the future, none of it."

"And now?"

"And now I still don't care, you damned oaf. But I'm starting to wonder about you. Back when we were alone, it was wonderful. I spent half of my time terrified out of my wits, but that aside, I've never been happier in my life. It was just what I'd always dreamed I'd have from you: adventure, love, and good squirming in the dark.

"But add a few people to the situation, and I'm suddenly like your bothersome little sister. *She* comes along, so much more like you than I can ever be——"

He interrupted her. "Winna, don't you ever want the normal things? A house? Children?"

She snorted. "I think I'll wait until the world isn't ending before I start a family, thanks."

"I'm serious."

"And so am I." Her green eyes were all challenge. "Are you saying I can't have those things with you?"

"I guess I never really thought about it."

"So this is you talking out loud, without thinking close about what you're saying?"

"Ah, I guess."

"Yah, werlic. You'll want to stop doing that."

An awkward silence descended over them.

"I don't think of you like a sister."

"No, of course not—less than a bell alone, and you're all after hiking up my skirt again."

"I was just saying that I was happy to be alone with you again, is all," Aspar said. "Just away from the others. And it's not what you think. I'm a holter; I've never been anything else. It's what I know how to do. I work alone, at my own pace, the way I want to, and I get things done. I'm not a leader, Winna. I wasn't cut out for that. Four of us was bad enough. Five was practically intolerable."

"I didn't think you minded it at all when Leshya joined us."

"This isn't about Leshya," Aspar said desperately. "I'm trying to *tell* you something."

"Go on."

"So, then all of a sudden there are fifty of us, and I don't know *what* I'm supposed to do. I'm not a knight, not a soldier. I work *alone*."

"So what does that say about me?"

He took a deep breath, feeling as if he were about to dive

into a very deep pool. "Being with you—and *just* you—is like being alone, but better."

She stared at him, blinking.

He saw dampness appear in her eyes, and his heart fell. He knew what he *wanted* to say, but clearly he didn't have the right words.

"Winna—" he started again.

She held up a finger.

"Hush," she said. "That's the best thing you've said to me in a long time—maybe ever—so you probably want to shut up now."

Relief took hold of Aspar. He followed her advice and settled into the ride.

Snow drifted fitfully, but he didn't have much worry that the trail would get covered; the tracks of one or two slinders he might lose in a heavy snowfall, yes, but not the several hundred that had come this way. And it wasn't just tracks they were finding but trails of blood and the occasional corpse. It might be that they didn't feel pain or fear, but they died just like everything else.

Daylight surrendered without much of a fight a few bells later, lead tarnishing to black, with a wicked promise of hard cold. They lit torches. The snowfall thickened, and the flames hissed and fussed in it.

Though Aspar didn't want to admit it, he was tired, so tired that his knees were quivering against Ogre's flanks. And though she didn't complain, Winna seemed on the verge of dropping, as well. It had been a very long day, a day lived almost entirely at the edge of death, and that could wear iron down to rust.

"How are you holding up over there?" Aspar asked.

"The snow will cover the tracks if we stop." She sighed.

"Not so I can't find the trail," Aspar said. "Even if there aren't any more bodies, they've scraped tree bark, broken branches—I can follow 'em."

"What if we stop and they kill Stephen while we're resting?"

"They won't, not if we're right."

"But we might be wrong. They might cut his heart out at midnight, for all we know."

"They might," Aspar agreed. "But if we find him now, in the shape we're in, do you really think we could do anything to help him?"

"No," Winna admitted. "Is that really the point?"

"Yes," Aspar said. "I'm not some kinderspell knight, ready to die because the story says I ought. We'll save Stephen if I think we'll survive it or at least have a decent chance. Right now, we need a little rest."

Winna nodded. "Yah," she said. "You've talked me into it. Do you want to camp here?"

"Nah, let me show you something. Just up ahead."

"Feel the notches?" Aspar asked, searching up through the darkness and finding Winna's rump.

"Yah. And watch your paws, you old bear. I'm not that forgiving, not with you making me climb another tree."

"This should be an easier climb."

"It is. Who cut the notches? They're old; I can feel bark that's grown back on 'em."

"Yah. I cut 'em, back when I was a boy."

"You've been planning this a long time."

Aspar almost chuckled at that, but he was too exhausted.

"Just a little higher," he promised. "You'll feel a jut."

"Got it," Winna said.

A few moments later Aspar followed Winna onto a hard flat surface.

"Your winter castle?" she asked.

"Something like that," he replied.

"It could do with some walls."

"Well, I couldn't see anything then, could I?" Aspar said.

"We can't see anything as it is," Winna pointed out.

"Yah. Anyway, it's got a roof to keep the snow off, and there ought to be a piece of canvas we can raise to hold the worst of this noar'wis off of us. Just mind the edge. I only built this for one."

"So I take it I'm the first woman you've brought home."

"Ah—" He stopped, afraid to answer that.

"Oh," she said. "Sorry, I was just joking. I didn't mean to bring that up."

"It was a long time ago," Aspar said. "It doesn't bother me. I just didn't . . ." Now he was *sure* he shouldn't say anything else.

But then he felt her mitten on his face. "I'm not jealous of *her,* Aspar," she said. "That was before I was born, so how could I be?"

"Raiht."

"Raiht. So where's the hearth?"

"Ah, I reckon you've just laid your hand on it," he said.

"Oh, well." She sighed. "I guess it'll be better than freezing."

It was considerably better than freezing, Aspar reckoned when the morning gray woke him. Winna was nestled into the crook of his arm, her bare flesh still hot against his, and the both of them were cocooned in blankets and skins. They'd found some energy neither thought they had, enough that it was a miracle they hadn't fallen off the platform during the night.

He kept his breathing slow and deep, not wanting to wake her yet. But he turned his gaze about, marveling still at what had struck him with wonder as a boy, all those years ago.

"There you are," Winna murmured.

"You're awake?"

"Before you were," she said. "Just looking. I never knew there was anyplace like this."

"I call 'em the tyrants," Aspar said.

"Tyrants?"

He nodded, looking up at the spreading and interlocking branches of the huge tree they rested in and those all around it.

"Yah. It's the biggest, oldest stand of ironoaks in the forest. No other trees can live here; the oaks shade 'em out. They're the kings, the emperors of the forest. It's a whole different world up here. There are things that live on these branches and never go down to the ground."

Winna leaned to peer over the edge. "How far down is— *eep!*"

"Don't fall," he said, gripping her a little tighter.

"That's farther than I thought," she rasped. "A lot farther. And we almost, last night we nearly—"

"No, never," Aspar lied. "I had us the whole time."

She smiled wryly and kissed him.

"You know," she said, "when I was a girl, I thought you were made of iron. Remember when you and Dovel brought in the bodies of the Black Wargh and his men? It was like you were Saint Michael made flesh. I thought that with you at their side, a person wouldn't have to worry about anything."

Her eyes were serious, as beautiful as he had ever seen them. Somewhere nearby a crow-woodpecker hammered at a tree, then vented a throaty warble.

"Now you know better," he said. "Fend took you from me, right out from underneath my nose."

"Yah," she said softly. "And you got me back, but it was too late. I already knew that you could fail by then, that no matter how strong and determined you were, the bad things could still get me."

"I'm sorry, Winna."

She gripped his hand. "No, you don't understand," she said. "A girl falls in love with a hero. A woman falls in love with a man. I don't love you because I think you can protect me; I love you because you're a man, a good man. It's not that you always succeed but that you'll always try."

She looked away, back down at the distant forest floor. It was a relief, because he couldn't think of any reply to that.

He remembered Winna as a kindling, a bundle of legs, hands, and blond hair racing around the village, always bothering him for stories of the wider world. Just one of a hundred children he'd watched flicker through mayfly childhood to become mothers, fathers, grandparents.

Aspar wasn't sure what love was. After his first wife,

Qerla, was murdered, he'd spent twenty years avoiding women and the entanglements they brought. Winna had snuck up on him, masquerading as a little girl well after he ought to have known better. But in the end the surprise had been a pleasant one, and for a short time he'd surrendered to it as much as he ever had yielded to anything.

That was before Fend had captured her. Fend had killed his first love; he seemed destined to kill all of them.

In any event, Aspar had been more and more uneasy since then, less and less sure of his feelings. He knew they were there, but what it came down to was that as long as they were on the move, fighting, always in danger of death, it was easy not to think about the future, easy to imagine that when this was all over, Winna would go back to her life and he would go back to his. He would miss her and have pleasant memories, but it would be something of a relief.

But now he suddenly realized how deep the water was, and he wasn't sure if he could swim in it.

Without meaning to, he recalled Leshya. The Sefry woman was tough and wise and kept what feelings she had close, very close. There wouldn't be any confusion with her; with her it would be honest and simple—

He suddenly felt the tree tremble. Not from the wind; the cadence was all wrong, and it came up from the roots.

Winna must have seen him frown.

"What?"

He held a finger to his lips and shook his head, then returned his gaze to the ground. The vibration in the tree continued, but he couldn't imagine what it was. It might be a few hundred horsemen, so many of them that the percussive thutter of hooves melted together. It might be slinders again, though it didn't feel like that, either. There was a sustained quality to the vibration that was like nothing he'd ever experienced before, but it was getting stronger.

He shallowed his breathing, waiting for the sound.

A hundred heartbeats later he heard the start of a scraping, a grinding sort of noise. A few dead leaves gave up their desperate hold on their branches and drifted down. Aspar still couldn't see anything, but he noticed that the woodpecker had stopped, as had all bird noises.

The sound was clearer now, and the shivering of the tree even more pronounced, so that at last he felt a heavy rhythm, a dull *whump-whump-whump-whump* almost below hearing. That said to Aspar that something very large and very heavy was running through the forest, faster than a horse could gallop.

And it was dragging something *huge*.

He noticed Winna's breath quicken as he reached carefully for his bow and arrows, so he found her hand again and squeezed it. He glanced at the sky; it was still gray, but the clouds were high and on the bright side. It didn't look like there would be more snow.

Whatever it was, it was coming from the same direction they had: north and west. The branches of the trees in that direction swayed visibly. He deepened and slowed his breath, trying to relax, focusing on the Old King's Road below them and slightly to the north.

He caught only glimpses at first of something huge, black, and gray-green winding through the trees, but his senses couldn't focus it into reality. He concentrated on two gigantic tyrants arching over a long clearing on the Old King's Road, reckoning that that would be where he would get his first good look at it.

A mist poured through the trees, and then something dark and sinuous, moving so quickly that Aspar first thought he was seeing some strange flood, a river flowing above ground. But then it stopped as suddenly, as did the sound of its passage and the shaking in the tree.

The mist coiled, and something like a viridian lamp burned through it.

Instantly, Aspar felt his skin prickle and ache like the onset of a fever, and he clapped a hand over Winna's face to stop her vision. For as the mist cleared, he saw that the green light was an eye, seen as just a sliver, above it as they were. But that might be enough.

Its head, he reckoned, was as long as a decent-sized man was tall. It had a long tapering snout with fleshy nostrils, something like that of a horse, but toward the neck its skull flared and thickened to resemble an adder's. Two black horny ridges jutted up just behind the eyes, which bulged out of round, bony sockets. It had no ears that he could see, but it had a ruff of spikes that started at the base of the skull and ran down its thorny spine.

It wasn't a snake, for he could see that after four kingsyards or so of very broad neck it was drawn up on immensely thick legs terminating in what resembled a huge hoof cloven five times. However, like a snake, it dragged its belly, and its body twisted behind it, so long that he couldn't tell whether it had rear legs, and he could see what he reckoned to be ten or twelve kingsyards of it.

The head lifted, and for an instant he feared it would turn its deadly eyes up toward them, but instead it lowered its nostrils to the ground and began to sniff at the trail. Its neck moved this way and that.

Was it following us or the slinders? he wondered. *And who will it follow now?*

It was then he noticed something he hadn't before. The body widened above the legs to accommodate a massive bunching of shoulder muscles, and there, at its thickest place, was something strange, a flash of color that didn't seem to belong, something sticking up.

Then he got it. It was a saddle, strapped around the girth of the thing, and there were two people sitting on it, one bareheaded and one wearing a broad-brimmed hat.

"Sceat," Aspar murmured.

As if in response, a flash of pale appeared as the man with the hat looked up. And though the distance was great and the mist obscuring, Aspar knew by the eye patch and the shape of the nose exactly who it was.

Fend.

CHAPTER SIX

HAUNTED

DUKE ERNST reached for his sword, but Neil's already was flying from its scabbard, feylight lapping up the length of its blade. Ernst froze and stared, as did his men, and Neil backed his horse so that he was not pressed, so that he could face both Ernst and Elyoner.

"By my fathers and their fathers," he snarled, "Anne Dare is under my protection, and I will slaughter any man who threatens to lay a hand on her."

Another sword hissed from its sheath, and Cazio bounded down, placing himself between Anne and Ernst, but with his back to the Craftsmen. At this point Neil thought that might be a mistake.

"Shinecraft!" Ernst said, still staring at Draug. "Witchery. The praifec shall deal with you, whoever you are."

"Much comfort that will be to your corpse," Neil shot back. "In any event, I took this sword from a servant of the praifec, which I'm sure is as strange to you as it is to me."

Ernst finished drawing his weapon. "I have no fear of your sorcery and no belly for your lies," he said. "I *will* carry out my lord's command."

"My uncle is an usurper," Anne said. "Your duty does not lie with him. It lies with me."

Ernst spat.

"Your father my have badgered the Comven into legitimizing you as his heir, but do not become confused, Princess. There is only one Dare whose blood is thick enough to rule Crotheny, and that is King Robert. Whatever childish adventure you have embarked upon, I assure you that it ends now."

"Oh, let the girl remain a child for a bit longer," Elyoner broke in.

"Duchess?" Ernst said.

"Anne, dear," Elyoner said, "you may want to close your eyes."

Neil heard the sudden strum of bowstrings, and his flesh went cold and hot as he cursed his stupidity.

But it was Duke Ernst who showed the most surprise— one arrow went through his throat, and another vanished a fourth of its length into his right eye socket.

More darts followed, and in the space of but a few heart-beats, all of Ernst's riders had fallen from their saddles. Only then did four men in yellow hose and orange surcoats appear from behind the wall. They began to slit the throats of the wounded with long wicked knives.

Anne gaped in astonishment.

"Oh, dear," Elyoner said. "I thought I told you not to look."

"It's not my first time to see men die, Aunt Elyoner," Anne replied. She looked pale and her eyes were watery, but she watched the murder with a steady gaze.

"Sadly, yes," Elyoner said. "Despite a residue of naïveté, I can see that you have grown up, haven't you? Well, enough of this unpleasantness," she continued, pulling on the reins of her horse. "Let's go see what my staff can find in the kitchens."

As they started up the avenue toward the mansion, Neil trotted his horse up next to Elyoner.

"Duchess—"

"Yes, sir knight, I know it was boorish to think me a trai-tor and a liar, but there's no need to apologize," she said. "You see, I hadn't expected the duke to arrive until tomor-row, and I had arranged for him to meet with an ill fate be-fore even reaching here."

"Robert will soon know that something has happened to them," Neil said.

"Tsk, tsk." Elyoner sighed. "These are evil times. Monsters and terrible people wander the roads. Even the king's men aren't safe."

"You think Robert won't see through that?"

"I think we have a *little* time, dove," Elyoner assured him. "Time enough to eat and drink and rest. The morning is early enough for plans, I should think. No, we need to be fresh when we discuss what to do next. After all, you didn't imagine that you were just going to ride up to Eslen and demand that they open the city gates, did you?"

Neil felt his mouth twist a bit.

"Well, that's the problem," he replied. "If I may be candid, Duchess . . ."

"You may be as candid with me as you like," she said wryly. "Or you may deceive and taunt me. Either way, I will find my amusement." Her lips bowed slightly.

"I've fought in many battles," Neil said, ignoring her flirtation. "My father first gave me a spear when I was nine, to kill Weihand raiders who were in the employ of Hansa. After my fah died, Baron Fail de Liery took me into his household, and I battled for him.

"Now I'm a knight of Crotheny. But I've little knowledge of how to wage a war, you see. I've led raids and defended redoubts, but taking a city and a fortress, especially one like Eslen—that's not something I know how to do. Nor, I fear, does Anne."

"I know," Elyoner agreed. "It's all so precious, this campaign of yours. But you see, my dear, that's all the more reason you should spend a little time with me. So I can introduce you to the right people."

"What do you mean?"

"Please have a little patience, dove. Trust Elyoner. Have I ever given you poor advice?"

"I can think of one instance," Neil said stiffly.

"No," Elyoner said softly. "I don't think so. That it didn't turn out well was no fault of mine. Your tryst with Fastia wasn't the cause of her death, Sir Neil. She was killed by evil men. Do you think a knight who did not love her could have saved her?"

"I was distracted," Neil said.

"I don't believe that. Muriele didn't, and I'm sure Fastia would never blame you. Nor would she want you to weep overlong. I know you have mourned her, but she is gone, and you yet live. You should—oh, my."

Neil felt his cheeks burn.

"Sir Neil?"

"Duchess?"

"Your face is so charmingly transparent. You looked so *guilty* just now. Who has taken your fancy?"

"No one," Neil replied quickly.

"*Hah.* You mean you *wish* no one had. You mean someone has, but you think it's wrong, somehow. Guilt is your real lover, sir knight. Name to me one woman you have loved when you did not feel guilty for the affection."

"Please, Duchess, I don't wish to discuss this."

"Perhaps you need more of my herbal concoction."

Neil gazed desperately ahead, hoping for relief from the conversation. The mansion was so very *far* from the gates. It hadn't seemed this far before.

Since finding Anne in Dunmrogh, he had managed to keep his heart silent, but Glenchest was waking it again. He remembered riding here the first time, on a much more carefree outing. He remembered Fastia, weaving him a chain of flowers to wear around his neck. And then later, after much drinking, she had come to his room . . .

The daughter of my queen, whom I was sworn to protect. A married woman.

She had died in his arms, and he had thought his heart was so shattered that it could never feel again.

Until he met Brinna, who saved his life and sacrificed her dream so he might pursue his duty. He did not love her, not as he had Fastia, but there was something there.

Where was she now? Dead also? Returned to the prison she had fled?

"Poor thing." Elyoner sighed. "Poor thing. Your heart is made for tragedy, I fear."

"That is why my one love must be my duty," he replied, speaking stiffly again.

"And that would be the greatest tragedy of all," Elyoner replied, "if I thought you could stick to that. But your heart is far too romantic to close all of its portals."

And finally, too late, they reached the gates of the manse.

Cazio put his hand against the wall to hold it up, belched, and lifted the carafe of wine to his lips, swallowing deeply.

The vintage was unlike any he had ever had: dry and fruity, with an aftertaste like apricots. The duchess had claimed its origin was in a nearby valley, which made it the first Crothanic wine he'd ever tasted.

He glanced up at the moonless sky and raised the carafe.

"Z'Acatto!" he said. "You should have come! We could have argued about this wine. To you, old man!"

Z'Acatto had claimed there was no vintage north of Tero Gallé worth drinking, but this one proved him wrong. Whether he was too stubborn to admit that was, of course, the issue. Cazio wondered how his mentor was doing. Surely he was still abed in Dunmrogh, considering his injuries.

He gazed around the garden he'd found. The meal had been excellent and exotic. The northern lands might be a bit barbaric, but the food was definitely interesting, and at the duchess's there was plenty of it. But after a few glasses of wine, the gabble around him had lost all intelligibility.

The duchess was able to carry on a passable conversation in Vitellian, but though she had flirted with him a bit on the ride, she quite naturally was concentrating on catching up with Anne. He was too tired to try to muddle clumsily through in the king's tongue, so after the meal he'd gone looking for a bit of solitude, and he had found it here.

Glenchest—such odd names they had in this part of the world—seemed to be more garden than anything else, rather like the grounds of the Mediccio in z'Irbina where he and z'Acatto had once pilfered a bottle of the fabled Echi'dacrumi de Sahto Rosa.

Of course, there hadn't been frozen rain all over the place in z'Irbina, nor did Vitellian gardens favor evergreen hedges trimmed to resemble stone walls as this one did, but the results were still pleasing. There was even a statue of Lady Fiussa, whose image had also graced the square in his hometown of Avella. It made him feel a bit at home.

He doffed his hat to the nude slip of a saint who stood in the paved center of a small, clover-shaped courtyard and rested on a marble bench to finish his wine. His hands ached with the cold, but the rest of him was surprisingly warm, courtesy not only of the wine but also of the excellent doublet and hose the duchess had given him. The orange leggings were thick and woolen, and the black upper garment was of supple leather lined with fur. Over all that was thrown a wide-sleeved quilted coat, and his feet were snugged in buskins.

He sat in the warm pool of light cast by his lamp and was lifting the carafe again in toast to the duchess's excellent taste in clothing, when a feminine voice interrupted his reverie.

"Cazio?"

He turned and found Austra regarding him.

Elyoner had given her presents, as well: an indigo gown over which she wore a robe of deep brown fur of some sort Cazio did not recognize, though he thought the hood was trimmed with white mink. Her face seemed ruddy, even for lamplight, probably from the cold.

"Hello, lovely," he said. "Welcome to my little kingdom."

Austra didn't answer for a moment. Cazio wasn't sure if it was a trick of the light that she seemed to be rocking back and forth on her heels, as if trying to keep balance on something narrow. He kept expecting her to put her arms out to steady herself.

"Do you really think I'm lovely?" she blurted, and Cazio realized that she'd had at least as much wine as he had.

That was something the duchess was good at, apparently: getting people to drink her wine.

"As the light of sunrise, as the petals of the violet," he answered.

"No," she said a bit angrily. "None of that. You say that sort of thing to every woman you meet. I want to know what you think of *me,* just me."

"I—" he began, but she rushed on.

"I thought I was going to *die,*" she said. "I've never felt so completely alone. And I prayed you would find me, but I feared you were already dead. I saw you fall, Cazio."

"And I *did* find you," Cazio said.

"Yes, you did," she said. "You did, and it was wonderful. Like that first time you saved me—saved us, back near the coven. You put yourself between us and harm without even asking why. I fell in love with you then. Did you know that?"

"I . . . No," he said.

"But then I got to know you better, and I understood that you would have done that for anyone. Yes, you were pursuing Anne, but even if you had known neither of us, you would have done the same thing."

"I wouldn't say that," Cazio said.

"I would. You are like an actor on a stage, Cazio, only what you're acting out is your own life. You contrive your speech and your mannerisms; you pose near constantly. But beneath all that, whether you know it or not, the thing you are pretending to be—you really *are.* And now that I understand that, I understand that I love you all the more. I also understand you don't love me."

Cazio's belly tightened. "Austra—"

"No, hush. You don't. You like me. You like kissing me. But you don't love me. Maybe you love Anne. I'm not sure about that part, but you understand now, don't you, that you can't have her?"

She was crying, and Cazio suddenly wanted nothing more than to stop those tears, but he felt strangely paralyzed.

"I know you dallied with me to make her jealous. And knowing you, the fact that Anne is unattainable probably makes her all the more enticing. But I'm here, Cazio, and I love you, and even if you don't feel the same, I want you, want whatever you can give me." She pushed the tears away and defiantly took a step closer.

"I've nearly died a dozen times in the last year. I've been lucky, but things are only going to get worse. I don't think I'll see my next birthday, Cazio. I really don't. And before I die, I want—I want to *be* with you. Do you understand? I won't expect marriage, or love, or even flowers, but I want you, now, while there's still time."

"Austra, have you really thought about this?"

"They were talking about *raping* me, Cazio," Austra said. "You think I want to lose my virginity like *that*? Am I so ugly that—"

"Stop," he said, holding up his hand, and she did. Her eyes seemed larger than usual, gentle shadows on her face. "You know better than that."

"I know better than nothing."

"Really? You seem to know quite a lot about me," he said. "What I feel, what I don't feel. Well, let me tell you, Austra Eleistotara—"

"Laesdautar," she corrected.

"However you pronounce it," he said. "My point is—"

"What is your point?"

"It—" He stopped, looked at her for a second, and the moment came back to him, just before the slinders attacked them, when he had seen her tied up, and the men who had taken her, saw that it was Austra and not Anne.

He took her by both shoulders and kissed her. Her lips were cold at first and unresponsive, but then they quivered against his, and her arms reached around him, and she sighed as her body butted against him.

"My point," he said, pulling away after a long, long time, and he was reasonably sure of what he meant to say. "My point is that you do not understand me half so well as you think you do. Because I *do* love you."

"Oh," she said as he pulled her close again. "Oh."

* * *

When the servant closed the door behind her, Anne collapsed onto the bed, listening to the faint wisp of buskins on stone until they vanished.

Dinner had been almost unbearable; it had been an age since she had eaten at a formal table, and though Elyoner's board was rowdier than most, still she felt the need to sit with her spine straight and attempt to make witty conversation. She'd eschewed the wine that might have helped relax her, because the idea of alcohol still sickened her a bit. The meal had been delicious, judging by the reactions of her companions, but she scarcely had noticed the taste of anything.

Now, finally, she had what she'd wanted for, well, months. She was alone.

She reached for the foot of the bed, where a wooden lion's head kept sentinel at the top of the post. She rubbed the glass-smooth crown of it.

"Hello, Lew." She sighed.

It was all so familiar and so strange at the same time. How many times had she stayed in this room? Once a year, nearly. The first time she remembered she'd been about six, and Austra five. Elseny, Anne's middle sister, had been eight. It was the first time Fastia, the eldest, had been put in charge of the three girls, and she must have been about thirteen.

Anne could see her now; to her younger eyes, of course, Fastia had seemed all but grown, a woman. Looking at her now, in her cotton shift, she was still just a slip, her breasts the slightest of bumps. Her face already had their mother's famous beauty, but still in girlish disguise. Her long dark hair was wavy from having been caught up in braids earlier that evening.

"Hello, Lew," Fastia had said, rubbing the lion's head for the first time.

Elseny had giggled. "You're in love!" she had accused. "You're in love with Leuhaert!"

Anne could barely remember who Leuhaert was. The son of some greft or duke who'd appeared at court during one

Yule season, a handsome boy whose manners were well intended but never quite right.

"Maybe I am," she said. "And you know what his name means? Lionheart. He's my lion, and since he's not here, old Lew here will have to do."

Anne put her hand on the lion's head. "Oh, Lew!" she said brightly. "Bring me a prince, too."

"And me!" Austra giggled, slapping the wood.

They'd made a habit of that for the next ten years, always rubbing Lew's head, even after Fastia married.

She'd closed her eyes in remembrance, but as a hand brushed hers, they flew open and she gasped. A girl stood there, a girl with golden hair.

"Elseny?" Anne asked, drawing her hand back.

It was Elseny, looking the age Anne had last seen her.

"Hello, Lew," Elseny said, ignoring Anne. "Hello, old fellow. I think Fastia is up to something naughty, but I won't tell if you won't. And I'm going to be married. Fancy that!"

Elseny patted the wooden head again and then walked back toward the door. Anne felt her breath rushing in her ears.

"Elseny!" she called, but her sister didn't answer.

She glanced back up and found Fastia standing there.

"Hello, Lew," Fastia said, giving the bedpost a brush with a hand that lingered. She looked almost the same as Anne had last seen her except that her face was relaxed, her public mask laid aside. It seemed soft, and sad, and young, not so different from the girl who had given Lew his name.

Anne felt her heart clutch. She'd said such angry things to Fastia the last time they'd spoken. How could she have known they would never speak again?

"What should I do?" Fastia murmured. "I shouldn't. I shouldn't . . ."

Anne suddenly recognized the glazed look in her sister's eyes. She was drunk. She stood there swaying, and she suddenly teared up. She looked straight at Anne, and for an instant Anne was sure Fastia saw her.

"I'm sorry, Anne," she whispered. "I'm so sorry."
Then Fastia closed her eyes and softly began to sing.

Here's my wish;
A man with lips as red as blood
With skin as white as snow
With hair of blue-black
Like a raven's wing.
That's my wish.

Here's my wish;
A man to hold me tight and warm
To hold no one but me
Until the stars dim
Until the sea dries up
That's my wish

She finished her song, and Anne was seeing her through a blur of tears.

"Good-bye, Lew," Fastia said. As she began to turn, Anne's silent weeping became sobs. Fastia walked to the tapestry of a knight astride a hippocampus and lifted it. Behind it, she tapped the wall, and a panel slid open.

Fastia paused at the threshold into darkness. "There are many more such hidden places where we are from," she said. "But that is for later. For now, you must survive this."

And then came the smell of rotting flesh, and Fastia's eyes were full of worms, and Anne screamed—

—and sat up screaming, her hand still on the bedpost, just in time to see the tapestry lifting.

CHAPTER SEVEN

✢

THE REVESTURI

THE MAN was so close, Stephen could feel breath on the back of his neck.

"I always thought that was just an expression," he murmured.

"What's an expression?" the man asked.

"Gozh dazh, brodar Ehan," Stephen said.

"Eh, yah, that's an expression: 'Good day,'" Ehan replied. "But you know that."

"May I turn around?"

"Oh, sure," Ehan said. "I was just trying to scare you."

"You did a fine job," Stephen allowed, turning slowly.

He found an almost dwarfish little man with bright red hair beaming up at him, fists on his hips and elbows jutting in a dark green robe. He suddenly thrust one of his hands out, and Stephen flinched slightly, until he saw it was empty.

"Jumpy, aren't you?" Ehan said as Stephen belatedly took the proffered hand.

"Well, it's just that you began by calling me a traitor, Brother Ehan."

"Well, it's true," Ehan replied. "There's some in the Church would consider you a traitor, but I'm not one of 'em. Nor will you find anyone in d'Ef that thinks that way. Not at the moment, anyway."

"How did you know I was going to be there?"

"Them below told me they was sending you up," Ehan said.

"Then you're allied with slinders?"

Ehan scratched his head. "The wothen? Yah, I reckon."

"I don't understand."

"Well, *I'm* not to explain it to you," Ehan replied, "for fear I'll get it wrong. I'm just here to take you to the fellow who *will* explain it to you, and to assure you that you're among friends—or at least not among enemies. No allies of the praifec here."

"So you know about that?" Stephen said.

"Oh, sure," Ehan replied. "Look, do you mind if we start walking? We're likely to miss the praicersnu if we don't hurry."

Stephen took a deep breath. He and Ehan had been friends, or at least he once thought they were. They had helped each other against Desmond Spendlove and the other corrupt monks of the monastery d'Ef. But Stephen had since undertaken a series of studies whose lesson was essentially that no one was what he seemed, especially in the Church.

Ehan had never given Stephen any reason to distrust him. He could as easily have stabbed him in the back as said hello.

But maybe what he wanted was subtler than murder.

"Let's go, then," Stephen said.

"This way."

Ehan motioned him along a trail that switched back through forest fringe and pasture, down across a little stream bridged by a log, out through the vast apple orchard, and up the next hill toward the sprawling monastery. Despite his bad memories of the place, he had to admit it was still a beautiful building. The high-steepled nave thrust up a double-arched clock tower of rose granite to catch the morning sun like pale fire, a prayer made architecture.

"What's happened since I've been gone?" Stephen asked as they climbed the last, steepest part of the approach.

"Ah, well, I reckon I can tell you some of it. After you saved the holter from Brother Desmond and his bunch, they went out after you. We learned later how that turned out, of course. In the meantime, we got word that the praifec had sent a new fratrex to carry on here at the monastery. Now, we knew Desmond was mean, but we didn't know he was working for the Hierovasi."

"Hierovasi?"

"I—right, supposed to let *him* explain. Don't worry about that just yet. The bad fellows, let's say. In fact, like you, most of us didn't even know about the Hierovasi until recently. But we did manage to work out that Hespero was one of 'em, which meant the fratrex he was sending would most likely be one, as well.

"He was, and we had a bit of a fight. We would have lost, but we had some allies."

"The slinders?"

"The dreothen, and yah, the wothen through them. You don't approve?"

"They eat people," Stephen pointed out.

Ehan chuckled. "Yah, that's a mark against 'em. But in this case they ate the right people, so we weren't complaining that much.

"Since then, our own numbers have grown as the word had gotten around. We've been attacked a few more times by the Hierovasi, but they've got other things on their table at the moment—the resacaratum, for instance."

"I heard something about that in Dunmrogh, mostly rumors."

"If only it were just rumors. But it's not; it's torture, burning, hanging, drowning, and all the rest. Anyone they don't like, anyone they think might be dangerous—"

"By *they,* you mean these Hierovasi?"

"Yah, but it's them that controls what most people think of as the Church, you understand."

"No," Stephen said. "I didn't know any of this."

But he felt a sudden spark of hope. Ehan was suggesting it was only a *faction* in the Church that was bad, albeit the most powerful faction. That meant there was a chance, after all, that he might find a side worth fighting on.

"Well, too few do," Ehan replied. "Know about it, that is. Anyhow, that's what we've been up to."

"Wait. These 'Hierovasi'—they control the Caillo Vaillamo in z'Irbina?"

"I should say so. Fratrex Prismo is one of 'em."

"Niro Lucio?"

"Ah, no." Ehan shook his head as they passed the higharched doors of the front entrance and moved toward the yard of the sprawling west wing. "Lucio died of a peculiar and unexpected stomach disorder, if you catch my meaning. It's Niro Fabulo now."

"So d'Ef is no longer obedient to the holy of holies?"

"Nope."

"Then who is in charge here?"

"Why, the fratrex is," Ehan said.

"Fratrex Pell? But I saw him die."

"No," a familiar voice averred. "No, Brother Stephen, you saw me *dying*. You did not see me die." Stephen's gaze leapt directly to the source of the words.

Fratrex Pell, the highest authority at d'Ef, was the first brother of that monastery whom Stephen had met. The fratrex had been posing as an old man, trying to lift a burden of firewood. Stephen had carried the burden, but he'd taken the opportunity to try to impress this person he'd imagined to be a simpleton. In fact, looking back on things, it was a bit painful to remember the condescension with which he had treated the fellow.

But the fratrex had been the one having sport with him, and the fratrex soon had revealed Stephen's foolishness.

He was there, now, seated at a wooden table in a rather peculiar-looking armchair, his violet eyes twinkling beneath bushy gray brows. He wore a simple umber robe with the hood thrown back.

"Fratrex," Stephen breathed. "I don't—I believed you dead. What I saw, and then the praifec's investigations—"

"Yes," the fratrex drawled casually. "Think carefully about that last one, won't you?"

"Oh," Stephen said. "Then you pretended to be dead to avoid the praifec."

"You always were a quick one, Brother Stephen," the

fratrex said drily. "Though it very nearly wasn't a pretense. Once Desmond Spendlove showed his true colors, I knew who he was working for. I wouldn't have guessed it, either. I trusted Hespero—I thought he was one of *us*. But everyone makes mistakes."

"Still," Stephen said. "When you saved my life, you were stabbed, and then the wall collapsed."

"I wasn't exactly left unscathed," Pell said.

That was when the details snapped into place: how sharp and thin the brother's legs were as they pushed through his robes, how his upper body moved strangely.

And the chair, of course, was wheeled.

"I'm sorry," Stephen said.

"Well, consider the alternative. And as I understand it, this is a particularly unpleasant time to be dead."

"But you were helping me."

"That is true," the fratrex allowed, "though I did it from more than personal regard. We need you, Brother Stephen. We need you alive. In fact, more than we need me, ultimately."

Somehow Stephen didn't like the sound of that.

"You keep referring to 'we,'" Stephen said. "I have a feeling you don't mean the Order of Saint Decmanus. Or the Church itself, for that matter, given what Brother Ehan has let on."

Fratrex Pell smiled indulgently. "Brother Ehan," he said. "I wonder if you would bring us some of the green cider. And maybe some of that bread I smell baking."

"It would be my honor, fratrex," he said, and scurried off.

"Can I help?" Stephen asked.

"No, stay, have a seat. We have a lot to talk about, and I'm not of a mind to delay. Time has gotten too short to be mysterious. Just give me a moment to collect my thoughts. They seem rather scattered lately."

Ehan brought the cider, a round of roglaef that smelled like black walnuts, and a hard white cheese. The fratrex took a little of each, bending with some difficulty; his right arm seemed particularly impaired.

The cider was cold, strong, and still a bit bubbly. The bread was warm and comforting, and the cheese sharp, with an aftertaste that reminded Stephen of oak.

The fratrex sat back, clumsily gripping a goblet of cider.

"How did our ancestors defeat the Skasloi, Brother Stephen?" the fratrex asked, sipping his cider.

That seemed an odd digression, but Stephen obliged.

"The Virgenyan captives started a revolt," he answered.

"Yes, of course," the fratrex said rather impatiently. "But even from our sparse records we know that there had been other revolts before that. How did the slaves led by Virgenya Dare succeed where the others failed?"

"The saints," Stephen said. "The saints were on the side of the slaves."

"Again," the fratrex asked, "why then and not before?"

"Because those who rose before had not been sufficiently devout," Stephen replied.

"Ah. Was that the answer you learned in the college at Ralegh?" the fratrex asked.

"Is there another?"

Fratrex Pell smiled benevolently. "Given what you've learned since leaving the college, what do *you* think?"

Stephen sighed and nodded. He closed his eyes and rubbed his temples, trying to think.

"I've never read anything that said it, but it seems obvious that Virgenya Dare and her followers walked faneways. Their powers, their weapons . . ."

"Yes," the fratrex said. "But what's beyond the obvious? The Skasloi had magery, as well—*powerful* magery. Did it come from the saints?"

"No," Stephen replied. "Of course not."

"You're certain?"

"The Skasloi worshipped the elder gods, whom the saints defeated," Stephen said. He brightened. "I suppose the saints didn't help any of the earlier uprisings because they hadn't yet defeated the elder gods."

Fratrex Pell's mouth widened a little farther. "Hasn't it

ever struck you as a little neat, a bit too tidy, that the elder gods and the Skasloi were defeated at the same time?"

"I suppose it just makes sense."

"It might make even more sense if the Skasloi and the elder gods were one and the same," the fratrex said.

Stephen gave that a moment, then nodded slowly.

"It's not impossible," he agreed. "I've never thought about it before because it's sacrilege, and I still have a habit of avoiding that when I can, but it's possible. The Skasloi had magicks that—" He frowned. "You aren't saying that the Skasloi got their power from the saints?"

"No, you lumphead. I'm suggesting that neither the elder gods nor the saints are *real.*"

Stephen suddenly wondered if the fratrex might have gone mad. Pain, coma, loss of blood and air to the lungs, the shock of being crippled . . .

He called back his fleeing wits. "But the— I've walked the faneways myself. I've *felt* the power of the saints." ·

"No," the fratrex said more gently, "you've felt *power.* And that is the only thing you or I know is real. The rest of it—where the power comes from, why it affects us as it does, how it differs from the power the Skasloi wielded—we know none of that."

"Again, when you say '*we*'—"

"The *Revesturi,*" Fratrex Pell said.

"Revesturi?" Stephen said. "I remember reading about them. A heretical movement within the Church, discredited a thousand years ago."

"Eleven hundred years ago," the fratrex corrected. "During the Sacaratum."

"Right. It was one of many heresies."

The fratrex shook his head. "It was more than that. History is often less about the past than it is about the present; history must be convenient to those who have power when it's being told.

"I'll tell you something about the Sacaratum I doubt very much you know. It was more than a holy war, more than a wave of conversion and consecration. At its very root it was a civil war, Brother Stephen. Two factions, equally powerful, fought for the soul of the Church: the Revesturi and the Hierovasi. The beginning of the argument was academic; the end of it was not. There are pits full of Revesturi bones."

"A civil war within the Church?" Stephen said. "Surely I would have heard something about that."

"There have been two such conflicts, actually," the fratrex continued. "In the first Church, the most high was always a woman, following the example of Virgenya Dare. The first Fratrex Prismo wrested his place by violence, and women were split from the hierarchy and thrust into their own temporally powerless and carefully controlled covens."

Again, the shift in perspective that changed the whole world. *Why wasn't there a word for that?* Stephen wondered.

"Then is all—is *everything* I know a lie?" he asked.

"No," the fratrex said. "It's history. The question you have to ask about any version of history is, Who *benefits* from that version? Over the course of a thousand years—or two thousand—the interests of the powerful change often, and thus, so do the stories that hold up their thrones."

"Then shouldn't I be asking who benefits from *your* version of events?" Stephen asked, feeling a bit sharp but not caring.

"Absolutely," the fratrex said. "But remember, there *are* absolute truths, things that actually happened. Genuine facts, actual bodies in the ground. Just because you've accepted some distortions, it doesn't mean there's nothing real in the world; it merely requires that you use some method to *discover* truth, wrestle it out of things."

"I've never been so naïve as to believe every opinion I hear," Stephen said. "There are always debates within the Church, and I've been among those who argued them. It isn't merely a matter of hearing and believing but of understanding how each proposition fits with the whole. And if

I'm told that something doesn't jibe with what I know, then I question it."

"But don't you see? That's just using one questionable source—or, worse, a body of them—to evaluate another. I asked you about the revolt against the Skasloi, the *central fact of our history,* and what did you have of substance to tell me? What sources could you refer me to? How do you know that what you've been told is true other than that it confirms other things you've been told? And what about the events of the last year? You know they happened; you witnessed some of them. Can you fit those things into what you've been taught?"

"The original sources from the time of the revolt have been lost," Stephen said, trying to wave aside the larger issue with the smaller one. "We trust the sources we have because that's *all* we have."

"I see. So if you lock three people in a room with a knife and a bag of gold, and when you open the door again, two of them are dead, do you accept the witness of the third merely because his is the only testimony available?"

"It's not the same thing."

"It's *exactly* the same thing."

"Not when the testimony is inspired by the saints."

"And if there are no saints?"

"Now we come full circle," Stephen said, becoming weary. "And you still leave me with the choice of supporting a faction that tortures and sacrifices children or one that co-operates with cannibals. Are you telling me there is no middle ground between the Hierovasi and the Revesturi?"

"Yes, of course there is. There's the largest faction of all: the ignorant."

"Which means me."

"Yes, until now. But you would have been approached, eventually, by one or both of the factions."

"First you tell me all the Revesturi were slaughtered in a civil war I've never heard of, and now you tell me they are a powerful cabal operating in the modern Church. Well, which is it?"

"*Both,* of course. Most of us were slain or banished during the Sacaratum. But while you can slay men and women, it is much more difficult to slay an idea, Brother Stephen."

"And what idea is that?" Stephen countered.

"Do you understand that name, Revesturi?"

"I presume it comes from the verb *revestum,* 'to inspect.' "

"Just so. Our very simple belief is that our history, our notions, the very world around us are properly subject to our own observation. All accounts must be considered and weighed; all facts must be included in any debate."

"That's a rather vague mandate to die for."

"Not when you consider the particular debates it inspires," the fratrex said. "To debate, for instance, whether there are actually saints isn't acceptable, is it?"

"Was that the debate that led to the civil war?"

"Not exactly. The simple fact is that that particular debate was so well suppressed that we actually don't know what it was about. But we do know the cause of it."

"And what might that be?"

"The journal of Virgenya Dare."

For several seconds Stephen couldn't think of anything to say at all. Virgenya Dare, the liberator, the savior of the human race, the woman who discovered the sedoi, the faneways, the paths to the saints. Her journal.

He shook his head and tried to focus on the moment.

"It would have been written in Old Virgenyan," he murmured. "Or perhaps elder Cavari. Her *journal*?"

The fratrex smiled.

Stephen rubbed his chin. "Then they actually had it," he mused in wonder, "her journal, as recently as the Sacaratum? Incredible. And yet they made no copies—oh. There's something in the journal, something the Hierovasi didn't like. Is that what you're going to tell me?"

"Indeed," Fratrex Pell confirmed. "Actually, there were several copies. All were destroyed. The original, however, was not."

"*What?* It still exists?"

"Indeed it does. One of our order fled with it and secreted it in a safe place. Unfortunately, the record of exactly *where* it was hidden was lost. That's a shame, because I believe the only thing that can save us—save the world—is what is contained in that journal."

"Wait. What? How does that follow?"

"Dreodh explained the doctrine of the wothen to you?"

"You mean their belief that the world itself has become ill?"

"Yes."

"He did."

"Did it make any sense to you?"

Stephen nodded reluctantly. "Somewhat. The forest, at least, seems to be dying. The monsters that now stalk the earth seem almost incarnations of sickness and death."

"Exactly. And you will not be surprised, I think, when I tell you that this has happened before, that such beasts have existed before."

"Legend suggests it. But . . ."

The fratrex raised a quieting hand. "There are no copies of Virgenya Dare's journal, but there are a very few, very sacred scrifti that reference it. I will show you those, of course, but let me summarize them now. This sickness comes to the world periodically. If it is not stopped, it will destroy all life. Virgenya Dare found a way to halt it once, but how she did so we do not know. If the secret exists anywhere, it will be in her journal."

"According to your own doctrine, however, lacking the journal, this story is just so much noise."

"Lacking the journal, yes," the fratrex said. "But we haven't been *completely* complacent. We have unearthed two clues as to its whereabouts; one is a very old reference to a mountain named Vhelnoryganuz, which we believe to be somewhere in the Bairghs. The other is this."

From his lap the fratrex produced a slender cedar box and pushed it toward Stephen. He reached for it gingerly and lifted off the top. Inside was a worn roll of lead foil.

"We can't read it," the fratrex said. "We're hoping you can."

"Why?"

"Because we need you to find the journal of Virgenya Dare," the fratrex said. "I repeat: Without it, I fear we are all of us doomed."

CHAPTER EIGHT

✛

A CHANGE OF SCENE

LEOFF WOKE to a faint rasping at his door.

He did not move but instead opened his eyes a slit, trying to think his way through the mind-mist that had followed him back from sleep.

His jailors never took so long at the door. They put their keys in, the keys turned, the door opened. And he had come to recognize the sound of a key in the lock. No, this was higher in pitch, a smaller piece of metal.

Before he could decide exactly what that meant, the scratching stopped, the door swung open, and in the low-guttering light of his oil lamp, he saw a shadow pass through it.

Leoff couldn't think of any reason to continue with the pretense that he was asleep. Instead, he swung his legs down from the bed and placed his feet on the floor.

"Have you come to kill me?" he asked the shadow softly.

It really was a shadow, or at least something his eye had difficulty penetrating. It resisted even being categorized as a particular shape. More than anything, it felt like the blind spot in the corner of his eye—except that this spot stood directly in front of him.

As he continued to stare, the umbra softened somehow, gaining definition, and figured into a human form clad in loose black breeches and a jerkin. Gloved hands reached up and brought down the hood.

Reality, Leoff had discovered, was the sum of a series of more or less consistent self-deceptions. His had been shattered by torture, privation, and loss, and he hadn't had time to deceive himself again.

Consequently, he wouldn't have been surprised if the face revealed had been the chimera mask of the queen of the phay, the pitying features of Saint Anemlen, or the fanged visage of an ogre come to devour him. The moment seemed absolutely pregnant with the impossible.

That the dropped cowl revealed the face of a young woman with sky-jewel eyes was thus unexpected but not surprising.

It did shift his perspective, however. She was slight and shorter than Leoff by more than a head. Her chestnut hair was pulled back, the line of her jaw soft. He doubted if she was yet twenty years old. She also looked familiar; he was certain he had seen her at court.

"I haven't come to kill you," she said. "In the name of Queen Muriele, I've come to set you free."

"To free me," he said slowly. Suddenly her face refocused, as if seen at twenty kingsyards, just next to the face of Muriele, the queen. That was where he had seen her; at the performance of his singspell.

"How did you do that? Make yourself invisible?"

"I am saint-blessed," she replied. "It's a coven secret. That's all I can tell you. Now, if you'll just follow me—"

"Wait," Leoff said. "How did you get in here?"

"With great difficulty and at considerable risk to myself," she said. "Now please, stop asking questions."

"But who are you?"

"My name is Alis, Alis Berrye, and I have the queen's confidence. She *sent* me. You understand? Now, please . . ."

"Lady Berrye, I am Leovigild Ackenzal. How *is* the queen?"

Alis blinked in what seemed to be incomprehension.

"She is passing well," she said, "for the moment."

"Why did she send you to free me?"

"That explanation would be lengthy, and we do not have much time. So please—"

"Humor me, my lady."

She sighed. "Very well. In brief, the queen is imprisoned in the Wolfcoat Tower. She has learned of your imprisonment, and also of the great affection in which the people of this city and Newland hold you. She believes that if you are free, it may improve her situation."

"How?"

"She believes the usurper might be overthrown."

"Really. All because of me. How very strange. And how did you get in here?"

"There are ways, secret ways that my—" She stopped, then started again. "That I know of. You will have to trust me. Trust also that if we do not move very soon, we will not leave this place alive."

Leoff nodded and closed his eyes. He thought about blue skies and warm winds from the south, the touch of rain on his face.

"I can't go." He sighed.

"What?"

"There are others held captive here: Mery Gramme and Areana Wistbirm. If I escape, they will suffer, and I can't have that. Free them, and prove to me they are free, and I will go with you."

"I don't know where the Gramme girl is being held. The young Wistbirm woman is beyond my reach, I fear, else I would certainly liberate her as well."

"Then I cannot go with you," Leoff said.

"Listen to me, Cavaor Ackenzal," Alis said urgently. "You need to understand your worth. There are people who will die—and see others die—to free you. What you did at Broogh is not forgotten, but your music at the Candlegrove unleashed a spirit that has not diminished. In fact, it has only continued to grow.

"Songs from your lustspell are sung throughout the country. The people are ready to come for the villain, the usurper, but they fear what he would do to you. If you were free, nothing would encumber them." Her voice dropped lower. "They say that a proper heir has returned to the kingdom: Princess Anne, daughter of William and Muriele. They will put her on the throne, but they fight for you. You are the most important man in the kingdom, Cavaor."

Leoff laughed at that. He couldn't help it; it seemed too ridiculous.

"I won't go with you," he said. "Not until Mery and Areana are safe."

"No, no, no, no, *no,*" Alis said. "Do you understand what I went through to reach you? It was nearly impossible—a miracle sufficient to qualify me for sainthood. Now you say that you won't go?

"Do *not* do this to me. Do not fail your queen."

"If you can work one miracle, then you can work another. Free Mery. Free Areana. Then I will happily go with you— so long as you have proof they are safe and well."

"Think, at least, of your music," Alis urged. "I told you your songs were famous. Did I also tell you that performing them is considered shinecraft? An attempt was made to do the entire play in the town of Wistbirm. The stage was put to the torch by the praifec's guards. But the performance was already a failure, because the subtler harmonies of your work eluded even the most gifted minstrel. If you were free, you could write it again, *correct* their performances."

"And doom more unfortunates to my fate?" he asked, lifting his useless hands.

"That's very odd," Alis said, seeming to notice his traction for the first time. She shook her head as if to clear it. "Look, it's a doom they *choose.*"

Leoff felt himself suddenly balanced very precariously. The woman—*and why a woman?* The woman's story was implausible at best.

Most likely this was Robert, having another go at him. So

far he hadn't done anything that would make matters worse; Robert knew that Leoff would never lift a finger for him unless Mery and Areana were in danger.

And if Alis was honest, his decision to stay was still consistent.

But here was a problem. What he might reveal here could give something to Robert that the usurper didn't already have, something that appeared to be of great value.

Yet the risk might be worth it. It probably was.

"In the Candlegrove," he said, breaking the silence.

"*What* in the Candlegrove?"

"Beneath the stage, on the far right, there is a space above the support. I knew they would burn my music, and I knew they would search my apartments for copies. But I hid one there; Robert's men might have missed it."

Alis frowned. "I'll find it if I get out. But I'd rather have you."

"You know my conditions," he said.

Alis hesitated. "It was an honor to meet you," she said. "I hope to meet you again."

"That would be nice," Leoff replied.

Alis sighed and closed her eyes. She drew the hood down. He thought she might have murmured something, and then she was again an absence, a shadow.

The door opened and then closed. He heard the lock being worked clumsily, then nothing for a long time.

Eventually he went back to sleep.

When the door rattled open the next day, it was in the usual way. Leoff had no way of knowing what time it really was, but he had been awake long enough that he reckoned it midday, in his sunless world.

Two men entered. Both wore black tabards over breastplates that had been enameled black, and each had a broadsword slung at his hip. They didn't resemble any of the dungeon wards Leoff had seen before, but they did look a great deal like Robert's personal guard.

"Hold still," one of them said.

Leoff didn't answer as one of them produced a dark cloth and wrapped it around his temples and eyes, tightening it until he couldn't see. Then they lifted him to his feet. Leoff's skin felt like cold wax as they began walking him down the corridor. He tried to concentrate on distance and direction, as Mery had, counting twelve steps up, then twenty-three strides through a corridor, twenty-eight up a passageway so narrow that occasionally both shoulders brushed the walls at the same time. After that it was as if they suddenly had stepped into the sky; Leoff felt space expand away from him, and currents of moving air. The reports of their footsteps stopped reverberating, and he guessed that they were outside.

Next they led him to a carriage and hoisted him up, and he felt a certain despair creep up on him. He kept suppressing the urge to ask where they were going, because obviously they had covered his eyes so he would not find out.

The carriage began rolling, first on stone, then on gravel. Leoff began to wonder suddenly if he hadn't been kidnapped by allies of the woman who had come to "rescue" him the day before. Adopting the livery of Robert's guard could be accomplished easily enough. His heart sank further as he began to contemplate what would happen when Robert discovered that he was missing.

It must have been dark when they'd left, but now light began to filter through the cloth. It grew colder, as well, and the air ripened with the scent of salt.

After an interminable period, the carriage ground to a halt. He was cold and very stiff now. He felt as if steel screws had been tightening into his kneecaps, in his elbows, and along his spine. His hands ached terribly.

They tried to carry him, but he fought to keep his feet on the ground, to count the steps on gravel, then stone, then wood, then stone again, and finally steps. He cringed as heat suddenly billowed against him, and the blindfold was removed.

He blinked in a cloud of smoke issued by a huge fire blazing in an extraordinarily large fireplace. A spitted side of venison sizzled merrily above it, filling the air with the scent of charred meat.

The room was round, perhaps fifteen kingsyards in diameter, and the walls were draped in tapestries whose subjects were not immediately obvious to him but that glowed in the firelight: umber, gold, rust, and forest green. A gigantic carpet covered the floor.

Two girls had just swung a huge wooden beam away from the fire. There was an iron kettle suspended on it from which they poured steaming water into a bathing basin that had been sunk into the floor.

A few yards away Robert, the usurper, reclined in an armchair, looking comfortable in a floral black-and-gold dressing robe.

"Ah," Robert said. "My composer. Your bath is just prepared."

Leoff glanced around. Besides Robert and the serving girls, there were the men who had fetched Leoff, two more similarly dressed soldiers, a Sefry on a stool plucking a large Safnian-style theorbo, a prim youngish fellow in red robes and a black cap, and finally, the physician who had been tending Leoff in the dungeon.

"No, thank you, Majesty," Leoff managed.

"No," Robert said, "I altogether insist. It's not just for your convenience, you know. We all have noses."

A general murmur of laughter followed that, but the joviality did nothing to relax Leoff; after all, these were Robert's friends, who might be even more amused by, say, the evisceration of a small child.

He signed, and the soldiers began stripping off his clothes. His ears burned, for the serving girls were of age, and he found it extremely inappropriate that they should have to look upon him. They seemed not to notice, however. He might just as well have been another object of furniture. Still, he felt exposed and uncomfortable.

He felt better in the water, though. It was so hot that it stung, but once he was immersed in it, he no longer felt naked, and the heat of it began to settle pleasantly toward his bones, ameliorating the aches that the cold had insinuated into them.

"There," the usurper said. "Isn't that better?"

Leoff had to reluctantly admit that it was. It was better yet when one of the girls brought him a cup of mulled mead and the other cut a great dripping slice of the venison and fed it to him in small bites.

"Now that you are settled," Robert said, "I would like you to meet our host, Lord Respell. He has graciously agreed to be your guardian while you work on the compositions I have requested of you, to offer whatever aid you might require, and to see to your comfort."

"That's very kind," Leoff said, "but I thought I was to work in my old room."

"*That* dank place? No, it has proved inconvenient in a number of ways." At that, his gaze became a bit more hawk-like. "You did not, by chance, have a visitor yesterday?" he asked.

Ah, Leoff thought. *Here it is. It* was *a ruse, and this is my reward for not falling into the trap.*

"No, Majesty," he said just to see what result that would get.

It wasn't what he expected. Robert frowned and placed his arms on the rests of the chair.

"The dungeons are not as secure as my predecessors believed," he said. "They were invaded yesterday by a sneak thief. The thief was caught, questioned, and garroted, but where one can come, others may follow.

"There are secret passageways, you see, that riddle the stone below Eslen castle, and many come—naturally, I suppose—through the dungeons. I have begun having them filled in."

"Is that true, Sire?" Lord Respell asked, sounding surprised. "Hidden passageways into the castle?"

"Yes, Respell," Robert said, waving him off impatiently. "I've told you before."

"Have you?"

"*Yes.* Composer, are you still with me?"

Leoff shook his head. Had he dozed off? He felt as if he had missed something.

"I-I've forgotten what you were saying," Leoff said.

"Of course. And you will forget again, I suppose, like Respell here."

"Forget what, Sire?" Respell asked.

Robert sighed and put a hand to his forehead.

"*The secret passages in the dungeons.* There are too many to locate and obstruct. Well, I needn't go into detail. In sum, Cavaor Leoff, I feel you will be more comfortable here, and safe from any further . . . incursions. Isn't that so, Lord Respell?"

The young man shook off his look of puzzlement and nodded. "Many have tried to invade this keep," he said proudly. "None has ever succeeded. You shall be quite safe here."

"And my friends?" Leoff asked.

"Well, that was to be a surprise," Robert replied. He motioned to the girls, who vanished for a moment, then returned with Mery Gramme and Areana Wistbirm.

Leoff's first reaction at seeing the two was one of pure joy, followed rapidly by mortification. Areana was a lovely lady, seventeen years in age, and it was hardly meet that she should see him in this situation.

Or in this shape. He was peculiarly aware of his hands and their terrible traction. He lowered them deeper beneath the water.

"Leoff!" Areana gasped, rushing forward to kneel by the tub. "Mery said she had seen you, but—"

"You are well, Areana?" he asked stiffly. "They have not harmed you?"

Areana looked up at Robert, and her face clouded. "I have been privated and locked in conditions most unpleasant," she said, "but no real harm has come to me." Her eyes suddenly filled with dismay. "Mery said your hands—"

"Areana," Leoff whispered desperately. "I am uncomfortable with this. They did not tell me you would be here."

"It's because he's naked," Mery put in helpfully. "Mother

says men aren't used to being naked and do not take to it very well. She says they aren't very smart without their clothes on."

"Oh," Areana said. "Of course." Again she glanced up at Robert. "Pay no mind," she said to Leoff. "He thinks by putting us in foolish situations he will make us smaller and weaken us."

"I knew by your singing you had quite the tongue, my lady," Robert said. "Cavaor Leovigild, I compliment you on your choice of vocalists."

Robert's voice sounded odder than usual now. Leoff had noticed its strangeness the first time he heard it. It was as if it strained to produce the notes natural to human speech, and yet there were very unnatural—even chilling—undertones the like of which his ear had never before experienced. He thought sometimes he heard whole other sentences in what the man said, not separate from his obvious speech but side by side with it, like a line of counterpoint.

At the moment it seemed to him that Robert was threatening to cut out Areana's tongue.

"Thank you, Your Majesty," he said, trying to sound co-operative. "I think you will be very pleased with the part I have written her for my new work."

"Yes, your new—what shall we call it? It isn't a lustpell, not really, is it? Nor is it a simple theatrical play. We need a name for it, I think. Do you have one?"

"Not yet, Majesty."

"Well, think on it. And so shall I. Perhaps that will be my contribution to this enterprise, discovering a name for it."

"What is he talking about, Leoff?" Areana asked.

"Didn't I tell you?" Robert answered. "Cavaor Leoff has agreed to write us another of his singing plays. I was so taken with the last, I just had to have another." He switched his regard to Leoff. "Tell me, have you found a subject?"

"I believe I have, Majesty."

"You can't be serious," Areana said, stepping back a bit. "That would betray everything you've done. Everything we've done."

"We are all very serious here," Robert said. "Now, tell us, my friend."

Hardening himself to Areana's distress, Leoff cleared his throat. "You are familiar with the story of Maersca?" he asked.

Robert thought for a moment. "I am perhaps not so familiar with it."

No, the counterpoint said, *and you had better not be trying to make me seem ignorant.*

"Neither was I, until I read the books you gave me," he said quickly. "It happened, as I understand it, in Newland, long ago—before that region was actually named Newland, when the first canals were being built and the poelen drained."

"Ah," Robert exclaimed. "A subject near to the hearts of the landwaerden, I shouldn't doubt. Isn't it so, Areana?"

"It is a popular story among us," Areana agreed stiffly. "I don't find it surprising, then, that you do not know it."

Robert shrugged diffidently. "Neither did your friend Leoff. He just said so."

"But *he* didn't grow up in the heart of Newland," Areana retorted. "Your Majesty did."

"Yes," Robert said a bit crossly, "and I did what I could for your kind, even fathering the occasional child to lighten your thick blood. Now *please,* young lady, tell us the story."

Areana glanced at Leoff, who nodded. He was starting to feel rather wrinkled but had no intention of asking to get out while the girls were still present.

"It happened when they were building the great northern canal," she said. "They did not know it, but when they diverted the channel of the river, they destroyed a kingdom, a kingdom of the Saethiod."

"Saethiod? A kingdom of Meremen? How delightful."

"Only one survived. Maersca, the daughter of the king, the granddaughter of Saint Lir. She swore vengeance, and so she put on human form to wreak it. When the canal was done, she went to the great sluice with the intention of flooding the newly drained land. But she saw Brandel Aethelson on the birm. She spoke to him, feigning womanly interest, asking how it was that the water was held back and how it might be loosed. She was clever, and he did not suspect her designs. In fact, he began to fall in love with her.

"Thinking that she could do more damage if she learned more, Maersca pretended to love him, as well, and soon they were married. She hid her sea-skin in a coffer in the roof beams of the house, and she gave him this condition: that each year on the day of Saint Lir she must bathe alone, and he could not watch her.

"And so for months she nursed her vengeance, and the months became years, and in that time a boy was born to them, and then a girl, and after a fashion she began to love her husband and to love Newland, and her thirst for vengeance faded."

"Oh, dear," Robert said.

"But the husband's friends chided him," Areana continued. " 'Where does your wife go on the day of Saint Lir?' They filled his head with the notion that she had a secret lover and that his own children were not indeed his. And so, over the years he became uncertain, and finally, one Saint Lirsdagh, he followed her. She went to the birm and cast off her clothes, then slipped on her fish skin, and he saw her for what she was—and she knew it.

" 'You've broken your vow,' she said. 'Now I must return to the waters. And if ever I come out into the air again, I shall die, for this changing can only happen once.'

"In despair, he begged her not to go, but go she did, leaving him with her children and his tears.

"Many years passed, and he searched for her in all the rivers and canals he knew. Once or twice he thought he heard her song. He became old, and his children grew up and married.

"Then the army of the Skellander swept down from the North Country, putting all before them to the torch, and next was Newland. The people gathered on the birmsteads and prepared to loose the waters and flood their country, for that was their only protection against the invader. But the capstone would not break; it had been built too well.

"And now the army was near.

"It was then the old man saw his wife again, as lovely as the day they'd met. She emerged from the waters, put her hand on the capstone, and it broke in half, and waters swept the invading army away. But the damage was done, for Maersca had been forced to take off her skin to leave the water, and in so doing took the curse of her ancestors on herself. She died in the old man's arms. And he died shortly after."

Her eyes cut over to Robert. "Their children were among the first of the landwaerden. Many of us claim our descent from Maersca."

Robert scratched his head and looked perplexed.

"This is a complicated story," he said. "I wonder if you might not be planning to hide some unflattering commentary about *me* in it, as you did before."

"I will not," Leoff promised. "I intend only to use a story beloved of the landwaerden, as I did the last time. It was a king of Eslen who rewarded the children of Maersca with their positions. He was the youngest son of the king before, and it is said he worked with the people on the dikes when he was young. In him, we could suggest you: a monarch whose heart lies with Newland and its guardians."

"And who is the villain of the piece?"

"Ah," Leoff said. "The Skellander was led into Newland by none other than the daughter of the old king, the sister of Thiodric, a shinecrafter most foul who poisoned her father and slew all her brothers save the youngest, who—as we shall see—was saved from drowning by none other than Maersca."

"And you could make this sister a redhead," Robert mused. "Very well, I like this.

"As I told you before, I've no doubt that you are clever enough to somehow betray me, even if I were to *assign* you a story. So know this: If you disgrace me further, I will hardly have anything to lose, and I will cut the throats of these young ladies myself, in your presence.

"Indeed, let me be even more candid. Even if your work

appears to have been composed in good faith, if your play fails to turn the landwaerden back to favoring me, their fate will be the one I've just described." He patted Leoff on the back.

"Enjoy your stay here. I think you will find it more than comfortable."

CHAPTER NINE

THE WOORM

ASPAR'S FINGERS felt as papery as birch bark as he set an arrow to the string.

Fend, who had killed his first love. Fend, who had tried to do the same to Winna.

Fend, who now rode the back of a monstrous woorm.

He measured the distance down the shaft. It seemed enormous, the arrow, and he was aware of every detail of it: the hawk-feather fletching wound on with waxed red thread, the almost imperceptible curve in the wood that had to be corrected for, a dull glint of sun from the slightly rusted iron head, the smell of the oil from the sheath.

The air ebbed and flowed around him, and dead leaves, like the signal flags of an army, showed him the way to Fend's flesh and blood and bone.

Yet he couldn't quite feel it. At this range, from this angle, it was an uncertain shot. And even if the shaft flew true, there was the improbable but terribly possible presence of the woorm. No arrow—or any number of arrows—could slay *that* thing.

But no, that wasn't entirely true. There was the black arrow of the Church given him by Praifec Hespero, the

one he had used to slay the utin. It was supposed to be able
to kill even the Briar King; it ought to be able to slay a
woorm.

Not that he knew the slightest thing about woorms.

Winna was trembling, but she didn't say anything. The
woorm and Fend both dropped their heads, and the creature
began moving again. Aspar relaxed a little, rolling completely out of sight, and held Winna tightly until the sound
of the thing's passage had faded.

"Oh, saints," Winna finally breathed.

"Yah," Aspar agreed.

"Just when I think I've seen every nightbale from all the
kinderspells." She shuddered.

"How do you feel?" he asked. Her skin felt clammy.

"Like I've been alvshot," she said. "A little feverish." She
looked up at him. "It must be poison, like the greffyn gave
off."

Aspar had first found the greffyn by its trail of dead and
dying plants and animals. Greffyns weren't much bigger
than horses, though. This thing—

"Sceat," he muttered.

"What?"

He placed his hand against the trunk of the tree, wishing it
had a pulse like a human being but feeling the truth somehow in his bones.

"It's killed this tree," he whispered. "All of these trees."

"And us?"

"I don't think so. The touch of it, the fog that it breathes—
that's down there. The roots are dead."

Just like that. Alive for three thousand years . . .

"What was it?" Winna wanted to know.

Aspar lifted his hands futilely. "Don't matter what we call
it, does it? But I reckon it's a woorm."

"Or a dragon, maybe?"

"Dragons are supposed to have wings, as I remember it."

"So are greffyns."

"Yah. True. So like I said, it doesn't matter what we call it.
Only what it is, what it does. And Fend—"

"Fend?"

Raiht, he'd had her eyes covered.

"Yah, Fend was riding the damned thing."

She frowned a little, as if he'd just told her a riddle and she was trying to reckon it out.

"Fend is riding the woorm," she said at last. "That's just, just so . . ." Her hands grasped at her sides, as if whatever word she was looking for might be caught there.

"Where did Fend find a woorm?" she finally settled on.

Aspar considered what he regarded as an essentially insane question.

For most of his forty-two years he had lived and breathed in the King's Forest, seen the darkest, most tangled corners of it, from the Mountains of the Hare to the wild cliffs and weevlwood swamps of the eastern coast. He knew the habits and sign of every living thing in all of that vast territory, and never—until a few months ago, anyway—had he ever seen so much as the droppings of a greffyn, or an utin, or a woorm.

Where *had* Fend found a woorm? Where had the woorm found itself? Sleeping in some deep cave, waiting in the depths of the sea?

Grim knew.

And Fend seemed to know. He'd found a greffyn; now he'd found something worse. But why? Fend's motives were usually simple, profit and revenge being chief among them. Was the Church paying him now?

"I don't know," he said at last. Then he peered over the edge. The mist the woorm had left seemed to have dissipated.

"Should we get down?" Winna asked.

"I think we ought to wait. And when we do go, we'll go down over there, farther from its path, to avoid the poison."

"What then?"

"It's following the slinders, I think, and the slinders have Stephen. So now I guess we're following the woorm."

What seemed like a safe amount of time passed, and Aspar was ready to suggest that they start climbing down, when he heard the muffled chatter of voices. He put a finger to his lips, but Winna already had heard them, too. She nodded to let him know she understood.

A few moments later six horsemen came riding along in the very furrow created by the woorm.

Three of them were narrow of shoulder and slim of body and wore the characteristic broad-brimmed hats that protected Sefry from the light of the sun. The other three were larger and uncapped, probably human. The horses were all smallish and had the scruffy look of northern breeds.

Aspar wondered where his own horses were. They might all three be dead if they had been near the woorm's exhalations, but horses, and Ogre especially, seemed to have good sense about things like that.

Anyway, the riders below weren't dead. Nor was Fend, and he was *riding* the thing. Maybe the woorm wasn't as poisonous as the greffyn. The utin, after all, hadn't been. On the other hand, the monks at the hill of the naubagm had seemed immune to the greffyn's influence, and a Sefry witch who called herself Mother Gastya had once provided Aspar with a medicine that neutralized the effect of the poison.

Aspar patted the branch and mouthed the words "wait here." Winna looked concerned but nodded.

He padded across the broad branch carefully. It was so thick here it wouldn't rattle smaller branches and give him away, like some gigantic squirrel. Working to a lower branch, he continued until he was just behind the riders and still comfortably above them. They had stopped talking now, and that presented him with something of a dilemma.

He'd been hoping they would say something to give away their purpose, something like "Don't forget, fellows, that we work for Fend," but that didn't seem likely to happen anytime soon. There were three reasons he could think of that might have sent these men chasing the woorm that was tracking the slinders. One, they were with Fend, following in his path—about the same wicked work but slower. Two, they were enemies of Fend, following him for the same reason as Aspar: to kill him. Third, they were a group of travelers following the trail out of stupid curiosity.

If the trail of the beast *was* poisonous, the last possibility could be left right out. Random wayfarers weren't likely to be carrying the antidote for woorm venom with them and would be pretty ill right now.

That left them with Fend or against him.

Well, he didn't have much longer to consider it, and the worst thing a man could do was dither. There were far too many of them for him to ask politely.

He sighted down his first shaft, aiming for the neck of the man in back: a human. If he could drop one or two of them before the others caught on, it would increase his chance of survival a good deal.

But . . .

With a sigh he shifted his aim and sent it into the fellow's right biceps instead. Predictably, the man screamed and fell off his horse, thrashing wildly. Most of the others just looked at him, puzzled, trying to work out what was wrong, but one—and now Aspar could see it *was* a Sefry—leapt from his horse and began stringing a bow, eyes scanning the trees.

Aspar shot him through the shoulder.

This fellow didn't scream, but his intake of breath was audible even at Aspar's distance, and his gaze immediately found the source of his wounding.

"Holter!" He bellowed. "It's the holter, you fools, in the trees! The one Fend warned us of!"

There, Aspar thought. *I could have hoped for that before they knew I was here, but . . .*

Another of the men had strung his bow, Aspar saw. He fired at the fellow, but the man was in motion, and the arrow only whittled a bit of ear. The man returned a shaft, a damned good shot, considering, but Aspar was already dropping to the next branch down.

He landed on slightly flexed legs, wincing at pain in his knees that wouldn't have been there five years ago, and loosed his third dart at the other archer. The man was cupping his wounded ear and just starting to scream when the arrow went through his larynx, effectively silencing him.

Aspar fitted another shaft and carefully shot another Sefry who was just putting arrow to string. He hit him in the inside of the thigh, dropping him like a sack of meal.

A red-fletched missile spanged against Aspar's boiled leather cuirass, just above his lowest rib, knocking most of the breath out of him. The world went all black spots and whirling, and he realized his feet weren't on the branch anymore, though they were still roughly beneath him.

His left foot caught the ground first, but his body had fallen too far back for him to land with balance or for his knees to absorb the shock. He did manage to twist and take part of the fall with his shoulder, but that caused more pain, this time with white sparks.

Grunting, he rolled out of it and noticed he no longer had his bow. He reached for his hand-ax and, as he came up, found himself looking down the shaft of the third Sefry. He threw the ax and spun to his left.

The ax missed by a hairsbreadth, but only because the Sefry flinched, throwing his aim wide. Snarling, Aspar hurled himself at his assailant, unsheathing his dirk. Ten kingsyards should have provided plenty of time for the Sefry to fit another arrow and take a close shot, but he apparently didn't know that, instead seeming to poise among shooting, drawing his blade, and running.

He finally settled on the blade, but by that time Aspar was there; he came in close, grabbing the Sefry's shoulder with his free hand and turning him to expose his left kidney. His first stab met mail, so he changed elevation and slashed the carotid, blinking his eyes against the spray of blood and running on past as his foe became a corpse.

He felt suddenly blind, because he knew there was one uninjured man he had lost track of. The first two he had shot might also be problems, but it was unlikely that either could wield a bow.

The fourth man announced himself in a huff of breath;

Aspar spun to find him charging, wielding a broadsword. Aspar's knees went wobbly, and he felt as if there were nettles in his lungs. The feeling was familiar, like when the greffyn had looked at him the first time.

Answers that, he thought. *Poison.*

A smart man with a sword ought to be able to kill a man with a dirk. This one, fortunately, didn't seem too smart. He had his weapon lifted for an overhead cut; Aspar feinted as if he were desperately leaping inside—an impossibility given the distance—and the fellow obliged by slashing hard and fast.

Aspar checked back, however, not actually coming into range, and as the whirling sword swept past on its way to the ground with too much momentum to reverse, he *did* leap in, catching the wielding arm with his left hand and driving his dirk deep into the man's groin, just to the left of his iron codpiece. The man gagged and stumbled backward, rowing the air with his arms to keep from falling, color draining from his face.

Aspar heard a choking sound at his back and spun unsteadily, only to find the first Sefry who had taken a shot at him staring in surprise. He had a short sword, but even as Aspar watched, it dropped from his fingers and he sank to his knees.

About ten kingsyards behind him, Winna grimly lowered her bow. She was looking pale, whether from poison or from nerves he wasn't sure.

Wonderful.

He could feel the fever burning in him now. Already he was nearly too weak to hold the dirk.

He forced himself to walk the round, though, making sure his foes were dead—all but one, the first one he had shot. The man was crawling across the ground, holding his arm and whimpering. When he saw Aspar coming, he tried to crawl faster. He already was weeping, and now his tears began to flow more freely.

"Please," he gasped, "please."

"Winna," Aspar called. "Search the other bodies for anything unusual. Remember the stuff Mother Gastya gave me? Anything like that."

He put his boot on the man's neck.

"Good morning," he said, trying to sound steadier than he was.

"I don't want to die," the man whimpered.

"Raiht," Aspar said. "Neither do I, yah? An' more, I don't want my lovely lass here to die. But we're going to, aren't we, because we've stepped in the path of this damned thing Fend conjured up. Now, all of your friends, I've sent them to Grim for his morning meal, and they're callin' for you, across the river. I can pitch you over there good and quick just by pushing this knife up into the bottom of your head." He knelt and thrust his fingers into the place where spine met skull. The man screamed, and Aspar smelled something foul.

"Feel that?" he said. "There's a hole there. Knife goes in as easy as into butter. But I don't have to do that. That wound in your arm isn't serious, and you could crawl off to the Midenlands, find a nice woman, and churn butter for the rest of your life. But first you have to make sure *I* don't die and my friend doesn't die."

"Fend will kill me."

Aspar laughed. "Now that's just silly. You don't help me, and you'll be mostly maggots before Fend even knows what happened to you."

"Yah," the man said miserably. "There is some medicine. Raff has it on him, in a blue bottle. One drink a day, as much as would go in a little spoon. But you have to leave me some."

"Do I?"

"Because I'll die, anyway," the man explained. "The medicine doesn't stop the poison; it just slows it down. Stop taking it for a few days and you're just as dead as you would have been."

"Really. And what kind of fool—*hah.* I see it now. Fend didn't tell you that until it was too late, did he?"

"No. But he has the antidote. When we're finished, he was going to give it to us."

"I see." He lifted his head with great difficulty. "Winna? It's in a blue bottle."

"I've got that," she called back.

"Bring it here."

He set the point of his knife against the man's head.

A moment later Winna fell to her knees beside him. Her eyes were red, and her skin a wormy white.

"Drink some," he told Winna. He pushed a bit with the knife. "If it kills her, you go next," he said.

"Give me some first," the man said. "I'll prove it's not poison."

Winna lifted the blue bottle, took a swallow, and made a face. For a long moment nothing happened.

"That feels better," Winna said. "Everything isn't spinning anymore."

Aspar nodded, took the bottle, and drank some himself. It was foul, like boiled centipedes and wormwood, but he felt almost instantly better. He stoppered the bottle carefully and put it in his haversack.

"What are you helping Fend with, anyhow?" Aspar asked. "What are you supposed to finish before he gives you the antidote?"

"We're just supposed to follow him and kill anything the woorm doesn't."

"Yah. Why?"

"He's after killing the slinders, is part of it," he said. "But there's also some fellow he's supposed to find; I don't know the name. Supposed to be with you, I think."

"Fend sent the utins after him?" Aspar asked.

"Yah. They went ahead and didn't come back."

"Where does Fend get these monsters?"

"He got the woorm from the Sarnwood witch, or so 'e said. But the monsters, they don't serve Fend. He and the monsters serve the same master."

"And who would that be?"

"None of us know. There's a priest, from Hansa, name of Ashern. I think he knows, but he's with Fend on the woorm. The Sefry just hired us for the loot. Said we could have anything that turned up in the woorm's trail. Then he told us we were poisoned and let Galus die to prove him werlic.

"Please, holter, I'm begging you."

"That's all you know?"

"That's all."

Aspar flipped him over on his back. He winced and shut his eyes. Aspar shook the bottle; it was more than half-full.

"Open your mouth."

The man did so, and Aspar dribbled in a few drops.

"Tell me something new," Aspar said, "and I'll give you a little more. If you last long enough, the woorm's venom might work out of your system on its own, yah? Or you could find a shinecrafter to help you. A chance for you to live to see another full moon, anyway. Better than you have now."

"Yah. What do you want to know?"

"Why did Fend have the girls kidnapped?"

"Girls?"

"On the border with Loiyes. Where he sent the utins."

The man shook his head. "Those men? We had nothing to do with them. The woorm and the utins found your man; they scented him somehow. Those other fellows—we killed some of them when we happened upon them. Fend told us if we saw a couple of girls to just kill them, too, but not to go out of our way. 'It's not our job, that,' he said. 'Let the others worry about that.'"

Aspar dribbled a few more drops onto the man's tongue.

"What else?"

"I don't know anything else. I didn't understand what I was getting into. I'm just a thief. I've never even killed anyone before. I never believed these things existed, but now I've seen 'em, I just want to go away. I just want to live."

"Yah," Aspar said. "Go, then."

"But the poison . . ."

"I've given you all I can. I'll need the rest to find Fend, kill 'im, and take his antidote. Do you know what it looks like?"

"No."

"I could still just kill you . . ."

"I really don't know."

Which means it might well not exist at all, Aspar thought grimly.

"Come on, Winna," he said. "I've a feeling we'd better get started."

CHAPTER TEN

BLADE MUSIC

PARALYZED BY TERROR, Anne watched the tapestry lift and darkness appear behind it.

The candles had all gone out, and though the only light was that of the moon, she could see every detail of the room clearly. The pulse in her head was so strong, she feared she would faint, and she wanted to look away from what was coming.

She had dreamed of Fastia with worms in her eyes, going behind that tapestry, opening a secret door. Now she saw that the door was really there and something was coming out of it. Here, in the waking world.

Or *was* she awake?

The figure that stepped into the room, however, wasn't Fastia. At first it seemed a shadow, but then the moonlight resolved someone dressed all in black, masked and hooded. A slight figure, a woman or perhaps a child, carrying something long, dark, and pointed in one hand.

Assassin, she thought, suddenly feeling numb and very slow.

Then the person's eyes appeared, and Anne knew she had been seen.

"Help!" she shouted quite deliberately. "Help, murder!"

Without a sound, the figure flung toward her. Anne's

paralysis ended instantly; she rolled off the bed and onto her feet, lurching toward the door.

Something cold and hard hit her in her upper arm, and she couldn't move that limb anymore. It seemed frozen in the act of lifting; she could neither lower nor raise it. She looked and saw that something dark and thin had stabbed through the flesh below the bone. It went straight through and out the other side, where it was stuck in Lew.

Anne raised her eyes and found a violet gaze fixed on her from only a handspan away. She looked back down and understood that the thin thing in her arm was the blade of a sword, held by the man. Somehow she knew it was a man, however slight in build.

Sefry, she realized.

He yanked at the sword, which was stuck solidly in the bedpost. Seeming to think better of that, he let his other hand drop to his waist. The pain of the sword in her arm suddenly hit her, but the fear proved stronger, because she knew he had to be reaching for a knife.

She put her head in the moon, buried her feet in the dark tangled roots of the earth, grabbed his hair with her free hand, and kissed him.

His lips were warm, hot even, and as she touched them, lightning seemed to strike down her spine and the taste of serpent musk and charring juniper burned in her throat. Inside, he was wet and damp, like all men, but terribly wrong, cold where he ought to be hot, hot where he ought to be cold, and nothing familiar. He seemed broken and re-formed, each curve in his bone like a healed shattering, every tissue a scar.

He screamed, and she felt a sudden hard yank at her arm as he pushed away. The sword pulled clean, and she slid to the floor, landing on her behind with her legs spraddled in front of her.

The Sefry stepped back and shook his head like a dog with water in its ear.

She tried to scream again but found she had no breath. She gripped her arm, and everything was sticky-wet with blood, which she understood was her own.

The door chose that moment to burst open, however, and two of Elyoner's guards charged in, carrying torches that seemed to burn so brightly that Anne was nearly blinded.

Her attacker, reduced to a dark stick figure by the brilliance, appeared to recover. His long sword darted out and hit one of the guards in the throat. The poor young man fell to his knees, dropping his torch and grasping at the wound, trying to hold his life in with his hands. Anne sympathized as blood squirted between her fingers.

The other fellow, bellowing for help, was a little warier. He wore half-plate armor and carried a heavy sword, which he thrust at the assassin rather than pulling back for a cut. The Sefry made a few experimental attacks, which the guard beat away.

"Run, Princess," the guard said.

Anne noticed that there was a gap between him and the door; she could run if she could make her legs work. She tried to get to her knees but slipped in the blood, wondering how close she was to bleeding to death.

The Sefry attacked and stumbled. With a roar, the guard cut hard; Anne couldn't follow what happened then, but steel rang on steel, and Elyoner's man went staggering past the Sefry and slammed into the wall. He collapsed there, unmoving.

The assassin was turning back toward her when another figure exploded through the open door.

It was Cazio. He looked odd, very odd, and for a moment Anne couldn't place why. Then she appreciated that he was as naked as the day he was born.

But he had Caspator in one hand. With only the slight hesitation it took for him to take in the situation, he flung himself at her attacker.

Cazio plunged Caspator toward the dark figure, but the blade was met with the quick, familiar parry of *perto,* followed by a strong bind in *uhtave.*

Without having to think, Cazio took the attack into a receding parry and replied with a thrust to the throat. His opponent avoided by withdrawing, and for a moment neither of them moved. Cazio had a distant moment of faint embarrassment that he was naked, yet he and Austra both had been in that state, a chamber away, when he had heard Anne's scream. If he'd stopped to dress, she might be dead now.

Truly, she was already wounded, and fear for her wiped away the embarrassment over his lack of clothing, that and the sudden realization that finally, after all these months, he was facing another student of dessrata.

"Come on," Cazio said, "Let's finish this before anyone shows up to interfere."

He could already hear more guards coming.

The man cocked his head to the side, then thrust. Cazio took a retreat, not trusting the verity of the move, and was taken aback when the fellow suddenly darted toward the wall, lifting a tapestry and vanishing into a dark opening beyond.

Cursing, Cazio leapt after him, brushing the tapestry back with his left hand. A blade snaked out of the darkness, and he just managed to deflect it. He stepped inside the point and pressed the weapon into the wall with his off hand—then ran straight into a fist. It hit him in the jaw; the blow wasn't so much strong as it was surprising. He released the blade.

Cazio stumbled back, weaving Caspator through the parries, hoping to catch a thrust he couldn't see. But receding footsteps told him that the fellow was running now, without renewing the attack.

Cursing, Cazio ran after him.

After a few seconds, reason reasserted itself and he slowed to a walk. After all, he couldn't see anything. He considered going back for a torch, but he still could hear soft footfalls ahead, and he didn't want to lose the trail. Keeping his left hand on the wall, he pressed forth quickly, Caspator held out before him like a blind man's cane.

He almost stumbled when the passageway became stairs, descending in a narrow series of turns. Ahead he heard a click and saw a brief moment of moonlight casting a human shadow on a landing below.

Then the light was gone.

He reached the landing and, after a brief search, discovered the door and pushed it open. The passage issued from a garden wall hidden by a hedge. A short path led to an open, grassy glade suffused in moonlight. He didn't see Anne's assailant anywhere.

He couldn't imagine that the man had had time to cross the open grass, so instead of walking out of the hedge, he rolled and found his deduction satisfied by the sough of steel where his head ought to have been.

He came back to his feet with a guard in *prismo*.

"This is disappointing," he said. "I've come across land and sea and land again and never met another dessrator. I am so *sick* of the meat cleaving that passes for swordplay in these barbarian lands. Now I finally find someone who might give me some entertainment, and I discover that he's a coward, unwilling to stand and fight."

"Sorry," the fellow replied in a muffled voice. "But you must understand that while I've no trouble fighting *you,* I can't be bothered to engage with the whole castle. And if I allow you to delay me, that will be my position."

That was right; they had been in Anne's room.

Cazio had heard the guards approaching behind him, and then—

They were outside. How had that happened?

He hazily remembered chasing the fellow, but if he had followed him out of Anne's room and down the stairs, shouldn't they have gone past the approaching soldiers? Had they leapt out of a window?

The man cut short Cazio's wondering by attacking. He was small and nimble, a Sefry, perhaps? Cazio had never fought a Sefry dessrator. His blade was lampblacked and difficult to see.

Cazio parried, but the attack turned out to be a feint, the real attack slipping in from a low line. Cazio took a step back to give him time to find the blade, which he did, catching it in the parry of *seft,* then twisting to one side to avoid the rapid renewal of the attack in the high line. The blade whispered through the air near his throat, and he straightened his arm.

His enemy deflected it with the flat of his palm, and suddenly they were at close quarters again. Cazio stepped in fast and hit the man with his shoulder, then followed with a short lunge that nicked an arm. He recovered, ready to press, when he became cognizant that the assassin once again was fleeing.

"Mamres curse you, stand and fight!" Cazio bellowed. He was getting cold now. His bare feet crunched on snow.

Once again he chased after the elusive swordsman, panting dragon breath. His fingers, nose, and other extremities were numbing with cold such as he had never known, and he began to remember stories he had heard of body parts freezing off. Could such a thing really happen? It had always seemed absurd.

They burst from the maze and sprinted through a garden where a thinly clothed statue of Lady Erenda presided over a pair of marble lovers in a frozen basin. Ahead, Cazio could see a canal and the swordsman's destination: a horse tethered in a small grove of trees.

He tried to redouble his speed, with limited success. The snow and his numb toes made it difficult to keep his balance.

The swordsman was trying to untie his beast when Cazio launched his attack. Giving up the task, the man turned to meet him. Cazio saw with surprise that he had pulled his mask down, probably to breathe better. The face was indeed Sefry, delicate and almost blue in the moonlight, with hair so fair that it looked as if he had no eyebrows or lashes, as if he were carved of alabaster.

He avoided Cazio's rush, turning his body aside and leaving his point for Cazio to impale himself on. Cazio checked his headlong rush, however, and picked up the extended blade in a bind. He was unable to riposte, but pushed past instead, and they both turned to face each other again.

"I'm really going to have to kill you," the Sefry remarked.

"Your Vitellian is odd, almost more Safnian," Cazio said. "Tell me your name, or if not that, at least where you hail from."

"Sefry hail from nowhere, as you must know," the assassin replied. "But my clan plied the routes from Abrinia to Virgenya."

"Yes, but you did not learn your dessrata in Abrinia or Virgenya. Then where?"

"In Toto da'Curnas," he replied, "in the Alixanath Mountains. My mestro was named Espedio Raes da Loviada."

"Mestro Espedio?" Z'Acatto had studied with Espedio. "Mestro Espedio has been dead for a long time," Cazio said.

"And Sefry live a long time," the fellow replied.

"Give me something to call you."

"Call me Acredo," he replied. "It is the name of my rapier."

"Acredo, I no more believe you studied with Mestro Espedio than that you've hunted rabbits on the moon, but let me see. I attack with the *caspo dolo didieto dachi pere*—" He launched an attack to the foot.

Acredo responded by instantly countering to Cazio's face, but that was anticipated, and Cazio changed his attack to countertime along the blade. Acredo receded into *prismo,* then cut over Cazio's blade for a *caspo en perto.*

Cazio voided to his right and counterthrust to Acredo's eyes. Acredo ducked and lunged to Cazio's foot, ending the attack as it had begun, except that Acredo's blade plunged through Cazio's numbed foot and into the chill soil below.

"The correct response?" Acredo asked, withdrawing his blooded blade and returning to guard.

Cazio winced. "Nicely done," he allowed.

"My turn," Acredo said, and commenced a flurry of feints and attacks.

"The cuckold's walk home," Cazio said, recognizing the technique. He replied with the appropriate counter, but again Acredo seemed to know one more move than he, and this time the exchange nearly ended with Acredo's blade in Cazio's throat.

Z'Acatto, you old fox, he thought. The old man had left out the final countermoves of Espedio's set pieces. That had never mattered before, because until now Cazio had never met anyone else who had mastered the old master's style; he had always managed to make his touch halfway through them. That wouldn't work here; in fact, it was an almost certain route to failure. Cazio would have to use his own tricks.

But for the first time in a very long time, he reckoned this was a duel he might lose. Dying was a thought he had become used to, fighting supernatural knights in heavy armor with magic swords. But in a duel of dessrata, only z'Acatto had been his match since he was fifteen.

He felt a bit of fear but even more exhilaration. *At last, a duel worth fighting.*

He feinted low and finished high, but Acredo retreated a step, put Caspator in a bind, and lunged. Cazio felt the tension run up his blade, and then, with a sudden dismaying ring of steel, Caspator finally snapped.

Acredo paused, then came on. Cursing, Cazio retreated, holding the stub of his old friend.

He was steeling himself for a last, desperate leap inside Acredo's sword point in hopes of grappling him, when the Sefry suddenly gasped and fell to one knee. Cazio's first thought was that it might be some odd gambit like the three-legged dog, but then he saw the arrow sprouting from the man's thigh.

"No!" Cazio shouted.

But men-at-arms were swarming along the canal now. Acredo defiantly lifted his weapon again, but an archer shot him from five kingsyards, hitting him in the shoulder, and in the very next instant a third shaft struck through his throat.

He clapped his hand to the wound and looked straight at Cazio. He tried to say something, but blood bubbled from his lips instead, and he fell face forward in the snow.

Cazio looked up in anger and saw Sir Neil. The knight was without armor, though he was a bit better dressed than Cazio, still wearing a white shirt, breeches, and, most enviable of all, buskins.

"Sir Neil!" Cazio cried. "We were dueling! He should not have died like that!"

"This rubbish stabbed Her Majesty," Neil replied, "in a

cold-blooded assassination attempt. He does not deserve the honor of a duel or any sort of honorable death."

He glanced down at Acredo.

"I did wish to take him alive, however, to discover who sent him." He gave Cazio a hard glance. "This isn't sport," he said. "If you believe that it is—if your love of the duel is more important than Anne's safety—then I wonder if you belong in her company."

"If I had not been here, she *would* be dead," Cazio replied.

"Fair enough," Neil said. "But my point still stands, I think."

Cazio acknowledged that with a curt nod.

Cazio picked up the Sefry's fallen blade. It had a beautiful balance but was a bit lighter than Caspator.

"I will take care of your weapon, dessrator," he told the fallen man. "I only wish I had earned it fairly."

Someone placed a cloak over Cazio's shoulders, and he realized he was shivering almost uncontrollably. It also occurred to him that he was being stupid, that Sir Neil was right.

But he could not shake the feeling that no matter what a villain he had been, any dessrator deserved to die by the point of a rapier.

"Sit me up," Anne commanded.

Just saying the words was almost enough to cause her to faint.

"You should lie back," Elyoner's leic said. He was a young man, handsome in a feminine way. Anne wondered just how much medicine he knew that didn't have anything to do with sex. He had stopped her bleeding and put something on her arm that caused it to throb a little less violently, but that was no guarantee she wasn't going to die of sepsis in a few days.

"I *will* sit up, against the pillows," she said.

"As Her Majesty wishes."

He helped her to that position.

"I need something to drink," Anne said.

"You heard her," Elyoner said. Her aunt was in a violet dressing gown of a complex weave whose name Anne didn't know. She looked drunk and worried.

More interesting was Austra, who was wearing nothing more than a bedcover pulled tightly around her shoulders. She had appeared only instants after Cazio had left; that was suggestive, since Cazio had been entirely naked.

"Austra, put something on," she said gently.

Austra nodded gratefully and vanished into the adjoining wardrobe.

A moment later, a young girl with hair in yellow ringlets wearing an umber skirt and a red apron appeared with a cup of what turned out to be watered wine. Anne quaffed it thirstily, her distaste for alcohol a thing of the past.

The girl went to Elyoner and whispered something in her ear. Elyoner sighed in apparent relief.

"The assassin is dead," she said.

"And Cazio?"

Elyoner looked at the girl, who blushed and said something too low for Anne to hear. Elyoner tittered.

"He's well, more or less, albeit perhaps in danger of losing bits to the frost."

"When he's clothed, I want to see him. And Sir Neil." Anne turned to watch Elyoner's men carrying off the corpses of the guards.

Austra emerged a few moments later, having hastily thrown on an underskirt and an ample dressing gown of Nahzgavian felt. Anne recognized it as one Fastia once had favored.

That had been Fastia, hadn't it? Her spirit or ghost, come in a dream. If she hadn't waked her, the Sefry would have completed his job without hindrance; she would have died in her sleep with no protest.

"Aunt Elyoner," Anne said. "You knew that passage existed?"

"Of course, dear," she said. "But few others do. I thought it secure."

"I wish you had told me of it."

"I wish I had, too, dove," she replied.

"Uncle Robert would have known about it, yes?"

Elyoner shook her head with great certainty. "No, my dear. That is an impossibility. I would not have thought . . . but then, I do not know as much about the Sefry as perhaps I believed."

"What do you mean?"

Cazio chose that moment to arrive. He hobbled into the room making a desperate show of not hobbling, but the bandage on his foot was plain proof that he had received some sort of injury.

"Anne!" he said, coming quickly to kneel by the bed. "How bad is it?" He took her good hand, and she was surprised to feel how cold it was.

"His blade went through the meat of my arm," Anne replied in Vitellian for his benefit. "The bleeding is stanched. There was no poison, fortunately. And you?"

"Nothing of consequence." His gaze flicked up and away, to where Austra stood behind her. "Austra?"

"I was never in danger, of course," Austra said, sounding a bit breathless.

Cazio released Anne's hand—a little too quickly, she thought.

"He stabbed you?" Anne asked.

"A small wound, in the foot."

"Cazio," Elyoner said. "They found the two of you down by the canal. How did you get there?"

"I followed him there from the hedge maze, Duchess," the swordsman replied.

"That's where the passage comes out?" Anne asked. "That wall in the grotto?"

"Passage?" Cazio asked. His brow furrowed.

"Yes," Anne said. "The passage there, in the wall. Behind the tapestry."

Cazio glanced at the tapestry. "There's a passage hidden behind there? Is that how he got in?"

"Yes," Anne said, beginning to be irritated. "And it's how he got out. You followed him, Cazio."

"I'm sorry, I did no such thing."

"I *watched* you."

Cazio blinked, and for perhaps the second or third time in the months she had known him, he actually seemed to have lost his tongue.

"Cazio," Elyoner said gently, "how did you get outside, do you suppose? To the grotto in the hedge maze?"

Cazio placed his hands on his hips. "Well, I—" he began confidently, then stopped, frowning again. "I . . ."

"Have you gone mad?" Anne said. "How drunk are you?"

"He can't remember, dove," Elyoner said. "No man can. It's a sort of glamour. Women can recall the passages in these walls. Women can use them. A man can be led through one, but it never impresses his memory. A few moments from now poor Cazio won't even remember what we were talking about, nor will any man here."

"That's absurd," Cazio said.

"What's absurd, dear?" Elyoner asked.

Cazio blinked, then looked a bit frightened.

"You see?"

"But the Sefry was male. I'm pretty sure of that."

"We will determine that for certain," Elyoner said. "There *are* ways of telling, you know. But I suppose the glamour was meant for humans. Perhaps it doesn't work on Sefry."

"This is all very strange."

"Then your mother never showed you the passages in Eslen castle?"

"Secret ones, you mean?"

"Yes. Austra?"

Anne turned to where Austra stood, looking mostly at the floor. "I've heard tell," she said softly. "I've only ever been in one of them."

"And you didn't tell me?" Anne said.

"I was asked not to," she said.

"So Eslen castle has passages like these?"

"Indeed," Elyoner said. "It's riddled with them."

"And Uncle Robert doesn't know about them," Anne mused. "An army could take the castle from inside."

Elyoner smiled wanly. "You would have difficulty if the army were made up of men, I should think," she said.

"*I* could lead them!" Anne said.

"Perhaps," Elyoner said. "I'll tell you what I know of them, of course."

"Do any of them open outside the city?"

"Yes," Elyoner replied. "There is one that I know of. And several emerge within the city, at various locations. I can tell you where they are, perhaps make a little map if my memory serves me."

"Good," Anne replied. "That's good."

Anne understood then that she was ready. Not because she knew what she was doing but because she had no choice.

Ten years of studying warcraft and building an army might make her better suited to the task, but in a few ninedays her mother would be married and she would have to fight not only what troops Robert could muster but Hansa and the Church, as well.

No, she was ready—because there was no other choice but to be.

CHAPTER ELEVEN

THE EPISTLE

THOUGH IT was made of lead, Stephen handled the manuscrift gently, as if it were the tiniest of babies, the sort born too early.

"It's been cleaned," he noted.

"Yes. Do you recognize the letters?"

Stephen nodded. "I've only seen them on a few tombstones, in Virgenya. Very, very old tombstones."

"Exactly," the fratrex said. "This is the ancient Virgenyan script."

"Some of it," Stephen cautioned, "but not entirely. This letter and this one here—both are from the Thiuda script, as adapted by the Cavari." He tapped a square with a dot pressed into the center. "And this is a very primitive variant form from Vitellian, where it was sounded as 'th' or 'dh,' as in *th*aurn, or, ah, dreo*dh*."

"It's a mixture of scripts, then."

"Yes," Stephen nodded. "It's . . ." He trailed off, feeling the blood rush to his scalp and his heart clout like a marching drum.

"Brother Stephen, are you well?" Ehan asked, staring at him with concern.

"Where did you get this?" Stephen asked weakly.

"It was stolen, actually," the fratrex said. "It was found in a crypt in Kaithbaurg-of-Shadows. A coven-trained recovered it for us."

"Well, don't keep the bag on my head," Ehan said in an attempt to lighten the mood. "What do we have here, Brother Stephen?"

"It's an *epistle*," he answered, still not believing it himself.

The fratrex's mouth formed a small "o." Ehan merely lifted his shoulders in puzzlement.

"It's a very old word in Virgenyan, no longer used in the king's tongue," Stephen explained. "It means a sort of letter. When they were planning their revolt, the Skasloi slaves passed these to one another. They were written in cipher so that if the epistles were intercepted by their enemies, the information, at least, remained safe."

"If it's in cipher, though, how can you read it?" Ehan wondered aloud.

"A cipher can be broken," Stephen said, excitedly now. "But if I'm to do so, I'll need some books from the scriptorium."

"Whatever we have is at your disposal," the fratrex said. "Which ones do you have in mind?"

"Yes, well," Stephen mused, "the *Tafliucum Eingadeicum*,

of course—the *Caidex Comparakinum Prismum,* the *Deifteris Vetis,* and the *Runaboka Siniste,* for a start."

"I had guessed those already," the fratrex responded. "They are packed and ready to go."

"Packed?"

"Yes. Time is short, and you cannot remain here," the fratrex said. "We've repelled one attack by the Hierovasi, but there will be more—either from them or from our other enemies. We remained here only to await you."

"To await *me*?"

"Indeed. We knew you would need the resources of the library, but we can carry no more than a fraction. So we had to keep it safe until you returned, because I didn't know everything you would need."

"Yet surely I'm not the only scholar of languages—"

"You are our foremost surviving expert," the fratrex said, "and the only one to have walked the faneway of Saint Decmanus.

"But there's more to it than that, I'm afraid. I don't want to burden you, but all auspex point to your *personal* importance in the coming crisis. I believe it has to do with you being the one to wend the horn and wake the king, though it's unclear whether you are important *because* you blew the horn or you sounded the horn because you were important. You see? The spetural world will always grip some secrets."

"But what am I to do, exactly?"

"Gather the books and scrolls you know you will need, though no more than can be packed on one mule and one horse. Be prepared to leave by morning."

"*Tomorrow?* But that's not enough time. I have to think! Don't you understand? If this is an epistle, it's likely the only one that has survived."

Ehan coughed. "Begging both of your pardons, but that's not right. My studies weren't thorough, I know—the virtues of minerals has always been my subject—but in the ahvashez in Skefhavnz, I studied John Wotten's letter to Sigthors. I didn't know the word 'epistle,' but that's what it would be, isn't it?"

"Yes," Stephen said, "if what you studied was really a letter from Wotten to Sigthors—but it wasn't. What you learned was a reconstruction of that text by Wislan Fethmann four centuries ago. He based it on a short summary of its content written by one of Sigthors's grandnephews sixty years after the victory over the Skasloi.

"Sigthors was killed in the battle. The grandnephew got his information interviewing the surviving son, Wigngaft, who was seven when his father read the letter aloud to his followers and sixty-seven when asked to recall what it said. There was also a single line recorded supposedly by Thaniel Farre, the courier who delivered the letter. But we don't have the original by Farre, only a thirdhand copy of a quotation of Farre in the *Tafles Vincum Maimum,* written a full thousand years after his death. '*Come what may, no grandchild of mine shall see a single sunrise under slavery. If we do not succeed, with my own hands I will end my line.*' "

Ehan blinked. "So that's not really what was written?"

"In truth, we have no way of knowing," Stephen said.

"But surely Fethmann must have been inspired by the saints to create an accurate reconstruction."

"Well, that's one school of thought," Stephen said drily. "In any event, he wrote in Middle Hanzish, not in the original encrypted form, so whether it was divinely inspired or not, that 'epistle' is of no help in translating this one. There are, by the by, a few other epistles with the same dubious provenance as the one you bring up. In fact, it's not uncommon to find them for sale in Sefry caravans, both as 'originals,' written in gibberish, and as translations."

"Fine, then," Ehan said brusquely. "So our epistle was a fraud, a local tradition not approved by the Church. So what? Are there no authenticated epistles?"

"There are two fragments, neither with more than three complete lines. Those seem to be originals, though neither is here. But they are supposedly faithfully reproduced in the *Casti Noibhi.*"

"We have the Dhuvien copy of that volume," Pell said.

"I could hope for a better edition," Stephen said. "But if it's the best you've got, it will have to do."

A thought occurred, and he met the gaze of the fratrex.

"Wait a moment," he said. "You said this epistle—if that is what it is—is a clue to the location of Virgenya Dare's journal. How can that be, when her journal was hidden centuries *after* the revolt was over?"

"Ah," the fratrex said. "Yes, that." He signed to Ehan, who lifted a leather-bound tome from behind his bench.

"This is the life of Saint Anemlen," the fratrex said. "While at the court of the Black Jester, Anemlen heard a rumor of Brother Choron, in whose hands the journal had been entrusted. Choron was supposed to have stopped in the kingdom ten years before the Jester won his bloody throne, serving as an adviser to the monarch who was reigning at the time.

"The book rested there for a while. In one passage, Anemlen records that Choron discovered—in a reliquary— the scroll you now hold. Without saying what it was, he stated that it spoke of a 'fastness' in a mountain some eighteen days' ride to the north and that this mountain was known as Vhelnoryganuz.

"He set out to find it, ostensibly because he felt that most sacred of documents would be safer there. He left for Vhel-noryganuz but never returned. As you know, the Black Jester had his court where the city of Wherthen now stands, though little remains of the original fortress. But when the Church liberated and consecrated the area, they gathered all the scrifti they found. The evil ones were destroyed, for the most part. Those which were not evil were collected and copied.

"And then there were a few that were kept in the scriftorium because no one was certain *what* they were. This was one such scroll. Brother Desmond acquired it for me; thank the saints he did not discern its nature. We received it just before your flight from this place. If things had proceeded as we hoped, you would have studied it months ago, and at a

more leisurely pace. Unfortunately, things have not proceeded as we hoped."

"Most unfortunately," Stephen agreed. He straightened
and put his hands on his knees. "Brothers, if my time is really so limited, I should go to the scriftorium now."

"By all means," the fratrex said. "Meanwhile, we'll see to
other preparations."

Death was following close behind the woorm.

The Oostish called the cold season winter, but the thing
about winter was that it gave farmers and villagers plenty of
time to think, shut up in their houses, waiting for the soil to
grow food again. When people had too much time to think,
Aspar noted, it usually resulted in too many words, Stephen
being the perfect case in point.

So the Oostish called winter winter, but they also called it
Bearnight and Sundim and Death's Three Moons. Aspar had
never found any reason to give it more than one name, but
the last had seemed particularly uninformed. The forest
wasn't dead in winter; it was just licking its wounds. Healing. Gathering its strength to survive the battle known as
spring.

Some of the ironoaks the woorm had brushed against had
been seedlings when the Skasloi still ruled the world. They
had watched in their sturdy, slow way as uncounted tribes of
Mannish and Sefry folk passed beneath their boughs and
vanished into the distance of years.

They would not see another leaf-bringing. Foul-smelling
sap already had begun to seep from cracks in their ancient
bark, like pus from a gangrenous wound. The woorm's venin
worked even faster in wood, it seemed, than it did in flesh.
The lichens, moss, and ferns that fleeced the trees were already black.

His hand dropped to touch the arrow case at his belt. The
weapon inside had come from Caillo Vallaimo, the temple
that was the very heart, center, and soul of the Church. He'd
been told it could be used only twice, and he had used it once
to slay an utin. He'd been ordered to kill the Briar King with it.

But the Briar King wasn't killing the forest Aspar loved. If anything, the lord of the slinders was fighting to save it. Yes, he was slaughtering men and women, but place their lives against the ironoaks . . .

Aspar glanced at Winna, but she was staring ahead, intent on the path. Winna understood a lot about him, but *these* feelings he could never share. Though more comfortable than most in the wild, she still came from the world of hearth and home, the world inside the fences of men. Her heart was tender when it came to other people. But though Aspar loved a few people well, most made little impression on him. Most folk were shadows to him, but the forest was real.

And if the life of the forest could be bought only by the extinction of Mannish kind . . .

And if he, Aspar, held that choice in his hands . . .

Well, he'd already had his shot not so long ago, hadn't he? It was Leshya who had convinced him not to do it, Leshya and the Briar King himself. How many villagers had died since he'd made that decision?

Would the woorm be here now if the Briar King had already perished by his hand?

He didn't know, of course, and he had no way of knowing. So when he saw the woorm again, should he use the arrow on it or not?

Grim, yes. The monster was killing everything it touched. And if that wasn't enough, Fend was riding it. If he'd had time to think a little more, he'd have killed it when he first saw it.

The horses slowed as they grew too weak to carry them, so Aspar and Winna dismounted and led them, trying to stay off the poisoned ground. Ogre's eyes were rheumy, and Aspar was afraid for him, but he knew he couldn't spare any of the potion, not with Winna at risk. He could only hope that the beasts hadn't been exposed directly to the woorm's breath, that they were suffering from a lesser, perhaps survivable, poisoning.

The trail ended at a hole in a hillside. With a faint shock, Aspar recognized the place.

"This used to be Rewn Rhoidhal," he told Winna.

"I wondered," Winna replied. She was familiar with the Halafolk dwellings, having been with Aspar in another such place: Rewn Aluth. That one had been abandoned. All of them had.

"Is this—is this where Fend was from?"

Aspar shook his head. "So far as I know, Fend never lived in a rewn. He was one of the wanderers."

"Like them that raised you."

"Yah," Aspar said.

Winna pointed at the gaping entrance. "I thought the Halafolk concealed their dwellings a little better than this."

"They do. This one used to be pretty small, but it looks like the woorm has burrowed a hole big enough for itself."

"Burrowed through rock?" Winna asked.

Aspar reached and snapped off a chunk of the reddish stone.

"Claystone," he said. "Not very hard. Still, it would take a lot of men a long time with picks and shovels to widen the hole *this* much."

Winna nodded. "What now?"

"I reckon the only way to follow it is to go in," Aspar said, dismounting and starting to work the saddle off Ogre.

"Have we any oil left?"

They left the horses again and picked their way down a talus slope. The debris was recent, most likely from the woorm's entry.

Their torchlight billowed as uncertain air wagged its flame, and Aspar was able to make out that they were descending into a large cyst in the earth. Even underground, the woorm's trail wasn't difficult to follow. They soon moved from the claystone antechamber down a sloping hall to ancient, sturdier rock, and even there the drag of the beast's belly had snapped stalagmites at their bases. In one place where the damp ceiling stooped low, the creature's back had shattered the downward-seeking stalactites, as well.

The rewn was silent except for the crunch of rock as they

descended and the sound of their breath. Aspar stopped to look for any sign that Fend had dismounted there—he must have, after all—but what sign hadn't been obliterated by the woorm was confused by evidence of the passage of hundreds of slinders.

They pressed on and soon heard a stir of voices, muffled by the enclosing stone. Ahead, Aspar could see that the passage was opening into something much larger.

"Carefully," he whispered.

"That noise," Winna said. "It must be the slinders."

"Yah."

"What if they're allies with the woorm?"

"They aren't," Aspar said, his foot slipping a bit on something slick.

"Can you be certain?"

"Pretty certain," he replied gently. "Mind your feet."

But it was a useless comment. The last few yards of the tunnel were smeared with blood and offal. It looked as if fifty bodies had been pounded fine in a mortar and then spread on the cave floor like butter on bread. Here and there he could make out an eye, a hand, a foot.

It smelled utterly foul.

"Oh, saints," Winna gasped when she realized what it was. She went double and began gagging. Aspar didn't blame her; his own stomach was heaving, and he had seen a lot in his day. He knelt by her and put his hand on her back.

"Careful, lubulih," he said. "You'll make me sick doing that."

She chuckled ruefully and shot him a look, then went back to it for a while.

"I'm sorry," she managed when she was done. "The whole cave knows we're here now, I guess."

"I don't think anyone cares," Aspar said.

The scriftorium had to be entered through a door so low that it forced him to crawl, to "come to knowledge on his knees." But it was in rising that Stephen felt humbled as he confronted the wonder of the scriftorium.

Stephen hadn't been born a poor man. His family, as he had once been wont to proclaim, were the Cape Chavel Dariges. His father's estate was an old one, situated on rambling sea-chewed bluffs above the Bay of Ringmere and built of the same tawny stone. The oldest rooms had been part of a keep, though only a few of the original curving walls remained. The main house boasted fifteen rooms, with several attached cottages, barns, and outbuildings. The family raised horses, but most of the income came from owning farmland, waterfront, and boats.

His father's scriftorium was considered a good one for a private collection. He had nine books; Stephen knew them all by heart. Morris Top, a league away and the most sizable town in the attish, had a scriftorium with fifteen books, and that was held by the Church.

The college at Ralegh, by far the largest university in Virgenya, possessed a grand total of fifty-eight scrolls, tablets, and bound books.

Here, Stephen stood inside a round tower containing thousands of books. It rose in four levels, with only the narrowest walkspaces at each story. Ladders bridged the vertical distances; books were moved up and down by means of baskets, rope, and winches.

Things had changed since the last time he'd been there. Before, it had bustled with monks copying, reading, annotating, studying. Now, besides himself, there was one lone monk who was frantically packing scrolls into oiled leather cases. The fellow waved but went quickly back to his work.

Stephen didn't recognize him, anyway.

His natural awe faded as the situation reasserted itself. Where to start? He felt overwhelmed.

Well, the *Casti Noibhi* was an obvious choice. He found it on the second tier and, leaning against the rail, thumbed through its pressed linen pages. He quickly found the epistle fragments written in what was supposed to be the original encrypted form. He saw right away that the symbols, as he had suspected, were mostly from the Old Virgenyan script with admixtures of Thiuda and early Vitellian. That was more by way of confirming his guess than anything else.

Nodding, he made his way to another section and selected a scroll of funeral inscriptions and elegiac formulae from Virgenya. The scroll itself was quite new, but the inscriptions had been copied from carved stones up to two thousand years old.

The epistle's cipher likely was built around one of the languages from the time of the insurrection. The major ones were ancient Vitellian, Thiuda, Old Cavari, and Old Virgenyan. From those four languages were descended most of the tongues spoken in the world Stephen knew.

But there were other languages with different lineages. Most were far away; the Skasloi had ruled lands beyond the seas, and their slaves had spoken languages very different from those in Crotheny. Those wouldn't have figured into the revolt here. There was also the slave cant, of which later scholarship knew almost nothing. Stephen rather doubted that his ancestors would have used that as their secret language, since the Skasloi themselves had had a hand in inventing it.

There were also Yeszik, Vhilatautan, and Yaohan. Yeszik and Vhilatautan had descendants spoken in Vestrana and the Iutin and Bairgh mountains, and a few tribes, like that of Ehawk, spoke Yaohan languages.

He stopped. Ehawk.

Stephen realized with a flash of guilt that he had forgotten him. What had happened to the boy? One moment he had been there, gripping his arm, and the next . . .

He would ask the fratrex to inquire with the slinders. It was all he could do. He should have done it already, but there was so much to do, so little time.

Right.

The more obscure the language, the better code it made, all on its own. So he needed what lexicons he could find concerning all the mother tongues. Indeed, his intended destination was supposed to be in the Bairghs; that meant some knowledge of the Vhilatautan daughter languages might also be useful.

Immediately he set about finding those tomes. When he had lowered them by basket to the floor, he had another, much more interesting thought and rushed to the geographies and maps. The Bairgh Mountains were very large indeed. Even after he had translated the epistle—*if* he translated it—he would need to plot the quickest route to Vhelnoryganuz Mountain or all his efforts would be moot.

Stephen wasn't certain how many hours had passed when Ehan found him, but the glass dome above had long since gone dark, and he was working by lamplight at one of the large wooden tables on the lowest floor.

"The new day is upon us," Ehan said. "Have you no need of sleep?"

"I've no time for it," Stephen said. "If I really must be away from here by sunrise—"

"It might be sooner," Ehan said. "Something's happening down in the rewn. We've got a watch, but we're not certain what it is. What are you about?"

"Trying to find our mountain," Stephen said.

"I don't suppose it's simple enough as to be on the map?" Ehan asked.

Stephen shook his head wearily and smiled. He realized that despite everything, this was the happiest he had been in a long time. He wished it didn't have to end.

"No," he said. He put his finger on a large-scale modern map that showed the Midenlands and the Bairghs. "I've made a guess how far someone could ride in eighteen days from Wherthen," he said. "The fratrex is right; the Bairghs are the only mountains that our 'fastness' could be in. But as you said, if there's such a mountain as Vhelnoryganuz, it's not marked here."

"Maybe the name has changed over time," Ehan suggested.

"Of course it has," Stephen said, then realized he'd sounded a bit pompous.

"What I mean, is," he explained, "that Vhelnoryganuz is

Old Vadhiian, the language of the Black Jester's kingdom. It means 'Traitorous Queen.' Vadhiian isn't spoken anymore, so the name would have been corrupted."

"But it's just a name; you don't have to know what it means to keep repeating it or teach it to your children. Why would it change? I mean, I can understand if it was *renamed* . . ."

"I'll give you a for instance," Stephen said. "The Hegemony built a bridge across a river in the King's Forest and called it the *Pontro Oltiumo,* which means 'the farthest bridge' because at the time it was on the frontier, the bridge most distant from z'Irbina. After a while, the name got transferred to the river itself but was shortened to *Oltiumo.* When new people settled there, speaking Old Oostish, they started calling it the *Ald Thiub,* 'old thief'—because *Oltiumo* sounded sort of like the way they pronounced it—which the Virgenyan settlers in turn corrupted into Owl Tomb, which is what it's called to this day.

"So a mouthful like Vhelnoryganuz easily could have ended up as, I don't know, Fell Norrick, or something like that. But I can't find anything on the map that looks like a simple corruption."

"I see," Ehan said. But he seemed distracted.

"So the next thing I thought of is that maybe the mountain is still called 'Traitorous Queen,' but in the current language of the area; that happens sometimes, though that's a weird name for a mountain."

"Not really," Ehan said. "In the north we often refer to mountains as kings or queens, and one that claimed the lives of many travelers might be referred to as traitorous. What's spoken in the Bairghs?"

"Dialects related to Hanzish, Almannish, and Vhilatautan. But to make matters more difficult, this map is based on one made during the Lierish regency."

"So you're stuck."

Stephen smiled wickedly.

"Oh, then you've figured it out," Ehan amended, starting to sound impatient.

"Well," Stephen said, "it occurred to me that Vadhiian was never spoken in the Bairghs, so the name we have for the mountain is already a Vadhiian interpretation of a probably Vhilatautan name. Once I started thinking that way, I pulled out the lexicon of Tautish and started comparing.

"Vhelnoryganuz in this case might be a mistranslation of *Velnoiraganas,* which in old Vhilatautish would mean something like 'Witchhorn.'"

"And is there a Witchhorn in the Bairghs?"

Stephen put his finger on the map next to the drawing of a mountain with an odd shape, a bit like that of a cow's horn. Next to it, in a tiny Lierish hand, was lettered *'eslief vendve.'*

"Witch's Mountain," he translated for Ehan's sake.

"Well," Ehan considered, "that was easy."

"And probably still wrong," Stephen said. "But it's the best guess I have until I've translated the epistle. I think I may have a start on that."

Off in the distance a clarion note soared.

"You'll have to finish it on horseback," Ehan said hurriedly. "That's the alarm. Come on, quickly now."

He gestured, and two other monks hurried over, packed the scrifti and scrolls Stephen had selected into weathersound bags, and stooped their way out of the scriftorium. Stephen followed, grabbing a few stray items. He didn't even have time for one last glance.

Outside, three horses stood stamping, their eyes rolling as the monks loaded them with the precious books. Stephen strained to hear what was upsetting them, but at first even his blessed senses found nothing.

The valley seemed quiet, in fact, beneath a cold, clear sky. The stars shone so large and bright that they seemed unreal, like those seen in a dream, and for a moment Stephen wondered if he *was* dreaming—or dead. There were some who said that ghosts were deluded spirits who did not understand their fate and tried desperately to continue in the world they knew.

Perhaps all his companions were dead. Anne and her army

of shades would batter insubstantially at the walls of Eslen, while its defenders felt little more than a vague chill at their presence. Aspar would slip off to fight for the forest he loved, a specter more terrifying than even Grim the Raver. And Stephen—he would continue to quest after mysteries at the behest of the dead fratrex and the dead Ehan.

When had he died, then? At Cal Azroth? At Khrwbh Khrwkh? Either seemed likely.

He heard it then, the rush of a breath through lungs so long that it sounded a note far below the lowest that could be stroked from a bass croth. It groaned just above the pitch sung by rocks and stones and had at first been hidden in those sounds. Now he *felt,* more than heard, sand rubbing from stone, limbs snapping, and a vast weight in motion.

The horn stopped blowing.

"What is that?" Stephen whispered.

Ehan stood a few feet away, whispering hastily with another monk, a gray-haired fellow Stephen had never seen before. The two briefly embraced, and the gray-hair hurried off.

"Just come on," Ehan said. "If it's what we think it is, we don't have time to spare. We've a few men waiting for us at the lower end of the valley, making sure nothing's coming that way."

"What about the fratrex?"

"Someone has to bait it to stay here for a while."

"What are you talking about?"

His mind raced back to recall the whispered conversation between Ehan and the other man; he hadn't been paying attention, but his ears ought to have heard it anyway.

He had it now. "A woorm?" he gasped.

Images crowded into his mind, all from tapestries, illustrations, children's tales, and ancient legends. He stared up at the hillside.

In the faint starlight he saw the motion of trees, a long, snaky line of them. How long was it? A hundred kings-yards?

"The fratrex can't stay and fight that," Stephen said.

"He won't be alone," Ehan said. "Someone has to delay it here, make it believe its prize is still in d'Ef."

"Its prize?"

"What it's after," Ehan said, the exasperation becoming plain in his voice. "You."

CHAPTER TWELVE

HEARTS AND SWORDS

"FIRE IS a wonderful thing," Cazio said happily. He used his native tongue so he would understand himself. "A woman is a wonderful thing. A *sword* is a wonderful thing."

He reclined on a velvet couch next to the great hearth in the grand salon of Glenchest, one half of him baking and the other pleasantly warm and cushioned. If the fireplace was not lit, a man easily could walk in and stand up; that was how big it was, a giant slice of orange, a half-moon on the horizon, Austra's smile inverted.

He reached lazily for the bottle of wine the duchess had given him. It wasn't wine, actually, but a bitter greenish tonic that had far more bite than the blood of Saint Pacho. He hadn't liked it at first, but between it and the fire, he felt as if his body were made of fur, and his mind was pleasantly reflective.

Esverinna Taurochi dachi Calavai. She'd been tall, as tall as Cazio, with limbs that seemed a bit long and awkward. Eyes like honey and hazelnut mixed together and long, long hair that sprouted almost black but paled to the color of her eyes toward the ends. He remembered that she always hunched just a little, as if ashamed of her regal height. In his arms, her length had felt luxurious, something he could stretch against infinitely.

She was beautiful but unaware of her beauty. Passionate but innocent of her desires. They both had been thirteen; she was already promised to marry a far older man from Esquavin. He had thought to duel the man, he remembered, but Esverinna had stopped him with these words: *You will never truly love me. He does not love me, but he might.*

Maio Dechiochi d'Avella had been a distant cousin of the Mediccio of Avella, the town of Cazio's birth. Like most young men of means in that place, he studied fencing with Mestro Estenio. Cazio had quarreled with him about the result of a game of dice. Swords had been drawn. Cazio remembered how surprised he had been to see fear in Maio's eyes. He himself had felt only exhilaration.

The duel had consisted of exactly three passes: an unconvincing feint by Maio, becoming an attack in *seft* to Cazio's thigh, and his parry of the attack and riposte in *prismo,* resulting in Maio's mad scramble out of distance. Cazio had renewed the attack; Maio parried violently but did not riposte. Cazio repeated the attack, exactly the same as before; again Maio blocked without responding, apparently happy just to have stopped the thrust. Cazio quickly redoubled and hit him in the upper arm.

He had been twelve, and Maio thirteen. It was the first time he had ever felt flesh give beneath his steel.

Marisola Serechii da Ceresa. Fine obsidian hair, the face of a child, the heart of a wolf. She knew what she wanted, and what she wanted was to watch Cazio fight for her and then exhaust what remained of his energy in the silk sheets of her bed. She was a licker, a biter, a screamer, and she treated his body as if it were a rare treat she would never have enough of. She had stood hardly to his chest, but with three touches she could rob him of his will. She had been eighteen, and he had been sixteen. He often wondered if she was a witch and thought for certain she was when she dismissed him. He couldn't believe that she didn't love him, and years later one of his friends told him her father had threatened to hire assassins if she did not break with Cazio and marry the man he had chosen. Cazio never got to question her about it; she died in childbirth a year after her marriage.

St. Abulo Serechii da Ceresa, Marisola's older brother, had spent time in their hometown of Ceresa, studying writing and swordplay with his grand-uncle's mestro. Aware of the relationship with his sister, St. Abulo had let drop a casually insulting remark regarding Cazio in the Tauro et Purca tavern, knowing it would get back to him. They had arranged to meet in the apple grove outside of town, each with a second and a crowd of admirers. St. Abulo was small, like his sister, but devastatingly quick, and he affected the somewhat antiquated tradition of using a *mano nertro,* a dagger for the left hand. The fight had ended when St. Abulo mistimed a counterthrust; he hit Cazio in the thigh, but Cazio skewered him in the ear. It was clear to both men that Cazio could as easily have stabbed him in the eye. St. Abulo conceded the point, but his second would not agree, and so he and Cazio's second had taken up the duel. Before long, the bystanders took to one another, as well. Cazio and St. Abulo retired to watch the brawl, bind their wounds, and drink several bottles of wine.

St. Abulo admitted that he wasn't really much concerned with his sister's virtue but that his father had put him up to it. He and Cazio shook hands and parted friends, which they remained until St. Abulo died of the wounds he received killing the man whose child had killed his sister.

Naiva dazo trivo Abrinasso. The daughter of Duke Salalfo of Abrinia and a courtesan from distant Khorsu, Naiva had had her mother's black almond eyes. She had tasted like almonds, too, and honey, and oranges. Her mother had fallen out of favor with the duke's court when he died, but he had provided a triva for her near Avella. Cazio had met Naiva in the vineyards, squishing fallen grapes with her bare feet. She was sophisticated and jaded. She believed she had been exiled to the farthest reaches of the earth, and he'd always believed that with him she was settling for something less than she imagined. He remembered her thighs in the sunlight, hot to the touch, the sigh that was nearly a giggle. She had simply vanished one day without a word. There was a rumor that she had returned to Abrinia and become a courtesan like her mother.

Larche Peicassa dachi Sallatotti. The first man who suggested in as many words that Naiva had been little more than a well-bred whore. Cazio had bound his blade and struck him through his left lung with such force that Caspator broke through his back. Larche was the first man Cazio had fully intended to kill. He had failed, but the man had been forever crippled by the fight, left to hobble on a crutch.

Austra. Skin so pale that it was white even by firelight. Amber hair that tousled pleasingly, cheeks that flushed as pink as a dawn-lily. She was more fearful of twining fingers than of kissing, as if the touch of two hands was somehow an embrace much riskier to the heart.

She had been clumsy, enthusiastic, fearful, and guilty. Happy but, as always, with an eye toward the end of happiness.

Love was strange and terrible. Cazio had thought he could avoid it after Naiva. Courting was fun, sex a lot of fun indeed, and love—well, that was a pointless illusion.

Maybe he still believed that, or part of him did. But if so, why did he want to twine his fingers with Austra's until she believed him, until she relinquished her fear, skepticism, and self-doubt and understood that he actually *did* care for her?

Acredo. Not really his name, of course; it just meant "sharp." The first swordsman in so long, so very long, to really test his point.

The duchess and some others were playing cards on the other side of the room, but he found that their voices had become like the piping of birds, melodic but incomprehensible. Thus, it took him a moment to realize that someone stood very near him and that the musical noises that were the loudest were intended for speech.

He lifted his head and saw that it was Sir Neil. Cazio grinned and raised the bottle.

"How is your foot?" Neil asked.

"I can't say it hurts at the moment," Cazio replied happily.

"I suppose not."

"The duchess told me not to, you see," Cazio finished by way of explanation, then laughed for a few moments at his own joke.

Oddly, Neil did not seem amused.

"What is it?" Cazio asked.

"I have the greatest regard for your bravery and swordsmanship," Neil started.

"As well you should," Cazio informed him.

Neil paused, then nodded, more to himself than to Cazio, and continued. "My duty is to protect Anne," he said. "Protect her from all things."

"Well, then, it should have been you fighting Acredo, eh, and not me. Is that it?"

"It should have been me," Neil agreed evenly, "but I had to confer with the duchess concerning what troops she has and what we can expect, and unfortunately I was not able to be in two places at once. Nor would it have been proper for me to have been in the room with her when she was attacked."

"No one was in the room with her," Cazio said. "That's how she came to nearly be killed. Maybe someone *should* be in the room with her, 'proper' or not."

"You weren't with her?"

"Of course not. Why do you think I was naked?"

"My question exactly. You were lodged in a different part of the mansion."

"I was," Cazio said. "But I was with Aus—" He stopped. "That's really not your business."

"Austra?" Neil hissed, lowering his voice. "But she was the one *supposed* to be in the room with Anne."

Cazio pushed himself up on one arm and leveled his gaze at the knight. "What are you saying? That you would rather they had both died? Acredo killed the guards. If I hadn't been nearby, how do you imagine it would have ended?"

"I know," Neil said, rubbing his forehead. "I didn't intend to insult you, only to understand why . . . what happened."

"And now you know."

"Now I know." The knight paused, and his face grew almost comically long. "Cazio, it is very difficult to protect someone you love. Do you understand that?"

Cazio suddenly felt like taking a sword to the knight.

"I know that very well," he said evenly. He meant to say more, but something in Neil's eyes told him he didn't have to. So rather than pushing it further, he just said, "Join me for a drink."

Neil shook his head. "No. I have too much to do. But thank you."

He left Cazio to increasingly more colorful memories, imaginings, and, soon enough, dreams.

When Neil left Cazio, he felt vaguely unclean. He had suspected from their first meeting that the Vitellian and Anne might have developed some sort of relationship; he remembered Anne's reputation. Her mother had sent her away to a coven in Vitellia precisely because she had been caught in a delicate position with Roderick of Dunmrogh.

Thus, it would be no surprise if, traveling together all this time, something had happened between the princess and the swordsman. Nor could Neil condemn Cazio for that; he himself had engaged in improper relations with a princess of the realm, and he was less well born than the Vitellian.

But he'd had to ask, hadn't he?

Still, he didn't like it, this role. It did not suit him to question grown men about their intentions, to worry about who was naked in bed with whom. These weren't the things he wanted to be interested in. It made him feel old, like someone's father. In fact, he and Cazio were about the same age, and Anne wasn't much younger.

He remembered Erren, the queen's bodyguard, warning him not to love Muriele, saying that loving her would get her killed. Erren had been right, of course, but had misplaced the person. It had been Fastia he loved, Fastia who died.

He suddenly missed Erren powerfully; he hadn't known her well, and when they had spoken, it had been mostly her putting him in his place. But Anne needed someone like Erren, someone deadly, competent, and female. Someone who could protect her with a knife and with wise words.

But Erren had died defending her queen, and there was no one to take her place.

He looked in on Anne. The duchess had moved her to another room, and though Neil couldn't remember the reasoning behind the change, he felt certain that it was to make her safer.

He found Anne apparently asleep, and Austra was sitting with her. The girl looked as if she had been crying, and her cheeks flushed brilliantly when she saw him.

Neil entered the bedchamber and walked as softly as he could to the far side of the room. Austra got up and followed him.

"She is sleeping?"

"Yes. The draft the duchess gave her seems to have worked."

"Good."

Austra bit her lip. "Sir Neil, I would talk with you for a moment, if I may. I have something I must confess. Will you listen to me?"

"I'm not a sacritor, Lady Austra," he said.

"I know that, of course. You are our guardian. And I fear I abandoned my lady when she most needed me."

"Really? You think you might have stopped the killer? Do you have resources that I don't know about?"

"I have a knife."

"The assassin killed two men who had swords. I can't imagine that you would have fared better than they."

"Yet I might have tried."

"Fortunately, that was not tested. I wasn't here, either, Austra. We are all very fortunate that Cazio happened by."

Austra hesitated. "He did not just . . . happen . . . by."

"Doubtless the saints guided him," Neil said, gently. "That is all I need to know."

A small tear began in the corner of Austra's eye. "It is too much," she said. "It is all too much."

Neil thought she would collapse into weeping, but instead the girl dried her eyes with her sleeve.

"But it can't be, can it?" she said. "I shall be with her, sir knight, from here on, I assure you. I will not be distracted. Nor will I sleep when she sleeps. If the only thing I can do is to scream once before I die, at least I will not die thinking myself an utter failure."

Neil smiled. "That's a fierce thing to say."

"I am not fierce," Austra said. "I am not much of anything, really—just a maidservant. I have no gentle birth, no parents, nothing to recommend me but her affection. I have forgotten myself and my station. I will not do it again."

Neil put his hand on her shoulder. "Don't speak with shame of your birth," he said. "My mother and father were steadholders, nothing more. There is no gentle blood in me, either, but I was born to good people, honorable people. No one can ask for better than that. And no one, no matter their birth, can ask for anything better than a loyal friend who loves them. You *are* fierce; I can see it in you. And you are a person of note, Austra. Hard wind and rain can wear down even a stone, and you have been in storm after storm. Yet here you are, still with us, worn but still ready to fight for what you love.

"Do not barter yourself away for nothing. The only shame comes in surrendering to despair. That's something I know all too well."

Austra smiled faintly. She had begun to cry again, but her face was steady. "I believe you do, Sir Neil," she said. "Thank you for your kind words."

He squeezed her shoulder and let his hand drop. He felt older again.

"I'll be outside the door," he said. "If you call, I'll be here."

"Thank you, Sir Neil."

"And you, milady. And despite your vow, I urge you to sleep now. I will not, I promise you."

Anne woke from a dream so incomprehensible as to be terrifying. She lay gasping, staring at the ceiling, trying to assure herself that the Black Marys she could *not* remember were the best kind.

As the nightbale faded, she gathered her surroundings. She was in the room she and her sisters had called "the cave" because it had no windows. It was also rather large and oddly shaped. She had never stayed in the room before, but they all had played in it when she was very young, pretending it was the lair of a Scaos where they might discover treasure, though only at great peril, of course.

Aunt Elyoner had moved her here, presumably, because she would be safer from another attempt at murder. She assumed that meant that there were no hidden passages to let her death in.

Austra lay back on a nearby couch, head turned up, mouth open, her scratchy almost-snore a comfortingly normal sound. A few candles burned here and there, and a very low flame burned in the hearth.

Anne wondered for the first time why the room had so many couches and beds. Upon further reflection, she decided she did not really *want* to know what entertainment Elyoner would plan in a room with no windows.

"How do you feel, plum?" a faint voice asked.

Anne jumped slightly, turned her head, and sat up. She regarded Elyoner, who sat on a stool studying some cards that lay on a small table.

"My arm hurts," Anne said. It did; it throbbed in time with her heartbeat beneath the tight bandages.

"I'll have Elcien examine you in a little while. He assures me that when it heals, you will scarcely know it happened. Not like that nasty place on your leg. How did you get that?"

"An arrow," Anne replied. "In Dunmrogh."

"You've had quite the adventure, haven't you?"

Anne coughed a weak laugh. "Enough to know that there's no such thing as adventure."

Elyoner smiled her mysterious little smile and dealt herself another card. "Of course there is, dove. Just as there is such a thing as a poem, an epic, a tragedy. It's just that it doesn't exist in real life. In real life we have terror, and problems, and sex. It's when it gets told as a story that it becomes adventure."

"That's exactly what I meant," Anne said. "I don't think I will ever be able to read such stories again."

"Perhaps not," Elyoner replied. "But however things go, it shall be some time before you are even afforded the chance. Though I hope for your sake, my dear, that you *are* eventually gifted with enough boredom to consider it."

Anne smiled. "Yes, I hope that, too, Aunt Elyoner. So tell me, has anything terrible happened while I slept?"

"Terrible? No. Your young knight had some questions for your young swordsman concerning his dueling apparel."

"I suppose he was next door with Austra," Anne murmured. She glanced warily at her friend, but her steady breathing continued.

"I suppose he was," Elyoner replied. "Does that trouble you?"

Anne considered that for a moment, her head cocked to one side. "Not at all," she replied. "She's welcome to him."

"Is she really?" Elyoner said, an odd lilt to her voice. "How liberal of you."

Anne gave her aunt a look that she hoped would bring an end to the subject. In point of fact, she wasn't that happy about it. That Austra and Cazio had been naked, almost certainly doing *that,* just a wall away from her, felt—well, disrespectful.

Still, Cazio's presence had been fortunate. Again. It was good to know she had someone who would throw himself naked at an enemy to defend her, especially when his heart seemed to be occupied elsewhere. She had profoundly misjudged Cazio when first they had met; she had thought him a braggart, a blowhard, and an incorrigible flirt. The latter was still true, and her chief concern for Austra was that he might prove himself fickle, as well.

But he had been so constant as their protector, so steadfast, that she was starting to believe that he might be less feckless in matters of the heart than he at first appeared. If she had suspected that when first they met . . .

She realized Elyoner was studying her now, and not the cards. Her aunt's grin had broadened.

"What?" she said.

"Nothing, dove." She looked back at her cards. "In any event, Austra is distraught. She stayed awake all night watching you; she only agreed to sleep when I arrived. Sir Neil is outside."

"Will you tell me what happened between him and Fastia?" Anne asked.

Elyoner shook her head slightly. "Nothing unnatural. Nothing so bad, and not nearly as much as either deserved. Let it stay at that, won't you? It would be far better that way."

"I saw her," Anne said.

"Saw who?"

"Fastia. In my dream. She warned me of the assassin."

"She would," Elyoner said without a trace of skepticism. "She always loved you."

"I know. I wish I had been nicer to her the last time I saw her."

"The only way to never have *that* regret is to be unfailingly nice all the time," Elyoner said. "I cannot imagine how terrible life would be if I had to live it like that."

"But you *are* nice all the time, Aunt Elyoner."

"Pish," she said. Then her eyes widened. "Why, look at that! The cards are predicting good news today."

Anne heard boots in the hall, and the hair on her arms suddenly prickled.

"How's that?" she asked.

"A beloved relation is coming and bringing gifts."

A rap sounded at the door.

"Are we ready to receive visitors?" Elyoner asked.

"Who is it?" Anne asked, hesitation in her voice.

Elyoner clucked and switched her finger about. "The cards aren't that specific, I'm afraid," she said.

Anne pulled the folds of her dressing gown tighter.

"Come in," she called.

The door creaked, and a tall male form stood there. It was several heartbeats before Anne recognized him.

"Cousin Artwair!" she cried.

"Hello, little saddle burr," Artwair replied, stepping to her bedside and reaching down for her hand. His gray eyes were stern, as they usually were, but she could tell he was happy enough to see her.

She hadn't been called "saddle burr" in a long time, and she remembered that it was Artwair who had coined that nickname for her. He'd found her in the stables hidden behind a heap of saddles when she was eight. She couldn't remember what she had been avoiding at the time, only Cousin Artwair lifting her up with his strong hands . . .

Something snapped into focus then, and she gasped.

Artwair had only one hand now. Where his right hand ought to be, there was only a bandaged stump.

"What happened to your— Oh, Artwair, I'm so sorry."

He lifted the stump, looked at it, and shrugged. "Don't be. That's the life of a warrior. I'm lucky that's all I lost. How can I complain when I still have another, and eyes to see you with? So many of my men lost everything."

"I-I don't even know where to begin," Anne said. "So much has happened . . ."

"I know a lot of it," Artwair said. "I know about your father and your sisters. Elyoner has been catching me up on the rest."

"But what about you? Where have you been?"

"On the eastern marches of the King's Forest, fighting—" He paused. "Things. It seemed important at first, but then we realized they never really come out of the forest. Then I got word of what Robert's been up to in Eslen, and I thought I ought to check into it."

"My uncle Robert's gone mad, I think," Anne said. "He's imprisoned my mother. Did you know that?"

"Auy."

"I've determined to do what I can to free her and take back the throne."

"Well," Artwair said, "I might be of some help there."

"Yes," Anne said. "I hoped you would say that. I don't know much about waging war, really, nor do any of my companions. I need a general, Cousin."

"I would be honored to serve you in that regard," Artwair replied. "Even one man can make a difference."

Then he smiled a little more broadly and fondly mussed her hair.

"Of course, I've also brought my army."

CHAPTER THIRTEEN

SONITUM

GRAY DAWN spilled into the valley as Stephen and Ehan raced toward the river. The horses proved unrideable, bucking and rearing uncontrollably, so they had to lead them.

The earth shivered beneath Stephen's boots, and sick unreasoning fear threatened to overwhelm him. It felt as if everything was too loud and too bright, and he wanted to tell everyone he just needed a rest, a day or so to himself.

Ehan, too, was flushed and wide-eyed. Stephen wondered if this was how field mice felt when they heard the screech of a hawk, knowing the terror in their bones even when they hadn't seen the predator itself.

He kept turning back, and just as they reached the base of the orchard, he saw it.

The monastery was raised up on a hill, its graceful, exuberant line etched against a lead sky faintly patinaed with amber. A peculiar violet light flickered in one of the highest windows of the bell tower; Stephen felt his face warming, as if he were looking at the sun.

An eldritch fog rose around the base of the structure, and at first Stephen thought what he saw was smoke rising up, until his saint-sharpened eyes picked out the details: the beetle-green lamps of its eyes, the teeth it showed as it opened its mouth, the long sinew of its body twining up the tower.

Everything else faded away: Ehan urging him on, the men at the bottom of the hill calling frantically, the distant tolling of the clock. Only the monster existed.

But "monster" wasn't nearly the right word. The greffyn was a monster. The utin, the nicwer—those were monsters, creatures from an elder time somehow restored to a world that had believed itself sane. But everything in Stephen screamed that this—this was a difference not only of degree but of kind. Not a monster but a god, a Damned Saint.

His knees trembled, and he dropped onto them, and as he did so, its eyes turned toward him. Across the distance of a quarter of a league their gazes met, and Stephen felt something so far beyond human emotion that his body could not contain it much less understand it.

"Saints," Ehan said. "Saints, it sees us. Stephen—"

Whatever Ehan meant to say was cut short as the violet light flared again. This time it didn't confine itself to the single window. Instead, it spewed from every part of the great monastery. It brightened unbearably, and d'Ef suddenly was gone, replaced by a sphere of intolerable radiance.

"Fratrex Pell!" Stephen heard Ehan gasp.

OBSERVATIONS ON THE VITELLIAN VERB, SONITUM
Having a very specific definition, "to deafen by thunder." It seems peculiar that the Hegemony would have had such a particular word; a verb "to make deaf" exists (ehesurdum), as does the word "thunder" (tonarus). It suggests that being deafened by thunder happened often enough to warrant its own verb. Was there more thunder in the past? Probably not of a natural sort. But when the saints and the old gods were at war, it was likely to have been rather noisy . . .

The first crest of sound brought tears of pain and horror to his eyes. Then he didn't hear anything at all, though he felt the blast against his face. When his other senses returned, Stephen grabbed Ehan and pushed him to the ground just as the second shock swept past, a horizontal sleet of stone and heat that sheared the upper branches of the trees and sent cascades of burning twigs down upon them.

Ehan's mouth was moving, but there was no sound except a long drawn-out tolling like the largest bell in the world.

Sonitum: "to deafen with thunder." Sonifed som: "I have by thunder been deafened" . . .

Stephen lifted himself gingerly, his gaze drawing toward where he had last seen the monastery. Now he saw only a cloud of dark smoke.

His first grief was for the books, the precious, irreplaceable books. Then he thought about the men who had sacrificed themselves, and a shiver of guilt ran through him.

He reached up to touch his ears, wondering if the drums had been burst, if his loss of hearing would be temporary or permanent. The ringing in his head was so loud, it made him dizzy, and the world his eyes saw seemed unreal. He was reminded of when he walked the faneway of Saint Decmanus; his senses had been stripped from him one by one, until he had been nothing more than a presence moving though space. Another time he apparently had been dead, and though he could see nothing of the quick world, he could feel and hear it. Here he was again, pushed a little beyond the bounds of the world, as if that was where he belonged.

He frowned, then remembered the time when his friends had thought him dead. There had been a face, a woman's face, with red hair but with features too terrible to gaze upon.

How could he have forgotten that?

Why did he remember it now?

Dizziness overwhelmed him, and he fell to his knees again and began to vomit. He felt Ehan's hand on his back and was ashamed at being down on all fours like a beast, but there was nothing he could do about it.

As his breath slowed and he felt a little better, he noticed that the vibration had returned, a quivering of the earth beneath his palms and knees. His mind, usually so quick, took a moment to grasp what his body was trying to tell him.

He came shakily back to standing and looked again toward d'Ef.

He still couldn't see anything but smoke, but it didn't matter. He could feel it coming. Whatever dread force the fratrex had released, it hadn't been enough to slay the woorm.

Shakily, he grasped Ehan by the arm and pulled him toward the horses. There were two other men there. One was a young fellow in burnt orange clerical robes. He had a large bulbous nose, green eyes, and ears that might have looked better on a larger head. The other man, Stephen recognized, a huntsman named Henne. He was a little older, maybe thirty, with a sun-browned face and broken teeth. Stephen remembered him as competent, uncomplicated, and friendly in a rough fashion.

At the moment they were all distracted by the discovery that they couldn't hear.

Stephen got their attention by waving his hands. Then he mimed feeling the ground, pointing back toward where d'Ef had stood; he shook his head no, then pointed to the horses. The other monk already understood; Henne suddenly nodded and mounted up, gesturing for them all to follow.

Probably also bereft of hearing, the horses actually seemed *less* skittish than before, though much inclined to depart. Mounted, Stephen couldn't feel the woorm through the earth anymore, but he had no doubt it was coming. *It must follow scent,* he mused, *like a hound, or perhaps it uses some faculty that has never been documented.* He wished he'd had a better look at it.

As they rode through a forest rendered eerily silent, he thought through what legend said of such creatures, but what he mostly remembered were tales of knights who fought and defeated them with sword or lance. Now that he had seen the woorm at a distance, that seemed so impossible that Stephen had to assume that if there was any reality at all in such tales, they spoke of some smaller cousin of the thing he had just seen.

What else could he recall?

They lived in caverns or deep water; they hoarded gold; their blood was venom but paradoxically could convey supernatural power under the right circumstances. They were much like dragons, but dragons were supposed to have wings.

And woorms weren't dumb beasts. Woorms were supposed to have the power of speech and terrible, crafty minds always devising evil. They were said to be sorcerers, and the very oldest texts he could remember suggested that they had enjoyed some special relationship with the Skasloi.

He also remembered an engraving of the Briar King gripping a horned serpent. The caption had read—

Had read—

He closed his eyes and saw the page.

Vincatur Ambiom. "Subduer of woorms."

So all he had to do was find the Briar King, and he would save them.

Stephen laughed at that, but no one heard him. Ehan might have thought he was in pain, though, for he looked more concerned than ever; at the moment that was quite a feat.

A bell later they descended into a lowland of white birches and crossed the worn track of the King's Road. The day had dawned crisp and clear. Away from the woorm, the horses had calmed enough to be ridden.

Stephen reckoned they were riding north more or less, paralleling the Ef River, which ought to be off to their right. The land got lower and wetter until the horses were slogging through standing water. The trees thinned, but fern and cattail rose head-high, obscuring vision beyond the narrow path they followed, which to Stephen's eye looked like no more than an animal path of some sort.

Finally Henne led them to slightly higher ground and a trail that had a well-traveled look. He took the horses to a trot, and they varied between that pace and a fast walk for perhaps two bells before they came quite suddenly upon a small cluster of houses.

Stephen didn't imagine it was a village, more likely a sort of extended family steading. It also was clearly abandoned. The pigpen had fallen into a ruin of rough wooden fence poles; the largest house had holes in its cedar-shake roof. Dead weeds had poked up through hard dirt, and there were hints of snow around the yard.

Henne rode past all of that, down a slight rise to a flowing stream that seemed too small to be the Ef. He dismounted and went over to something suspended between two trees, covered with a tarp. For a moment Stephen feared that he would reveal a corpse when he drew away the cloth, that it was a burial such as he had heard some of the mountain tribes performed.

In fact he had gotten the scale wrong; it was a boat hung by rope above the highest watermark on the witaecs. It looked in fair shape and was large enough to accommodate them.

But not their horses.

Henne set them to the task of removing the harnesses and saddles, and those they placed in the boat. That made sense: the Ef flowed north, which was the direction they wanted to go, but at the city of Wherthen it would join the White War-lock and turn west toward Eslen. They might go upriver from Wherthen if they could find the right sort of vessel, but at some point they would have to find new horses and con-tinue north and east to reach the Bairghs. Better that they didn't have to buy new tack, as well.

Their task completed, they climbed into the craft. Henne went to the tiller, and Ehan and the other monk took the oars. Stephen watched the horses, which regarded them curiously as they started downstream. He hoped they had enough sense to scatter before the woorm reached them.

He tapped Ehan and made a rowing motion, but the little

man shook his head, pointing instead to the packages of scrifti and books. Stephen nodded and set about securing them with twine in case the boat should capsize. When he was done with that, he dipped his hand in the icy-cold water, not long from the mountains.

He thought he felt the faint vibration of the woorm, but he couldn't be certain. As he watched the prow of the boat cut the river, a few flakes of snow began to fall, vanishing without a ripple as they struck the quicksilver surface.

There seemed a world of meaning in that, but he was too tired, far too tired to search for it.

He wondered how Winna was. And Aspar, and poor Ehawk.

His limbs were made of stone; he couldn't move and was able to open his eyes only with terrific effort.

He was in his own bed, at home in Cape Chavel, but the familiar mattress was draped in soft black sheets, and the curtains hung about it were also black, though diaphanous enough for him to make out the suffused glow of candlelight in the room beyond.

He felt as if he were sinking into himself, growing heavier. He knew he must be dreaming, but he couldn't make it stop any more than he could move his limbs or scream.

Beyond the curtain but between his eyes and the light, something moved: a darkness cast upon the cloth, walking around his bed, a shape sometimes human and sometimes something else. Something no more large than small, something that was whatever it wanted to be. His eyes—the only things he could move—followed it until it was behind him.

He couldn't shift his head to follow it there, but he could hear its heavy step, smell the air thickening as the curtains rustled ever so softly and the shadow fell across his face.

He was suddenly, acutely aware of his manhood, of a warmth and tingling that grew along with his terror. It was as if something were touching him, something soft.

He lifted his eyes and saw her. His heart expanded like his lungs, and it was exquisitely painful.

Her hair was effulgent copper, so bright that it burned through his lids when he closed them. Her smile was wicked and erotic and beautiful, and her eyes were like jewels of a bright but unknown color. Taken together, her face was so terrifying and so glorious that he could bear it for only an instant.

His entire body shook with unfamiliar sensations as she pressed down upon him, her flesh melting on him like butter and honey, and still he couldn't move.

My child, my man, my lover, she crooned in a voice that was no more a voice than her features formed a face.

You will know me.

He awoke gasping or, rather, with the sensation of gasping. There was no sound.

Ehan's face resolved, as did Henne's. He was back in the boat, and he could move again.

And he remembered something, something important.

"What river is this?" he asked, feeling the words but not hearing them. Ehan saw his lips move and looked angry, touching his ears.

Stephen pointed to the river. The stream they had started on was probably a tributary, but they were on a river of some size now, bounded by substantial banks.

"Is this the Ef River or some tributary?"

Ehan frowned, then mouthed a word that looked like Ef.

Stephen sat up. How long had he been asleep?

"Are we near Whitraff?" he asked. "How far are we from Whitraff?" He exaggerated the shape of the words, but Ehan's puzzled expression wasn't replaced by anything else.

Exasperated, Stephen started working at the cords of one of the oiled leather bags, digging around for parchment and ink. It was stupid to have to waste parchment like this, but he couldn't think of any other way.

The ink wasn't where he thought it was, and by the time he found it, houses were becoming suspiciously common along the banks of the river. Desperately, working on his knees, he scribbled out the message.

*There is a monster near Whitraff village, a nicwer. It lives
in the water. It is very dangerous.*

He passed the note to Ehan. The little man blinked, nodded, and gestured for Stephen to take his oar. Then he went
back to the tiller to talk to Henne.

Or gesture at him, rather. When he showed Henne
Stephen's note, Henne merely shrugged. Ehan pointed
toward the bank.

Around the bend, Stephen saw the familiar buildings of
Whitraff coming into view. Aspar, Winna, Ehawk, Leshya,
and he had been there less than two months before and had
barely survived the nicwer's attentions.

Henne steered them over to one of the ruined docks,
where Ehan began trying to explain to him by signs what
was the matter. Stephen searched the waters for any indica-
tion of the beast but couldn't make anything out.

It was difficult to argue without words, but Henne pointed to
the river and then held his hands about a handspan apart. Then
he pointed in the direction they had come and stetched his hand
as far apart as he could. After a bit more pantomime, Stephen
gathered that the gist of Henne's sentiment was that whatever
might be lurking in the waters around Whitraff, it couldn't possibly be as bad as the woorm, and their best chance of outrun-
ning the woorm was on the river. So despite Stephen's
warning, a few moments later they were back on the water.

They passed the ruins of Whitraff without incident, however.

Stephen wondered once again where Aspar and Winna
were. Had they come looking for him? Winna would want
to. Aspar might, although if he was beginning to sense
Stephen's feelings for Winna, he might *not*. In any event,
both were bound to do whatever Anne Dare commanded,
and she needed every knife, sword, and bow she could get if
she meant to retake her throne.

Maybe Winna had come after him alone. After all, she had
set out alone to find Aspar. But then again, she loved Aspar,
or thought she did.

To Stephen it seemed a bit ridiculous. Aspar was two decades Winna's senior. She would spend her middle years wiping the drool from his face. Would he give her children? Stephen couldn't imagine that, either. The holter was admirable in most ways, but not in the ways that make for a good husband.

Then again, Stephen wasn't really any better, was he? If he *really* loved Winna, he would be searching for her right now, eager to be at her side. And he wanted to be, he really did. But he wanted this more: to unravel the mysteries of language and time.

That was why he was doing this; not because the fratrex had asked him to, not because he feared the woorm, not even because he believed he could prevent whatever new horror was to be released upon the world, but because he had to *know.*

They never saw the nicwer. Perhaps it had died of its wounds; perhaps it simply had become wary of men. Maybe it could sense that its prey couldn't hear its deadly song.

But the next day, when fish began floating to the surface of the river, Stephen reckoned that maybe the nicwer knew when to make way for its better.

CHAPTER FOURTEEN

WAR COUNCIL

ANNE HAD SEEN the great hall of Glenchest many times. Sometimes it had been empty when she and her sisters had sneaked into it to enjoy the echos that boomed in the dark and the cavernous reaches of its high-arched roof. On other occasions she had witnessed it full of light, glittering with decorations, packed with lords in elegant suits and ladies in dazzling gowns.

She had never seen it full of warriors before.

Elyoner had ordered a huge, long table brought in, and a large armchair placed at the head of it.

That was where Anne sat now, feeling uncomfortable, staring around at the faces, trying to fit names even to the familiar ones. She wished she had paid more attention at her father's court, but there was nothing to do about it now.

The men—and they were *all* men, all thirty-two of them—looked back at her, some staring frankly, others averting their gaze when they thought she was looking. But she knew that all of them were studying her, probing her, trying to figure her out.

She was wondering what to say when Artwair stood up and bowed.

"May I, Your Majesty?" he asked, gesturing at the assembly.

"Please," she said.

He nodded, then raised his voice.

"Welcome, all of you," he said, and the murmur of voices receded. "You all know me. I'm a plain man, not given to long speeches, especially at times like this. This is a time for spears, not words, but I reckon a few words have to be spoken to gather the spears together.

"Here's what it comes down to, as I see it. Not a year ago, our liege, king, and emperor was murdered, and so were two of his daughters. Now, whether that was Black Robert's work I don't know, but I do know that Crotheny had a king, a perfectly legitimate one, and now an usurper sits the throne. I might be still for that, but he's invited Hansa in for a visit and offered them our former queen, Muriele. You all know what that means."

"Maybe we do and maybe we don't," one fellow shouted back. He was of medium build, with a hairline crept halfway back to the crown of his skull and startling blue eyes. "Maybe peace with Hansa is all it means."

"And maybe the crows only perch on the dead to give 'em

blessings and pay respects, auy, Lord Kenwulf? I know you're not so foolish as that, my lord."

Kenwulf shrugged reluctantly. "Who knows *what* Robert has planned? The praifec endorses him. It might be we know too little about his designs. Maybe they only seem sinister from afar. And you have to admit—no offense to Archgreffess Anne—that we might ask for a better sovereign than Charles."

"I think we all understand your point about Charles," Artwair agreed. "The saints chose to touch him, and I'm sure even his mother would allow that the throne does not suit him. But there is another legitimate heir to the throne, and she sits right here."

Most of the gazes had gone to Artwair, but now they returned to Anne, sharper and hungrier than ever.

A portly man with shockingly red hair and black eyes heaved himself to his feet.

"May I speak on that, my lord?"

"By all means, Lord Bishop," Artwair replied.

"King William did manage to persuade the Comven to legislate the article that would allow a woman to take the throne. But this is something that has never actually been done before. It has never been *tested*. The only reason such a thing was ever considered was, in fact, young Charles' condition.

"By the older, more established rule, if the son proved unfit to be king, the crown would pass to his son, which, of course, Charles does not have. Failing that, the crown quite legitimately goes to Robert as the only remaining male heir."

"Yes, yes," a sallow-faced man interrupted testily. Anne remembered him as the Greft of Dealward. "But Lord Bishop, you leave out the fact that we had our doubts not only about Charles but about Robert, as well. That was why we voted as we did."

"Yes," Bishop acknowledged, "but some would argue it were better to have a devil on the throne than an untested girl, especially in times like these."

"When devils roam freely, you mean?" Artwair asked drily. "You would have evil inside *and* outside the walls?"

The man shrugged. "The rumors about Robert grow darker. I've even heard that he doesn't bleed as other men. But we have heard things about Anne, as well. The praifec himself has condemned her as a shinecrafter, the product of education in a coven turned wholly to evil.

"And the stories we hear of her actions at Dunmrogh are . . . disturbing," he added.

Anne felt an odd dislocation then, as if she were watching the proceedings from far, far away. Could they be talking about her? Could things have become so twisted?

Or *were* they twisted? She'd been to only one coven, the Coven Saint Cer. It was true that her education had been in such subjects as poison and murder. Wasn't that evil? And the things she could do—*had* done—wouldn't they qualify as shinecraft?

What if the praifec was right, and . . .

No.

"If you wish to accuse me of something, Lord Bishop, please have the decency to address me directly," Anne heard herself say. She suddenly felt distilled back into her body, and she leaned forward from the makeshift throne.

"Was Virgenya Dare a shinecrafter because she wielded the power of the saints?" she continued. "The man who accuses me, Praifec Hespero—I have evidence, a letter, in fact, that proves he was in league with churchmen who participated in a pagan abomination and performed cruel murder in the process. If you have heard anything of Dunmrogh, you know it was not I who nailed men, women, and children to wooden posts and disemboweled them.

"It was not I who chanted over that innocent blood to awaken some horrible demon. But my companions and I stopped them and their hideous rite. So perhaps, Lord Bishop—and all of you—well, perhaps I *am* a shinecrafter. Perhaps I am evil. But if that is the case, then there is no good here at all, for certainly the praifec and those churchmen who attend him do not serve the holy saints.

"Nor does my uncle Robert. He will give our country over to the darkest forces you can imagine, and you all know it. That's why you're here."

She sat back and, in the momentary silence that followed, felt her sudden burst of confidence waver. But then another of the men she recognized—Sighbrand Haergild, the Marhgreft of Dhaerath—chuckled loudly.

"The lady has a tongue in her," he said to the assemblage. He stood, a lean old man who somehow reminded her of the trees on the coast cliffs, an oak shaped by wind and spray, with wood as hard as iron.

"I'll admit that I'm the first to wonder if a woman ought to be sovereign," he said. "I opposed William's campaign and the Comven's decision. And yet here we are, and it is done. I don't understand all this talk of shinecraft and saints. The only saint I've ever trusted is the one who lives in my sword.

"But I *have* spent my whole life staring across the Dew River at Hansa. I've borne the brunt of the marchland plotting, and I would not see William's wife wed to a Hansan, would not see one of *them* sit on even a chamber pot in Eslen. Robert has certainly gone mad to make any deal with the Reiksbaurgs, and that's proof enough to me that William was right, that the only hope for Crotheny lies in this girl.

"I think it no coincidence that her sisters were murdered on the same day as William, do you?" He stared around the room, and none responded to his challenge. "No, Black Robert was clearing his path to the throne."

"We don't know that," Kenwulf cautioned. "It might as easily have been she who arranged all that." He pointed at Anne.

That struck through her like a bolt.

"What . . . did . . . you say?" she managed to choke out.

"I'm not—I'm just saying, lady, for all we know—I'm not actually accusing . . ."

Anne pushed herself to her feet, acutely aware of the sudden throbbing in her arms and legs.

"Here I look you in the eye, Lord Kenwulf, and I tell you that I had *nothing* to do with the death of my family. The very idea is obscene. I have been hounded by the same murderers over half this world. But *you* look in my eye. Then you do the same with my uncle and see who holds your gaze and does not blink."

She felt a sort of rushing in her ears and heard the cackle of demonic laughter somewhere behind her.

No, she thought. Would even so many men be enough to protect her? Probably not . . .

She suddenly realized that she was sitting again, and Austra was offering her water. She also felt as if she had missed something. Everyone was staring at her with concerned expressions.

"—injuries sustained both at Dunmrogh and in an assassination attempt here in Glenchest three nights ago," Artwair was saying. "She is weak yet, and vile slanders such as Lord Kenwulf conceives do her no good, I assure you."

"I never meant—" Kenwulf sighed. "I apologize, Your Highness."

"Accepted," Anne said frostily.

"Now that that's done," Artwair said, "let's get back to the point, shall we? Lords, Marhgreft Sighbrand speaks the truth, doesn't he?

"Most of you are here because you are already convinced of what we must do. I am most familiar with this sort of bickering, and I know its root. I also know we do not have time for it. Here is my suggestion, my lords. Each of you speak—in plain king's tongue—what advantage you desire from Her Majesty once she has been placed on the throne. I think you will find her fair and generous in her treatment of her allies. We will begin with you, Lord Bishop, if you please."

The rest of the day was a Black Mary for Anne. She hardly understood most of the requests; well, she *understood* them, but not their importance. The Greft of Roghvael, for instance, asked for a reduction on the tax on the trade of rye, which Artwair advised her to deny him, giving him instead a seat on the Comven. Lord Bishop's desire was for a position and title in the emperor's household, an hereditary one. This—again at Artwair's behest—she granted.

And so it went. That brief moment when she had felt something like a queen had vanished, and she was once again a little girl who hadn't done her lessons. For all she knew, she was making Artwair the king, and given what her aunt had said about trusting relatives, that was no idle worry.

But she also knew that by herself she could never organize something so complicated as a war.

The proceedings ended only because Artwair declared a break for the night. Elyoner had prepared an entertainment for the guests, but Anne avoided that, sending Austra to the kitchen for some soup and wine and retiring to her quarters.

Neil MeqVren went with her.

"Did you understand any of that?" she asked him once they were seated.

"Not a lot, I'm afraid," he admitted. "War was much simpler where I come from."

"What do you mean?"

"My family served Baron Fail. If he told us to go and fight someplace, we did, because that's what we did. There wasn't much more to it, thank goodness."

"I suppose I imagined I would make some sort of speech about right and wrong and the honor of fighting for the throne, and men would just fall in line." She sighed.

Neil smiled. "That might work for a battle. Not for a war, I think. Then again, I mostly know battles. And I thought you did quite well, you know."

"But not well enough."

"No, at least not yet. It's one thing, I suppose, to ask men to risk their lives. It's quite another to ask them to risk their families, their lands, their aspirations, their dreams . . ."

"Most of them are just greedy, I think."

"There's that, too," Neil granted. "But the fact is, there's a very good chance we're going to lose this war, and they all know it. I wish that loyalty to Your Majesty could be enough to make them accept that risk, but—"

"But it isn't. I'm really just a symbol for them, aren't I?"

"Maybe," Neil conceded. "For some of them. Maybe even for most of them. But if you win, you'll be queen in fact as well as in name. In that case, you can even let Artwair or whoever advises you make all the important decisions. But I don't think that's how things will go. I think you will lean only until you can stand."

Anne stared down at her lap.

"I never wanted this at all, you know," she said faintly. "I only wanted to be left alone."

"That's not really your choice," Neil said. "Not anymore. I'm not sure it ever was."

"I know that," Anne said. "Mother tried to explain it to me. I didn't understand then. Maybe I don't now, but I'm starting to."

Neil nodded. "You are," he agreed. "And for that I'm sorry."

CHAPTER FIFTEEN

✤

AN AMBUSH

WINNA LOST her mind within a bell of entering the Halafolk rewn.

Aspar had noticed her breath coming quicker and quicker, but suddenly she began choking, trying to talk but not getting any words out. She sat heavily on an upjut of stone and rested there, quaking, rubbing her shoulders, trying to find her breath.

He couldn't blame her. The cavern had become a charnel house, a place of death on a scale that paled anything Aspar had ever seen. The dead lay embanked on either side of a river of blood, and it was easy to imagine what had happened: the woorm crawling along, the slinders throwing themselves at it from either side, tearing at its armor with bare fingers and teeth. Those who weren't crushed by its passage had succumbed to its poison.

Of course, they weren't all dead yet; a few still were moving. He and Winna had tried to help the first few, but they were so clearly beyond all hope that they now just avoided them. Most didn't even seem to see them, and blood ran freely from their mouths and nostrils. He could tell from the way they breathed that something was wrong inside, in their lungs. Surely it was too late for the Sefry medicine to have any effect. Anyway, he and Winna needed what was left.

If they came across Stephen or Ehawk . . .

"Stephen!" Aspar shouted into the hollowness. "Ehawk!"

The two of them might be anywhere. It could take months to find them if they were among the dead.

Aspar put his hand on Winna's shoulder. She was trembling, mumbling.

"We're . . . we're not . . ."

Over and over again.

"Come on," he told her. "Come on, Winn; let's get out of this place."

She looked up at him, her eyes filled with greater despair than he had imagined her capable of.

"We can't get out," she said softly. Then something seemed to explode in her. "We *can't* get out!" she shrieked. "Don't you understand? We can't get out! We've been here! We've already been here, and it just gets worse and worse, everything, we're . . . we're not . . ." Her words tapered off into an incoherent wail.

He held her shoulders, knowing all he could really do was wait until it passed.

If it passed.

With a sigh he sat next to her.

"I've been in this rewn before," he said, not sure if she was listening. "It's not much farther to the city. We could— it should be cleaner there. You could rest."

She didn't answer. Her teeth were gritted and her eyes squeezed shut, and her breath was still racing with her heartbeat.

"That's it," Aspar said. He picked her up. She didn't resist but buried her head in the crook of her arm and wept.

He dithered briefly, torn between continuing on and going back, but then it struck him how utterly stupid it would be to go after Fend and a woorm, carrying Winna all the while. True, he might hide her in the Sefry city, but that might be exactly where Fend and his pet had come to a stop. With his luck, the instant he left to look for them, Fend would sneak in from behind and make off with Winna again.

So he started back the way they had come.

The woorm had gone into the rewn; it had to come out. Aspar knew of only three entrances to the rewn: this one, another many leagues north, and a third just over the next ridge.

And suddenly he had a plan that made sense.

The horses were still outside—and alive—when he exited the cave. He got Winna up onto Tumble, made sure she had enough awareness to stay on, then took the horses' reins to lead them. They started winding their way up the hillside.

Half a league up, he felt his breath coming easier and he started to sweat, even though it was bitterly cold. His step strengthened, and at first he thought it was just that he had removed himself from the woorm's venomed trail.

Then he realized it was more than that. He was surrounded by life again, by sap that was slow but not dead. Squirrels scampered through the branches above, and a flight of fluting geese sang by high overhead. He watched them, smiling in spite of himself, but felt a slight chill as they suddenly changed course.

"There we are," he said, urging Ogre up the slope in the direction the geese had avoided. "It's there, just as I thought."

Two bells later, about a bell before sunfall, they reached the top of the ridge. Winna had calmed, and Aspar got her down, then situated her in the roots of a big tree. Reluctantly, he left the horses saddled, because for all he knew they might have to bolt at any moment. Could a horse outrun a woorm? Maybe for a little while.

"Winna?" He knelt and tucked another blanket around her.

"I'm sorry," she whispered. It was faint and she didn't sound good, but it lifted the strongest fear off his heart: that her spirit had gone away. He had known such things to happen; he'd rescued a boy whose family had been slaughtered by the Black Wargh. He'd left the lad in the care of a widow in Walker's Bailey. She'd tried to take care of him, but he never spoke, not for two years, and then he drowned himself in the mill creek.

"These are mirk and horrible things," Aspar said. "I would be more worried if they *didn't* upset you."

"I was more than upset," she said. "I was—useless."

"Hush. Listen, I'm going to climb up for a better view. You stay here, watch Ogre. If something's coming, he'll know before you do. Can you do that?"

"Yah," Winna said. "I can do that."

He kissed her, and she answered with a sort of desperate hunger. He knew he ought to say something, but nothing seemed right.

"I won't go far" was what he settled on.

He'd taken them up to a section of the ridge too rocky to support many trees. For his watchtower he chose a honey locust perched on the edge of a broken stone shelf. From there he'd be able to see down to this new entrance to the rewn. Though he couldn't make out the opening itself, he was close enough that he would be able to see the monstrous serpent-thing should it appear.

Looking the other way, he had an even better view. The River Ef wound through a pleasant valley checkered with pastures and orchards. On a rise about a league away he made out the bell tower of the monastery where Stephen had been headed when first they had met. The last time Aspar had been here, he'd been wounded and half out of his mind, and if it hadn't been for Stephen, he would have died.

At the moment the valley looked peaceful in the twilight, cloaked in a slight mist drifting through the neat rows of apple trees where they waited for spring's kiss to bud them.

Where was Stephen now? Dead, probably, since he had been with the slinders. Ehawk was probably dead, too.

He ought to feel something, *had* felt something back when he saw the boys fall. But his heart had tightened up inside him, and the only emotion he recognized was anger.

That was a good thing, he reckoned.

Night seeped down through the clouds, and as the world his eyes knew faded, the deeper domain of scent and sound intensified. Winter sounds were spare: the chilling shrill of a screech owl, the wind catching its belly on bony branches, the scuff of small claws on bark.

Smell was the more palpable sense: leaves steeping in cold pools, the smell of rot kept slow by cold, the grassy scent of cow dung from the pastures below, and smoke—hickory and old apple burning down in the valley, wormy witaec when the wind shifted from the Midenlands, and something nearer—oak, yes, but he also made out the minty scent of sassafras, sumac, and huckleberry: understory plants.

And pine kindling.

He strained his ears and heard the faint ticking and popping of a fire. It was downslope, not too far away.

He eased out of the tree, afraid to breathe. If there was a monk down there who had walked the same faneway as Stephen . . .

Then they already would have heard him, probably. The Order of Mamres—from which most of their churchish enemies had come—fought like mad lions but did not have senses any sharper than his. It was they who had walked the faneways of both Decmanus and Mamres who presented the greatest danger.

He found Winna sleeping and again had a moment's indecision, but the fear of leaving her unguarded was overridden by the need to know who was just down the hill. Besides, Ogre was still there; he would at least create a fuss, even in his weakened state, if someone came around.

He began his slow creep down the slope, going hand to

hand and foot to foot with shrubs and small trees that clung to stone and shallow earth. He wasn't in a hurry; he reckoned he had all night. That was good, since he had to move by feel and instinct.

He reckoned it was two or three bells past midnight when he finally saw the touch of orange glow on a tree trunk below. He couldn't make out the fire itself, but he could guess where it was. He knew he'd come down too far east, with a sheer drop keeping him from getting the position he wanted.

So he worked his way back uphill and west. The glimpse of light vanished, but he knew where he was going now, and shortly before sunup he found it.

By then the fire was mostly embers, with just a few licks of flame. Aspar could make out someone sitting and someone lying flat but not much more. The campsite was about twelve kingsyards below him, beneath a long, shallow rock shelter.

Would he be able to get a clear shot at them? The angle was bad.

The clouds were gone, but there was no moon, only the distant, unhelpful lamps of the stars. Maybe when the sun cracked his eye, Aspar would be able to find a better position. He settled in to wait, hoping Winna didn't wake and panic. He didn't think she would, but after today . . .

The earth below him was rumbling.

He heard a stone crack and then the sudden rush of rocks sliding down a slope. It wasn't close, but it wasn't far, either.

Quickly he heard the rush and roar of breathing and smelled the faint, sickening scent of its breath.

As he'd thought, the woorm had gone through the rewn and was now exiting on the Ef side of the hill. That meant it was about a quarter of a league to his left.

He still couldn't see it, though he could easily hear it moving down the slope and toward the valley floor.

"There she is," an unfamiliar male voice said. He had a funny northern-sounding accent.

"I told you," a second man answered.

That voice wasn't unfamiliar at all. It was Fend, which was what Aspar had more than half expected. After all, it was all well and good to ride a woorm when it was traveling over open ground, but when your mount burrowed into a cave, you didn't really want to be on it. Nor would it have been safe riding through a sea of hostile slinders. No, Fend was smarter than that.

The woorm was moving away from him now. Fend was just below.

First things first.

Aspar felt about for a ledge, a branch, anything to allow him the perspective for a clear shot. To his delight, he found a jut of stone he hadn't known was there. Carefully—very carefully—he let himself onto it belly first, then put an arrow to the string.

"Should we follow it down?" the unknown voice said.

Fend laughed shortly. "The Revesturi won't all flee. Some of them will fight."

"Against the waurm?"

"Remember who they are. The Revesturi know some very old faneways and some very potent sacaums. It's true that none of them is likely to be able to slay our little lovely, but imagine what sort of sacaum they might attempt in the effort."

"Ah. So once again it's better for us to stay out of the way."

"Precisely. If all goes well, the creature will slay the Revesturi, and if the Darige boy is there, it will bring him to us. But if the priests have some surprise in store . . ."

Aspar froze at the mention of Stephen.

"What if Darige is slain in the process?"

"They no more wish him dead than we do," Fend replied. "But if it happens, it happens."

"*He* won't like it."

"No, he won't—it would certainly be a serious setback. But *only* a setback."

Aspar listened carefully, anxious to catch their every word. Why would Fend be after Stephen? How could a monster like the woorm "bring him"? In its mouth? Who in

Grim's name were the Revesturi, and *who did Fend work for*?

One of the two figures poked at the fire, and it suddenly flared brighter, providing enough light for him to locate Fend's face. Aspar sighted down the arrow, his breathing slow and controlled. This was a shot he could make—of that he had no doubt. And Fend, finally, would be dead.

There was a chance that Fend's death might leave some unanswered questions, but he'd just have to take that chance. Whoever the fellow with him was, he seemed to know who their master was. A second shaft would wound him but leave him alive to provide the answers.

Then Aspar would take the antidote and cure himself, Winna, and the horses. When the woorm returned, he'd have the Church's arrow for that. And maybe Stephen would be with it.

He drew back the string.

Something flashed in his peripheral vision, a purple light.

Fend saw it, too, and straightened.

Everything went white as Aspar released the string. His eyes closed reflexively, and he heard Fend cry out in pain. He tried to open his eyes, to see . . .

Something struck the mountain like a fist. His belly went queer, and he suddenly realized that the rock he was lying on was sliding out from under him. He was falling.

He flailed, trying to find something to grab, but there was nothing, and he fell for the space of a whole breath before he hit something that bent, broke, and let him keep falling until he fetched hard against a boulder.

He opened his eyes without knowing how long they had been closed. His mouth tasted like dust, and his eyes were full of grit. His ears were ringing as if thunder had just clapped a tree a yard away. He was looking at his hand, which was illuminated by a pale gray light.

Someone nearby was screaming. That was what had wakened him.

He raised his head, but all he saw was a confusion of

crumpled vegetation. He hurt everywhere, but he couldn't tell if anything was broken.

The screaming dropped off to harsh panting.

"That's got it," he heard the strange voice say. "The bleeding's bad."

"Keep an eye out for him," Fend's voice instructed tersely.

"That was Aspar. I know bloody well it was, and you'll never hear him coming, not after that."

Aspar allowed himself a tight grin. He'd lost the bow in the fall, but he still had his dirk and ax. Grimacing, he pulled himself to his feet.

That sent a dizziness through him that nearly sat him back down, but he waited through it, breathing as deeply as he could. Fend was right; he could hear their voices—barely—but the belling in his ears would hush over the small sounds of someone creeping up on him.

Now, where exactly were they? He took a step in what he thought was the right direction and for an instant thought he had caught a glimpse of someone ahead, but the light was still dim.

He was starting to move closer when someone grabbed him from behind and wrapped a forearm across his face. He grunted and tried to throw him off, but he was already off balance and he fell rather heavily with his face pressed against the earth. He twisted and kicked, vaguely aware that the ground was shuddering, and a face came into view. It was a familiar face, but not Fend's.

Ehawk.

The boy pressed a finger to his lips and pointed.

Four kingsyards away a massive wall of scale was sliding though the trees.

PART III

✢

THE BOOK OF RETURN

Nothing is ever destroyed, though often they are changed. Some things may be lost for a very long time, it is true—but the waters beneath the world will eventually carry them home.
—FROM THE *Ghrand Ateiiz, or The Book of Return,*
    AUTHOR ANON.

Each fane I visited robbed me of some sense—feeling, hearing, sight, sound, and eventually self. But in the end it all came back, and more, much more.
—FROM *The Codex Tereminnam,* AUTHOR ANON.

CHAPTER ONE

LABYRINTH

ALIS MEANT to cut the man's spine just below his skull, but her fatigue-numbed feet slipped on the slick stone, and the point of her dagger plunged into his collarbone instead.

He screamed and whirled around. She had just enough presence of mind to duck his flailing arms, but his booted foot caught her in the shins, and she gasped as pain shot jagged lines across her vision and she stumbled back into the wall.

He hadn't dropped his lantern, and they peered at each other in its sanguinary light.

He was a large man—over six feet—all in black, one of the usurper's Nightstriders. His face was surprisingly feminine for such a big fellow, with a gently tapered chin and round cheeks.

"Bitch," he snarled, drawing his knife.

Behind him a girl—she might have been eleven—cowered against the wall.

Alis tried to summon the shadow; sometimes it was easy, like snapping a finger inside her head, and sometimes it was very hard, especially when someone had already seen her.

It didn't come immediately, and she didn't have time to work at it. So she blew out her breath and let her shoulders sag, let her knife hand drop to her side.

He in turn relaxed for an instant, and with what remained of her strength she struck, launching from the wall, her empty left hand snapping toward his face. She felt a liquid, parting sensation as she plunged her knife into his left side and worked it in and out.

He shrieked again, and a fist clubbed against her head, but she kept pumping the blade until her hand was so slick with blood that she couldn't keep her grip on the weapon. Then she pushed herself away, gasping, and felt a weird wrenching in her arm. She realized that her arm *hurt,* that she had been cut, too. She backed into the shadows.

Despite his wounds, the man didn't stop, either. He lumbered after her, and she ran, feeling her way through the dark, until she reached the mouth of the tunnel. She ducked into it, hearing only the whine of her breath, then tugged at her breeches, trying to tear a piece to tie on her arm. She couldn't get it to rip, so she just clamped her hand over the wound and waited.

She could still make out the glow of firelight around the corner; he was there, waiting.

She needed that knife to cut a strip of cloth. She couldn't wait much longer, either, or she would lose so much blood that she wouldn't be able to do anything at all.

Cursing under her breath, she rose unsteadily and minced back toward the light.

He was lying facedown, and something about his position suggested to her that he wasn't faking. The lamp had fallen but hadn't shattered; it lay on its side guttering, nearly out. She propped it up. He'd dropped his knife, too, and hers was still poking out from between his ribs.

Trying not to faint, Alis took his knife and carefully drove it into his spine, as she had intended to do earlier.

That drew a gasp from beside the stairs. Then a whimper.

The girl. She had forgotten the girl.

"Stay there," Alis said tersely. "Stay just where you are or I'll kill you like I killed him."

The girl didn't answer; she just continued whimpering.

Alis righted the lantern, cut a piece of her breeches, tied a tourniquet, then sat down to catch her breath and listen. Had anyone heard the Nightstrider scream? If they had, would they be able to determine where it came from?

Eventually, yes. That meant she needed to get back into the tunnels, the ones men couldn't remember. They would have a hard time following her there.

"Girl, listen to me," she said.

A face peered up from the bundle of gray cloth.

"I don't want to die," she said softly.

"Do what I ask, and I promise you that you will live," Alis told her.

"But you killed him."

"Yes, I did. Will you listen to me?"

A small pause.

"Yes."

"Good. Do you have food? Water? Wine?"

"Reck has some food, I think. He had some bread earlier. And wine, I think."

"Then get it for me. And anything else he has on him. But don't try to run. You've heard how knives can be thrown?"

"I saw a man on the street do it once. He split an apple."

"I can do better than that. If you try to run, I'll put this right in your back. Do you understand?"

"Yes."

"What's your name?"

"Ellen."

"Ellen, do what I asked you. Get his things and bring them here."

She watched the girl approach the body. When she touched him, she began to cry.

"Did you like him?" Alis asked.

"No. He was mean. But I've never seen someone dead."

And I've never killed anyone before, Alis thought. Despite her training, it still didn't seem real.

"Ellen," Alis asked, "do all the guards have girls with them?"

"No, lady. Only the Nightstriders."

"And what are you doing with them, exactly?"

The girl hesitated.

"Ellen?"

"The king says there are secret tunnels down here, tunnels

that only girls can see. We're supposed to find them for him. The men are to protect us."

"Protect you from me?" Alis asked, feigning a little smile.

Ellen's eyes gleamed with terror. "N-no," she stuttered. "The king said a murderer was loose in the dungeons. A man. A big man."

Ellen had worked as she spoke and had assembled a little pile of things. She picked them up but seemed more reluctant to approach Alis than she had the dead man, which made good sense.

"There," Alis said. "Good girl."

"Please," Ellen whispered. "I won't tell."

Alis hardened her heart. The only advantage she had was Robert's belief that she was dead. If the girl described her—or, worse, knew who she was—that advantage would be lost. She tightened her grip on the knife.

"Just come here," Alis told her.

Blinking away tears, the girl approached.

"Do it quick, please," Ellen said, so low that Alis almost couldn't hear.

Alis looked into the young woman's eyes, imagined the life going out of them, and sighed. She gripped her shoulder and felt it trembling.

"Keep your word, Ellen," she said. "Don't tell anyone you saw me. Just say he excused himself to answer nature's demands, and then you found him dead. I swear by all the saints it is the right thing to do."

Ellen's face shone with wary hope.

"You won't throw the knife at me?"

"No. Just tell me how you came into the dungeons."

"Through the Arn Tower stair."

"Right," Alis muttered. "Is it still guarded?"

"By ten men," Ellen confirmed.

"Is there anything else you know that might help me?"

The girl thought for a moment. "They're filling the dungeons in," she said.

Alis nodded wearily. She already knew that, too.

"Go on," Alis told her. "Find your way out."

Ellen stood and took a few trembling steps, then ran. Alis listened to her skittering footfalls recede, knowing she should have killed the girl—and glad she hadn't.

Then she turned her attention to the Nightstrider's things.

He didn't have much; after all, he hadn't come down there to stay. It was more luck than anything else that he'd had a kerchief with a piece of hard bread and cheese wrapped in it and greater luck still that he'd brought a wineskin. She took those items, his knife, a leather strap from his baldric, the lamp, and his tinderbox.

Alis had a little bread and wine, then hauled herself up and returned to the relative safety of the ancient passageway.

When she felt she was far enough away, she stopped and dressed her arm again. The wound wasn't as bad as she feared; the knife had been forced into the two bones of her forearm and had lodged there until she tore free. That was why he hadn't been able to stab her again and again, as she had him, or turn the knife in the wound.

Yes, this had been, all things considered, a lucky day. Or night. She no longer had the faintest sense of when it was.

She reckoned it had been more than a nineday that she'd been trapped down there. But it might be more than twice that, since she had gone there to free Leovigild Ackenzal.

It was probably best that he had refused to accompany her. On her way back out of the dungeons she'd found that the passage was heavily guarded. That wasn't good, because it meant her presence had been detected, and it was the only sure way she knew to get out.

Even so, the labyrinth of passages obvious and obscure was so baroque that there had to be another point of egress. She wondered how they knew she had entered the dungeons, but Prince Robert wasn't stupid. And due to his . . . condition . . . he was able to remember the hidden ways. He must have posted guards or set up some sort of alarm. Possibly Hespero or some other churchman had helped with that, but it may have been as simple as flour on the floor to record her tracks. She had been moving in darkness, after all, and wouldn't have seen it.

For the last nine days the usurper had been finding the passages and blocking them up. The dungeons shuddered with the work of royal engineers, mining and sapping.

There were plenty of passages that he hadn't found, but none of them seemed to go anywhere except back to the dungeon. And the dungeon was being systematically filled in and closed off, at least those sections which might allow her access to the castle. One whole section—complete with prisoners—had been sealed off already. Those trapped there weren't dead yet; sometimes she could still hear them pleading for food and water. Their cries were getting weaker, though. She wondered what they had done to end up in the dungeon in the first place and whether they deserved their fate.

Feeling a little better as the food dissolved in her belly, she headed back into the depths. There was one area of the dungeons she had avoided, hoping against hope that she wouldn't have to brave it, even though it was one place Robert dare not cut off entirely. But she could no longer bow to that fear; the food she'd just taken was probably the last she would get. Whether Ellen said anything or not, a Nightstrider was dead, and Robert doubtless would increase the size of his patrols.

She had lived until now by taking scraps from prisoners, and she'd had a fresh source of water up until two days before, when the walls had blocked it off. Now the only water she had access to was dirty and diseased. She knew that mixing the wine with it would allow her to drink it for a while, but the wine would last only for a few days at best.

From here on out, she would only get weaker.

So she turned toward the whispering.

It wasn't like the voices of the prisoners. At first she'd thought it was her own thoughts, talking to her, a sign that she was going mad. The voice didn't make much sense, at least not in words, but what words it spoke were freighted with images and sensations that did not belong in a human head.

But then she remembered a trip to the dungeons with Muriele and knew that the voice she heard was that of the Kept.

The Kept was called that to avoid naming what it really was: the last of the demon race that had enslaved both Men and Sefry—the last of the Skasloi.

As she drew nearer to his domain, the whispering grew louder, and images brightened, scents sharpened. Her fingers felt like claws, and when she put her hand against the wall, she felt a rough scraping, as if her hands were made of stone or metal. She smelled something like rotting pears and sulphur, saw in bright flashes a landscape of scaly trees without leaves, a strange and huge sun, a black fortress by the sea so ancient that its walls and spires were weathered like a mountain. Her body felt at turns small and enormous.

I am me, she insisted soundlessly. *Alis Berrye. My father was Walis Berrye; my mother was born Wenefred Vicars* . . .

But her childhood seemed impossibly far away. With effort she remembered the house, a rambling mansion so poorly kept that some rooms had floors that had rotted through. When she tried to picture it, however, she envisioned a stone labyrinth instead.

Her mother's face was a blur surrounded by flaxen hair. Her father was even dimmer, though she had seen him only a year ago. Her elder sister, Rowyne, had blue eyes, like her, and rough hands that stroked her hair.

She'd been five when the lady in the dark dress came and took her away, and after that it was ten years before she saw her parents again, and then they had just been bringing her to Eslen.

Even then they hadn't known the truth of the matter, that the reason she had been returned to them was so that the king would notice her and take her for his mistress.

Her mother died the next year, and her father came to visit two years later, hoping Alis could persuade the king to grant him funds to drain the festering swamp that had crept over most of the canton's once-arable land. William had given him the money and an engineer, and that was the last she had seen of anyone in her family.

Sister Margery with her crooked smile and curly red hair; Sister Grene with her big nose and wide eyes; Elder Mestra Cathmay, iron-haired and whip-thin, with eyes that saw into everything—they had been her family.

All now dead, the voice taunted. *So very dead. And yet death is no longer very distant . . .*

Suddenly there was a sense of floating, and it took Alis a moment to understand that she was *falling,* so many and strange were the sensations that came with the voice.

She put out her arms and legs in a flailing attempt to find something to grab. Incredibly, she succeeded as her palms struck flat against walls before they were half-extended. Pain shot up her arms as if they were trying to yank from her shoulders, and the agony of her wound wrenched a scream out of her. Then she fell again, her knees and elbows scraping against the walls of the shaft until white light blossomed in the soles of her feet and struck up through her, knocking her cleanly out of her body and into the black winds high above.

Singing brought her back, a rough, raspy canting in a language she did not know. Her face was pressed against a damp, tacky floor. When she lifted it, pain shot across her skull and down her spine.

"Oh!" she gasped.

The singing stopped.

"Alis?" A voice asked.

"Who is that?" she answered, feeling her head. It was sticky, and she found a cut at the hairline. None of her bones seemed to be broken.

"It is I, Lo Videicho," the voice replied.

The darkness was absolute, and the walls made strange the sound, but Alis guessed the speaker was no more than four or five kingsyards away. She reached down to her girdle and the dagger she kept there.

"That sounds Vitellian," she said, trying to keep him talking so she would know where he was.

"Ah, no, my *dulcha,*" he said. "Vitellian is vinegar, lemon juice, salt. I speak honey, wine, figs. Safnian, *midulcha.*"

"Safnian." She had the knife now, and securing her grip on it, she sat up. "You're a prisoner?"

"I was," Lo Videicho said. "Now, I do not know. They bricked in the way out. I told them they should kill me, but they did not."

"How do you know my name?"

"You told it to my friend the music man, before they took him away."

Leoff.

"They took him away?"

"Oh, yes. Your visit was quite upsetting, I think. They took him off."

"Where to?"

"Oh, I know. You think I did not know? I know."

"I don't doubt it," Alis said. "But I would like to know, as well."

"I have lost my mind, you understand," Lo Videicho confided.

"You sound fine to me," Alis lied.

"No, no, it's quite true. I am mad. But I think I should wait until we are out of these dungeons before I tell you where our friend was taken."

Alis began feeling around for a wall. She found one and put her back to it.

"I don't know the way out," she said.

"No, but you know the way in."

"The way in is—you mean the way into *here,* don't you?"

"Yes, sly one," Lo Videicho said. "You fell down it."

"Then if you know that, why don't you just leave? Why do you need me?"

"I would never leave a lady," the man said. "But more than that . . ." She heard a metallic rattling.

"Oh. You *can't* leave. You're in a cell." She must have fallen into an anteroom rather than the cell itself.

"It's a palace, *my* palace," Lo Videicho said. "But the doors are all locked. Do you have a key?"

"I might be able to get you out. We might come to some agreement. But first you must tell me why you are here."

"Why am I here? Because the saints are filthy bastards, every one. Because they favor the wicked and bring grief to the kind."

"That's probably true," Alis acknowledged, "but I'd still like a more specific answer."

"I am here because I loved a woman," he said. "I am here because my heart was torn out, and this is the grave they put me in."

"What woman?"

His voice changed. "Beautiful, gentle, kind. She is dead. I saw her finger."

A little chill went up Alis' spine.

Safnian. There had been a Safnian engaged to the princess Lesbeth. She had gone missing, and word was that she had been betrayed by her fiancé. She remembered William mumbling his name in his sleep; it almost seemed he had been apologizing to him.

"Are you . . . are you Prince Cheiso?"

"Ah!" the man gasped. There was a pause, and then she heard a quiet sound she thought might be weeping.

"You are Cheiso, who was betrothed to Lesbeth Dare."

The snuffling grew louder, but now it sounded more like laughter. "That was my name," he said. "Before, before. Yes, how clever. Clever."

"I heard you had been tortured to death."

"He wanted me alive," Cheiso said. "I don't know why. I don't know why. Or maybe he forgot, that's all."

Alis closed her eyes, trying to adjust her thinking, add the Safnian prince to her plans. Did he command troops? But they would have to sail here, wouldn't they? A long way.

But he would surely be useful.

Cheiso shrieked suddenly, a throat-tearing howl of rage that hardly sounded human. She heard a meaty thud and guessed that he was throwing himself against the walls even as he continued to scream in his own language. She realized she was gripping the knife so hard that her fingers were numb.

After a time his shrieks subsided into full-belly sobbing. On impulse, Alis took her hand from the knife and felt her way through the darkness until she encountered the iron bars of his cell.

"Come here," she said. "Come here."

He might kill her, but death was so near, she had begun to lose respect for it. If a moment's kindness was what sent her from the lands of fate, then so be it.

She could feel him hesitate, but then she heard a sliding sound, and a moment later a hand brushed hers. She gripped it, and tears started in her eyes at the contact. It felt like years since anyone had held her. She felt his hand tremble; the palm was smooth and soft, the palm of a prince.

"I am less than a man," he gasped. "I am much less."

Alis' heart gripped; she tried to disengage her hand, but he held it all the tighter.

"It's all right," Alis said. "I only want to touch your face."

"I no longer have a face," he replied, but nevertheless he let her hand go. Tentatively, she reached up until she felt the beard on his cheek, then traced higher, where she found a mass of scars.

So much pain. She reached for her knife again. A single motion into the bowl of his eye and he would forget what they had done to him, forget his lost love. She could hear in his voice and feel in his grip that he was broken. Despite his bravado and talk of revenge, there wasn't much left of him.

But her duty wasn't to him. It was to Muriele and her children—and in a way to poor dead William. She had loved him in her fashion; he had been a decent man in a position no decent man ought to hold.

Like this Safnian prince.

"Prince Cheiso," she whispered.

"I was," he replied.

"You *are*," she insisted. "Listen to me. I will free you from your cage, and together we will find a way out of here."

"And kill him," Cheiso said. "Kill the king."

With a faint prickling she realized he meant William.

"King William is already dead," Alis said. "He is not your enemy. Your enemy is Robert. Do you understand? Prince Robert's word put you here. Then he killed his brother, the king, and left you to rot. He probably doesn't even remember that you exist. But you will remind him, won't you?"

There was a long pause, and when Cheiso finally spoke again, it was in a surprisingly passionless and even voice.

"Yes," he said. "Yes, I will."

Alis drew out her lock-picking tools and set to work.

CHAPTER TWO

THE POEL

ANNE TOOK a few deep breaths, closing her eyes against her tent and its spare furnishings. She'd sent Austra away, and the girl had gone with what had seemed to Anne a sense of relief.

Did the little tart just want to get away from her, or did she want to get *to* Cazio?

Hush, she told herself. *Hush. You're just getting angry with yourself. Small wonder Austra would rather spend time with someone else.*

Anne settled into the darkness and then looked deeper, trying to find her way to the place of the Faiths so she could ask their counsel. In the past she had been wary of their advice, but she felt she needed *something—some guidance from someone who knew more about the recondite world than she.*

Faint light appeared, and she focused on it, trying to draw

it nearer, but it slipped to the edge of her vision, tantalizingly out of reach.

She tried to relax, to coax it back, but the more she tried, the farther off the light drew, until in a sudden rage she reached out for it, yanking it toward her, and the darkness in turn squeezed, tightened until she couldn't breathe.

Something rough seemed to press about her body, and her fingers and toes went numb with cold. The chill crept up her, stealing all sensation until only the pulse of her heart was left, beating dangerously hard. She couldn't draw breath or utter a sound, but she heard laughter and felt lips against her ear, murmuring warm words that she couldn't understand.

Light flared, and suddenly she saw the sea rolling out before her. On the broad waves rode ships by the dozens, flying the black-and-white swan banner of Liery. Her view shifted, and she saw that they were approaching Thornrath, the great seawall fortress that guarded the approach to Eslen. It loomed large enough to make even so vast a fleet seem tiny.

Then, suddenly, the light was gone and she was on her knees, with her hands pressed against stone, the smell of decay and earth in her nostrils. Gradually a faint light sifted down from above, and slowly, as if waking from a dream, she began to understand where she was.

She was in Eslen-of-Shadows, in the sacred grove behind the tombs of her ancestors, and her fingers were pressed against a stone sarcophagus. And she *knew,* was certain that she had always known, and she screamed in the most utter despair she had ever experienced.

Hush, child, a small voice said. *Hush and listen.*

The voice calmed her terror, if only a little.

"Who are you?" she asked.

I am your friend. And you are right; she is coming more for you. I can help, but you must seek me out. You must help me first.

"Who is she? How can you help?"

Too many questions, and the distance is too great. Find me, and I will help you.

"Find you where?"

Here.

She saw Castle Eslen, watched it ripped open like a ca-
daver to expose its hidden organs and humors, nests of dis-
ease and thrones of health, and after a moment she
understood.

She awoke screaming, with Neil and Cazio staring down
at her. Austra was next to her, holding her hand.

"Majesty?" Neil asked. "Is something wrong?"

For several long heartbeats she wanted to tell him, to reverse what was to come.

But she couldn't, could she?

"It was a dream, Sir Neil," she said. "A Black Mary, nothing more."

The knight looked skeptical, but after a moment he accepted her explanation with a nod.

"Well, then, I hope the rest of your sleep is dreamless," he
said.

"How long until we break camp?"

"Four bells."

"And today we shall reach Eslen?"

"If the saints will it, Your Majesty," Neil replied.

"Good," Anne said. Images of ships—and more terrible
things—still burned behind her eyes. Eslen would be the
start of it.

The men left, but Austra remained, stroking her forehead
until she fell asleep.

Anne had made the trip from Glenchest to Eslen many times.
She had ridden there on her horse Faster when she was four-
teen, accompanied by a guard of Craftsmen. That had taken
her two days, with a stop in the Poel of Wife at her cousin
Nod's estate. By carriage or canal, it might take a day longer.

But it had taken her army a full month, even though most
of their supplies were floated downstream on barges.

And a bloody month it had been.

Anne had seen tournaments: jousting, men battering about

with swords, that sort of thing. She had seen real combat, too, and slaughter aplenty. But until the day they marched from Glenchest, everything she knew about armies and war she'd had from minstrels, books, and theater. Those had led her to imagine that they would march straightaway to Eslen, blow the horns of battle, and fight it out on the King's Poel.

The minstrels had left out a thing or two, and Castle Gable had been her first lesson in that.

Armies in songs didn't have to keep their supply lines open so they didn't have to stop and "reduce" every unfriendly fortress within five days' ride of their march. Most of them were unfriendly, it turned out, because Robert had either coerced or cajoled the castle owners to fight for him or had simply occupied them with his own handpicked troops.

Anne had never heard the word "reduce" used to describe the conquering of a castle and the slaughter of its defenders, but she quickly came to the opinion that a better word was needed. The siege of Gable cost them more than a hundred men and almost a week, and when they left it, they had to leave another hundred men behind to garrison it.

Then came Langraeth, Tulg, Fearath . . .

The old songs also didn't talk much about women throwing their children over the walls in an insane attempt to save them from the flames or about the smell of a hundred dead men as the morning frost began to thaw. Or how a man could have a spear all the way through him and appear not to feel it, keep talking as if nothing were wrong, right up until the moment his eyes lost sight and his lips went lazy.

She had seen horrible things before, and these were differences in scale rather than in kind.

But scale made a difference. A hundred dead men were more horrific than a single dead man, as unfair as that might seem to the single fellow.

In ballads, women keened in grief over the loss of their beloved ones. In the march to Eslen, no one close to Anne had died. She didn't keen in grief; instead she lay awake at night, trying to stop the cries of the wounded from her ears, trying not to remember the images of the day. She found that the brandy Aunt Elyoner had sent with her was helpful in that regard.

The minstrels also tended to leave out the drearier aspects of politics: four hours listening to the aithel of Wife drone on about the comparative virtues of dun-colored cows; an entire day spent in the company of the spouse of the Gravwaerd of Langbrim and her not-so-subtle attempts to present her hopelessly dull son as a possible suitor for "someone—not Your Majesty of course, but *someone* of note"; two hours in Penbale watching a production of the musical theater that had "opened the eyes" of the landwaerden to the evils of Robert.

Only the fact that most of the singers were so terribly off-key kept *her* eyes open, though it did leave her wondering what the original could have been like. The only thing amusing in it was the physical portrayal of Robert, which involved a mask made of some sort of gourd and a nose that was noticeably, inappropriately made to resemble another, netherer, body part.

All because occupying the castles wasn't enough; the countryside had to be wooed. Besides drumming up more troops, she had to make sure her canal boats could come and go to Loiyes, which was where her provisions came from. While Artwair and his knights reduced castles, she spent her time visiting the neighboring towns and villages, meeting with the landwaerden, garnering their support, and asking permission to leave behind even more soldiers to watch the dikes and malends that kept them drained. That turned out to be almost as grueling as her flight from Vitellia, although in an entirely different way, a daily march of audiences and dinners with town aithels and gravwaerds, flattering them or frightening them, whichever seemed more likely to work.

In the end most of them were willing to give her passive support—they wouldn't hinder her progress, they would let her leave troops to occupy the birms so the canals couldn't be flooded or chained—but few were willing to relinquish manpower. Over the course of the month only about two hundred joined their forces; that came nowhere near offsetting their losses.

Despite all of that, she somehow had it in the back of her mind that when they reached Eslen, they would still stage the final battle on the poel. What she found instead was what she was looking at now from the birm of the north dike. Artwair, Neil, and Cazio stood beside her.

"Saints," she breathed, not certain what exactly she felt.

There was home: the island of Ynis, her stony skirts draped in fog, her high-peaked hills overlooking Newland, the city of Eslen rising on the greatest of those hills. Within the concentric circles of her walls were the great fortress and palace whose spires seemed to thrust into the lower provinces of heaven. It looked both impossibly huge yet ridiculously tiny from this strange vantage point.

"That's your home?" Cazio asked.

"It is," Anne said.

"I never saw such a place," Cazio said, his voice timbred with awe, something Anne wasn't sure she had ever heard before. Thanks to Elyoner's tutors and Cazio's quick mind, he did so in the king's tongue.

"There is no other place like Eslen," Neil said. Anne smiled, realizing that Neil himself had seen Eslen for the first time less than a year ago.

"But how do we get there?" Cazio asked.

"That will be the problem," Artwair said, scratching his chin absently. "It's the same problem we were always going to face, only multiplied. I had hoped he wouldn't do this."

"I don't understand," Cazio said.

"Well," Anne said, "Ynis is an island in the confluence of two rivers: the Warlock and the Dew. So there is always water around it. The only way to reach Eslen is by boat."

"But we have boats," Cazio asserted.

That was true enough; they still had, in fact, every one of the fifteen barges and seven canal wolves they'd had at the beginning of the journey. There had been no river battle.

"Yes," Anne said. "But normally we'd just be crossing a river, you see. This lake you're looking at now used to be dry land." With a wave of her hand, she indicated the vast body of water that now lay before them.

Cazio frowned. "Maybe I didn't understand you," he said. "Did you say dry land? *Tero arido?*"

"Yes," Anne replied. "Eslen is surrounded by poelen. That's what we call land we've claimed from the water. You've noticed that our rivers and canals all flow above the land, haven't you?"

"Yes," Cazio said. "It seems very unnatural."

"It is. And so when a dike is broken or opened up, it all floods again. But why didn't they wait until we were here, marching across the poel, before they opened it? That way we might have been drowned."

"That would have been too risky," Artwair explained. "If the wind is blowing the wrong way, it can take a long time for the poel to fill, and we might have made it across. This way Robert has made our task very, very difficult."

"Yet we still have our boats," Cazio pointed out.

"Auy," Artwair replied. "But look there, though the mist."

He pointed at the base of the great hill. Anne recognized the shadowy shapes, but Cazio didn't know where to look.

"Are those ships?" he finally asked.

"Ships," Artwair confirmed. "I'll wager that when the fog lifts, we'll see nearly the whole fleet. Warships, Cazio. They couldn't have maneuvered very well in the river channel, but now they've got a lake. We might have slipped across the Dew and set up a beachhead, but now we have to cross all of that, in full view of the imperial fleet."

"Can we?" Cazio asked.

"No," Artwair said.

"There's more than one approach to Eslen, though," Neil said. "What about the south side, the Warlock side? Have they flooded the poelen there, as well?"

"That we don't know, not yet," Artwair admitted. "But even if that side hasn't been flooded, it's a very hard approach. The rinns are difficult to march through and easily defended by a few archers on the heights. And then there are the hills: difficult to take but easy to defend.

"But you're exactly right. We need to send someone around the island. A small group, I think, one that can move quickly, quietly, unseen."

"That sounds like the sort of thing I might be able to do," Cazio volunteered.

"No," Anne, Neil, and Austra said at the same time.

"What good am I otherwise?" the swordsman asked irritably.

"You're an excellent bodyguard," Neil said. "Her Majesty needs you here."

"Besides," Anne said, "you don't know the terrain. I'm sure the duke will have good men chosen for the task."

"Yes," Artwair said. "I'll pick a few parties. But you know Eslen as well as anyone here, Anne. What do you think? Have you any ideas?"

"You've sent word to our kin in Virgenya?"

"Yes," Artwair said. "But the well has been poisoned, you know. Robert's cuveiturs went ahead of us with stories of how your mother was in the process of handing the throne to Liery."

"And yet my uncle would give the country to Hansa. Which would they prefer?"

"Neither, let us hope," Artwair replied. "I've told them that if they fight with you, we can keep a Dare on the throne, one who will lean toward Virgenya. But it's complicated. Many in Virgenya would prefer to see a high king back on their own throne, with no emperor in Eslen to lord over them. Even if he—or she—is one of their own.

"That group reckons that Hansa would be content with Crotheny and let Virgenya go its own way."

"Oh," Anne said.

"Auy. And even if they started today, it would be months before Virgenyan troops could arrive over land, and almost as long by sea, considering that they'd have to sail the Straits of Rusimmi to get here. No, I think we must plan this without counting on Virgenya."

Cazio pointed. "What's that?" he asked.

Anne followed the direction of the Vitellian's finger. A

small craft was approaching, a canal boat flying the colors of Eslen.

"That will be Robert's emissary," Artwair said. "Probably come to arrange a meeting. We might as well see what my cousin has to say before we make too many plans."

As the boat approached, Anne realized with a tightening of her gut that the emissary was none other than Robert himself.

His familiar face peered at her from underneath a black cap and the golden circlet her father used to wear for less formal state occasions. He was seated in the center of the boat, in an armchair, attended by figures in black. She couldn't see any archers or, in fact, any weapons at all.

She had the sudden profound feeling that some mistake had been made. Robert was only four years older than she; he had played with her when she was little. She'd always thought of him as a friend. It was impossible that he had done the things they said, and she was suddenly sure that he was about to clear things up. There wouldn't be any need for a war at all.

As the boat arrived, a slender figure in black hose and surcoat leapt off to secure the moorings; it took an instant for Anne to realize that the figure was female, a girl of perhaps thirteen. In the next blink she understood that all but one of Robert's retainers were unarmed young women. The single man wore a gold filigree brooch on his mantle that identified him as a knight, but he was likewise weaponless.

Robert certainly didn't seem very worried.

When the craft was secure, he rose from his makeshift throne, grinning.

"My dear Anne," he said. "Let me look at you."

He stepped out upon the stone, and Anne felt a shock run through her feet. The rock beneath her went suddenly soft, like warm butter, and everything blurred. It was as if the world around her were melting.

And then, just as suddenly, all was firm again, re-formed. But *different.* Robert was still there, handsome in a black sealskin doublet sequined with small diamonds. But he stank like rotting meat, and his skin was translucent, revealing the dark riverine network of vessels beneath. Even more peculiar, his veins did not end at his flesh but trailed off into the earth and air, joining the otherworldly waters of her vision.

But unlike the man she had seen dying, leaking the last of his life into the headwaters of death, everything was flowing *into* Robert, filling him, propping him up like a hand thrust into a stocking puppet.

She realized she had stepped back, and her breath was coming fast.

"That is near enough," Artwair said.

"I only want to give my niece a kiss," Robert said. "That is not so much, is it?"

"Under the circumstances," Artwair replied, "I think it is."

"None of you see it, do you?" Anne asked. "You can't see what he is."

The puzzled gazes that brought confirmed her guess, and even in her own vision the dark rivulets were fading, though not entirely vanished.

Robert met her gaze squarely, and she saw something weird there, a sort of recognition or surprise.

"What *am* I, my dear? I am your beloved uncle. I am your dear friend."

"I don't know what you are," Anne said, "but you are not my friend."

Robert sighed dramatically.

"You are distraught, I can see that. But I can assure you I am your friend. Why else would I protect your throne as I have?"

"*My* throne?" Anne said.

"Of course, Anne. Liery has kidnapped Charles, and in his absence I have acted as regent. But you are the heir to the throne, my dear."

"You admit this?" Artwair said.

"Of course. Why wouldn't I? I have no reason to go against the Comven's decision. I have only been awaiting her return."

"And now you plan to give me the crown?" Anne asked, staring in disbelief.

"Indeed I shall," Robert agreed. "Under certain conditions."

"Ah, now we're to the viper's bargain," Artwair said.

Robert looked annoyed for the first time since his arrival.

"I'm surprised by the company you keep, Anne," he said. "Duke Artwair was commanded to protect our borders. He has abandoned that duty in order to march upon Eslen."

"To return the throne to its rightful owner," Artwair said.

"Oh, really?" Robert replied. "When you began your march west, you knew that Anne was alive, well, and ready to take her place in Eslen? But that was before you had seen her, or spoken with her. In fact, how *could* you have known that?" He switched his gaze to Anne.

"How do you imagine he knew you were alive, my dear? Have you ever asked yourself exactly what our dear duke might want from this bargain?"

Anne had, in fact, wondered just that, but she withheld her confirmation.

"What are your terms?" she asked.

Robert nodded appraisingly. "You've grown up, haven't you? Though I have to say, I'm not sure I like your hair cut short. It seems mannish. When it is long, you look almost like—" He stopped abruptly, and what little color there had been in his face suddenly drained.

He looked away, first at the western sky, then at the distant rise of the Breu-en-Trey. Finally he cleared his throat.

"In any event," he said, his tone more subdued, "you'll understand if I'm a bit concerned, given the manner of your coming."

"I can see that," Anne said. "Your men resisted our march here, and you've flooded the poelen. Clearly, you are prepared for war. So why would you suddenly capitulate?"

"I had no idea this army was led by you, my dear. I assumed it was more or less what it appeared to be: a revolt by greedy and disaffected noblemen of the provinces. People who would use this time of troubles as an excuse to place an usurper on the throne. Now that I see they have chosen you as their poppet, it changes things substantially."

"Poppet?"

"You don't really think they will let you be queen, do you?" Robert said. "I think you are brighter than that, Anne. All of them had to be promised something, didn't they? After they have lost blood, men, and horses, do you think their appetites will lessen?

"You have an army here you cannot trust, Anne. What's more, even if you *could* trust it, you can't take Eslen easily—if at all."

"I've yet to hear what you propose."

He held up his hands. "It isn't complicated. You come into the city, and we arrange a coronation. I shall function as your chief adviser."

"And how long, I wonder, would I survive that honor?" Anne asked. "How long before some poison or dagger of your design finds my heart?"

"You may bring a retinue of reasonable size, of course."

"My army is of reasonable size," Anne replied.

"It would be foolish to bring all of them in," Robert said. "In fact, I cannot allow it. I do not trust them, nor, as I've mentioned, should you. Bring in a strong bodyguard. Leave the rest of them out here. When the adjudicator from the Church arrives, he will sort this out, and we will abide by his decision."

"That's an easy promise for you to make!" Artwair exploded. "It's well known that you and the praifec are villains together in all of this."

"The adjudicator comes directly from z'Irbina," Robert said. "If you cannot trust our most holy fathers, I cannot imagine who you would trust."

"I'll begin by not trusting *you* and work my way out from there."

Robert sighed. "You aren't really going to insist on fighting this silly war, are you?"

"Why is my mother imprisoned?" Anne asked.

Robert's gaze dropped down.

"For her own protection," he said. "After the deaths of your sisters, she became first melancholy, then inconsolable. She was unbalanced, and it showed to her detriment in governing. You have heard of the slaughter of innocents at Lady Gramme's, I presume. Still, it wasn't until she attempted the unthinkable that I felt I had to step in."

"The unthinkable?"

His voice lowered. "It is a most closely guarded secret," he said. "We kept it quiet to prevent embarrassment and, frankly, despair. Your mother tried to kill herself, Anne."

"Did she?" Anne meant to sound skeptical, but something caught at the back of her throat. Could it possibly be true?

"As I say, she was inconsolable. She remains so, but under my protection she is at least safe from herself."

Anne had been considering Robert's offer.

She didn't trust him, but once in the castle she would be able to find the passages. She would be safe from Robert and his men there, and she could open the tunnel that led into the rinns and move men into the city, if not the castle itself.

There was an opportunity here, and she wasn't going to let it pass.

"I should like to see her," she said.

"That is easily arranged," Robert assured her.

"I should like to see her *now*."

"Shall I send for her?" Robert asked.

Anne took a deep breath, then let it out. "I rather think I should like to go to her."

"I've already said that you could bring a retinue into the castle. We can see your mother first thing."

"I would rather that you stayed here," Anne replied.

Robert's eyebrows arched up. "I've come here under a flag of truce, unarmed and unguarded. I never imagined you would be so dishonorable as to take me captive. If you do, I warn you, you will never enter Eslen. My men will burn it first, if anything happens to me."

"I'm asking this as a favor," Anne replied. "I'm asking you to *agree* to stay here while I speak to my mother. I will take only fifty men. In turn, you will send word to your men to allow me free access to the castle so I can verify the truth of these things you say. Then—and only then—might you and I come to some sort of agreement."

"Even if I trust you," Robert said, "I have already made it plain I don't trust your followers. How can you be sure they won't murder me while you're gone?" He glanced significantly at Artwair.

"Because my personal bodyguard, Neil MeqVren, will defend you. You may trust him absolutely."

"He is only one man," Robert pointed out.

"If anything happens to Sir Neil, I will know I have been betrayed," Anne said.

"That would be a small comfort to my corpse."

"Robert, if you are serious about your good intentions, here is your chance to prove it. Otherwise, I will not trust you, and this war *will* begin in earnest. Most of the land-waerden are on my side. And Sir Fail will arrive soon with a fleet, do not doubt it."

Robert stroked his beard for a moment.

"One day," he said at last. "You return to Eslen with my word, on my boat, and I will stay here under the care of Sir Neil, whom even I do not doubt. You will speak to your mother and determine her condition. You will assure yourself that I am honest in my intention to give you the throne. Then you will return, and we will discuss the way in which you will take your place.

"One day. Agreed?"

Anne closed her eyes for a moment, trying to see if she had missed something.

"Your Majesty," Artwair advised, "this is *most* unwise."

"I agree," Sir Neil said.

"Nevertheless," Anne said, "I am to be queen, or so you all say. It is my decision to make. Robert, I agree to your terms."

"My life is in your hands, Majesty," Robert said.

CHAPTER THREE

IN THE BAIRGHS

DANGER TINGLING at his back, Stephen paused to catch his breath.

Behind him Ehan said something, but although his ears had begun to heal, it was still too muddled to make out, as if he had water in his ears. He tapped the side of his head to indicate as much, something they had all gotten used to in the past two ninedays.

"Rest?" the little man repeated a little louder.

Stephen nodded reluctantly. During his time with the holter he'd thought his body had hardened to travel, but the trail was too steep to ride the horses, so they had to lead them. His legs, it seemed, had not been strengthened by months on horseback.

He settled onto a boulder as Ehan produced a waterskin and some of the bread they'd bought in the last village they'd passed through, a gathering of a dozen huts named Crothaem. That lay someplace far below them now, beyond the unnamed valley below and the folds of the Hauland foothills that ran along it.

"How far up do y' think we are?" Ehan asked. Now they were facing each other, and it was easier to communicate.

"It's hard to tell," Stephen replied, because it was, even in the most visceral sense. "We must be in the mountains themselves by now."

"The trouble is there aren't any trees," Ehan offered.

Stephen nodded. That *was* the problem, or at least one of them. It was as if some ancient saint or god had ripped up a monstrous expanse of pasture from the Midenlands and settled them over the Bairghs like a sheet. Stephen reckoned that what he saw was the result of two thousand years of Mannish activity: cutting trees for house timbers and firewood and to clear pasture for the sheep, goats, and hairy cows that seemed to be everywhere.

The effect, though, was a disorienting loss of perspective. The grass soothed over the steepness of the slopes and tricked the eye about distance. Only when he focused on something specific—a herd of goats or one of the occasional sod-roofed steadings—did he have some appreciation of the vastness of it all.

And of the danger. Inclines that appeared gentle and friendly—which he imagined he could roll down like a child on a small hill—actually hid fatal drops.

Fortunately, the same millennia and the same men that had produced the treeless landscape had also created well-worn tracks to tell them where it was safe to walk—and where it wasn't.

"You still reckon the woorm is following us?" Ehan said.

Stephen nodded. "It's not following us exactly," he said. "It didn't follow us across the Brogh y Stradh uplands; it swam up the Then River to meet us."

"Makes sense that it would prefer traveling in rivers, a thing that size."

"That's not the point, though," Stephen said. "While we followed the Ef down to the Gray Warlock, it was actually getting ahead of us, as we discovered in Ever."

"Yah," Ehan said, his brow furrowing at the memory. Ever had been a village of the dead. The few survivors had told them of the woorm's passage just a few days before.

"From there we could have gone anywhere. And even if it was determined to dog us using the rivers, it might have gone up the Warlock, down to the confluence at Wherthen. It might have gone to Eslen. But it didn't. It went upstream on the Then to cut off our overland flight, and it very nearly got us."

He shuddered at the memory of the monster's head breaking the iced surface of the stream like a boat made of iron.

The impression was enhanced by the pair of passengers, bundled in furs, who rode on its back. He'd been wondering what those two would do if the woorm ever dove below the surface when its gaze—its terrible gaze—had found him, and he'd known in his heart that it was the end.

But they'd turned away and nearly killed their horses riding that night. And they hadn't seen it since.

"But we know it came through Ever on its way *to* the monastery," Ehan said. "Maybe it was just going back the way it came, and we were unlucky enough to have chosen the same path."

"I wish I could believe that, but I can't," Stephen said. "The coincidence would be far too great."

"Then maybe it's not coincidence," Ehan pressed. "Maybe it's all part of some larger design."

"I wouldn't put too much weight on that leg," Henne interjected, peering intently at them both. "It's got two fellows riding it, don't it? If either of 'em knew the lay of the land and a thing about tracking, they could've reckoned which way we were headed. Saints, they could have stopped to question them poor folk near Whitraff, the ones we talked to. They'd remember us, since we were near deaf at the time, and I don't think they'd hold out on a woormrider.

"Once they knew what road we were on, they could figure out where we'd have to cross the Then; there're only a couple of fords and no bridges."

"That's possible," Stephen acknowledged. "It didn't meet us at the ferry on the White Warlock. If it's following us now, it's coming overland again."

"Unless you're right," Henne said, "and it canns where we're going. In that case, it would have gone on up the Welph, and it'll be waiting for us two valleys over."

"What a wonderful thought," Ehan muttered.

Midafternoon they reached the snow line, and soon the wet, muddy trail froze as hard as stone.

At Henne's suggestion, they'd found a tailor in Crothaem

and bought four paiden, a sort of local quilted felt coat lined with sheepskin. The paiden cost them more than half of what remained of the funds the fratrex had sent with them, and to Stephen the price seemed exorbitant.

His mind was firmly changed now as they walked up into low-lying clouds and found them to be a freezing mist. The horses slipped too often for them to ride, and walking became more difficult both because the path steepened and because the air seemed somehow less substantial.

Stephen had read about the bad air at the tops of mountains. In the Mountains of the Hare, the highest peaks—those known as *Sa' Ceth ag Sa'Nem*—the atmosphere was said to be completely unbreathable. Up to now, he had doubted the veracity of those accounts, but this part of the Bairghs wasn't very high as mountains went, yet he already was becoming a believer.

It was growing dark when they chanced across a goatherd driving his flock along the trail back the way they had come. Stephen greeted him in his best Northern Almannish. The herdsman—really a lad of perhaps thirteen with raven-dark hair and pale blue eyes—smiled and answered in something akin to the same language, albeit with such odd pronunciation that Stephen had to take his time to understand it.

"Dere be a *vel* downtrail, het Demsted," the boy informed them, "'boot one league. Du't be-gitting one room-hoos dere. Mine fader-bruder Ansgif'l git du'alla one room," he added cheerfully.

"Danx," Stephen replied, guessing at the local expression of gratitude. "I wonder—have you ever heard of a mountain named *eslief vendve*?"

The boy scratched his head for a moment.

"Slivendy?" he asked at last.

"Maybe," Stephen said cautiously. "It's farther north and east."

"Je, very far," the boy replied. "Has 'nother namen—eh, *net gemoonu*—not 'member? Du ask mine fader-bruder, je? He is talking better Almannish."

"And his name is Ansgif?"

"Je, at room-hoos, named svartboch. Mine namen is Ven. Du spill 'im du seen me.

"Mekle danx, Ven," Stephen said.

The boy smiled and waved, then continued on his way, vanishing into the fog, though they continued to hear the sound of the bells on his goats for some time.

"What was all that?" Ehan gruffed after the boy was out of earshot. "I started off understanding you, but then you started talking like the boy, and it all turned to gibberish."

"Really?" Stephen thought back. He'd only been adjusting his Almannish based on the boy's dialect, guessing at how the words ought to sound in his version of the tongue.

"Didn't understand a word after you said hello and asked him if there was anyplace to spend the night."

"Well, there is, a town called Demsted in the glen up ahead. We're to look for an inn called the svartboch—'Black Goat'—and his uncle Ansgif will rent us a room. He'd heard of our mountain, as well, and he said it had another name, one he couldn't remember. He said to ask his uncle about that, too."

"Is it going to be like this from here on out, people gabbling near nonsense?"

"No," Stephen said. "More likely, it'll get worse."

Their day did get worse, if not in the way Stephen had predicted. A bit after the pass dropped back below the snow line and began its slow downward snaking, Stephen was drawn from reviewing his reasoning on the location of the mountain he sought by a strangled cry from Ehan that immediately brought his wits back to his feet and sent a jolt through his heart and lungs.

Peering in the direction Ehan was pointing, he at first found it impossible to sort out what he saw. It was a tree, especially noticeable because it was one of the few he had seen in many leagues. He didn't know the variety, but it was leafless, and the branches gnarled and twisted by the mountain winds. But there was a large flock of birds perched in its branches.

Birds, and *people,* climbing . . .

No, not climbing. Hanging. Eight corpses with blackened faces depended from thick ropes tied to the boughs. Their eyes were gone, presumably eaten by the crows that now cawed and muttered at Stephen and his companions.

"Ansuz af se friz ya s'uvil," Ehan swore.

Stephen swept his gaze around the narrow pass. He didn't see or hear anyone, but his hearing was still damaged, so that was no surprise.

"Keep watch," he said. "Whoever did this may still be nearby."

"Yah," Ehan said.

Stephen approached the corpses for a better look.

Five were men, and three women, of various ages. The youngest was a girl who could hardly have been more than sixteen, the oldest a man of perhaps sixty winters. They were all naked, and each seemed to have died by strangulation. But they all had other wounds: backs flayed nearly to the bone, burns and abrasions.

"More sacrifices?" Brother Themes offered.

"If so, they aren't like the ones I saw before, at the fanes," Stephen said. "Those had been eviscerated and nailed to posts around the sedos. I don't see a sedos fane here, and these people look as if they were simply tortured, then hanged."

He thought he ought to feel sick, but instead he felt oddly giddy. It was an irrational reaction, he supposed, brought on by the horrible sight.

"There are certain old gods and even saints who take their sacrifices hung on trees," he continued. "And it was common even in Church lands to hang criminals like this, at least up until a few years ago."

"Maybe that's why the boy didn't mention it," Themes suggested. "Maybe this is just where his town brings its criminals."

"Probably," Stephen agreed. "That makes sense."

But despite the logic, the creak of the ropes swaying in the wind and the eyeless faces were still very much with Stephen a few bells later, when Demsted came into view.

* * *

To Stephen's eye, most of the towns he had seen since leaving the ruins of Ever hadn't been what he considered proper towns, and he didn't expect much out of Demsted. He was, however, pleasantly surprised when they came down through the fog and were greeted by a myriad of lights in the glen below. In the twilight he could make out the outline of a clock tower, the peaked roofs of at least a few houses that boasted more than one story, and a squat cylinder that might be an old keep.

The entire town was encircled by a stout stone wall. It was no Ralegh or Eslen, but considering where they were, Stephen was nothing short of amazed. How could a handful of sheepherders support a town of this size?

The mountain way joined an older, embanked road shortly before they reached the town. Another surprise: It resembled the sort of road the Hegemony had built, though as far as Stephen knew, the Hegemony hadn't expanded all the way into the Bairghs.

They soon found themselves at the city gate, a pair of ironbound wooden portals about four kingsyards high. They weren't closed yet, but a hoarse shout from above warned them to halt. Or at least Stephen supposed it was a warning.

"We're travelers," Stephen shouted up. "Do you speak the king's tongue or Almannish?"

"I can speak the king's tongue," the man shouted back down. "You're out awfully late. We were about to close the gates."

"We might have camped in the mountains, but we met a boy who told us we could find lodging here."

"What was the boy's name?"

"Ven, he called himself."

"Je," the man said reflectively. "Do you swear you're not warlocks, wirjawalvs, or other creatures of mischief or evil?"

"We're monks of Saint Decmanus," Ehan called up, "or three of us are. The fourth is our friend and a huntsman."

"If you'll allow the test, you can come in, then."

"Test?"

"Step on through the gate."

The gate didn't open directly into the town but into a walled-in yard. Even as they entered it, Stephen watched the opposite gates close. He waited for those they had just passed through to shut as well, but apparently if Stephen and his companions were warlocks or wirjawalvs, the townsfolk would just as soon leave one door open for them to exit through.

A door opened to their left, at the base of the wall, and the hairs on Stephen's neck pricked up as two large four-legged shapes stepped out, their eyes glinting red in the torchlight. He couldn't tell if they were dogs or wolves, but they were something from that clan and *big*.

It was a moment before he noticed that there was someone with the beasts. Whoever it was wore a weather cloak and a paida like his, and his face was in shadow.

The beasts were coming closer now, growling, and Stephen reckoned they were some sort of mastiff, albeit the size of a pony.

"This don't make me feel easy," Henne said.

"Just hold still," said the person with the dogs. Stephen thought it sounded like a woman, though the voice was a bit husky. "Make no sudden move."

Stephen tried to obey, but it wasn't easy when the huge, wet, toothy muzzles of the animals were snuffling against him.

"This is the test?" he asked to try to curb his nervousness.

"Any dog can scent what isn't natural," the woman said. "But these have been bred for it."

The dog sniffing Stephen suddenly bellowed out a bark, bared its teeth, and backed away, the hair on its back standing visibly.

"You're tainted," she said.

"Yes," Stephen said. "We ran across something back in the Midenlands. A woorm. We may have its scent on us still."

His hearing was only now approaching normal; he had yet

to recover—if he ever would—the saint-touched ability to hear a whisper a hundred kingsyards away. But he didn't need to have such hearing to imagine the creak of bows bending all around them. As the woman backed away, though, the dogs quickly quieted down, and she seemed to relax a bit. He heard her whisper something to them, and the beasts came back for a second smell. This time they seemed content.

Clearly these people made a habit of testing strangers to make certain they weren't monsters; that meant either that they had good practical reasons for doing so or that they were hopelessly mired in primitive superstition.

Stephen wasn't sure which he preferred.

"They're tainted," the woman said loudly, "but they're Mannish, not monsters."

"Good enough," the voice from the wall responded.

Stephen imagined the wood of bows relaxing, and he felt his shoulders loosen a bit.

"My name is Stephen Darige," he said to the woman. "Whom do I have the honor of addressing?"

The hood lifted a bit, but Stephen still couldn't make out any features.

"A humble servant of the saints," she said. "I am called Pale."

"Sor Pales?"

She chuckled. *"Pro suveiss nomniss . . ."*

". . . sverruns patenest," he finished. "What coven did you attend?"

"The Coven Saint Cer of Tero Gallé," she replied. "And you made your studies at d'Ef?"

"Indeed," Stephen replied cautiously.

"May I ask if you are on the business of the Church? Were you sent to aid the sacritor?"

Stephen didn't know how to answer that except with the truth.

"We're on a mission for our fratrex," he admitted, "but we're just passing through your town. I don't know your sacritor."

His words were followed by a long, odd silence.

"You mentioned Ven," the woman said at last.

"Yes. He said his uncle would give us a room at, ah, *svart-boch*."

"You would rather stay at an inn than at the church, where you would be lodged without fee?"

"I've no wish to impose on the sacritor," Stephen replied. "And we'll leave with the dawn. Our fratrex has provided us with funds sufficient for the journey."

"Nonsense," a male voice interrupted. "We have room for you in plenty."

Stephen glanced toward the new voice and found himself regarding a knight in brass-chased armor. His helm was off, and in the wan torchlight his face was mostly beard.

"Sister Pale, you really should know better. You should have insisted."

"It was my intention to, Sir Elden," Sister Pale replied.

Sir Elden made a small bow. "Welcome, good brothers, to the attish of Ing Fear and the town of Demsted. I am Sir Elden of Saint Nod, and it would be my great honor to escort you to your secure beds."

Though he desperately wanted to, Stephen could think of no possible way to refuse.

"That's very kind," he said.

The streets of Demsted were narrow, dark, cluttered, and mostly empty. Stephen caught a few curious souls peering at them from darkened windows, but for the most part the town was eerily still.

The single exception was a sprawling building from which the sound of pipes and harp skirled, along with clapping and singing. A lantern hung on a peg outside the door identified it—as Stephen imagined—as the svartboch.

"You'd not want to stay there," Sir Elden offered, contra-dicting Stephen's tacit wish. "It's no place for men of the saints."

"I'm happy to take your word for it," Stephen lied.

"Very sensible," Sir Elden said. "You'll find the temple much more to your taste. Demsted itself can be quite a trial."

"I was surprised to find a town of this size in such a remote place," Stephen said.

"I *don't* find this to be a town of much size," the knight
said, "but I suppose I know what you mean. They mine silver in the hills north of here, and Demsted is the market
where merchants buy the ore. The Kae River starts here, as
well, and flows into the lower reaches of the Welph, and
thence to the Warlock. If you came from the south, over the
pass, it's easy to understand your surprise at finding anything at all."

"Ah. And how long have you been here, Sir Elden?"

"The space of a month, not more. I came with the sacritor
to do the work of the resacaratum."

"In this remote place?"

"The worst infections fester in the places most difficult to
reach," the knight replied. "We have discovered heretics and
shinecrafters in plenty. You may have seen some of them on
the tree in the pass."

For an instant Stephen was so startled that he couldn't
reply.

"I did," he said finally. "I thought them criminals."

It was too dark to make out Sir Elden's face, but his tone
suggested that he had heard something in Stephen's comment he didn't care for.

"They *were* criminals, Brother, of the very worst sort."

"Of course," Stephen said carefully.

"These mountains are fairly crawling with the get of
shinecraft," the knight went on. "Foul beasts conjured from
beneath the earth. I myself witnessed a woman give birth to
a most hideous utin, proving that she had had intercourse
with unclean demons."

"You *saw* this?"

"Oh, yes. Well, the birth, not the intercourse, but the one is
reasoned from the other. These lands are under siege by the
armies of evil. What, did you think Sister Pale's inspection
of you was spurious? The first nineday I was here, a wir-
jawalv entered the town, murdered four citizens, and injured
three more." He paused. "Ah, here we are."

"I should like to hear more of these things," Stephen said. "We must travel farther into the mountains. If there are dangers we may encounter there . . ."

"There are dangers in plenty," the knight assured him. "What business takes you into this heathen land? What fratrex sent you hence?"

"My mission must remain confidential, I fear," Stephen replied. "But I wonder, is there a collection of scrifti and maps to be found in Demsted?"

"There are some," the knight replied. "I myself have not examined them, but I'm certain the sacritor will allow you to see them once you've satisfied him as to your need and the authenticity of your claim. Meanwhile, come, let us stable your horses and see you to your lodging. I'll fetch the sacritor, and you can become acquainted."

It was too dark to make out much of the temple from the outside; it was bigger than Stephen thought it might be, with a domed nave in the style of the Hegemony. He wondered briefly if it might actually be that old, if some forgotten mission had pushed farther into the mountains than the histories knew.

But as Sir Elden had pointed out, though Demsted was remote, it wasn't isolated. And if its church was really that ancient, one of the many sacritors or monks who had lived there would have noticed and made note of the fact.

The knight opened the door, and they entered. The marble floor was worn to polished, and the paths where feet were used to tread actually were slightly channeled, heightening Stephen's impression of great age.

But the architecture wasn't that of the Hegemony, at least no temple of the Hegemony he had ever seen, whether depicted or manifest. The doorways were high, arched, and narrow, and the columns that held the high ceilings oddly delicate. Instead of the usual hemispheric dome, the central nave seemed to have a steep cone, though the flickering candles and torches that lit the altar and the prayer niches weren't sufficient to illuminate the upper reaches of it.

More than anything, he realized, the building reminded

him of the few sketches he had seen of the audacious construction from the era of the Warlock Wars.

They went beyond the nave into a quiet corridor lit by only a few candles, though the stone still was so polished that it shone like glass, making the most of the light. Then they passed through a door into a comfortable room that Stephen quickly recognized as a scriftorium. Behind a heavy table, a man sat hunched over an open book, an Aenan lamp brightening the pages but not his face.

"Sacritor?" Sir Elden ventured.

The man glanced up, and the focused light of the lamp grazed his face, revealing middle-aged features lengthened by a small beard. Stephen's heart suddenly picked up a few beats, and he had the sudden understanding of what the wolf feels when the trap closes on its foot.

"Ah," the man said. "How good to see you, Brother Stephen."

For an instant he'd hoped to be wrong, hoped the face was a trick of light and memory. But the voice was unmistakable.

"Praifec Hespero," Stephen said. "What a surprise."

CHAPTER FOUR

A NEW MODE

LEOFF REMEMBERED blood spattering on the stone floor, each drop like a garnet until it struck the slightly porous rock, where it soaked and spread, jewels transformed into stains.

He remembered wondering how long his blood would be part of the stone, if he had in some sense become immortal by spilling his life there. If so, it was a humble sort of immortality, a common one, judging by the quantity of stains already there.

He blinked and rubbed his eyes with the knobbed backs of his wrists, torn oddly between a fit of rage and utter exhaustion as he watched splashes of ink soak into the parchment, so like blood on stone. He seemed to vibrate between the two moments: then, the lash across his back, the exotic pain so total that it was difficult to recognize, and now, ink spraying from his shivering quill.

For a long instant the difference between *then* and *now* collapsed, and he wondered if he was still there, in the dungeon. Perhaps the *now* was just a pretty illusion his mind had created to help him die more easily.

If so, his illusions were of poor quality. He couldn't actually hold a quill, but he'd had Mery tie one to his hand. At first his arm had cramped quickly and agonizingly, but that was only a fraction of the pain he was enduring.

To write music, he had to *hear* it, and doing that in his mind had always been his great gift. He could close his eyes and imagine each note of fifty instruments, weaving counterpoint, insinuating harmony. Everything he wrote he heard first, and that had never been anything but a joy to him—until now.

A wave of nausea swept through him. He rose jerkily from his stool and stumbled to the narrow casement of the window. His belly crawled as if it were full of maggots, and his bones felt as rotten as termite-infested branches.

Could it kill him merely to imagine these chords? But if that was the case . . .

Speculation was swept aside as he leaned out of the window to retch. He had eaten hardly any supper, but his body didn't care. When his belly was empty, it reached deeper, convulsing him until his legs and arms gave way, and he crumpled until his face was against stone.

He imagined himself as a drop of blood, a garnet becoming a stain . . .

He wasn't sure how long it was before he found the

strength to stand again. He pulled himself back up to the
window, heaving in great gulps of the salty air. The moon
had risen, cold and round, and the freezing air numbed his
face. Far below, silver lapped against ebony in little
wavelets, and Leoff suddenly yearned to join them, to free
himself through the window, break his ruined skeleton on
the rocks, and leave the lands of fate to those who were
stronger and braver. To those who were well.

He closed his eyes, wondering if he was mad. Certainly, if
he had never been tortured, broken, humiliated as he had
been, he would never in his wildest dreams be able to imagine the music that so sickened him now. He knew that vis-
cerally.

The obscure notation in the book he'd found would have
remained as incomprehensible as the script in which it was
written. It was related to no system of music he knew, but
once he'd seen that first chord, he'd somehow *heard* it in his
head, and the rest of it fell into place. But a sane man—a
man who had not experienced the horror he had—could
never have *heard* that chord. He certainly could never have
gone on, never purposefully hurt himself the way he was
doing now. Anyone who loved his life, who imagined a future, could never write this music.

His dreams for his music had been grandiose; his dreams
for himself had never been particularly ambitious. A wife to
love him, children, evenings singing together, grandchildren
in a comfortable house, and old age coming on kindly, a
long, pleasant, comfortable reflection before life's end. That
was all he'd asked.

And he would have none of it.

No, any such hopes for himself were dead, but there was
his music. Yes, he might still accomplish something if he
was willing to destroy himself. And there was so little left to
destroy, it was almost a pleasure.

No fall to the rocks for him. Back to the paper and ink.

He'd just begun the next progression when he heard a
light knock at his door. He stared at it blankly for a moment,
struggling to remember the significance of the sound. He

was sure he should know; it was like a word almost remembered, stuck at the bottom of the throat.

It happened again, slightly louder this time, and he got it.

"Come in if you wish," he said finally.

The door creaked open slowly, revealing Areana, and for a
long moment he couldn't speak. The pain in him fled as
shadows flee light, and he had a sudden happy memory of
his first meeting with her at the ball in Lady Gramme's mansion. They'd danced; he could remember the music, a country dance known as a whervel. He hadn't known the steps,
but she had shown him easily enough.

She stood framed in the doorway like a painting by a master of the brush, her blue kirtle glowing in the moonlight, the
darkness of the hall behind her. Her red-gold hair seemed
molten, dark, sensuous.

"Leoff," she said tentatively. "Have I come at a bad time?"

"Areana," he managed to croak. "No, please. Come in.
Find yourself a seat." He tried to push back his disheveled
hair and nearly stabbed himself in the eye with the pen.
Sighing, he let his hands drop to his sides.

"It's just—you haven't been coming out," she said, walking across the room to stand beside him. "I'm worried about
you. Are they keeping you confined?"

"No, I have freedom to roam the castle," Leoff said. "Or
so I'm told. I haven't tested it."

"Well, you should," she said. "You can't spend *all* your
time up here."

"Well," he said, "I've a lot of work to do."

"Yes, I know," she said, smiling. "Your singspell about
Maersca." She stepped closer and lowered her voice to a
conspiratorial level. "And what will you do this time? *Really?*"

"Exactly what he asked."

Her dark eyes widened. "Do you think I would betray
you?"

"No," he said. "You've been very brave about all this. I
never got a chance to tell you how perfect your singing was
that night. It was a miracle."

"The miracle was the music," Areana said. "I felt—I thought I *was* her, Leoff. I really did. My heart was breaking, and when I leapt from the window, I felt I would die. There is so much magic in you . . ."

She reached to stroke his face. He was too stunned to react until she touched him, and then he jerked away.

"What they *did* to you . . ." She sighed.

"Yes, well, I knew it could happen," he said. "But I promised you better. I'm so sorry."

"No, you warned me," she said. "You warned us all, and we were all with you. We believed in you." She moved nearer, and her breath was sweet. "I still believe in you. I want to help with whatever it is you're really doing."

"I told you," he murmured. Her hand was warm, and if he moved his face a fraction, he could kiss it. A small movement more and he could reach her lips.

But he couldn't put his hand against hers. Not like this. So he turned away slightly.

"I'm doing what he asked," he said. "Nothing more."

She withdrew her hand and stepped back. "You *can't*," she said. "Don't fool with me."

"I *must*. He'll kill you and Mery," he replied. "Don't you understand?"

"You can't give in because of me," she said.

"Oh," he replied. "Oh, yes—yes I can. And I will."

"Don't you think he'll kill us, anyway?"

"No," Leoff said, "I don't think he will. That would undo everything. He's trying to win your family—and the other landwaerden—back to him."

"Yes, but the truth is that you were tortured, then *forced* to do this. Prince Robert can't allow that fact to get out. And yet there are three of us who know. Not to mention what they did to—well, never mind. Do you really think we can be allowed to survive, knowing what we know?"

"We've a better chance than if I go against him," Leoff argued. "You know that. If I defy him, he'll torture you to death right in front of my eyes; then he'll start with Mery. Or maybe he'll go the other way around, I don't know, but I can't bear—"

"I can't bear to see you doing his bidding," Areana exploded, and he saw sudden real fury in her eyes. "It's obscene, a perversion of your talent."

He stared at her for a moment, unblinking, as he registered something she hadn't quite said.

"What did they do to you?" he asked at last.

She blushed and took a further step back. "They did not hurt me, not as they did you," she said quietly.

"I can see that," he said, growing angry. *"But what did they do to you?"*

She flinched at his tone.

"Nothing," she said. "Nothing I want to talk about."

"Tell me," he said more softly.

Her eyes teared up. "Please, Leoff. Please leave it be. If I don't tell you—"

"Don't tell me what?"

Her mouth parted. "I've never seen you like this," she said.

"You've barely seen me at all," Leoff hissed. "You think you *know* me?"

"Leoff, please don't be angry with me."

He took a deep breath. "Were you raped?"

She looked away, and when she turned back, her face had a grimmer cast. "Would that make a difference to you?"

"What do you mean?"

"I mean, could you still love me if I had been raped?"

Now he was aware that his jaw was hanging completely open. "Love you? When did I ever say I loved you?"

"Well, you didn't, did you? You're too shy and too preoccupied. I don't know; maybe you aren't even aware you love me. But you do."

"I do?"

"Of course. And it's not that I think everyone loves me, you know. But sometimes a girl knows, and with you I know. Or did."

Leoff felt tears streaming down his face. He held his hands up. She shook her head.

"That doesn't matter to me," she said softly.

"It matters to me," he replied. "What did they do to you?"

She lowered her head. "What you said," she admitted.

"How many times?"

"I don't know. I really *don't* know."

"I'm so sorry, Areana."

"Don't be sorry," she said, looking back up. Her eyes were smoldering now. "Make them *pay*."

For a precious moment he wanted to tell her his plan, to take her in what remained of his arms. But that would only weaken him, and now, more urgently than ever, he needed the worst he had in him.

"Robert doesn't pay," Leoff said. "Robert gets away with it, and *we* pay. Now, please go. I have work to do."

"Leoff—"

"Go. Please."

He turned away, and a few heartbeats later he heard footsteps retreating slowly and then picking up speed.

When he looked again, she was gone, and his feeling of sickness returned, stronger than before.

He settled back in front of the score and began again.

CHAPTER FIVE

RETURN TO ESLEN

ANNE SURVEYED herself dubiously in the looking glass. "You look every inch a queen," Austra assured her.

To that Anne could only answer with a dour chuckle, thinking of her mother with her alabaster skin, flawless hands, and long, silky hair. What she gleaned from the flecked mirror Artwair had found somewhere was a very different image.

Weather had chapped and reddened her face, and her freckles—always ubiquitous—were fatted on Vitellian sunlight. Her shorn hair was tucked underneath a wimple of the sort that hadn't been popular outside of covens since before she was born. The gown was nice, though, a red-and-gold brocade, not too fancy, not too simple.

Even so, she felt like a toad in a silk slip.

"You have the bearing," Austra amplified, clearly understanding her doubts.

"Thank you," Anne replied, having nothing else to say. Would anyone in Eslen agree? She supposed she would find out.

"Now, what should I wear?" Austra mused.

Anne raised an eyebrow. "It shouldn't matter, I think. *You* aren't going."

"Of course I'm going," Austra said firmly.

"I thought I asked you never to question me again," Anne said.

"You never said that," Austra protested. "You said I might argue with you, try to persuade you, but in the end your word would be my law. That is still the case. But it would be foolish not to take me."

"And how is that?"

"How will it look, a queen with no servants?"

"It will look as if I do not feel the need for them," Anne replied.

"I don't think so," Austra countered. "It will be a sign of your weakness. You must take an entourage. You must have a maidservant, or else no one will take you seriously."

"I'm taking Cazio. Or is *that* what this is about?"

Austra pinkened, and her brows lowered in anger.

"I won't pretend I don't want to stay near him," Austra said, "but I want to be near you, too. And I stand by my reasoning. You claim to be queen, you've come to take the throne—you *must* act the part. Anyway, are you really so afraid?"

"I'm terrified," Anne admitted. "Robert agreed so readily, so confidently. I don't know what it means."

"That, at least, is a wise assessment," Artwair's voice came from outside the tent. "May I enter?"

"You may."

The flap brushed open, and her cousin ducked in, accompanied by a man-at-arms.

"You have reservations, then?" Anne asked.

"Holy saints, yes. You have no idea what Robert is playing at, Anne. You might be slain the moment you leave our sight."

"Then Sir Neil will chop off Robert's head," Anne said reasonably. "How will that benefit him?"

"Perhaps instead you will be taken prisoner and tortured until you give the order for his release. Or merely held until Hansan troops arrive."

"I've made it clear to my uncle that if I am accosted in any way, his head will roll. Besides, I'm taking fifty men with me."

"Robert has thousands in Eslen. Fifty is a only gesture, nothing more.

"Think, Anne! Why would Robert allow you to place him in this position? He could easily have held Eslen against us until his support came."

"Then maybe he isn't so certain that his support *will* come in time," Anne suggested. "Or maybe he's not so confident that his allies will support him at all. What if the Church should claim a Hansan as regent and send my uncle to the gallows?"

"That's possible," Artwair said, then he sighed. "But if that's the case, why not open the gates and let all of us in? I believe he must have some dark design. Or perhaps it's worse than that; perhaps Robert isn't actually the master here, and he's being sacrificed to lure you into the grip of whoever *is* in control."

"And who would that be? Praifec Hespero?"

"Possibly."

"Possibly," Anne echoed.

She held her cousin's gaze, wishing she could explain her visions to him, how she had seen the secret ways that lay within the walls of Eslen. Whatever her enemies had planned, they were men, and men could not know about the hidden passages.

Unfortunately, the same glamour made it impossible to explain that to Artwair.

"Perhaps to any and all of that," she admitted. "But what alternative do you see? You've just admitted that we cannot easily take Eslen by brute force. Besides, whatever Robert's plan may be, I have an advantage he cannot know about."

"What advantage?"

"I could tell you," Anne said, "but you would not remember."

"What does *that* mean?" Artwair asked irritably.

Anne bit her lip. "I have a way of getting troops into the city."

"That cannot be. *I* would know of such a thing, were it true."

"But you are wrong," Anne told him. "Only a very few know of this way."

He rubbed at the stump of his hand for a moment.

"If this is true, so . . ." He shook his head. "You have to be more specific."

"I can't," Anne replied. "I've sworn an oath."

"That's not good enough," Artwair said. "I can't allow it."

Anne felt suddenly light. "What are you saying, Cousin?"

"If I must protect you from yourself, I will."

Anne drew a long breath, surveying the guards. How many more did he have outside?

Well, there it was.

"How do you intend to protect me, Artwair? What do you imagine you will do?"

Artwair's face twisted with some emotion, but Anne couldn't see what it was.

"We need you, Anne. Without you this army has no cause."

"What you mean is that without me, *you* have no army."

He stood silent for a long moment.

"If you must put it that way, Anne, then yes. What do you know of these things? I've always liked you, Anne, but you're just a girl. A few months ago you hadn't the least care for this kingdom or anyone in it besides yourself. I don't know what naïve notion you have—"

"It doesn't matter," Neil MeqVren interrupted, shouldering into the tent. Cazio came in just behind him, and beyond them Anne could see a dozen or more of Artwair's guard, watching intently. "Anne is your queen."

"You're supposed to be watching Prince Robert," Artwair said.

"He is in safe hands. I came, like you, to try to talk her away from this dangerous course of action."

"Then I urge you not to involve yourself."

"You have involved me already," Neil replied. "She will not be convinced, and you must not attempt to force her."

"I hardly think you can enforce that," Artwair said drily.

"He'll have my help," Cazio said. The two brushed past Artwair's men to stand at Anne's side. She knew that even with Neil's strange weapon, he and Cazio hadn't a chance against her cousin's men. But it felt good to have them there.

Artwair grimaced. "Anne—"

"What is your plan, Duke Artwair?" Anne interrupted. "How do you plan to claim your throne?"

"I want no throne for myself," Artwair said, hotly now. "All I want is what's best for Crotheny."

"And you think I don't?"

"I've no idea what you want, Anne, but I believe your desire to rescue your mother has clouded your judgment."

Anne walked over to the tent flap, threw it open, and speared her finger toward the mist-covered island. The men outside stepped back.

"*There* is the throne, across that water, on that island. That's what we've come here for. I've a chance to—"

"You've no chance at all. Robert is too devious. Better we withdraw, build our strength, join with Liery."

"Liery," Anne said, "is already out there. Do you honestly believe Sir Fail does not have a fleet in the water, even now?"

"Then where are they?"

"On the way."

"They will never reach us," Artwair said. "What fleet can survive—much less take—Thornrath?"

"No fleet," Anne replied. "But *you* could."

Artwair opened his mouth, then closed it.

"It's possible," he said, "but not bloody likely. Yet if there is a Lierish fleet . . ." He looked thoughtfully into the distance.

"There is," Anne said. "I've seen it. Two days from now they arrive. If we do not control Thornrath, they will be destroyed, crushed between the wall and a Hanzish fleet."

"*Seen* it?"

"In a vision, Cousin."

Artwair barked a little laugh. "Visions are of no use to me," he said.

Anne gripped his arm and stared up into his eyes. "What you said about me was true," she admitted. "But I have changed. I am not the girl you knew. And I *know* more than you, Cousin Artwair. Not about tactics and strategy, I grant you, but about other things of perhaps greater importance. I know how to get troops into Eslen. I know Fail is coming. You *do* need me, but not as the figurehead you imagine.

"I will not be, as Robert put it, your poppet. We will do this the way I want it done, or we will not do it at all. Unless you think this army will follow my corpse. Or yours."

Her anger was grown now, a kernel of rot in her belly. Once again she felt the waters of life and death pulsing around her and followed them through the seams of Artwair's armor, past the scratchy surface of his skin, into the tangle of bloody tissue and the flexing muscle of his heart. She felt it beat for a moment, then, gently, she caressed it.

The result was immediate. Artwair's eyes bulged out, and

his knees started to buckle. His man caught him as he clutched at his chest.

"No," he gasped. "No."

As if she were still watching herself through the looking glass, Anne heard herself talking.

"You say I am your queen, Artwair," she murmured. "Say it now. Say it. Say it again."

His face was bright red, but his lips were going blue.

"What . . ."

"Say it."

"Not . . . like . . . this."

She felt his heart spasm and realized he would die soon if she did not stop. How marvelously delicate the heart was.

But she didn't want Artwair dead, so with a sigh she released him. He gasped and sagged, then tried to straighten, his eyes brimming with shock and fear.

"I am not what you think I am," she said, releasing her grip on his arm.

"No," he managed weakly, eyes still bulging. "You aren't."

"The fleet is coming—I know that. You know how to fight wars. Can we work together?"

Artwair held her gaze for a long moment, then nodded.

"Good," she said. "Let's discuss this, but quickly. In one bell I'm going to Eslen."

A bell later, as she approached Robert's boat, Anne felt a sudden jolt. It was like waking from one of the dreams she'd had as a child, a dream of falling. What made those dreams so disconcerting was the fact that they often happened when she didn't know she was asleep.

She felt a bit of that now. She remembered her confrontation with Artwair well enough, and the conversation that followed, but the memory possessed an unreal quality, suddenly thrown into focus as the sights, smells, and sounds around her returned with such acuity that they were distracting. The iron-and-iodine scent of water was overpowering, and falls of liquid gold seemed to drop through the clouds.

She noticed the fine wrinkles in the corners of Artwair's eyes and the soft crush of her feet on yellowed grass, followed by the hushed friction of stone and leather.

And Eslen. Above all Eslen, her white towers burning here in sunlight and ghostly pale there in shadow beneath the broken clouds, her pennants fluttering like dragon tails in the sky. Off to the right the lesser twin mounds of Tom Cast and Tom Woth showed fawn crowns above shoulders of evergreen. She felt lifted and at the same time disoriented.

She had not feared Artwair at all, but now her terror was back.

What was she doing?

She wanted to run back to her cousin, place herself in his care, let him take the responsibility and power he so clearly desired. But even that wouldn't save her, and for the moment that was what kept her going. She had seen the arrival of the Lierish ships, just as she had told Artwair. She had seen the passages only women could see.

But she had seen something else, as well: the monstrous woman of her Black Marys, crouching beneath the cold stone in the city of the dead.

She'd been eight when she and Austra first had found that crypt, and like the little girls they were, they had imagined it to be the tomb of Virgenya Dare, though no one really knew where the Born Queen had been buried. They had scratched prayers and curses on lead tissue and pushed them through the crack in the sarcophagus, and they more than half believed their pleas were effective.

As it had turned out, they had been right. Anne had asked for Roderick of Dunmrogh to love her, and he had been driven completely mad by love. She had asked for her sister Fastia to be nicer, and she had been—most apparently to Neil MeqVren, if Aunt Elyoner was to be believed.

What they had been *wrong* about was who lay in the crypt, who was answering their prayers.

She came out of her reverie and realized that Robert was leaning against the stone retaining wall of the dike, watching her.

"Well, dear niece," he said, "are you ready to return home?"

Something about the way he said it seemed odd, and she wondered again if this had somehow been all his idea.

"Pray that I find my mother well," she answered.

"She is in the Wolfcoat Tower," Robert offered helpfully. He nodded toward his only male companion, a short man with wide shoulders and blunt features garnished by the same prim mustache and beard Robert wore. "This is my trusted friend Sir Clement Martyne. He carries my keys and my authority."

"I am your humble servant," the man said.

"If harm comes to her, Sir Clement," Neil said, "you shall know me better, I promise you."

"I am a man of my word," Sir Clement said, "but I should be happy to become further acquainted with you, Sir Neil, under whatever conditions you might care to set."

"Boys," Robert said, "be nice." He reached for Anne's hand. She was so startled, she let him take it. As he raised it to his lips, she had to choke back the urge to vomit.

"A good journey to you," he said. "We shall all meet back here in a day, yes?"

"Yes," Anne replied.

"And discuss our future."

"And discuss the future."

A few moments later she was on a canal barge with her men and their mounts, moving across the water toward Eslen. She felt in her bones as if it were a place she had never been.

When they reached the docks, they mounted and that impression grew.

The castle of Eslen was built upon a high hill, protected by three concentric walls. The Fastness, its outmost wall, was the most impressive, twelve kingsyards high and watched by eight towers. Outside of it, on the broad lower ground between the first gate and the docks, a town had grown up over the years: Docktown, a collection of inns, brothels, warehouses, alehouses—everything a wandering seafarer might want, whether he arrived when the city gates were open or closed. It was usually a bustling, rowdy place, considered dangerous enough that the few times Anne had seen it had been when she had sneaked out of the castle incognito and against her parents' wishes.

Today it was quiet, and the only seafarers she saw were those wearing the royal insignia. There weren't many, though; most were on the fleet her boat had passed through on their way in.

Through open doorways and windows, Anne caught glimpses of men, women, and children—the people who actually lived there—and wondered what would happen to them if and when the fighting started. She remembered the little villages around the castles her army had reduced. They had not fared well.

After some explaining by Sir Clement and the presentation of a letter in Robert's hand, the gates were opened, and they proceeded into Eslen itself.

The city was a bit livelier than Docktown. Anne imagined it had to be. Even if war threatened, bread still had to be baked and bought, clothes had to be washed, beer brewed. Despite the bustle, though, her party drew a lot of curious stares.

"They don't know me," Anne noticed. "Do I look so different?"

Cazio chuckled at that.

"What?" she asked.

"Why *should* they know you?" the Vitellian asked.

"Even if they don't know me as their queen, I have been their princess for seventeen years. Everyone knows me."

"No," Austra corrected. "Everyone in the *castle* knows you. The nobility, the knights, the servants. Most of those would recognize you. But how would the people in the street identify you unless you actually wore a symbol of office?"

Anne blinked. "That's incredible," she said.

"Not really," Cazio replied. "How many of them have had the opportunity to meet you face to face?"

"I mean it's incredible that I never thought of that." Anne turned to Austra. "When we used to come into the city, I always wore disguises. Why didn't you say anything then?"

"I didn't want to spoil your fun," Austra admitted. "Anyway, there *are* people who would have known you, and some of them might have been the wrong people."

Watching her companions grin, Anne felt unaccountably conspired against, as if Austra and Cazio had somehow planned for this bit of stupidity on her part. She quashed the irritation, however.

The winding way steepened before they reached the second gate. The city of Eslen was laid out somewhat like a spider's web draped over an anthill, with the avenues paralleling the broad circles of the ancient walls and streets running down the hills like streams. The largest thoroughfares, however, the ones used by armies and merchants, wound up the hill to prevent them being too steep for wagons and armored horses.

They followed just such a route—the Rixplaf—and so their path carried them through most of the Westhill neighborhoods. Each was distinctive, or so she was told. With some it was obvious; the houses in the old Firoy ward had the steepest roofs in town, all of black slate, so as the road wended above them, it was like looking down on stony waves. The people were pale, with lilting accents. The men wore two-color plaid jerkins, and the women's skirts rarely had fewer than three bright shades.

The ward of Saint Neth, on the other hand, *felt* distinctive, but there was nothing Anne could actually point to to explain why. Still, of most of the city's eighteen wards, Anne had seen only the houses fronting them to the streets, with tantalizing glimpses down the narrow alleys. Once she and Austra had slipped into Gobelin Court, the Sefry quarter, which she believed to be the most exotic part of the city with its vibrant colors, alien music, and odd, spicy smells. Now, after her experiences in the countryside of Crotheny, Anne wondered if the Mannish neighborhoods were not perhaps as strange and distinct.

In short, who *were* the people of Eslen?

She realized she didn't know and wondered if her father had. If any king or emperor of the Crothanic empire ever had, and if in fact such a thing were really knowable at all.

At the moment they were in the Onderwaed district, where the sign of the ridge-backed swine was everywhere in evidence: in door knockers, on small paintings above the doors, as wind vanes on the roof. The plastered houses tended all to be the same umber hue, and the men wore brimmed hats pinned up on one side. Many of them were butchers, and in fact, Mimhus Square was dominated by the impressive facade of the butcher's guild, a two-story building of yellow stone with black casements and roof.

As they entered the square, Anne's attention was drawn more to the spectacle than to the buildings around it. A large crowd was gathered around a raised podium in the center of the plaza, where many oddly clothed persons seemed to be under guard by soldiers. The soldiers wore square caps and black surcoats with the sigil of the Church on them.

Above them—quite literally, perched on a precarious-looking stilt-legged wooden chair—a man dressed as a patir seemed to be presiding over some sort of trial. A gallows loomed behind him.

Anne had never seen anything like it.

"What's going on here?" she asked Sir Clement.

"The Church is using the city squares for public courts," the knight replied. "Heretics are common in the city, and it looks as if the resacaratum has discovered more."

"They look like actors," Austra noted. "Street performers."

Sir Clement nodded. "We've found that actors are most particularly susceptible to the lures of certain heresies and shinecrafting."

"Are they?" Anne asked. She spurred her horse toward the attish.

"One moment!" Sir Clement cried in alarm.

"I heard my uncle state that you were at my command," she responded over her shoulder. "I wonder if you heard the same thing."

"Yes, of course, but—"

"Yes, *Highness,*" Anne said icily. She noticed Cazio placing himself so he could come between her and Robert's knight should the need arise.

"Yes . . . Highness," Sir Clement gritted.

The patir was watching them now.

"What's going on here?" he called.

Anne drew herself up. "Do you know me, patir?" she asked.

His eyes narrowed, then widened.

"Princess Anne," he replied.

"And, by law of the Comven, sovereign of this city," Anne added. "At least in my brother's absence."

"That is debatable, Highness," the patir said, his gaze flickering nervously to Clement.

"My uncle gave me passage into the city," Anne informed him. "Thus, it would seem he has some belief in my claim."

"Is this so?" the patir asked Clement.

Clement shrugged. "So it would seem."

"In any case," the churchman said, "I'm engaged in the business of the Church, not that of the crown. It is immaterial who sits on the throne so far as these proceedings are concerned."

"Oh, I assure you that isn't the case," Anne replied. "Now, please tell me of what these people are accused."

"Heresy and shinecraft."

Anne looked the company over.

"Who is your leader?" she asked them.

A balding man of middle years bowed to her. "I am, Your Majesty. Pendun MaypValclam."

"What did you do to come before this court?"

"We performed a play, Majesty, nothing more—a sort of singspell."

"The play by my mother's court composer, Leovigild Ackenzal?"

"Yes, that one, Majesty, as best we could."

"The play has been judged to be shinecraft most foul," the patir erupted. "That confession alone consigns them to the necklace of Saint Woth."

Anne arched her eyebrows at the patir, then turned and gazed around the square at the faces of the assembled on-lookers.

"I've heard of this play," she said, raising her voice. "I hear it is very popular." She sat straighter in the saddle. "I am Anne, daughter of William and Muriele. I have come to take my father's throne. I've a mind to let my first act be the pardoning of these poor actors, for my father would never have tolerated this sort of injustice. What do you say to that, people of Eslen?"

She was met by a moment of stunned silence.

"It is 'er, you know," she heard someone call out from the crowd. "I've seen 'er before."

"Free 'em!" someone else yelled, and in a moment every-one but the soldiers and churchmen had taken to shouting for the troupe to be let go.

"You are free to go," Anne told the players. "My men will escort you from this court."

"Enough," Sir Clement shouted. "Enough of this non-sense!"

"Anne!" Cazio said.

But she saw them, as she had half expected: footmen in Robert's colors, entering the square from every direction, pushing through the indignant crowd.

Anne nodded. "Well," she said. "Better to know this now than inside the Wolfcoat Tower, don't you think?"

"What shall we do?" Cazio asked.

"Why, fight of course," she replied.

CHAPTER SIX

✛

CROSSROADS

"WINNA'S NOT doing well," Ehawk murmured.

Aspar sighed, tracking his gaze across the distant hillside.

"I know," he said. "She's been coughing blood. So have you." He pointed at a line of blackened vegetation. "See, there?"

"Yes," Ehawk replied. "It came out of the water over there."

Something that left a trail like that ought not to be hard to track, but the woorm used rivers for a lot of its traveling, and that was a problem, especially when the river branched. They might have lost it when it turned up the Then River, but for the dead fish flowing from its mouth into the Warlock.

They followed the trail at the greatest distance possible, never actually stepping on it or taking water downstream of it, and Aspar had hoped that the poison already in them would work its way out.

It hadn't.

The medicine they'd gotten from Fend's men sustained them, but they were forced to take less and less of it each day to stretch it out. The horses seemed better, but then, none of the beasts had actually stood on poisoned ground or breathed the monster's breath.

Not far away, Winna coughed. Ehawk knelt and searched through the remains of the campfire.

"You think this is Stephen's trail?"

Aspar glanced around. "Four of 'em, and they didn't come from the river. They came down from the Brogh y Stradh. If it's Stephen, the woorm isn't following him, but their paths keep crossing."

"Maybe it knows where he's going."

"Maybe. But at this point I'm more concerned with finding Fend."

"Maybe he died."

Aspar barked a sharp laugh that became a cough. "I doubt it. I should have finished him."

"I don't see how. By the time we found your arrow, the woorm was gone. You can't imagine you were going to kill it with your dirk."

"No, but I could have killed Fend."

"The woorm is his ally. We were lucky to escape."

"So now we die slow."

"No," Ehawk said. "We'll catch it. It's on land now, so it won't be as fast."

"Yah," Aspar said, a bit doubtfully. Ehawk was probably right, but they, too, were slower every day.

"See to the horses and the camp," Aspar said. "I'll find us something to eat."

"Yah," Ehawk said.

Aspar found a game trail and a convenient perch in a sycamore. He settled there and let weariness have his body while trying to keep his eyes and wits sharp.

It had been ten years since Aspar had been in the low marshes around the Then, on one of his rare ventures outside the boundaries of the King's Forest. He'd gone to deliver some bandits to the magistrate of Ofthen town, and while there he had heard interesting tales about the Sarnwood and the witch who was supposed to live there. He'd been at his most footloose back then and reckoned he'd see what the ancient, supposedly haunted forest was really like. He'd made it only about halfway before news about the Black Wargh turned him back south, and he hadn't ever taken up the trip again.

But he'd stopped there for a few days to hunt. That had been in the summer, with everything lush and green. Now it all appeared thin, a landscape of rushes and broken cattails, brittle sheens of ice in the standing places that clutched any color the sky might give them. To his right he made out the black stone remains of a wall, and farther up a mound that looked suspiciously regular. He'd heard there had been a mighty kingdom there long ago. Stephen probably could go on about it at distracting length, but all Aspar knew was that it was long gone, and once you got a few leagues from Ofthen, this was one of the most desolate parts of the Midenlands.

The soil was poor even when the land was drained, and what few people lived in the area were mostly river fishers or goat herders, but there wasn't much sign even of them. He vaguely remembered hearing something about the land having been cursed during the Warlock Wars, too, but he'd never paid much attention to that sort of thing, though in hindsight maybe he should have.

Something caught his eye: not movement but something weird, something that ought not be there . . .

A sick prickling crept up his shoulders as he realized what it was. Black thorns had sprouted from a dead cypress and had clawed their way into nearby trees. He'd seen such thorns before, of course, first in the valley where the Briar King slept and later as infestations in the King's Forest. And here they were, too.

Did that mean that the Briar King had come this way? Or that the briars were now spreading everywhere?

He shuddered, then went dizzy and nearly fell from his roost. He clung desperately to the branches, his breath coming in fits. Spots danced before his eyes. He'd only pretended to drink his fraction of the medicine for the last few days, and that was starting to take its toll.

He had to catch Fend. Where was the sceathaoveth going?

Something had been nagging at him, and he suddenly realized what it was.

Before he could think much about it, movement caught his eye. Barely breathing, he waited until it resolved itself into a doe. Calming his shaking hand, he took aim and put an arrow through her neck. She bolted, and with a sigh he climbed down from the tree. Now he would have to follow her for a while.

"I've got a new plan," he told Winna and Ehawk, as they roasted the venison. Winna looked even worse than she had earlier in the day, and she clearly was having trouble eating. "But seeing as how it concerns all of us, I'll want you two to mull it over."

"What?" Winna asked.

"It's something Leshya said, when we first met her. She said she'd heard that Fend had gone to see the Sarnwood witch."

"Yah," Winna said. "I remember that."

"And the fellow we captured—he said that's where Fend got the woorm. She's supposed to be the mother of monsters, so I guess that makes sense."

"You think Fend's going back there?" Winna asked.

"Maybe. Maybe not. That's not my point, though. If he got the woorm from the witch, he probably got the antidote there, too."

"Oh," Winna said, looking up.

"Ha," Ehawk said.

"Yah. Maunt you both, we're not catching this woorm. Not before we die. It's days ahead of us, and yah, it may go slower on land, but I've seen it move, and it's still as fast as a horse. And if it takes to another river . . ."

"So instead you want to go find the mother of monsters and ask her for the remedy for her child's poison?" Winna said.

"I wasn't planning on asking Fend for it," Aspar replied. "I won't ask her, either."

"But we *know* Fend has it."

"Not really. Or, rather, if I know Fend, he's just got enough for himself."

"Or maybe there is no antidote," Winna went on. "Maybe Fend is like Stephen, and the venom doesn't eat at him at all."

"That's possible," Aspar admitted. "But Mother Gastya had a real remedy. Mother Gastya was a witch, so maybe this Sarnwood woman . . ." He trailed off and shrugged.

Winna considered that for a moment, then smiled weakly. "It's worth going just to see you chase a kinderspell," she finally said. "I'm for it."

Ehawk didn't answer for a long time.

"She eats children," he finally said.

"Well," Aspar replied, "I'm not a child."

They forded the Then upstream of the woorm's path just at dawn, with Ogre breaking the way through the thin sheen of ice. The ground was firmer beyond and quickly rose in low terraced hills thick in willow and sassafras. By the time the sun was far up, they were on rolling prairie broken up by pasture and fields, brilliant green in calf-high winter wheat. Trees were few and far between, and stands greater than half a dozen were rare indeed. Aspar didn't like so much openness; it felt as if something might swoop up on him from the sky. Who knew, maybe it could happen? If there could be a snake half a league long, maybe there were eagles that big, too.

There were also too many people in the Midenlands, at least there had been. They didn't build huge towns as they did toward either coast, but farmsteads were common—a house, a barn, a few smaller buildings—and every few leagues or so there was a market square with half a dozen buildings. Almost anything that looked like a hill had a castle on it, some in ruins, some puffing smoke to show they were still inhabited. That day they saw three from sunup to sundown. That seemed like a lot, seeing as how there weren't many rises in the land that imagination might make a hill of.

But they didn't actually see anyone, not that first day, because they were still pretty much along the woorm's trail, and it seemed to have made a detour every time it came within sight of houses. They didn't see any cows, sheep, goats, or horses, either. The thing had to eat, and considering its size, it probably had to eat a lot.

Early the next day, though, the monster's trail turned more

northerly than Aspar wanted to go, putting them at a cross-road. The time came to test his resolve. A glance at Winna kept his mind made up, and they went northeast, toward the Sarnwood.

Within a bell they came across some foraging cows and a couple of people with them. As they got closer, Aspar saw it was a boy and girl, neither one older than thirteen or so. They looked at first as if they might run, but they stood their ground until Aspar and his companions were fifty or so kingsyards away.

"Hello!" the girl shouted. "Who is that?"

Aspar held up empty hands. "I haet Aspar White," he called back. "I'm the king's holter. These are my friends. We mean you no harm."

"What's a holter?" the girl returned.

"I ward the forest," he replied.

The girl scratched her head, then looked around as if searching for a forest. "Are you lost?" she asked.

"No," Aspar replied. "But can I come closer? All this shoutin' is wearing out my throat."

The two looked at each other, than back at the trio. "I don't know," the girl said.

"We should dismount," Winna said. "They're frightened."

"They're scared of me," Aspar said. "I'll dismount. Winna, why don't you go closer first. But stay on your horse, at least until you get there."

"That's a good idea," she assented.

Aethlaud and her brother Aohsli were both fair-haired, pink-cheeked youths. She was thirteen, and he was ten. They had some bread and cheese, to which Aspar added a generous portion of the last day's venison. He hadn't had time to cure it properly, so what they hadn't eaten would soon spoil, any-way. They sat on a gentle rise beneath a solitary persimmon tree and watched the cows.

"We're taking 'em down to Haemeth," Aethlaud ex-plained, "to my uncle's place. But we're supposed to graze them on the way."

"Where is that?" Aspar asked.

Her expression said that anyone who didn't know where Haemeth was didn't know much of anything.

"It's about a league that way," she said, pointing northeast. "On the Thaurp-Crenreff road."

"We're going that way," Winna said. Aspar wanted to shush her before she offered to accompany them. He didn't want to be kept to the speed of cows. But she looked so gaunt and brittle, it froze his voice.

"Are you sick?" Aohsli blurted.

"Yes," Winna said. "We all are. But it isn't catching."

"No, it's from the waurm, isn't it?"

They were out of Oostish country, and her pronunciation was a little different, but there wasn't any mistaking what she meant.

"Yah," Aspar said.

"Haudy *saw* it," the boy confided.

His sister popped him on the back of the head. "*Aethl*aud," she snapped. "I'm too old for that nickname. I'll be married by next year, and Mom will send you to live with me, and I'll make you eat kalfsceit if you call me that."

"Mom still calls you that."

"That's Mom," the girl said.

"You saw the woorm?" Winna interrupted. "West of here?"

"No," she said. "That's it coming back, I think."

"How do you mean?" Aspar asked, leaning closer.

"It was back before Yule," she said. "I went with my mom's brother Orthel to Mael to have some rye ground. That's on Fenn Creek, what flows into the Warlóck. We saw it in the river. The people around there, a lot of 'em took sick, like you."

"Before Yule."

"Yah."

"So it *did* come out of the Sarnwood."

"Oh, yah," the girl said, her eyes rounding. "Where else would it come from?"

That lifted Aspar's spirits, if only a little. He'd made one good guess; perhaps the rest of his "maybes" were true.

"What do you know about the Sarnwood?" Aspar asked.

"It's full of ghosts and alvs and booygshins!" Aohsli said.

"And the witch," Aethlaud said. "Don't forget the witch."

"Do you know anyone who's been there?" Winna asked.

"Eh . . . no," the girl replied. " 'Cause anyone who ever went—they never came back."

" 'Cept Grandpa," the boy corrected.

"Yah," Aethlaud agreed. "But he's gone west t' the wood."

"Is that where you're going?" Aohsli asked Aspar. "The Sarnwood?"

"Yah." Aspar nodded.

The boy blinked, then glanced at Ogre. "When you are dead, may I have your horse?"

Ehawk, not usually given to outbursts, exploded at that. He was laughing so hard that Winna caught it, and in the end even Aspar found himself grinning.

"Now you're wishing for things you'd might rather not have," he said. "Ogre might be a little much for you."

"Nah, I could handle 'im," Aohsli said.

"How much longer do you expect it'll take you to get to Haemeth?" Winna asked.

"Another two days," Aethlaud said. "We don't want to walk the fat off 'em."

"Is it safe, just the two of you out here?"

Aethlaud raised her shoulders. "Used to be safer, I guess." She frowned, then continued a little more defiantly. "But there's not much choice. There's nobody else to do it, not since our father died. And we've done it before."

Winna glanced at Aspar. "Maybe we could—"

"We can't," he said. "We can't. Two days—"

"A moment over here, Aspar?" Winna asked, gesturing with a toss of her head.

"Yah."

There wasn't anyplace to go except away, and Winna was

having trouble moving, so they didn't go all that far. But whispering made it feel a little private.

"You aren't as sick as I am," Winna said. "Something happened when the Briar King saved your life, something that made you stronger. You don't really drink the medicine you got from Fend's man anymore, do you?"

He acknowledged that with a small nod. "I still feel it," he admitted, "but yah, I'm not so sick as you."

"How much farther to the Sarnwood?"

He considered. "Three days."

"At the pace we're traveling, I mean."

He sighed. "Four, maybe five."

She coughed, and he had to catch her to keep her from falling.

"I'm pretty sure I won't be sitting a horse in two days, Aspar. You'll have to tie me on. Ehawk's got a little longer, I'd guess."

"But if we dally here . . ."

"Just me and Ehawk, Aspar," Winna said. Her eyes were brimming with tears. "If I'm only going to live a few more days, I'd rather use them helping these two get where they're going than chasing after some cure that isn't there."

"It *is* there," Aspar insisted. "You heard 'em: Fend got the woorm in the Sarnwood. I'm sure he got the antidote there, too."

"I also heard them say that most everyone who has ever gone into the Sarnwood never came out."

"That's because it's never been me before."

She shook her head wearily. "No," she said. "Let's take them to Haemeth. You can ask questions there, learn more about the witch."

"We can do that, anyway, without dallying to drive cattle."

"I want to help them, Aspar."

"They don't need help," he argued, desperation creeping into his words. "They've done this before. They said so."

"They're terrified," Winna contradicted. "Who knows what they'll come across out here in two days. If not a woorm or greffyn, then maybe just cattle thieves."

"They aren't my concern, Winna—you are."

"Yah. I know. But do this for me."

She was crying freely but silently. Her face was red, her lips tinted blue.

"I'll go," he said. "I'll go by myself. It'll be easier that way; you're right about that. Ehawk won't be in any condition to fight by then; you're right. I wasn't thinking."

"No, love," Winna said. "No. Then I'll die without you, you see? I want to breathe my last in your arms. I want you to be there."

"You aren't going to die," he said evenly. "I'll be back, with your cure. I'll meet you in Haemeth."

"Don't. Can't you hear me? I don't want to die alone! And she'll kill you!"

"What about Ehawk? You've given up on yourself, but there still might be time to save him, even by your reckoning."

"I . . . Aspar, please. I'm not strong enough for this."

His throat was clotted, and his pulse pounded in his ears.

"Enough," he said. He lifted her, strode back to her mount, and pushed her up on it, then brushed away her clinging hands.

"Ehawk," he shouted. "Come here."

The boy obeyed.

"You and Winna'll go with these two to the town. Then you find a leic, you hear? The folk around here may know more about monsters and their venom than we think. You wait there, and I'll be back."

"Aspar, no!" Winna wailed weakly.

"You were right!" he shouted back. "Go with them."

"You come, too!"

Instead of answering, he clapped his mouth and mounted Ogre.

"I'll tell him to find you when I am dead," he told Aohsli. "But you take care of him."

"Auy, sir!"

He turned to regard Winna and found her and her horse only a few paces away.

"Don't leave me," she whispered. Her lips moved, but he scarcely heard the sound.

"Not for long," he promised.

She closed her eyes. "Kiss me, then," she said. "Kiss me one more time."

Grief welled up like a monster, climbing out of the caves of his guts, trying to claw its way out of his eyes.

"Keep that kiss," he said. "I'll get it when I return."

Then he turned and rode and did not—could not—look back.

CHAPTER SEVEN

THE MAD WOLF

ROBERT DARE stroked his mustache, sipped his wine, and sighed. From their vantage on the dike he glanced out over the flooded lands toward Eslen.

"I've always favored the Galléan wines," he commented. "You can all but taste the sunlight in them, you know? The white stone, the black soil, the dark-eyed girls." He paused. "You've been there, Sir Neil? Vitellia, Tero Gallé, Hornladh—you've had quite the tour of this continent. I really hope you can arrange to see the rest of it. Tell me—they say that traveling opens the mind, broadens the palate. Did you learn any new tastes in your travels? Or anything at all?"

Watching the prince, Neil had the strange impression he was seeing some sort of an insect. It wasn't anything obvious but something subtle about the way he moved.

A dog, a stag, even a bird or lizard—all those things moved smoothly, in time with the larger world around them. Beetles, in contrast, moved weirdly. It wasn't just that they were quick or had six legs; it was more that they seemed to move to the rhythms of a different world, a smaller one, or perhaps to the smaller rhythms of this world that giants such as Neil could not feel.

That was how it was with Robert. His gestures studied normality but could not reproduce it. Seen from the corner of the eye, even the parting of his lips seemed oddly monstrous.

"Sir Neil?" Robert prompted politely.

"I was just thinking," Neil said, "how best to sum it up. I was overwhelmed at first by the *size* of the world, how many parts it has. I was amazed by how different people are, and at the same time how they are all the same."

"Interesting," Robert said in a tone that suggested it was anything but.

"Yes," Neil said. "Until I came to Eslen, I thought my world was large. The sea, after all, seems endless when one is upon it, and the islands seem uncountable. But then I came to discover all of that could fit into a cup, if the world were a table."

"Poetic," Robert said.

"In the little cup of the world I lived in," Neil went on, "things were pretty simple. I knew who I fought for, I knew why. Then I came here, and things became confusing. As I traveled farther into the world, they became more confusing yet."

Robert smiled indulgently. "Confusing how? Did you lose your sense of right and wrong?"

Neil returned the smile. "I grew up fighting, and mostly I fought Weihand raiders. They were bad people because they attacked my people. They were bad people because they fought for Hansa, people who once kept my people in bondage and would do it again if they could. And yet looking back on it, most of the men I killed were probably not that different from me. They probably died believing their cause was just, hoping their fathers would look from beyond the world and be proud of them."

"Yes, I see," Robert said. "You may not know this, but

there is a philosophy of considerable weight built on that same premise. It is not a philosophy suited to the weak-minded, however, because it suggests—as, in fact, *you* just suggested—that there is really no such thing as good or evil, that most people do what they think is right. It's just the lack of agreement on what is right that leads us to believe in good and evil."

He leaned forward almost eagerly.

"You traveled great distances, Sir Neil. Leagues. But one can also travel, so to speak, in time, through the study of history. Consider the argument that sits before us now; I am vilified for trying to strengthen our bonds of friendship with Hansa and thus avert a war we can ill afford. My detractors point out that by doing so I create conditions that *might* allow a Reiksbaurg to take the throne a few years hence.

"Now, why should that be considered wrong? Because Hansa is evil? Because they desire control of this kingdom? And yet my family, the Dares, wrested Crotheny from Hansa in a bloody conflict. My great-great-grandfather murdered the Reiksbaurg emperor in the Hall of Doves. Who was good and who was evil then? It's a meaningless question, don't you think?"

"I'm not as learned as you," Neil acknowledged. "I know little about history, even less about philosophy. I am a knight, after all, and my job is to do as I am told. I have killed many men I might have liked if we had met under other circumstances, because they weren't—as you say—evil. We were merely serving masters at cross-purposes. In some cases, it wasn't even that. To do my duty, I had to stay alive, and to stay alive sometimes means killing others.

"As you say, most people in this world are just trying to do the best they can, protect the ones they love and the life they know, live up to their duties and obligations."

"All perfectly reasonable."

"Yes," Neil continued. "And so when I meet real evil, it stands out all the more, like a tall black tree in a field of green heather."

Robert's eyes fluttered, and then he chuckled. "So after all that, you still believe there are genuinely evil men. You somehow possess the ability to read their hearts and see that they aren't like most people, who think they are doing the right thing."

"Let me put it another way," Neil said.

"Oh, please do."

"Do you know the island of Leen?"

"I'm afraid I don't."

"There's no reason you should. It's not much more than a rock, really, though a rock with a thousand small valleys and crevices. There are wolves there, but they keep to the heights. They don't come down to where people dwell.

"In my fifteenth year I was on Leen for most of a summer, part of a Lierish garrison. And that year a wolf did come down—a big one. At first it only killed kids and ewes, but soon enough it started in on children, and then grown women and men. It didn't eat what it killed, mind you; it just mauled them and left them to die. Now, there might have been any number of reasons for it doing that; maybe its mother died, along with its brothers and sisters, and it grew up outside the pack, a loner hated by its own kind. Maybe it was bitten by something that gave it the water-fearing madness. Maybe a man mistreated it once, and it had sworn revenge on all of our kind.

"We didn't ask those questions. We didn't have to. This thing looked like a wolf, but it didn't behave like one. It couldn't be frightened away, or appeased, or reasoned with. The only way to make the world a better place was to take that beast out of it, and that we did."

"One might argue that you did not make the world a better place for the wolf."

"One might reply that to ask the world to accommodate itself to the needs of a single mad wolf can never make it a better place for anyone. And the wolf that would ask such a thing of the world—well, that's my black tree in a field of heather, you see?"

"Why not a green tree in a field of black heather?" Robert mused.

"Why not?" Neil agreed. "It's not the color that matters, really."

"Here's my question, then," Robert said, quaffing the rest of the wine and reaching for the bottle. He stopped in midgrasp.

"May I?"

"If you wish."

Robert poured himself more wine, took a sip, then returned his regard to Neil.

"My question. Suppose you felt someone was this black tree of yours, this truly evil person. A mad wolf that needed killing. Why ever would you entrust the safety of, say, a young woman to his promise?"

"Because he serves only himself," Neil replied. "Never something higher. So I can be sure he would never sacrifice himself."

"Really? Not even out of spite or revenge? I mean, we all must die. I see no escape from that, do you? Let us suppose this man of yours had ambitions, and seeing them thwarted was just, well, impossible for him. If a man cannot inherit a house he covets, might he not burn it down? Wouldn't that be in keeping with the sort of person you've been describing?"

"I'm tired of this," Neil said. "If anything happens to Anne, you will not die quickly."

"What is her signal? I wonder. How will you know she is well?"

"There is a signal," Neil assured him. "Something we can see from here. If we do not see it before sundown, I will cut off one of your fingers and send it to your men. That will continue until she is either free or proved dead."

"You're going to feel so foolish when this is all over and Anne and I are fast friends. What do you suppose will happen to a knight who threatened his liege?"

"At the moment," Neil said, "that isn't my concern. When it is, I will of course accept whatever fate the queen thinks I deserve."

"Of course you will." Robert sneered.

Robert glanced up at the sky and twitched a smile. "You haven't asked about your last queen, Muriele. Aren't you curious about her?"

"I'm more than curious," Neil replied. "I haven't asked about her because I've no reason to trust anything you say. Whatever you tell me about her will leave me in doubt. I will find out how she is in good time."

"And suppose she complains about my treatment of her? Suppose everything else goes well here—I step aside, Anne takes the throne—and yet Muriele still has some protest concerning her treatment?"

"Then you and I will have another discussion about mad wolves."

Robert drained his cup and reached for the bottle again. When he tried to pour, however, he found it empty.

"Surely there is more of this around," he said in a loud voice.

At Neil's nod, one of Artwair's squires hurried to fetch another bottle.

"This isn't about Fastia, is it?" Robert asked. "These feelings of yours? That's not what this is really about, I hope."

Neil had managed to feel mostly contempt for Robert until that point. That was good, because it kept his murderous inclinations toward the man in check. But now rage came howling up, and it was only with great effort that he forced it back into his marrow.

"Such a tragedy," Robert said. "And poor Elseny, just about to be wed. If only William had had more sense."

"How can you blame the king?" Neil asked.

"He forced the Comven to legitimize his daughters. How could he imagine that they would not become targets?"

"Targets for whom, Prince Robert?" Neil asked. "An usurper?"

Robert sighed heavily. "What are *you* suggesting, Sir Neil?"

"I thought it was you doing the suggesting, Prince Robert."

Robert leaned forward, and his voice dropped very low.

"How did it feel? Royal wool? Different from the lesser sort? I've always found it so. But they buck and cry like animals, all of them, don't they?"

"Shut up," Neil grated.

"Don't get me wrong; Fastia really was in need of a good thumping. She always seemed the sort to like it from behind, on all fours, like a dog. Was that the way it was?"

Neil was aware that his breath was coming harshly, and the world was taking on the bright edge that came with the quetiac, the battle rage. His hand was already gripped on the hilt of the feysword.

"You should be quiet now," Neil said.

The boy arrived with a new bottle of wine.

"This will quiet me," Robert said. But as he took the bottle, he suddenly stood and shattered it against the boy's head.

It seemed to go very slowly: the heavy glass container cracking against the squire's temple, the spray of blood. Neil saw one eye pop from its socket as the skull deformed under the impact. At the same time, he saw Robert reaching for the boy's sword.

And he was happy. Happy, because now the feysword hummed from its sheath and he lunged forward. Robert twisted the dying lad in front of him, but the blade cut through and deep into the prince. Neil felt an odd jolt, almost a protest from the weapon, and his fingers loosened reflexively.

From the corner of his eye he saw Robert's fist coming, still holding the neck and upper third of the bottle. He brought his hand up without thinking.

Too late. The side of his head seemed to explode in a white-hot concussion. He fell away from the blow, his rage sustaining his consciousness, but when he came back to his feet, Robert was already two yards away, holding the feysword, a demonic smirk on his face.

Dizzily, Neil reached for his knife, knowing it wouldn't help much against the ensorcelled weapon.

But an arrow struck the prince high in the chest, and then another, and he stumbled back, shouted, and pitched over the side of the dike into the water. Neil lurched after him, gripping the knife.

Artwair's men caught him at the birm, preventing him leaping the eight kingsyards down into the water.

"No, you fool," Artwair shouted. "Let my archers have him."

Neil fought his captors, but blood had filled one of his eyes, and his muscles felt horribly loose.

"No!" he screamed. But following that, a deep silence fell. They waited for the prince to surface, dead or alive.

But after many long breaths he did not. Artwair sent men into the water then, but they found nothing.

A cold mist ran up the river that evening, but the Pelican Tower stood above all that, its north face clearly visible and dark.

"Even if she puts out the light," Neil said, pressing a clean rag to his head wound, "it might only mean she was tortured into telling her signal."

"Auy," Artwair agreed. "The only thing that will have real meaning is if she doesn't put out the light at all."

"You'd like that, wouldn't you?" Neil snapped. "Dead at the hand of Robert's men, Anne might be more useful to you than alive—at least now that you know her mind."

Artwair was silent for a moment, then took a pull on the green glass bottle he'd put beside them on the boards. The two men sat on the upper story of a half-burned malend, watching for Anne's signal.

He offered the bottle to Neil.

"I won't pretend she left me happy this morning," the duke said. "She reached right inside me. I could feel 'er there. What happened to her, Sir Neil? What has that girl become?"

Neil shrugged and reached for the bottle. "Her mother sent her to the Coven Saint Cer. Does that mean anything to you?"

Artwair stared skeptically as Neil took a drink from the bottle, tasting fire, peat, and seaweed. He looked at the bottle in surprise.

"This is from Skern," he said.

"Auy. *Oiche de Fié*. The Coven Saint Cer, eh? A coven-trained princess. Muriele is an interesting one."

He took the bottle and swallowed more of the stuff as Neil let the aroma filter up his nose. He'd never drunk much; it dulled the senses. Right now he didn't much care, because his senses had proved pretty useless and every piece of him hurt.

"But you've got me wrong, Sir Neil," Artwair said. "Just because I think a girl of seventeen winters doesn't have the skills to lay siege to the greatest fortress city in the world, that doesn't mean my aim is the throne. I'm unhappy enough with my duller duties as duke without being saddled and ridden by the Comven. Believe me or not, I do think she's the one ought be on the throne, and I'm trying to put her there." He drank again. "Well, she got her way, and see what's happened."

"Because of me," Neil said, taking the bottle back and swallowing hard. He thought he would gag for a moment, but then it went down, feeling smoother this time. "Because of my rage."

"Robert provoked your rage," Artwair said. "He wanted to die."

"He wanted me to fight him," Neil said, ignoring Artwair's outstretched hand long enough to take another drink. Then he relinquished the bottle. "That part is true, and I fell for it like the fallow-brained fool I am. I let the anger take me away from common sense. But he isn't dead; that's the thing."

"I didn't see it, but they say you fair skewered him, and it's for sure he didn't come up," Artwair pointed out.

"Well, these days that's nothing certain at all," Neil said. "In Vitellio and in Dunmrogh both I fought a man who couldn't die. The first time he nearly killed me. The second time I cut off his head, yet he kept moving. In the end we chopped him into a hundred pieces and burned them. A friend of mine told me he was a thing called a nauschalk, that he could exist because the law of death had been broken. Now, I'm far from an expert on this, but I have fought one nauschalk, and I'm pretty sure Prince Robert is another."

Artwair swore in a language Neil didn't know, then said nothing for the time it took each of them to have three drinks. It was the customary silence after one had spoken of something unnatural—at least while in cups.

"There are rumors," he said finally, "rumors that suggest such a thing, but I discounted them. Robert always had unhealthy appetites, and people exaggerate."

Neil took another drink. By now the oiche felt like an old friend drawing a blanket up from his toes to warm him.

"That was what we were missing," he said. "He probably told his man to have Anne killed or taken captive the moment they passed through the gates. Then all he had to do was make sure we didn't lock him up or slice him into pieces. All he had to do was provoke me into attacking him, which he did right well."

"Yes, but whatever you might have done, the result to Anne would have been the same, you see."

"Unless she's safe until he returns," Neil said. "That would have been the wiser plan. When he's back, safe in the city, *then* the trap is sprung."

"Auy," Artwair replied. "That would make more sense, I'm supposing. But Anne isn't helpless, either. I'll bet Robert doesn't know what *she* can do. And she has fifty good men with her."

Across the water they heard the first, melodious chime of the Vespers bell.

The window of the Pelican Tower remained dark.

"She might make a fight of it, for a while, if she found the right place to defend. If she isn't lulled into taking poison or has an arrow sunk into her eye."

"I doubt she's lulled," Artwair said. "The tower isn't lit. That means she's dead, captured, or for some other reason not in the castle. Whichever it is, our duty is clear."

"What's that?"

"We have to strike, and now. The rumor has gone out by

now of what happened with Robert. Even if he lives, everyone believes him dead. If we give him time to reappear, it
will prove confusing. So we strike immediately, while we
can."

"Strike what?" Neil asked.

"Thornrath. After what she did to me this morning, I'm
tempted to believe Anne's prophecy concerning Baron Fail
and the Lierish fleet. We have two days to take control of
Thornrath. If we manage that—and if Fail arrives as
foretold—then we have a chance to take Eslen and save her."

"Unless she is already dead."

"In which case we will avenge her. In no case would I see
Robert on the throne, nor, I'm sure, would you."

"You have that right," Neil said, lifting the bottle. The
liquor was now a tide, lifting his anger even as the night
darkened and the water deepened. "*Can* we capture Thornrath?"

"Possibly," Artwair said. "It will be costly, though."

"May I lead the charge?"

Artwair swirled the bottle, then sipped at it. "I'd meant to
have you do that," he said, "on account of that feysword of
yours. It's a narrow approach, and that sword might have
made a difference. Now . . ."

"I'd still prefer to lead it," Neil said. "I'm a warrior. I can
kill. About strategy I know little. Without Anne here, that
would be the best use for me."

"You'll probably die," Artwair said. "Anne would think
I'd sent you to your doom to avenge myself on her. I can't
have her thinking that."

"I'm not too attached to this life," Neil confessed. "And I
don't much care anymore what Her Highness thinks, if she's
still able to think anything. She's the one put me in this situation. I'm tired of being set up to fail, only to live and lament
it. Let me lead that charge, and I'll write a note in my own
hand for you to give to whoever might care. I suspect that'd
be no one."

"You've a better reputation than you think," Artwair said.

"Then let me better it yet and live on in song," Neil

replied. "I don't need a feysword. Just get me a few spears and a broadsword that won't break at the first swing. Then find me some men who love death, and I'll give you Thornrath."

Artwair handed him the bottle. "As you wish, Sir Neil," he said. "I'd never deny a good man his destiny."

CHAPTER EIGHT

✢

A WELL-MANNERED VIPER

HESPERO SMILED and rose from his chair.

"Praifec?" Ehan gasped.

"You seem chagrined," Hespero said, raising an eyebrow at the little man.

"Surprised, perhaps," Stephen quickly replied. "Sir Elden led us to expect a humble sacritor."

"But I *am* a sacritor," Hespero said, stroking his goatee. "And a fratir, a patir, a peslih, an agreon."

"Of course, your grace," Stephen said. "It's only that one usually is known by one's most exalted title."

"Generally true, depending on one's purpose." His brows knitted. "Brother Stephen, are *you* unhappy to see me?"

Stephen blinked.

OBSERVATIONS QUAINT & CURIOUS: CONCERNING THE
WELL-MANNERED VIPER
Perhaps the most deadly of its sort, the well-mannered viper is capable of great charm, luring its prey near with honeyed words. It is a most unusual predator in that it has the habit of convincing other animals to kill for its sustenance and amusement. It is only by observing the middle

of the eye where the icy fluid that passes for its blood co-
agulates visibly that one can identify its true nature, and
when one is that close, it is often too late to save oneself.

It is in the perfection of its knowledge—or lack
thereof—that survival often hinges, for if the viper believes itself well served, it may allow the servant to live
and perform another task. But if it believes itself betrayed, and its real nature is discovered, woe to the hapless
titmouse or toad that finds itself confronting those gleaming, venoméd teeth . . .

"Brother Stephen?" the praifec said impatiently.

"Praifec, I—"

"Perhaps your anxiety stems from what you have to tell
me. I have had no word of you. Where are the holter and
your friend Winna? Have you failed in the task with which I
entrusted you?"

Stephen felt the first sense of relief he'd experienced
since meeting Sir Elden. It wasn't much, but it was something.

"They were slain, your grace," he said, putting on the most
doleful face he could manage.

"Then the arrow did not work?"

"We never had a chance to use it, your grace. We were
beset by slinders. We never even saw the Briar King."

"Slinders?"

"I beg your pardon, your grace. That is the Oostish term
for the wild men and women Ehawk reported to you."

"Ah, yes," Hespero said. "Did you at least learn more
about them?"

"Nothing of note, your grace," Stephen lied.

"A pity. But still I don't understand. How did you know to
find me here? I came to this place in secrecy."

"Your grace, I hadn't the slightest idea I would find you
here," Stephen replied, his mind spinning down the false
road he was building, wondering what he would find over
the next hill.

The praifec frowned. "Then why are you here? You failed in the mission I assigned you. I should think your first priority would be to report that failure, and the logical place to do that would be Eslen. What on earth brought you to this remote place?"

Stephen's road had narrowed to a rope of the sort jugglers walked to amuse children. He'd tried it once, in the town square of Morris Top, and the relief at managing to take two steps had felt like a triumph. But it hadn't been; it had only been two steps, and then he had lost his balance and fallen.

"We came here at my request, your grace," Brother Ehan interrupted.

Stephen tried to keep his face neutral. He hoped he had succeeded, even though the praifec's glance already had shifted to the Herilanzer.

"Pardon me," Hespero said. "I don't believe I know you."

Ehan bowed. "Brother Alfraz, your grace, at your service. I was with Fratrex Laer when he went to the monastery d'Ef to cleanse the heretics there."

"Really. And how is Fratrex Laer?"

"Then you haven't heard, your grace. Word should have reached you by now; we sent messengers to Eslen. He was slain by the slinders, the ones Brother Stephen spoke of. We were fortunate to escape."

"So *many* fortunate escapes," the praifec commented. "Still, how does that explain your presence here?"

"We arrived at the monastery and found only piles of bone. Everyone had vanished—or so we thought. But that evening we discovered Fratrex Pell, locked away in the uppermost meditation room. He was quite mad, raving about the end of the world and how the only hope was to find a certain mountain in the Bairghs. Less than a bell later, the same fate that befell the monks of d'Ef befell us, and the slinders attacked. But Fratrex Laer thought there might be something to Brother Pell's ravings, and so he charged us with the mission of saving the books he had with him in the tower and finding the mountain of which Pell spoke.

"Almost too late, we discovered Brother Stephen, locked in a cell in the tower. The fratrex had him captive, forcing him to translate the more obscure texts."

"I'm confused. How did you come to be in the tower, Brother Stephen?"

"When Aspar, Winna, and Ehawk were slain, I went to the only place I knew," Stephen said, trying to get both feet planted on the wildly swaying rope. "The only place I knew in the King's Forest was d'Ef. But the instant I arrived, Fratrex Pell took me captive."

"I believe you earlier reported to me that Pell was dead," Hespero said, suspicion in his voice.

"I was wrong," Stephen replied. "He was crippled—his legs destroyed—but he was alive. And as Brother Alfraz said, quite mad."

"Yet you believed his wild speculations?"

"I—" Stephen broke off. "I had failed, your grace. My friends were dead. I suppose I was grasping at any hope for redemption."

"This is all very interesting," the praifec said. "Very interesting, indeed." His eyes tightened at the corners, then relaxed.

"I'll hear more of this in the morning. I'm most particularly interested in learning what Fratrex Pell considered so pressing. For tonight, I'll have someone show you to your quarters and see what can be done about a meal. I'm sure you're hungry."

"Yes, your grace," Stephen said. "Thank you, your grace."

A monk named Brother Dhomush appeared and showed them to a small dormitory somewhere in the building. It had no windows and only one door, and that left Stephen feeling intensely claustrophobic.

As soon as they were alone, he turned to Brother Ehan.

"What was all that?" he asked, his heart thundering in his chest. His deeply submerged panic had found a way up now that the immediate danger seemed past.

"Something had to be said," Ehan replied defensively.

"Brother Laer led the expedition to replace us at d'Ef—he was a Hierovasi, of course, like Hespero. With the help of the slinders, we destroyed them all. I reckoned he might know that, but not the details. It looks like I was right."

"I don't know," Stephen said dubiously. "The one thing I do know, I don't like."

"What's that?"

"That we're here. And Hespero is here. Do you really think that's a coincidence?"

Ehan scratched his head. "I suppose I thought it was just bad luck."

"It's impossible," Stephen asserted. "He's either following us or he's after the same thing we are. I can't think of any other explanation. Can you?"

Ehan was still mulling that over when Brother Dhomush reappeared with bread and mutton broth.

Dhomush and two other monks slept in the dormitory with them, but by the time the night had half turned above their heads, their breathing indicated to Stephen that they were asleep. He quietly reached his feet down from the hard wooden cot and padded to the door, fearing it would be locked or would squeak loudly if it wasn't.

Neither was true.

Padding lightly on marble was as close to absolutely silent as anyone could be. Another initiate of Saint Decmanus might hear him, but as they had passed, he'd noticed that the church's altar was dedicated to Saint Froa, whose gifts usually didn't involve acute senses.

It wasn't difficult to find his way back to the library. He approached it tentatively, fearing Hespero would still be there, but found it dark. A moment's listening disclosed no breath or heartbeat, but he still didn't feel as if he could trust his ears. Henne had regained more or less normal hearing, as had Ehan and Themes, but none of them had begun with the ability to hear a butterfly's wing.

Knowing he had to take the risk eventually, he entered

the room and felt along the wall for the window ledge where he'd earlier seen a tinderbox. He found it and managed to light a small candle. In its friendly light he began his search.

It didn't take long to find the first item he sought: a volume detailing the history of the temple itself. It was large, massively thick, and prominently displayed on a lectern. He loved it immediately because he could see that it had been rebound many times to accommodate new pages. All the layers of time were there in the type and the condition of the scrifti bound into it.

The most recent pages were smooth and white, crafted in Vitellia of linen rag, using a secret Church process. The next layer back was more brittle and yellowed, rough at the edges; it was Lierish bond made mostly of pulped mulberry fibers.

The oldest sheets were vellum, thin and flexible. The writing was worn in some places, but the scrift itself would outlast its younger neighbors.

Smiling despite himself, he flipped through the first few pages, hoping to discover when the temple was founded.

The first page was of no use, a dedication to Praifec Tysgaf of Crotheny for his vision in establishing the church in Demsted. Tysgaf had been praifec a bare three hundred years ago; that meant that despite the seeming age of the building, it had not been established in Hegemonic or pre-Hegemonic times.

That meant he wasn't going to find anything useful here.

Or so he thought, until he reached the last paragraph of the introduction.

It is also fitting that we laud the good sense and basic decency of those who kept this place before us. Though lacking the inspired teachings of the true Church, they preserved for many generations a light of knowledge in what is otherwise a dark wilderness. The legend among them is that in ancient times, before the coming of the Hegemony, they lived in a most pagan state, sacrificing to stones and trees and pools of water. During that time, a holy man came from the south who taught them medicine, writing, and the basic tenets of true religion, then departed, never to be seen again. Dark days followed as the armies of the Black Jester came to control the region, yet they kept faith with their teacher. Without guidance, the centuries have corrupted their doctrine, but rather than resisting our coming, they have embraced us with open arms as the bearers of the faith of their revered one, Kauron.

Stephen almost laughed out loud. Choron, the priest who was carrying Virgenya Dare's journal. Not only had he stopped here, he had in essence founded a religion!

Stephen flipped ahead and discovered to his delight that the next page was older, written in a strange but comprehensible version of Old Vitellian script. The language, however, was not Vitellian but rather a Vhilatautan dialect. Translating it might be possible, given time, but reading it wasn't, so Stephen scanned through it.

He found the name "Kauron" many times, but it was only after two bells that he spotted what he was really searching for: the word *"Velnoiraganas"* juxtaposed with a verb that seemed to mean "he went." Stephen backed up and concentrated on that section. After a moment he went rummaging about the room until he found a scrap of paper, an inkwell, and a quill. He copied most of the page word for word, then scratched out the best translation he could manage.

He departed, and not (would? could?) *said why* (where?) *he was going. But his guide later said they went along the stream* (river, valley?) *Enakaln* (uphill?) *to hadivaisel* (a town?) *and thence the Witchhorn. He had talk with the* (old? belly?) *hadivara*(?)

I went (followed?) *to the base* (lower part) *of the horn called be-zawle* (where the sun never falls?) *and there he bade me leave. I never saw him again.*

Never, someone whispered in his right ear. He felt the aspiration, and his muscles stiffened and spasmed from the sheer terror of finding someone so close without his knowing it. He batted at the sound, swinging his right arm and stumbling away at the same time.

But there was no one there.

His mind refused to accept that, and he sent his gaze searching through the shadows. But no one could move that quickly, have his mouth against his ear in one moment and be gone the next.

But he'd felt it, a double puff of breath, because "never" had been *"nhyrmh,"* in Vadhiian dialect, as clear as could be, and it hadn't been his voice.

"Who's there?" Stephen whispered, turning constantly, unwilling to put his back to anything.

No answer came. The only sound not made by his body was the faint lisp of the candle, the only motion the play of light and shadow from that small flame. He tried to relax, but some part of him felt seized in the moment, like a fish striking bait and finding itself on a hook.

Helplessly he studied the random shifting from dim to black to lumined and gradually saw what he feared the most: that the play of light and darkness wasn't random. That from the moment he had lit that candle he had been surrounded by *something* studying him more intently than he had been studying the book. Horrified, he watched glyphs and letters trace themselves on the walls and fade, always hinting at sense, never quite forming it.

"What are you?" He thought speaking aloud would help, but it didn't. It only made things worse, as if he'd been attacked by a brute, pulled a knife, and found it made of a green leaf.

The woorm reared up. The utin crouched in the corner. The greffyn stalked out of the edge of his sight. He felt as if he were in a house painted in gay colors, yet when he leaned against the wall, it crumbled, revealing the rotten wood full of termites and weevils.

Only it wasn't a room but the walls of the world, the

bright illusion of reality shattering to reveal the horror that lay behind.

Nearly weeping, he dragged his eyes from the shadow and back to the candle.

The flame had formed a little face with black round eyes and a mouth.

With a stifled shriek he snuffed the light, and darkness poured in to comfort him. He moved to the window and crouched there on the cold stone, chest heaving, trying to collect his wits, trying to believe it hadn't happened. He drew his legs and arms up and hugged himself, feeling his heartbeat gradually slow, afraid to move lest he somehow bring it all back.

He heard another voice, but this one wasn't in his ear. It was a perfectly normal voice, up the corridor.

The book. He reached up and found it with his fingers. He could feel the old vellum section. This might be his last chance to see it, but he dared not light the candle again. Could he tear the pages out? The very thought sickened him, but the answer was no, anyway; the vellum would require cutting, and he didn't have anything sharp enough to serve. He quickly flipped back toward the beginning, and as he did so, something wisped by his hand. He jerked back, but it touched against his robe and then went to the floor.

He heard footfalls now. He quickly scooted underneath another table.

The footsteps rang closer, and momentarily the doorway was framed in candlelight.

"Who's there?" A voice he didn't recognize echoed his own earlier query.

Stephen almost answered, thinking he might be able to make up some sort of excuse, but then he heard a commotion farther away. He froze, and his palms felt chill and damp against the floor.

He could hear Ehan shouting his name, telling him to flee, the clumping of booted feet, the sound of steel drawing. The man at the doorway made a sound like a curse and ran off.

Ehan stopped shouting.

"Saints," Stephen murmured under his breath. He patted the floor, searching for the paper that had fallen out. The man in the hall was returning, now, at a dead run.

Stephen's finger touched the paper, and then he had it and was up, dashing toward the window. It was narrow, and he had to turn to squeeze his way into the cold night air before dropping two kingsyards to the ice-hardened ground. The fall hurt more than he had expected it to, but he felt as if he had fire in his veins.

He ran around the building, searching for the stables. He had the horrible Black Mary feeling of running without getting anywhere, and his pulse deafened him to whoever might be coming after him. The thing from the room seemed all around him, and all he could think to do was run until he found someplace where the sun was up and would never go down.

He found the stables more by their smell than by memory, and once inside, he began hunting for the horse he'd been riding since Ever.

He wished he had light.

That wish suddenly was granted as he heard the grating of the shutter on an Aenan lamp and its fiery eye turned to reveal him. He couldn't see who held it, but whoever it was had a sword; Stephen could see it projecting into the cone of illumination.

"Hold there," the voice commanded. "Hold by the word of his grace the praifec of Crotheny."

For an instant, Stephen stood frozen. The lamp started toward him, wavered, and then dropped to the ground, casting its beam sideways.

Stephen bolted for the open door of the stable. He'd gotten only a few paces before someone grabbed his arm. Gasping, he tore at it, and it fell away.

"You'll want my help," a soft voice said urgently. He knew instantly who it was.

"Sister Pale?"

"Your Decmanian memory doesn't fail you," she replied.

"I've just killed a man for you. I think you should listen to me."

"I believe my friends are in danger," Stephen said.

"Yes. But you can't help them now. Maybe later, if they live. Not now. Come on, we have to go."

"Where?"

"Wherever you're going."

"I need some things from my horse."

"The books? The praifec has them. His men had taken them before you even met with him. Come, or he'll have you, too."

"How can I trust you?"

"How can you not? Come along."

Helplessly, mind whirling, Stephen did as he was told.

CHAPTER NINE

SKIN

LEOFF WOKE to screaming and a damp rag on his brow. The screams, of course, were his own, and for a moment he didn't care about where the rag had come from. But when it moved, he swatted at it and jerked himself up in the bed.

"Hush," a feminine voice whispered. "You've nothing to fear. Just wait a moment."

He heard the sound of a lantern. A tiny light appeared, then brightened into a flame, illuminating ash-blond curls framing a heart-shaped face. It was odd, Leoff thought, how he'd never really seen the origins of Mery in her mother, but in this light the resemblance was obvious.

"Lady Gramme," he mumbled. "How—" He suddenly

realized that his upper body was exposed and drew the covers up.

"I'm sorry to trouble you, Cavaor Ackenzal," Lady Gramme said, "but I really need to speak to you."

"Have you seen Mery? How did you find us?" An ugly thought occurred as the words slipped off his tongue, that Lady Gramme somehow was involved in the whole affair. It made a certain sense. She was a highly political creature, after all.

He didn't voice it, but she must have seen it in his eyes. She smiled, dabbing his brow again.

"I'm not in league with Robert," she assured him. "Please believe me when I say I would never lend him Mery for any purpose."

"Then how did you come to be here?"

She smiled again, a melancholy grimace, really.

"I was mistress to the emperor for almost twenty years," she said. "Did you know that? I was fifteen when I first shared his bed. I did not spend all that time on my back. There are few places on Eslen, Ynis, or Newland where I don't have eyes, ears, and pending favors. It took me a while to find you and my daughter after you were moved from the dungeons, but I managed it. After that it was merely a matter of paying the right bribes."

"How was Mery when you saw her?"

"Sleepy. Concerned about you. She doesn't think you've been well. Now that I see you, I understand why."

"I've been working. It's taxing."

"I daresay. Roll over."

"Milady?"

"Onto your belly."

"I really don't see—"

"I've risked my life to speak to you," Lady Gramme said. "The least you can do is obey my every whim, especially when it's for your own good."

Reluctantly, Leoff complied, careful to keep the sheet over him.

"Do you always sleep without a nightshirt?" she asked.

"It is my habit," he said stiffly.

"Lack of habit, I would rather say," she replied.

His back felt cold. He wondered if she had been sent by someone to slip a knife or poisoned needle into his spine so he couldn't write Robert's singspell.

He should have cared, but he didn't; his outrage was still around someplace, but his dreams tended to misplace it. It took some waking distance from them for him to recall it.

Lady Gramme's fingers brushed against his back, and to his horror he heard himself moan. It was the first really nice thing his skin had felt in a long time, and it was incredibly good. The tips began to tease gently into his muscles, pressing out soreness and tension.

"I was never trained for much of anything," she said softly. "No coven education for me. But William hired me tutors, to train me in certain arts. The one who taught me this was from Hadam, a thick-fingered girl with dark, dark hair named Besela."

"You shouldn't—it isn't—"

"Proper? My dear Leovigild, you've been imprisoned by a mad usurper. You think that proper? We'll decide—you and I—what is proper. Do you like this?"

"I like it very much," he admitted.

"Then relax. We have things to discuss, but I can practice this upon you while we do so. Are we agreed?"

"Yes," he groaned as she worked up either side of his spine, then sent each hand kneading in a different direction along his shoulders and upper arms.

"It's nothing very complicated," she went on. "I think I can help you escape, all three of you."

"Really?" He tried to sit up and engage her gaze, but she pushed him back down.

"Just listen," she said.

When he didn't protest again, she went on.

"An army has laid siege to Eslen," she said. "An army commanded, or so it seems, by Muriele's daughter, Anne. What chance they have of defeating Robert I do not know. He will have help shortly from both the Church and Hansa, but if Liery weighs in, this war could last for quite some time."

Both of her hands had gone to his right arm now, her fingers digging deeply into the twisted tendons of his forearms. He gasped as he felt small spasms in his fingers, where he thought no feeling remained. His eyes dampened with mixed pain and pleasure.

"My larger point being that Robert is at the moment quite distracted. I have a few friends in this castle, and I believe I can take advantage of them to spirit you, Mery, and the land-waerden girl to someplace safe."

"Surely that is too much to hope for," Leoff said. "I would see Mery and Areana safe. As for me—"

"It is all the same," she said flatly. "If I can get them out, I can liberate you, as well. But it is a noble thought. And there is only one thing I would ask of you."

Of course, Leoff thought.

"What is that, lady?" he asked.

"Muriele likes you. You have her ear. I admit that once I thought I might place my son on the throne—he is, after all, William's son—but now I only wish protection for my children. If Anne wins and Muriele is again queen mother, I only ask you to put it in her ear that I helped you. Nothing more."

"I can do that without reservation," Leoff said.

She was massaging him with only one hand now, and he was wondering about that when she pressed down on him and he felt something sticky and warm against his back that sent a thrill all the way to his toes. A ridiculous gasp escaped him. She'd been using her other hand to undo her bodice and was pressing her naked breasts against him. What kind of bodice could be opened with one hand? Did all women have them, or did courtesans have specially designed clothing?

Then she was straddling him, moving down his back, kissing along his spine, drawing the covers down with her torso, and his whole body was instantly awake, on fire. He couldn't take it; he twisted beneath her, and she was neither heavy nor strong enough to stop him.

"Lady," he gasped, trying to keep his eyes averted. She still wore her gown, but it was pulled up around her waist, and he could see the ivory skin of her thighs above her stockings. And of course her breasts were there, lily and rose . . .

"Hush," she said. "Part of the treatment."

He held up his hands. "Look at me, Lady Gramme," he pleaded. "I am a cripple."

"I should think you might call me Ambria under the circumstances," she replied. "And you seem to be functional in the parts and territories that interest me." She leaned down and kissed him with a warm, familiar, very practiced kiss. "This is not love, Leovigild, and it is not charity. It is something between—a gift for what you have done for Mery, if you wish. And to deny it would make you uncharitable indeed."

She kissed him again, then on the chin, the throat. She rose up and after a bit of bustling was suddenly all flesh upon him, and he certainly couldn't protest anymore. He tried to be active, to be a man, but she gently guided him away from everything but experiencing her.

It was slow, and mostly quiet, and very good indeed. Ambria Gramme wasn't the first woman he'd been with, but this was far beyond anything he'd ever experienced, and he suddenly understood something about her that he never had imagined before. What *he* could do with music, she could do with her body.

For the first time he understood that love could be art, and a lover an artist.

For that insight he would be grateful for however many days he had left in the lands of fate.

And so he felt a bit of guilt when, at his most helpless moment, it was Areana's face he saw and not Ambria's.

When they were done, she poured them wine and reclined, still nude, against a pillow. She had seemed tall when he first met her, but she really wasn't. She was quite small—almost as narrow-waisted as she appeared in a corset—but her body curved luxuriously, and he could just make out the tiger-stripe marks on her belly from bearing William's children.

"And now you feel better, don't you?" she said.

"I admit it," he replied.

She reached over and shuttered the flame so that she became an alabaster goddess in the shaft of moonlight seeping in the window. She finished the wine and crawled under the covers, turning him so she was spooned against his back.

"In three days," she whispered into his ear. "Three nights from now, at midnight. You will meet me in the entrance hall. I will have gathered up Mery and Areana. Be prepared."

"I will," Leoff said. He thought for a moment. "Should you—will you be discovered here?"

"I will be safer here for the next few hours than anywhere I can imagine," she said. "Unless you want me to leave."

"No," Leoff said. "I don't."

Her warmth against him was pleasant, still sexual but in a subdued mode that allowed him to drift off into an agreeable, comforting sleep.

When he awoke again, he wasn't sure why, but he looked up at a faint sound. At first he thought it was Ambria again, looking down at him in the darkness, but Ambria was still nestled against his back.

And then, even in the feeble light, he recognized Areana, tears glistening.

Before he could think of anything to say, she hurried away in her stocking feet.

CHAPTER TEN

GOBELIN COURT

CAZIO THOUGHT he understood what was going on pretty well, until Anne stood up in her stirrups, flourished a short sword, and shouted, "I am your Born Queen! I shall avenge my father and sisters; I shall have my kingdom back!"

For one thing, the sword she brandished was so silly; he'd rather fight with a piece of stale bread. But then again, she wasn't fighting with it; she was *leading* with it.

Men in surcoats who didn't look friendly were pouring into the square, and Anne didn't seem surprised. From his point of view, she *ought* to be surprised, and if she wasn't, by Lord Mamres, he ought to know why.

Had this been her plan all along, to be ambushed in a public square? It wasn't a plan that made a lot of sense.

"What shall we do?" he shouted.

"You stay close to me," Anne replied, then, raising her voice, gestured toward the men entering the square. "Keep them back!"

Forty of the fifty men in Anne's company responded by charging across the square toward the city guard, or Robert's guard, or whatever it was. It was a messy business right away, as the plaza was full of people, and though they were trying to clear the way between the two armed forces, there was a good deal of pushing and tripping and falling down.

Anne's remaining guardians clumped around her as she dismounted and strode toward the actors. Taken by surprise, Cazio dismounted so quickly, he nearly fell.

As his feet hit the square, he was suddenly very pleased to

have cobbles under them again. Not grass, not tilled land or
wild forest floor or a lord-forsaken beaten desert of a track
in the middle of nowhere, but a city *street*. He nearly
laughed with joy.

He realized then that he had mistaken Anne's target. It
wasn't the actors but Sir Clement, who had leapt from his
horse and run to stand by the patir, arming himself with a
sword from one of the churchman's guards. The other
Church soldiers lowered their spears into a hedge around the
patir, keeping their swords in reserve.

But Clement, their betrayer, was a knight, so he *would*
prefer a sword.

Cazio sprinted to put himself between Anne and the
knight.

"Allow me, Highness," he said, noticing the somewhat
unnatural look in Anne's eye, not unlike her aspect that evening in Dunmrogh. He realized he was doing Clement a
favor.

She nodded curtly, and Cazio drew his steel as Clement
rushed at him.

It wasn't Caspator, but Acredo, the rapier he'd taken from
the Sefry dessrator. It felt unfamiliar, too light, oddly balanced.

"Zo dessrator, nip zo chiado," he reminded his opponent.
"The swordsman, not the sword."

Clement ignored him and came on.

To Cazio's delight, the fight wasn't as simple as it might
have been. Knights, Cazio had discovered, were extraordinarily hard to fight when they were in armor, but that had
nothing to do with their swordplay, which was uniformly
clumsy and boring to the point of tears. Part of it was the
weapons they used, which were really more like flattened
steel clubs with edges.

The sword Clement bore was a little lighter and thinner
than most he had seen since leaving Vitellio, but it was still
essentially the same sort of cutting tool. What was really
different was the way the fellow held his blade. Knights in
armor tended to cock their weapons back, to swing from the

shoulder and hips. They didn't fear the swift stop-thrust to the hand, wrist, or breast since they were usually sheathed in iron.

But Sir Clement dropped into a crabwise stance not so different from that of a dessrator, although he put a little more weight on his back leg than Cazio would recommend. The sword he held in front of him, arm extended toward Cazio's head, so that he was looking straight at the knight's knuckles, while the tip of the sword slanted curiously *down,* aimed roughly at Cazio's knees.

Curious, Cazio lunged for the exposed top of the hand. Moving the sword far faster than Cazio would have guessed was possible, Clement merely flipped his wrist, with only a slight motion of his forearm and none from his shoulder at all. That quick, simple turn brought the forte of his blade up to intersect Cazio's thrust. The tip came up, too, and sliced quickly down along Cazio's rapier, forcing it away and exposing his wrist to a cut that would have arrived if Cazio hadn't been ready to take a step back.

"That's very interesting," he told Clement, who was following up his riposte by bounding forward, inside the point of Cazio's weapon, dropping his tip again and raising his hand to keep Cazio's sword parried to the outside. With that odd twist of the wrist, he cut at the right side of Cazio's neck. Cazio lengthened his retreat and parried swiftly, bringing his hilt nearly to his right shoulder, then quickly threw himself to his left, dropping his point toward the knight's face.

Clement ducked and made a stronger, arm-driven slash at Cazio's flank as he closed. Cazio felt the wind of it, and then he was past his opponent, turning in hopes of a thrust to the back.

But he found Clement already facing him, on guard.

"Zo pertumo tertio, com postro pero praisef," he said.

"Whatever that means," Clement replied. "I'm certain I'm fortunate your tongue isn't a dagger."

"You misunderstand," Cazio said. "If I were to comment on your person and call you, for instance, a mannerless pig with no notion of honor, I would do it in your own tongue."

"And if I were to call you a ridiculous fop, I would do that in *my* own language for fear that speaking yours would unman me."

Someone nearby shrieked, and with chagrin Cazio suddenly realized he wasn't in a duel but a battle. Anne had gotten away from him, and he couldn't look for her without risking being hamstrung.

"My apologies," he said. Clement looked briefly confused, but then Cazio was attacking him again.

He started the same as before, lunging for the top of the hand, and drew the same result. The cut came, just as before, but Cazio avoided the parry with a deft turn of his wrist. To his credit, Sir Clement saw what was coming and took a rapid step back, dropping the point of his blade again to stop the thrust now aimed at the underside of his hand. He let his blade recede a bit and then cut violently up Cazio's blade toward his extended knee.

Cazio let the blow come out, withdrawing his knee quickly, bringing his front foot all the way back to meet his rear foot so that he was standing straight, leaning forward a bit. He took his blade out of the line of the cut at the same time and pointed it at Clement's face. The cutting weapon, a handsbreadth shorter than Cazio's rapier, sliced air, but Clement's forward motion took him onto the tip of Cazio's extended blade, which slid neatly into his left eye.

Cazio opened his mouth to explain the action, but Clement was dying with a look of horror on his face, and Cazio suddenly had no desire to taunt him, whatever he had done.

"Well fought," he said instead as the knight collapsed.

Then he turned to see what else was happening.

He got it in sketches. Austra was still where she ought to be: away from the fighting, watched over by one of the Craftsmen. Anne was standing, looking down at the patir, who was holding one hand to his chest. His face was red and his lips were blue, but there was no evidence of blood. His guards were mostly dead, although a few still were engaged in a losing battle with the Craftsmen guarding Anne.

Their forces seemed to be winning across the square, as well.

Anne glanced up at him.

"Free the players," she said crisply. "Then mount back up. We'll be riding in a few moments."

Cazio nodded, both elated and disconcerted by the strength of her command. This wasn't the Anne he remembered from when he'd first met her—a girl, a person, someone he liked—and for the first time he feared that she was gone, replaced by someone else entirely.

He cut the actors free, smiling at their thanks, then got back up on his horse as Anne had commanded. The battle in the square was all but over, and her warriors were rallying back to her. By his quick count of the fallen, they'd lost only two men—quite a good bargain.

Anne sat tall.

"As you can all see, we were betrayed. My uncle intended our murder or capture from the moment we entered the gate. I've no idea how he intends to escape his own punishment, but I've no doubt he does. We are fortunate we discovered this before setting foot in the castle, for we could never have fought our way out of there."

Sir Leafton, the head of her detail of Craftsmen, cleared his throat.

"What if that isn't what happened here, Majesty? What if those troops attacked us by mistake?"

"Mistake? You heard Sir Clement; he gave the order. He knew they were there."

"Yes, but that's my point," Leafton said, pushing his long black hair from his sweaty brow. "Perhaps Sir Clement was, ah, incensed by your conversation with the patir and gave an order Prince Robert would not have wished him to give."

Anne shrugged. "You are too polite to say it, Sir Leafton, but you suggest that my poor judgment may be to blame. That is not the case, but it hardly matters now. We cannot continue to the castle, and I strongly suspect we could not fight our way back out of the gate. Even if we could, the fleet stands between us and our army.

"We certainly cannot remain here any longer."

"We might take the east tower of the Fastness," Sir Leafton offered. "Perhaps hold it long enough for the duke to come to our aid."

Anne nodded thoughtfully. "That's rather along the lines of what I was thinking, but I was considering the Gobelin Court," she said. "Could we hold that?"

Sir Leafton blinked, opened his mouth, then fingered his ear, a puzzled expression on his seamed face.

"The gate is sturdy, and the streets within are all narrow enough to throw up workable redoubts. But with this many men, I don't know how long we could keep it. It would depend on how determined they were to stop us."

"A few days, at least?"

"Perhaps," he replied cautiously.

"Well, it will have to do. We'll go there now, and quickly," she said. "But I need four of you to volunteer for something a bit more dangerous."

As they made their way down the crooked street, Anne had to resist the temptation to take her mount to a run, to leave Mimhus Square and its surroundings as quickly as possible.

The patir had known what was happening to him. She hadn't meant to kill him, only to put the fear of her in him. But the more she squeezed his fat, corrupt heart and the more he begged and pleaded for her to spare him, the angrier she got.

Still, she thought she'd released him in time. His heart must already have been weak.

"He probably would have died soon, anyway."

"What?" Austra asked.

Anne realized then that she must have spoken aloud.

"Nothing," she replied.

Thankfully, Austra didn't push the matter, and they continued their downhill clatter, passing through the south Embrature gate into the lower city.

"Why so many walls?" Cazio asked.

"Ah, I'm not sure," Anne replied, a bit embarrassed but

happy to have a harmless topic before them. "I never paid proper attention to my tutors."

"They——" Austra began, but then she stopped.

Anne saw that her friend's face was white. "Are you well?"

"I'm fine," Austra replied unconvincingly.

"Austra."

"I'm just scared," Austra said. "I'm always scared. This never stops."

"I know what I'm doing," Anne said.

"That worries me more than anything," Austra said.

"Tell Cazio about the walls," Anne requested. "I know you remember. You always paid attention."

Austra nodded, closed her eyes, and swallowed. When her lids lifted again, they were damp.

"They . . . the walls were built at different times. Eslen started out as just a castle, a tower, really. Over the centuries they built it bigger, but most of it was constructed all at once by Emperor Findegelnos the First. His son built the first city wall, called the Embrature wall; that's the one we just rode through. The city kept growing outside the wall, though, so a few hundred years later, during the de Loy regency, Erteumé the Third built Nod's wall.

"The outer wall, what we call the Fastness, went up during the Reiksbaurg reign by Tiwshand II. It's the only one that's completely intact; the inner walls have gaps where stones were pulled for other construction."

"Then the only real wall is that last one."

"The last time the city was invaded, it was by Anne's great-great-grandfather, William I. Even after he broke through the Fastness, it took him days to get to the castle. The defenders threw up barricades in the elder wall gaps. They say the streets ran with blood."

"Let's hope that doesn't happen this time."

"Let's hope it's not our blood," Anne said, hoping to be amusing. Cazio smiled, but Austra's smile seemed more like a grimace.

"Anyway," Anne went on, "I may not know the history,

but I've been to the Gobelin Court before, and my father once told me the most unusual thing about it."

"And what is that?" Cazio asked.

"It's the only place in the city where two of the walls meet. Nod's wall goes right into the Fastness. It makes a sort of long cul-de-sac."

"You mean there's only one way out," Cazio said.

"More or less. There's a gate near the place where they meet, but it's not too large."

"So that's why you choose Gobelin Court?" Austra asked. "I didn't know you knew so much about strategy. Did you and Artwair discuss this before you came? Was this all a secret plan of yours?"

Anne felt a surge of anger. Why did Austra have to question *everything* she did?

"I did *not* discuss it with Artwair," Anne said flatly. "And this wasn't a plan, it was an option. I would have rather gone into the castle as we had agreed, but I didn't really think Robert would be faithful to his word. So yes, I had thought of this beforehand."

"But why did you come in at all if you were so sure we would be betrayed?" Austra wondered aloud.

"Because I know something no one else does," Anne replied.

"But you're not going to tell me what that is, are you?"

"Certainly I am," Anne said, "because I'm going to need your help. But not here. Not now. Soon."

"Oh," Austra said. Anne thought she looked a little more content after that.

Given Anne's description, Cazio had no problem recognizing the Gobelin Court when they entered it, passing through a modest gate in a rather more impressive wall of reddish stone. Beyond a cobbled square, a single row of outlandish buildings butted up against another wall only about thirty kingsyards away. The second wall was even more impressive, of a nearly black stone, and Cazio recognized it as the Fastness.

Following his sword hand, he saw that the two walls indeed

met, and right in the corner a weird, narrow manse seemed almost to lean into the juncture, looking sinister. The space between the walls widened a bit but stayed uncomfortably close as the walls climbed up around the hill and out of sight.

He didn't know much about war and stratagems, but it didn't seem like the sort of place easily held by fifty men. For one thing, the outer wall was surely controlled by the castle. What was to prevent hot oil and arrows being dropped on them from above? Or warriors from swarming down on ropes?

Nod's wall was high enough, but houses had been built close on the other side of it, providing stepping-stones that might allow attackers to come within a few yards of the top even if there weren't stairways up, which there probably were.

In short, Cazio felt a good deal more trapped than protected.

Despite his misgivings, he was fascinated. The buildings, the signs, and the pale faces peeping out from beneath broad-brimmed hats and veils all seemed exotic.

"Echi'Sievri," he said.

"Yes," Anne acknowledged. "Sefry."

"I've never seen so many in one place."

"Just wait," Anne said. "Most of them don't come out until night. That's when Gobelin Court really comes alive. People also call this the Sefry quarter. There are hundreds living here."

Cazio knew he was gawking, but he couldn't help it. The neighborhoods on the other side of the wall were dingy, to say the least: dilapidated huts with leaky roofs, stone buildings whose days of grandeur were decades if not centuries in the past, streets full of rubble, rubbish, and dirty children.

But Gobelin Court was neat, clean, and colorful. The buildings were tall and narrow, with roofs so high-pitched that they were comical. They were all tidily painted: rusty red, mustard, burnt orange, violet, teal, and other muted but cheerful shades. Bright clothing flew like banners from lines stretched between upper windows, and umber signs with black lettering proclaimed the shops of diviners, card readers, apothecaries, and other outlandish businesses.

"Majesty," Sir Leafton said, breaking the spell, "we've little time to spare."

"Very well," Anne said. "What do you suggest?"

"The Fastness is the most important thing," Leafton said. "We'll need to scale it and take control of the Saint Ceasel and Vexel towers and everything in between. Next we need to throw up a barrier north of here; I think Werton Cross would be the best place. And we'll need men on Nod's wall, too. That's easy; we've stairs on this side. The Fastness will be a bit more difficult."

Who says I don't know anything about strategy? Cazio thought to himself. Aloud, however, he offered a suggestion.

"That mansion in the corner goes almost to the top," he said. "We might be able to climb the rest of the way."

Leafton nodded. "Possibly. I'll have some men strip their armor."

"That will take time," Cazio said. "Why not let me get a start?"

"You have to guard Anne," Austra pointed out.

"But I'm already without armor," he said. "If we give anyone time to position themselves up on that wall, they'll be dropping stones on us before we know it."

"He's right," Anne said. "Sir Leafton can guard me until he's done. Go on, Cazio. The Craftsmen will be with you as soon as they've stripped."

They rode up to the house, where Cazio dismounted and knocked at the door. After a moment a Sefry woman answered. She was so swaddled in red and orange cloth that Cazio couldn't see much of her save a single pale blue eye surrounded by a patch of skin so white that he could make out the veins through it. She didn't even give them a chance to speak.

"This is my house," the woman said.

"I am Anne Dare," Anne said from horseback. "This is my city, so that is also *my* house."

"Of course," the woman said matter-of-factly. "I've been expecting you."

"Have you?" Anne asked a little coldly. "Then you know that my man needs to find the shortest route to your roof."

"No, that I did not know," the woman replied, "but of course I will help." She focused her eye again on Cazio. "Go straight in. There is a central stairway that spirals to the top. The small door opens onto the uppermost balcony. You'll have to climb from there to the roof."

"Thank you, lady," Cazio said pleasantly. He doffed his hat and waved it at the girls. "I won't be long."

Anne watched Cazio vanish up the stairs, feeling Austra stiffen next to her.

"He'll be fine," Anne whispered. "This is the sort of thing Cazio lives for."

"Yes," Austra said. "And the sort of thing that will kill him."

Everyone dies, Anne thought, but she knew it wasn't the politic thing to say at the moment. Instead, she turned her attention back to the Sefry woman.

"You said you were waiting for me. What did you mean?"

"You mean to use the Crepling passage. That is the reason you have come."

Anne glanced at Sir Leafton. "Can you repeat what she just said?" Anne asked the Craftsman.

Leafton opened his mouth, then looked puzzled.

"No, Your Highness," he said.

"Sir Leafton," Anne said. "Organize the rest of our defense. I'll be fine here for the moment."

"I'm not very comfortable with that, Majesty," he said.

"Do it. Please."

He puckered his lips, then sighed. "Yes, Majesty," he said, and hurried off to direct his men.

Anne turned back to the Sefry. "What is your name?" she asked.

"They call me Mother Uun."

"Mother Uun, do you know what the Crepling passage is?"

"It is the long tunnel," the woman said. "It begins in the depths of Eslen castle, and it ends in Eslen-of-Shadows. I am its watcher."

"Watcher? I don't understand. Did my father appoint you? My mother?"

The old woman—or at least Anne had the impression that she was old—shook her head. "The first queen in Eslen appointed the first of us. Since then, we have chosen from among ourselves."

"I don't understand. What are you watching for?"

The eye grew wider. "*Him,* of course."

"Him?"

"You do not know?"

"I've no idea what you're talking about now."

"Well, now. How interesting." Mother Uun stood back a bit. "Would you mind continuing the discussion inside? The sunlight hurts my eye."

She stood farther aside as six Craftsmen approached, wearing only their padded gambesons. The old woman repeated the instructions she'd given Cazio, and they went past her into the house.

"Your Highness?" the Sefry prompted.

But before Anne could answer, Austra's stifled shriek drew her attention. Her blue eyes were focused high above, and Anne quickly followed the arrow of her gaze.

She saw a tiny figure—Cazio—somehow working himself up the wall above the high, steepled roof. It didn't look like he had far to go, only a couple of kingsyards.

But on the wall, two armored soldiers with spears were rushing to meet him.

CHAPTER ELEVEN

SARNWOOD

THE MAN looked Aspar up and down with piercing gray eyes and one eyebrow lifted.

"You're a dead man," he said.

The fellow didn't look far from dead himself. He was as spindly as a skeleton, and his gray hair was thin and mussed. The flesh of his face was sun-browned and hung from his skull like an unshaped mask. His words were simple, unironic, and unthreatening, an old man telling things as he saw them.

"You ever seen her?" Aspar asked.

The old man gazed off at the green line of the forest.

"Some say it's best not to even speak of these things," he replied.

"I'm going in after her," Aspar said. "You can help me or not." He paused. "I'd rather you helped me."

The old man raised an eyebrow again.

"That wasn't a threat," Aspar said quickly.

"Eyah," the fellow said. "I've lived all my life a stone's throw from the forest. So eyah, I reckon I've seen her. Or what she wanted me to see."

"What do you mean by that?"

"I mean she's not always the same, 'swhat I mean," he replied. "One time a bear came down into the hollow. Big black bear. I might have shot it—*would* have shot it—till she looked at me, let me know. Sometimes she's a flock of crows. Sometimes a Sefry woman, they say, but I've never seen that. Them that see her in Sefry or human shape don't usually have many breaths left in the lands of fate."

"How would you know? I mean if anyone saw her . . ."

"Some of 'em live a little while," the man said. "So they can tell us. So the rest of us can know." He leaned nearer. "She only talks to the dead."

"Then how do people talk to her?"

"They die. Or they take someone dead."

"What the sceat does that mean?"

"It's just what they say. She can't talk the way we do. Or leastwise, she *won't.* I reckon she might, only she prefers murder as often as she can get it." He looked glum. "I reckon every day she's gonna come out to claim me."

"Yah." Aspar sighed. "Anything else you can tell me?"

"Eyah. There's a trail'll take you to her. Stay on it, though."

"Good enough," Aspar said, turning back toward Ogre.

"Traveler!" the old man called out.

"Yah?"

"You could stay here tonight. Think it over. Have some soup; that way at least you won't die on an empty stomach."

Aspar shook his head. "I'm in a hurry." He started to turn, then glanced back at the man. "If you're so scared of her, why do you still live here?"

The man looked at him like he was crazy. "I told you. I was *born* here."

The old man wasn't the only one who worried about the Sarnwood. A long picket of poles topped with cow, horse, and deer skulls suggested that others might have given the place an anxious thought or two. Aspar wasn't sure what the bones were supposed to accomplish, but some of the poles had little platforms about halfway up, made of plaited willow branches, and on them he saw the rotting remains of sheep and goats, bottles he reckoned to be filled with beer or wine, even bunches of blackened flowers. It was as if they figured the witch might be appeased by *something* but didn't know exactly what.

The forest itself lay just beyond, slouching down from the hills into the wide valley of the White Warlock. The river itself vanished into its ferny mouth a couple of bowshots north of him. He crawled his regard across every bit of the tree line he could see, trying to take its measure.

Even at a glance it was different from the King's Forest. The familiar fringe of oak, hickory, witaec, larch, and elm was replaced by high green spears of spruce and hemlock, thickly bunched though currently leafless heads of ironwood, and stands of birch so white that they resembled bones against the dense green conifers. Off toward the river black alder, twisting willow, crack willow, and pine dominated his view.

"Well, Ogre," he grunted. "What do you think?"

Ogre didn't opine until they were closer, and then he did it silently, with a bunching of muscles and a studied hesitation that was uncharacteristic of the stallion. Of course he was tired, hungry, and still feeling the effects of the woorm's poison, but even so . . .

Aspar found himself trying to recall how old Ogre was as the trail led them beneath the first branches of the Sarnwood. He remembered, didn't like the answer, and started wondering instead why there should be a path in a forest no one dared enter. What kept it clear?

He had a few hours of daylight left, but the overcast sky and high-reaching evergreens brought dusk early to Aspar and his mount. He strung his bow and rested it on the pommel of his saddle, felt the shifting of massive muscles beneath his thighs as Ogre continued his reluctant way forward, trudging through the frequent streams that Aspar reckoned came from snowmelt in the foothills. Despite the cold, the understory was already verdant with fern, and emerald moss carpeted the ground, as well as the trunks and branches of trees. The forest appeared healthy to the eye, but it didn't smell right. Even more than the King's Forest, it seemed somehow diseased.

He thought they were probably about a league in when it finally got dark enough to make camp. It was cold, and

Aspar could hear wolves waking up not far away, so he decided he didn't much care how the witch felt about fire. He gathered tinder, twigs, and branches, set them up in a cone, and with a spark brought it all to life. It wasn't a big fire, but it was enough to keep one side of him warm. He sat on the corpse of a linden tree and watched the flame feed, wondering glumly if Winna was still alive, if he should have stayed as she had asked.

To hear her last words? Sceat on that.

The horrible thing was, part of him was already thinking about how life would be without her. The same part that was shy about the idea of a permanent arrangement in the first place. What were men made of, he wondered, that they thought such thoughts? In his deepest heart, did he want her to die? When Qerla—

"No," he said, loudly enough that Ogre looked at him.

There it was.

He'd met Qerla when he was very young, younger than Winna. He'd loved her with an absolute madness he'd never imagined feeling again. He could still remember the smell of her, like water caught in the bloom of an orchid. The touch of her skin, a little hotter than Mannish flesh. Looking back on it, she had been even madder than he, for whereas Aspar had little to lose in the way of community and friends, Qerla had been born to a family famous for seers. She had property, and prospects, and all the best marriage opportunities.

But she'd run away with him to live alone in the forest, and for a time that had been enough.

For a very short time. Maybe if they could have had children. Maybe if either the Sefry or the Mannish world had been a little more accepting.

Maybe. Maybe.

But instead it was hard, and it grew harder every day, so hard that Qerla slept with an old lover. So hard that when Aspar found her body, part of him was relieved that it was over.

He hated Fend for killing Qerla, but he saw now that he

hated Fend more for showing him this dirty thing about himself. Aspar had spent twenty years without a lover, but it hadn't been because he feared losing her. It was because he knew he hadn't been worthy of loving someone.

He still wasn't.

"Sceat," he told the fire. When had he started all this thinking? Much good it was doing him.

The wolves had found him. He could hear them rustling in the dark, and now and then a pair of eyes or a gray flank would pick up the firelight. They were big, bigger than any wolves he'd seen before, and he had seen some pretty big ones. He didn't reckon they would come after him, not with the fire going, but that would depend on how hungry they were. It also depended on whether they were like the wolves he was familiar with. He'd heard tell of some northern varieties that hadn't the same worries about men that the common sort did.

For now they were keeping their distance. They might be more trouble in daylight.

He brightened the fire with a few pokes, turned for one of the logs he'd placed beside him—and stopped.

She was only four kingsyards away, and he hadn't heard anything, not the slightest sound. But there she sat, crouching on the balls of her feet, watching him with sage-colored eyes, her long black hair settled on her shoulders, skin as pale as the birches. She was naked and looked very young, but the top pair of her six breasts was swollen, which happened in Sefry only after the age of twenty.

"Qerla?"

She only talks to the dead.

But Qerla was *very* dead. Bones. Town people saw the dead, or so they claimed, on Temnosnaht. Old Sefry women pretended to speak to them all the time. And he himself had seen something in the deep mazes of Rewn Aluth that had been either an illusion or—something else.

But this . . .

"No," he said aloud. "Her eyes were violet." But other

than that, she was so like Qerla: the faint turn of her lip, the trace of veins on her throat, in one place shaped almost like those of a hawthorn leaf.

Very like.

Her eyes widened at the sound of his voice, and he hardly dared breathe. His right hand was still reaching for the log; his left had gone instinctively for his ax, and it still rested there on its cold steel head.

"Are you her?" he asked.

Them that see her in Sefry or human shape don't usually have many breaths left in the lands of fate, the old man had said.

She smiled very faintly, and the wind started, jittering his fire and wisping her fine hair.

Then she was gone. It was as if he had been seeing her reflected in a giant eye, and the eye had blinked.

He was still breathing the next morning and set out at the earliest hint of the sun. He worried about the wolves, but pretty soon he noticed they wouldn't cross, or even come onto, the trail he was following.

That bothered him more in some ways. Wolves belonged in the forest. What could be so bad about this bit of ground that they wouldn't walk on it?

He counted a pack of about twelve. Could he and Ogre take that many in the state they were in? Maybe.

The forest opened up for a while as the girth of the trees increased, revealing small, mossy meadows here and there. The sky was blue when he saw it, dazzling when a shaft or two of it fell through to the forest floor. The wolves paced him until midday, then vanished. Not much later he heard wild cattle trumpet in alarm and knew the predators had found prey they reckoned worth their while.

He was glad to be rid of the wolves, but something was still following him. It bent branches not like a wind but like a weight settling on them from above. As if it was walking on them, all of them at once, or at least all of them around him. If he stopped, it stopped, and he was reminded of a very stupid entertainment given by a traveling troupe in Colbaely. One fellow walked stealthily behind another, mimicking his motions exactly, and whenever the person being followed turned, the stalker would freeze in place, and the fool in front wouldn't see him. Aspar had found it annoying rather than funny.

But deer couldn't see you when they were feeding. When they had their heads down to the ground, you could walk straight toward them so long as they were upwind and couldn't smell you. Frogs couldn't see you unless you moved, either.

So maybe to whatever was following him, Aspar was basically a frog.

He chuckled under his breath. It might have been the fatigue, but that actually *did* seem funny. Maybe he should have given the actors a little more credit.

A rasping wheeze caught his attention, something off the trail a bit. He didn't forget the old man's warning to stay on the path, but he didn't much trust it, either. After all, if no one lived through coming here, what was the point of following directions? With only a little hesitation he turned Ogre toward the sound.

He didn't go far before he saw it: a large black hairy form quivering in the ferns. It raised a bristly head when it saw him and grunted.

Ogre whinnied.

It was a sow, a big one, bigger because she was pregnant. It was a little early for that—the piglets usually came with the first flowers—but something much more fundamental was wrong, he could see. Whatever was pushing from inside its belly was a lot larger than a piglet. And there was blood, a lot of it, around the sow, leaking from her wheezing nostrils, from her eyes. She didn't even know he was there; her grunt had been one of pain, not of perception.

She died half a bell later even as he watched, but whatever was inside her kept moving. Aspar noticed that he was shaking, but he didn't know with what, only that it wasn't fear. He felt the weight above him, the thing bending the branches, and suddenly the side of the boar split open.

Out pushed a bloody beak, a yellow eye, and a slimy scaled body.

A greffyn.

Very deliberately he dismounted as the thing fought to release itself from its mother's womb.

"Stop me if you can," he said to the forest.

Its scales were still soft, not hard like an adult's, but its glare took a long time to dim even after its head was off.

He wiped his ax on dead leaves, then doubled over, retching.

But at least he knew something now. He knew why he'd passed forty years in the King's Forest without seeing a trace of a greffyn, an utin, a woorm, or anything of the like, yet now the whole world was lousy with them.

People had said they were "waking up," like the Briar King, which implied they'd been sleeping like a bear in a hollow tree—except for a thousand years.

They hadn't been sleeping anywhere. They were being *born*. He remembered an old tale about basil-nix coming from hen's eggs.

Sceat, they probably did.

He waited for the wrath of the witch to descend on him, but nothing happened. Still shaking, he remounted and went on.

It was almost without surprise that he saw buds on the trees. They were not natural buds but black spikes splitting through trunks and branches. It was easy enough to recognize the black thorns he'd seen in the King's Forest and again in the Midenlands. Here they sprouted from galls on the trees themselves, and the deeper he went, the more growth he saw, and the more variety.

The thorns in the King's Forest had all looked the same, but here he saw many sorts, some narrow, their spines almost feathery in their delicacy and number, and others that bore blunt knobby growths. Within a bell he didn't even recognize the parent trees anymore; like the sow, they were giving birth to monsters and were being consumed in the process.

Then he came to the end of the trail and an eldritch mere beneath the boughs of the strangest forest he had ever seen.

The largest of the trees were roughly scaled, with each branch spawning five smaller ones and each of those five spawning more, endlessly, so that the fringes were cloudlike. Aspar was reminded of some sort of pond weed or mossy lichen more than of any real tree. Others looked something like weeping willows save that their fronds were black and serrated like the tail of a fence lizard. Some of the saplings looked as if a mad saint had taken pinecones and stretched them out ten yards high.

Other plants were a bit more natural. Pale, nearly white ferns and gigantic horsetails sedged the edges of the pool stretched out before him. Beyond and to his left and right, rocky walls rose up to place him and the mere in the bottom of a gorge. The entire grotto had been decorated with human skulls, which japed down at him from the trees, from the crannies in the rock, and along the ground bordering the pool.

Everything bent toward him.

"Well," Aspar said. "Here I am."

He felt the presence, but the silence stretched until, very quietly, the water started to mound, and something rose up out of the mere.

It wasn't the Sefry woman but something larger, a mass of black fur matted with pond weed, dead leaves, and fish bones. It stood more like a bear than a man, but its face was froglike, with one bulging, blind white eye visible and the other occluded by a mane of oily strands that seemed almost to pour from the crown of its head. Its mouth was a down-turned arc that took up most of the bottom of its face. Its arms dangled down to the water, depending from massive sloping shoulders. There was nothing feminine—or masculine, for that matter—about it.

Aspar faced the thing for a few moments, until he was certain it wasn't going to attack, at least not yet.

"I've come to see the woman of the Sarnwood," he finally said.

Silence followed for several long tens of heartbeats. Aspar was starting to feel a little foolish when something else stirred in the water just in front of the whatever it was.

A head emerged. At first Aspar thought it was just another, smaller version of the creature, but the resemblance was superficial. This once had been a man, though his eyes were now filmed and his flesh an ugly shade of bluish-gray. Aspar couldn't see what had killed him, but aside from the fact that he was standing up, he was clearly long dead.

The corpse suddenly started jerking, and water spurted from his lips. As this continued, a sort of wet gasping sound emerged and grew louder.

Finally, after the last of the water, Aspar began to recognize speech, soft around all the edges but understandable if he concentrated.

"They bring blood who come to see me," the corpse said. "Blood and someone to speak for me. This one has almost been dead too long."

"I had no one to bring."

"The old man would have done."

"But I didn't bring him. And you're talking to me."

The witch shifted her monstrous head, and even without human expression, he felt her anger.

"I wish to kill you," she said.

Aspar lifted what he held in his hand: the arrow given him by Hespero, the treasure of the Church said to be capable of killing anything.

"This was meant to slay the Briar King," he said. "I reckon it will murder you."

The corpse started gasping, as if for air. It took a while for Aspar to recognize laughter.

"What will you slay?" the witch asked. "This?" The massive paw reached up to touch its breast. "You might kill *this*."

The trees around him suddenly creaked and groaned, and he felt the presence that had followed him since he'd entered the forest press down with incredible weight, then push *through* him so that he fell roughly to his knees. He tried to bring the arrow to the bow, but both were suddenly too heavy to hold.

"Everything around you," the corpse gurgled. "Everything

you see that grows or creeps or crawls in the Sarnwood—that is me. Can you put an arrow in that?"

Aspar didn't answer, concentrating his will in a fierce effort to stand, to at least not die on his knees. Muscles trembling, groaning, he lifted first one knee, then the other, and from a squat tried to come upright. He felt as if he had ten men standing on his shoulders.

It was too much, and he collapsed again.

To his vast surprise, the pressure suddenly eased.

"I see," the witch said. "*He* has touched you."

"He?"

"Him. The Horned Lord."

"The Briar King."

"Yes, him. What have you come here for?"

"You sent a woorm from here with a Sefry named Fend."

"Yes, I did that. You've seen my child, haven't you? Isn't he beautiful?"

"You gave Fend an antidote to its poison. I need that."

"Oh. For your lover."

Aspar frowned. "If you already knew—"

"But I didn't. You say certain things, I see others. If you never say anything, I never see anything."

Aspar decided to let that pass.

"Will you help me?"

The leaves rustled around him, and he heard a murder of crows cawing somewhere in the trees.

"We do not have the same purposes in this world, holter," the Sarnwood witch told him. "I can think of no reason to help someone who is determined to slay my child, who has already slain *three* of my children."

"They were trying to kill me," Aspar said.

"That is meaningless to me," the witch replied. "If I give you the medicine you seek, you will return to the trail of my woorm and with that arrow of yours you will try to slay him."

"The Sefry with your child, Fend—"

"Killed your wife. Because she *knew*. She was going to tell you."

"Tell me? Tell me what?"

"You will try to slay my child," the witch repeated, but this time in a very different tone, not so much stating a fact as reflecting, musing. "*He* has touched you."

Aspar let out a deep breath. "If you save Winna—"

"You shall have your antidote," the witch interrupted. "I have changed my mind about killing you, and you will hunt my son whether I give you the cure for his poison or not. I see no reason to help you, but if you will agree you owe me a service, I see no reason to refuse you."

"I—"

"I won't ask you for the life of anyone you love," the witch assured him. "I won't ask you to spare one of my children."

Aspar thought that over for a moment.

"That'll do," he said finally.

"Behind you," the witch said, "the thorny bush with the cluster of fruit deep in the leaves. The juice of three of those should be sufficient to cleanse a man of venom. Take as many as you like."

Still suspecting a trick, Aspar looked where he was told and found hard, blackish purple fruit about the size of wild plums. Defiantly, he popped one in his mouth.

"If this is poison," he said, "I'll find out now."

"As you wish," the witch said.

The fruit had a sharp, acidic bite with a bit of a putrid aftertaste, but he felt no immediate ill effects.

"What are you?" he asked.

Again the corpse laughed. "Old," she replied.

"The black thorns. Are they your children, too?"

"My children are being born everywhere now," she said. "But yes."

"They're destroying the King's Forest."

"Oh, how sad," she snarled. "*My* forest was destroyed *long* ago. What you see here is all that remains. The King's Forest is a stand of seedlings. Its time has come."

"Why? Why do you hate it?"

"I don't hate it," the witch said. "But I am like a season,

Aspar White. When it is time for me, I arrive. I've nothing to do with the order of the seasons, though. Do you understand?"

"No," Aspar replied.

"Nor do I, really," the witch replied. "Go now. In two days your girl will be dead, and all of this will have been for nothing."

"But can you see? Will I save her?"

"I see no such thing," the witch replied. "I only tell you to make haste."

Aspar took as much of the fruit as his saddlebag would hold, fed a handful to Ogre, and left the Sarnwood.

CHAPTER TWELVE

SISTER PALE

SISTER PALE led Stephen through the night without benefit of a torch. She somehow knew where she was going and kept one hand clasped firmly on his. It was a peculiar sensation, that contact of flesh against flesh with a strange woman. He hadn't held the hands of many women: his mother's, of course, and his older sister's.

Embarrassingly, this recalled that; he felt very much the little boy, protected from things he did not understand by the caring grip of fingers in his own. But because this *wasn't* his mother or his sister, it brought out other, more adult feelings that didn't contrast very well with the childish ones. He found himself trying to translate the pressure of her fingers, the shift of grip from intertwined digits to clapped palms into some sort of meaningful cipher, which of course it wasn't. She just wanted him to keep up with her.

He didn't know what she looked like, but he teased himself with an image based on the shadowed glimpses he'd gotten. It was only after a bell or so that he realized that the image was that of Winna, almost precisely.

They weren't alone on the trail; he heard the snuffling of her dogs moving around them, and once one of them nosed into his free hand. He wondered what faneway the sister had walked that allowed her to move in such utter darkness; even his own saint-blessed senses didn't allow for that.

The moon finally rose; it was half-gone and a strange, astringent yellow Stephen had never quite seen before. Its light revealed a little more of his companion and surroundings: the hood and back of her paida, jagged lines of landscape that seemed impossibly far above them, the silhouettes of the dogs.

Neither of them had spoken since leaving the town through a secreted gate Stephen was certain he could never find again. He'd been concentrating too closely on not stumbling, on straining for sounds of pursuit, and on the hand holding his. But finally the muffled sounds of Demsted faded into the wind's south quarter, and he couldn't make out any hoofbeats or footsteps pursuing them.

"Where are we going?" he whispered.

"A place I know," she answered unhelpfully. "We'll find mounts there."

"Why are you helping me?" he asked bluntly.

"Sacritor Hespero—the man you know as the praifec—he's your enemy. Did you know that?"

"I know it well," Stephen said. "I just wasn't certain *he* knew it."

"He knows," Pale replied. "Did you think it a coincidence that he arrived shortly before you did? He's been waiting for you."

"But how could he know I was coming here? That doesn't make sense unless . . ." He allowed the words to trail off.

Unless the praifec and Fratrex Pell were in league.

Pale seemed to pluck the thought from his mind.

"You weren't betrayed by whoever sent you," she told him.

"At least, that isn't required to explain why he's here. He may not have even known you were the one who was coming."

"I don't understand."

"I suppose you wouldn't," she said. "You see, before he was praifec in Crotheny, Hespero was sacritor in Demsted for many years. We liked him at first; he was wise, caring, and very smart. He used Church funds to make improvements in the village. Among other things, he expanded the temple a bit to include a ward for the care of aged persons with no kin to tend them. The elders tried to stop him from doing that."

"Why? It seems a worthy endeavor."

"Nor would the elders disagree. It was the location they objected to. To build the addition, he broke down an old part of the temple, a part that had once been the sanctuary of the older pagan temple that was here before. And he found something there, something our forefathers hid instead of destroying. The *Ghrand Ateiiz*."

"Book . . . ah, returning?"

She squeezed his hand in what felt like affection, and he nearly swallowed his tongue.

"The *Book of Return*," she corrected. "After he found it, Hespero changed. He became much more distant. He still managed the attish—managed it better than ever, in fact—but his love for us seemed forgotten. He took to long trips into the mountains, and his guides came back changed with fear. They would not speak of what had happened or even where they went. Eventually he tired of that and focused all his energies on advancing his rank in the Church.

"When he was promoted and finally left, we were relieved, but we shouldn't have been. Now the resacaratum is upon us, and I fear he will hang everyone in Demsted."

"Are you all heretics?" Stephen asked.

"In a way, yes," she replied with surprising frankness. "We understand the teachings of the Church a little differently than most others."

"Because your Church was founded by a Revesturi?"

She laughed quietly.

"Brother Kauron did not found our Church. *Because* he

was Revesturi, he saw that we already followed the saints in our own way. He merely helped us shape our outward image so that when the Church finally came, they would not burn us as heretics. He helped us preserve our old ways. He cherished them, and he cherished us."

"So the *Book of Return* . . ."

"Is about Kauron's return. Or, more properly, the coming of his heir."

"Heir? Heir to what?"

"I don't know. None of us have ever seen the book. We thought Kauron took it with him. Our traditions were passed down mouth to ear, and we know its writings foretold these times. That much has been made clear by the things that have come to pass. And we know that Kauron's one heir is destined to come, driven by a serpent into the mountains. The one who comes will speak with many tongues, and it is he who will find the Alq."

"The Alq?"

"It means a sort of holy place," she explained. "A throne or a seat of power. We've debated endlessly whether it is a physical place or a position, like that of sacritor. Whichever is true, it was fated to remain hidden until the day the one returned."

"And that one seems to be you. *We* knew you were coming, and we have only the scraps of knowledge remembered from the *Book of Return*. Hespero has the book itself, so his knowledge of the signs is more precise. He was waiting for you because he knew you could lead him to the Alq."

"Then all he need do is follow us," Stephen said, instinctively glancing over his shoulder into the darkness.

"True. But this way we have a chance of arriving ahead of him and preventing him from becoming the heir."

"But how could he ever do that? You just admitted you don't even know what that means," Stephen said.

"No, we don't, not exactly," Sister Pale allowed. "But we do know that if Hespero becomes the heir, no good can come of it."

"And how do you know I would be any better?"

"That's obvious. You aren't Hespero."

There was a logic there that Stephen had no way to contradict. Besides, it served his purposes.

"Does your tradition tell you who sent the woorm or why it's following me?"

"About the khirme—what you call the waurm—little is said, and what we've gleaned can be contradictory. One legend says that it is your ally."

Stephen vented a humorless laugh. "I don't expect I'll count on that," he said.

"It *is* a debated tradition," she admitted. "Besides the khirme, there is also mention of a foe called the Khraukare. He is a servant of the Vhelny, who does not wish you to have the prize."

Stephen's head was beginning to swim.

"Khraukare. That translates as 'Blood Knight,' doesn't it?"

"That's right."

"And the Vhelny?"

"Vhelny. It means, ah, a king, of sorts, a lord of demons."

"And where are these people? Who are they?"

"We don't know. We didn't know who Kauron's heir was, either, until you showed up."

"Could Hespero be the Blood Knight, the servant of the Vhelny?"

"It's possible. The Vhelny has other names: Wind-of-Lightning, Sky-Breaker, Destroyer. His only desire is to see the end of the world and everything in it."

"Perhaps you mean the Briar King?"

"No. The Briar King is lord of root and leaf. Why would he destroy the earth?"

"There are prophecies that say he might."

"There are prophecies that say he might destroy the race of Man," she corrected. "That isn't the same thing."

"Oh. True. But why would Hespero want to destroy the world?" he asked.

"I don't know," Sister Pale replied. "Perhaps he is insane. Or very, very disappointed in things."

"And you, Sister Pale? What's your interest in this? How do I know you aren't an agent of Hespero, tricking me into leading you to the Alq? Or a disciple of the Destroyer, or whoever else wants this thing?"

"You don't, I suppose. And there's nothing I can say to convince you. I could tell you that I am descended of the line of priestesses Kauron met when he came here. I could tell you that I was trained in a coven but that it was not the Coven Saint Cer. And I could tell you I am here to help you because I have waited all my life for you to come. But you have no reason to believe these things."

"Especially when you've already lied to me once. Or perhaps twice," he replied.

"The once I understand: what I told you about Saint Cer. But that wasn't for your benefit; it was for the benefit of others. But when did I lie to you a second time?"

"When you told me you attended a different coven. There are many covens, but *all* are of the Order of Saint Cer."

"If that's true, then it would mean I told the truth the first time and am only lying now. So it's still only one lie, not so much, really, between friends."

"Now you're making fun of me."

"Yes. What did I tell you earlier about assuming that you know everything?"

"Then there really is a coven dedicated to a saint other than Cer? And it isn't a heretical sect?"

"I never claimed that it wasn't heretical," Pale replied. "Unsanctioned by z'Irbina, certainly. But neither are the Revesturi sanctioned by the Church, yet you are one."

"I'm not!" Stephen snapped. "I'd never even heard of the Revesturi until a few ninedays ago, until I started on this bloody quest. And now I don't understand anything at all!"

He jerked his hand away from her and groped away into the dark.

"Brother Darige—"

"Stay away," he said. "I don't trust you. Every time I think I have some inkling of what's going on, this happens."

"What happens?"

"*This!* Blood Knights, Destroyers, prizes, treasure troves, prophecies, and Alqs, and . . ."

"Oh," she said. He could almost see the shape of her face in the moonlight now and the liquid shimmer of her eyes. "You mean *knowledge*. You mean learning. You think you'd be more content if the world continued to bear out what you believed to be true when you were fifteen."

"Yes!" Stephen shouted. "Yes, I think I would!"

"Then there's something I don't understand. If learning is so painful to you, why do you pursue it? Why were you there in the scriftorium tonight?"

"Because . . ."

He felt like strangling someone, possibly himself.

"Don't do that," he said sullenly.

"Do what?"

"Make sense. Even better, don't talk to me at all."

He closed his eyes, and when he opened them, he found her much nearer, near enough that he could feel her breath on his face. He could make out the curve of her cheek, rounded so she looked young. Ivory in the moonlight. One eye was still dark, but the other shone like silver. He could see half her lip, too, either pouting or naturally made that way.

Her breath was sweet, faintly herbal.

"You started this," she breathed. "You started talking. I was perfectly happy holding your hand in silence, helping you, taking you where you need to go. But you had to start asking all the questions. Can't you just let things happen?"

"That's all I *have* been doing," Stephen said, his voice cracking. "It's like one of those dreams where you're trying to do something, but you keep getting distracted, pulled off the track, and your original purpose falls farther and farther away. And I'm losing people. I lost Winna and Aspar. I lost Ehawk.

"Now I've lost Ehan, and Henne, and Themes, and I keep trying to pretend it doesn't matter, but it does."

"Winna, Aspar, Ehawk. Are they all dead?"

"I don't know," he said miserably.

"Winna was your lover?"

That went in like an arrow.

"No."

"Ah, I see. But you wanted her to be."

"What's this got to do with anything?"

"Nothing, maybe." He felt her hand wrap around his again. They were both cold.

"Were they with you on this quest of yours?" she pressed. "Did the waurm kill them?"

"No," Stephen said. "That's what I'm trying to tell you. I came to Crotheny to join the monastery d'Ef. On the way I was kidnapped by bandits. Aspar—he's the king's holter— he saved me from them."

"And then?"

"Well, then I went on to d'Ef, but only after learning about terrible things in the forest and about the Briar King. And then at d'Ef—" He stopped. How could he explain in a few words the betrayal he'd felt at finding the corruption at d'Ef? At the first beating Brother Desmond and his cohort had given him?

Why should he?

She squeezed his hand encouragingly.

"Things went wrong there," he finally said. "I was asked to translate terrible things. Forbidden things. It was as if the world I thought I knew ceased to exist. Certainly the Church was different than I believed it to be. Then Aspar showed back up, nearly dead, and it was my turn to save him, and suddenly I was off on *his* quest, off to rescue Winna—and save the *queen,* of all things."

"And you did that?"

"Yes. And then the praifec sent us out after the Briar King, but halfway through that business we figured out that the real evil was Hespero himself, and we ended up trying to foil their plans to awaken a faneway of the Damned Saints. After doing that we were thrown in with a princess off to reclaim her throne from an usurper—something I really had no idea how to do—and the next thing I know I've been snatched by slinders and I'm sitting with my old fratrex, whom I thought dead, and he tells me the world's only hope is for me to come up here . . . I just wanted to study books!" He couldn't continue then. Why was he going on like this, anyway?

He sounded like a child.

"I'm sorry," he finally managed. "That must all sound ridiculous."

"No," she said, "it sounds reasonable. I knew a girl who wanted to study letters at the Coven Saint Cer. She'd wanted to do so since she was five, when she was in the care of her aunt, who dusted the temple library in Demsted. Everything looked hopeful, but then a boy she'd known forever but never thought twice about seemed suddenly to shine like a watchstar, and she couldn't bear the thought of not knowing his touch.

"And then she found herself with child, and her dreams of a coven education dropped away. Suddenly marriage— something she had always wished to avoid—became her only path.

"She'd just begun to settle in to that, to lose the edge of her resentment, when her husband died and then her child. Just to live, she had to become the maid of a foreign noble, tending children who were not hers. Then one day a woman appeared and offered her another chance at her dream, to study in a coven . . ."

Her voice had become hypnotic, and he could see both of her eyes now, small half-moons.

"That's how life is, my friend. Yours seems strange because it is full of wonders fantastic, but the fact is that few people remain on the path they begin on. The truth is, we have dreams like you describe because our dreams are dark mirrors of waking.

"But here is where you are lucky," she continued. "*I* have come to put you back on your path. You joined the Church because you loved knowledge, yes? Loved mystery, old books, the secrets of the past. If we find the place you're looking for—if we find the Alq—you'll have all of that, and more."

Stephen felt as if he couldn't breathe, couldn't think of anything to say.

"The girl, the one who wanted to study—"

She leaned forward, and her lips met his, caressed them slightly. A shock ran down his spine, a very pleasant one.

But he pulled away.

"Don't do that," he said.

"Why? Because you like it?"

"No. I just told you. I don't trust you."

"Hmm," she said, leaning back in. He meant to stop her, he really did, but somehow her lips were on his again, and he *did* like it, of course, and as if he had gone mad, he suddenly let go of her hand and reached around her, drew her body against his, realizing with a shock how small she was, how good she felt.

Winna, he thought, and touched her face, ran his fingers under her hood into her blond hair, seeing her in his mind's eye with the perfect clarity only an initiate of Decmanus could conjure.

She placed both hands on his chest then and pressed him away gently. "We can't stay here," she said. "It's not much farther, and we'll be safe."

"I—"

"Hush. Try not to think too much about it."

He couldn't help it. He laughed quietly. "That will be very difficult," he said.

"Think about this instead," she told him, taking his hand again and beginning to lead him back to the trail. "Soon the sun will rise, and you will see that I am not *her*. You should be prepared for that."

Sunrise found them on a rocky white path winding through a high, treeless moor. The clouds were low, wet and cold, but the ground cover was brilliant green, and Stephen wondered what it was. Could Aspar name it, or were they too far from the plants the holter knew?

Snow capped the surrounding peaks, but it had to be melting, for the path was often crossed by rivulets, and virtual waterfalls cascaded down the sides of many of the hills. They stopped at one of them to drink, and Sister Pale pushed back her weather cloak.

In that gray light he finally saw her.

Her eyes really were silver or, rather, a blue-gray so pale that they caught the light that way at times. Her hair, however, wasn't blond but a thick auburn, cut simply and short. Her cheeks were rounded, as had been hinted in the darkness, but whereas Winna's face was an oval, Pale's tapered sharply to the chin. Her lips were smaller than they had seemed when he was kissing them, but they had the natural pout he'd imagined. She had two large pox marks on her forehead and a long, raised scar on her left cheek.

She kept her eyes averted as she drank, then studied their surroundings, knowing he was studying her, giving him his chance.

It was disappointing. Not only was she not Winna, she wasn't as beautiful as Winna. He knew it was a terrible thought, but he couldn't deny his reaction. In the phay stories, the hero always won the beautiful virgin and everyone else had to settle for what was left.

Aspar was the hero of this tale, not Stephen; he'd known that for some time. Winna wasn't a virgin, but she had that air about her, the aura of the hero's prize.

Pale tilted her head to look at him then, and he almost gasped. He recalled the time Sacritor Burden had been trying to explain the saints to him; he'd produced a piece of crystal, triangular in cross section but long, like the roof of a lodge house. It seemed interesting, even unusual, and when he put it into the sunlight, it sparkled fetchingly. But it was only when he turned it just so that it threw out the colors of the rainbow and revealed the beauty that had been hidden in white light.

When he met her eyes now, there was suddenly so much more than his first glance had found, and her features came into clearer focus. For the first time he saw them as her own.

"Well," she said, "that's what you get for kissing a girl before you've seen her."

"You kissed *me*," he blurted, realizing in the same breath that it wasn't what he was supposed to say.

She just shrugged and pushed the hood of her cloak back on her head.

"Yes," she allowed.

"Wait," he said.

She turned and cocked her head.

"What's happening here?" he asked desperately.

"Most likely the praifec and his men are just starting after us," she replied. "We'll need mounts, and we can get some just ahead. After that, we might stay ahead of them."

"That's *not* what I meant."

"I know that," she replied.

"Well, then? I mean, I hardly know you. It's simply not reasonable."

"Where I come from," Pale said, "everything isn't reasonable. And we don't wait a lifetime for a perfect kiss from the perfect person, because then we die alone. I kissed you because I wanted to, and you wanted me to, and maybe we both needed it. And until the sun came up, you seemed to be happy with that and maybe ready to do it some more.

"But here we are instead, and that's life, too, and not worth dwelling on. We can only get so much done before we die, yes? So let's go."

CHAPTER THIRTEEN

CREPLING

CAZIO HEARD someone shout his name; it was a thin, distant thing.

He'd had most of his attention on climbing, wedging boot tips and fingers into the precarious notches that had been cut into the stone and mortar. He'd been delighted to find them there and wondered who had carved them originally. Some ancient thief? Children exploring the wall, or perhaps a Sefry magician? It didn't matter, really. He could probably have managed the climb at the intersection of the walls using only the meager purchase offered naturally by the masonry, but the ancient climbers had helped him considerably.

They increased his chances of survival only slightly, however, when he spotted the soldiers who were rushing toward him. He still had a kingsyard to go, and at the rate he was climbing, he wasn't going to make it before cold iron married him.

With a silent prayer to Mamres and Fiussa, he flexed his knees and leapt as hard as he could up and to his right, toward the first spearman.

The problem with that was that the jump threw him away from the wall. Not much, but enough that he wouldn't be able to reach it again. He felt the cobbles of Gobelin Court below him, eager to smash his spine, as he stretched his arms nearly out of their sockets.

As he had prayed, the spearman was taken aback, seeing a crazy man leaping toward him. If logical thought was his guide, he would step away, watch Cazio grasp at empty air, and laugh as he fell.

Instead, the man reacted instinctively and thrust the spear at his attacker.

Cazio caught the thick shaft just above the wickedly pointed steel, and to his delight, the guard's second reaction was to yank back. That pulled Cazio toward the wall, and he let go so he could catch the top of the edifice with his arms and upper chest.

The spearman, overcompensating, tumbled backward. The wall was sufficiently wide that he didn't fall off, but with him down and his companion still a few strides away, Cazio had the time to jerk himself to his feet and draw Acredo.

Heedless, the second fellow lowered the sharp of his

weapon and prepared for the attack. Cazio was pleased to see that he was wearing only chain, a breastplate, and a helm rather than a knight's plate.

As the thrust came, he parried *prismo* and stepped quickly toward his opponent, lifting his left hand to seize the shaft and then flipping the tip of his blade up for a long lunge that ended in the man's throat. If it hadn't been for the armor, he might have tried for a less lethal spot, but the only other exposed place was the thigh, where his sword point might become lodged in bone.

As the man dropped his spear and whistled in despair through novel lips, Cazio turned to the first fellow, who was regaining his feet.

"Contro z'osta," Cazio said, *"Zo dessrator comatia anter c'acra."*

"What are you babbling about?" the man screamed, clearly distressed. "What are you saying?"

"My apologies," Cazio said. "When I speak of love, wine, or swordplay, I find it easier to use my native tongue. I quote the famous treatise of Mestro Papa Avradio Vallaimo, who states—"

He was rudely interrupted as the man screamed and lunged forward, leaving Cazio wondering exactly how much training these men had been given.

He threw his rear leg back and dropped his body and head below the line of the attack while extending his arm. Carried by momentum, the attacker more or less threw himself onto the tip of Cazio's blade.

"'Against the spear, the swordsman shall move inside the point,'" Cazio continued as the man folded over on his side.

Here came another one out of the tower to his left. He set his stance and waited, wondering how many of them he would have to fight before the Craftsmen joined him.

This one proved more interesting, because he understood that Cazio had to come within reach. So he used his feet like a dessrator, allowing Cazio what looked like a good chance to close the distance, when in fact it was a ruse designed to make him commit to his own foolish charge.

Even more interesting were the shouts he heard coming from behind him and the next man running along the wall in the direction he was facing.

With a grim smile, he began teaching the rest of Mestro Papa's chapter *"Contro z'osta."*

Anne watched breathlessly as Cazio, in typical form, did the craziest thing imaginable and somehow survived.

Austra stood there, fists at her sides, growing whiter and whiter as the battle went on, until at last the Craftsmen appeared, swarming up the wall and joining the Vitellian. Then they split up and ran toward the towers. They appeared there a short time later, waving pennants.

Cazio had his broad-brimmed hat clutched in one hand.

"Saints," Austra breathed. "Why must he always—" She didn't finish but sighed instead. "He loves fighting more than he loves me."

"I'm sure that's not true," Anne replied, trying to sound convincing. "Anyway, at least it's not another woman."

"I'd almost rather that," Austra replied.

"When it happens," Anne said, "I'll take your bearings again."

"You mean *if* it happens," Austra said, sounding a bit defensive.

"Yes, that's what I meant," Anne said. But she knew better. Men took mistresses, didn't they? Her father had had many. The ladies of the court had always agreed that it was the nature of the beast.

She glanced back at the Sefry house. She and Austra had backed up to witness the action on the wall, but Mother Uun was still waiting in the shadow of her doorway.

"I apologize for the distraction, Mother Uun," she said, "but I would be pleased to discuss the Crepling passage now."

"Of course," the old woman replied. "Please come in."

The room where the Sefry took them was disappointingly ordinary. It had touches of the exotic, to be sure: a colorful rug, an oil lamp made of some sort of bone carved into the form of a swan, panes of dark blue glass that gave the room a pleasant, murky underwater feel. Except for that last feature, however, the room could have belonged to any merchant who traded in goods from far away.

Mother Uun indicated several armchairs arranged in a circle and waited until they were settled before she herself took a seat. Almost the instant she did so, another Sefry—a man—entered the room with a tray. He bowed without upsetting the teapot and cups he was carrying, then placed it all onto a small table.

"Will you have some tea?" Mother Uun asked pleasantly.

"That would be nice," Anne replied.

The Sefry man seemed young, no older than Anne's seventeen winters. He was handsome in a thin, alien way, and his eyes were a striking cobalt blue.

He then departed, only to return moments later with walnut bread and marmalade.

Anne sipped the tea and found it tasted of lemons, oranges, and some spice she wasn't familiar with. It occurred to her that it might be poison. Mother Uun was drinking from the same pot, but since she'd touched the Sefry assassin and found him so *wrong* inside, she thought it possible that what was poison to a human might be pleasing to a Sefry.

Her next sip was feigned, and she hoped Austra was doing the same, although if her maid drank it, at least she would know if it was poisoned.

Horror followed swiftly on the heels of that thought. What was *wrong* with her?

Austra's face crinkled in concern, and that only made matters worse.

"Anne?"

"It's nothing," she replied. "I had an unpleasant thought."

She remembered that her father had had someone to taste his food. She needed someone like that, someone she didn't care about. *But not Austra.*

Mother Uun sipped her tea.

"When we arrived," Anne began, "you said something about watching someone. Will you explain that?"

In the dense blue light from the windows, Mother Uun's skin seemed less transparent, because the fine veins were no longer visible. Anne wondered idly if that was why she'd chosen indigo for her glass rather than orange or yellow. She also seemed somehow larger.

"You've heard him, I think," Mother Uun said. "His whispers are loud enough now to escape his prison."

"Again," Anne said impatiently, "of whom do you speak?"

"I will not say his name, not just yet," Mother Uun replied. "But I ask you to recall your history. Do you remember what once stood where this city now stands?"

"I was a poor student in every subject," Anne replied, "history included. But everyone knows *that*. Eslen was built on the ruins of the last fortress of the Scaosen."

"Scaosen," Mother Uun mused. "How time deforms words. The older term, of course, was 'Skasloi,' though even that was merely an attempt to pronounce the unpronounceable. But yes, here is where your ancestress Virgenya Dare won her final battle against our ancient masters and pressed her booted foot on the neck of the last of their kind. Here the scepter passed from the race of demons to the race of woman."

"I know the story," Anne said absently, interested by the Sefry's odd turn of phrase.

"When the Skasloi ruled here, it was known as Ulheqelesh," Mother Uun continued. "It was the greatest of the Skasloi strongholds, its lord the most powerful of his kind."

"Yes," Anne said. "Why do you say 'woman,' though, and not 'man'?"

"Because Virgenya Dare was a woman," Mother Uun replied.

"I understand that," Anne said. "But the name of her race was not 'woman.'"

"I meant the race to which women belong, I suppose," the Sefry said.

"But you are a woman, are you not, though not of Mankin?"

"Indeed," she said, the corners of her mouth lifting faintly.

Anne frowned but wasn't sure she wanted to crawl farther into this odd warren of semantics, not when the Sefry seemed perfectly content to be drawn farther and farther from the original question.

"Never mind," she said. "This person you say whispers to me. I want to know about him."

"Ah," Mother Uun said. "Yes. Virgenya Dare did not kill the last of the Skasloi. She kept him alive in the dungeons of Eslen.

"He is there yet, and it is my charge to make certain that he *stays* there."

An unexpected vertigo seized Anne; she felt as if her chair were nailed to the ceiling and she must grip its arms tightly to keep from falling out as the room slowly revolved.

Again she heard unintelligible words breathed into her ear, but this time she thought . . . almost . . . that she understood them. The voices of strange birds warbled beyond the window.

No, not birds at all, but Austra and Mother Uun.

She focused on them.

"That's impossible," Austra was saying. "The histories clearly say that she killed him. Besides, that would make him more than two thousand years old."

"He was older than that when his kingdom fell," Mother Uun replied. "The Skasloi did not age as your kind does. Some of them did not age at all. Qexqaneh is one of those."

"Qexqaneh?"

As she said the name, Anne suddenly felt something rough sliding against her skin, and her nostrils filled with a scent like burning pine. It happened so quickly that she burst into a fit of coughing.

"I should have warned you to be careful with that name," Mother Uun said. "It draws his attention, but it also gives you power to command him, if your will is strong enough."

"Why?" Anne asked hoarsely. "Why keep such a thing alive?"

"Who knows the mind of the Born Queen?" Mother Uun said. "Perhaps, at first, to gloat. Or perhaps from fear. He made a prophecy, you know."

"I've never heard of such a thing," Anne said.

Mother Uun closed her eyes, and her voice changed. It dropped lower and canted somewhere between song and chant.

"You were born slaves," she said. "You will die slaves. You have merely summoned a new master. The daughters of your seed will face what you have wrought, and it will obliterate them."

Anne felt as though a hand were cupped across her mouth and nose. She could hardly draw breath.

"What did he mean by that?" she managed.

"No one knows," the Sefry replied. "But the time he spoke of has come; that much is certain." Her voice was of normal pitch now, but she was almost whispering.

"Even bound, he is terribly dangerous. To enter the castle, you must pass him. Be strong. Do nothing he asks and do not forget that it is in your blood to command him. If you ask him a question, he cannot lie, but he will nevertheless do his best to mislead you."

"My father? My mother? Did they know of him?"

"All the kings of Eslen have known the Kept," Mother Uun replied. "As will you. As you *must*."

Well, at least that wasn't something I missed when I wasn't paying attention, Anne mused to herself.

"Tell me," she said, "do you know anything about a certain tomb beneath a horz in Eslen-of-Shadows?"

"Anne!" Austra gasped, but Anne shushed her with a motion of her hand.

Mother Uun paused, the cup just inches from her lips, and her smooth brow wrinkled.

"I can't say that I do," she replied at last.

"What of the Faiths? Can you tell me anything about them?"

"I suspect you know them better than I," the old woman said.

"But I would be more than moderately pleased to learn what you know of them," Anne countered in what she hoped was an insistent tone.

"Sorceresses of the most ancient sort," the old woman offered. "Some say they are immortal; others say that they are the heads of a secret order and are replaced with each generation."

"Really? Which explanation do you fancy?"

"I do not know if they are immortal, but I suspect they are long-lived."

Anne sighed. "This is no more than I have already heard. Tell me something I don't know. Tell me why they wish me to be queen in Eslen."

Mother Uun was silent for a moment, then she sighed.

"The great forces of the world are not aware of themselves," she said. "What drives the wind, what pulls the falling rock to earth, what pulses life into our shells and pulls it away—these things are senseless, with no will, no intelligence, no desires or intentions. They simply are."

"And yet the saints control these things," Anne said.

"Hardly. The saints— No, leave that aside. Here is what is important: Those forces might be diverted by art, certainly. The wind can be harnessed to pump water or drive a ship. A river can be dammed, its currents used to drive a mill. The sedos power can be tapped. But the forces themselves dictate the ultimate shape of things, and they do so by their nature, not by their design.

"The Skasloi knew this; they did not worship gods, or saints, or any other such creatures. They found the sources of power and learned how to use them to their advantage. They fought for control of these sources, fought for millennia, until their world was all but destroyed.

"Finally, to save themselves, a few banded together, slaughtered their kin, and began remaking the world. They discovered the thrones and used them to keep the powers in check."

"Thrones?"

"It's not a good term, really. They aren't seats or even places. They are more like the position of king or queen, an office to be filled, and once filled it confers the powers and obligations of the throne on the person who is filling it. There are several sorts of arcane power in the lands of fate, and each possesses a throne. These powers wax and wane in relative puissance. The throne that controls the power you know as sedos has been strengthening for millennia."

"But you say there are others?"

"Of course. Do you think the Briar King is nurtured by the sedoi? He is not. He sits a very different throne."

"And the Faiths?"

"Counselors. Queenmakers. They fight to see *you* receive the power, sit the sedos throne, rather than seeing it fall into the hands of another. But they have enemies, as do you."

"But the sedoi are controlled by the Church," Anne said.

"Up until now, yes, insomuch as they were controlled at all."

"Then surely Fratrex Prismo already sits on that throne," Anne said.

"He does not," Mother Uun said. "No one does."

"But why?"

"The Skasloi *hid* it."

"Hid it? But why?"

"They forbade the use of the sedos power," she replied. "Of all the forces they knew, it was the most destructive and could be used most effectively against the other thrones. Whoever sits the sedos throne can destroy the world. Virgenya Dare found that throne, used it to free your people and mine, and then abdicated it for fear of what it might do. For two thousand years men have been searching for it in vain. But now, like a season long in coming or a slow tide rising, the sedos power waxes again, and the throne will reveal itself. When that happens, it is important that the right person seize it."

"But why me?" Anne asked.

"The throne isn't open to just anyone," Mother Uun

replied. "And of the possible candidates, the Faiths probably consider you the best chance for preserving the world."

"And the Briar King?"

"Who knows what his desires may be? But I should think his intention is to destroy whoever fills the throne before the sedos power can destroy him and everything he embodies."

"And what is that?"

Mother Uun raised an eyebrow. "Birth and death. Germination and decay. Life."

Anne set her cup down. "And how do you know all this, Mother Uun? How do you know so much about the Skasloi?"

"Because I am one of his keepers. And along with him, my clan preserves the knowledge of him from generation to generation."

"But what if none of this is true? What if it's all lies?"

"Why, then I know very little at all," the Sefry said. "You must decide for yourself what is true. I can only tell you what I believe to be so. The rest is up to you."

Anne nodded thoughtfully. "And the Crepling passageway? There is an entrance in this very house, isn't there?"

"Indeed. I can show you if you are ready."

"I'm not yet prepared," Anne said. "But soon." She settled her cup down. "You seem very helpful, Mother Uun."

"Is there something else, Your Majesty?"

"Male Sefry can remember the passages, can't they?"

"They can. Our kind are different."

"Are there Sefry warriors here in Gobelin Court?"

"It depends on what you mean. All Sefry, male and female, have some training in the arts of war. Many who live here wander far in the world, and many have known battle."

"Then—"

Mother Uun raised a hand. "The Sefry of Gobelin Court will not help you. In showing you the passageway, I fulfill the only obligation we have."

"Perhaps you should not think in terms of obligations," Anne said, "but of rewards."

"We make our own way in the world, we Sefry," Mother Uun said. "I don't ask you to understand us."

"Very well," Anne said. *But I will remember this once I am on the throne.*

She rose. "Thank you for the tea, Mother Uun, and for the conversation."

"It was my pleasure," the Sefry replied.

"I'll return shortly."

"Whenever you wish."

"You said you were going to tell me what was going on," Austra reminded her as they reentered the sunlight. They shielded their eyes from the glare.

Something seemed to be happening at the far end of the square, but Anne couldn't tell what it was. A small group of men broke off from the rest and moved in her direction.

"I have dreams," Anne said. "You know that."

"Yes. And your dreams told you about this Crepling passage?"

"I saw all the passages," Anne said. "There's a sort of map in my head."

"That's rather convenient," Austra replied. "Who showed you this map?"

"What do you mean?"

"You said you had a vision. Was it the Faiths again? Were they the ones who told you about the passages?"

"It isn't always the Faiths," Anne replied. "They are, in fact, more confusing than helpful. No, sometimes I just know things."

"Then no one actually spoke to you?" Austra pressed, sounding doubtful.

"What do *you* know about this?" Anne said, trying to keep a sudden burst of anger leashed.

"I think I was there, that's all," Austra said. "You were talking in your sleep, and it seemed as if you were talking to someone. Someone who frightened you. And you woke up screaming, remember?"

"I remember. I also remember telling you that you aren't to question me so boldly."

Austra's face went stony.

"Begging your pardon, Your Majesty, but that isn't what you said. You said I was free to question you and make my arguments in private but that once you had *spoken* on a subject, I was to be obedient to that word."

Anne suddenly realized that Austra was shaking and very near to tears. She took her friend's hand.

"You're right," Anne said. "I'm sorry, Austra. Please understand. You're not the only one under a strain, you know."

"I know," Austra said.

"You're right about the vision, too. There *was* someone in the dream, and it was he who showed me the passages."

"He? A Sefry, then?"

"I don't think so," Anne said. "I think it was something else. Something neither Sefry nor human."

"The Kept, you mean? The Scaos? But how could you ever trust *that* creature?"

"I don't. I'm sure that what he wants in return for his help is to be released. But remember what Mother Uun said—that I command *him*. No, he'll give me what I want, not the other way around."

"A real Scaos," Austra murmured, wonder in her voice. "Living below us all this time. It makes me sick to even think about it. It's like waking up to find a snake coiled around your feet."

"If my ancestors kept such a thing alive, they must have had their reasons," Anne said.

While they were speaking, five of her Craftsmen stepped up and formed a hedge around her. She noticed that Sir Leafton also was approaching.

"What's going on at the other end of the square?" Anne asked.

"You'd best find a safe place, Majesty," Leafton said. "Someplace that is easily defensible. We are already attacked."

PART IV
✠
THRONES

The Sefry are known almost everywhere except the islands, for they dislike crossing water. But oddly, in history they are nearly invisible. They do not fight battles; they do not found kingdoms. They do not leave their names on things. They are everywhere and nowhere.

One wonders what they are up to.
—*FROM THE AMENA TIRSON OF PRESSON MANTEO*

If you wish to know what a man really is, give him a crown.
—*PROVERB FROM THE BAIRGHS*

CHAPTER ONE

✣

THE CHARLATAN

ASPAR HEARD the death knells before he ever saw the town of Haemeth.

The sound carried in long, beautiful peals along the waters of the White Warlock River, startling a flock of hezlings into furtive flight. The southern sky was dark with smoke, but the wind was going that way, so Aspar couldn't smell what was burning.

She's a stranger. Would they ring the bell for a stranger?

He didn't know. He didn't know much at all about village customs on the north side of the Midenlands.

He urged Ogre to a trot. The great horse had strengthened steadily during the ride down the Warlock, grazing on rye and early fengrass, and after only a couple of days he was nearly his old self. This was cause for hope, but Aspar tried to keep away from that dangerous emotion. Winna had been far sicker than Ogre, and no medicine could bring back the dead.

The road wound along the low lip of the river valley, and after a few moments, Haemeth finally came into sight. Situated on the next large hill, it was a town of surprising size, with outlying farms and steadings spread out into the lowlands and along the road. He could see the source of the woeful music now, too, a spindly bell tower of white stone capped in black slate, so peaked that the whole thing looked rather like a spear.

A second tower, this one thicker and crenellated on top, stood on the highest point at the other end of town, and it seemed as if the two towers were joined by a long stone wall. Most likely the wall went all the way around the town, but since Aspar was looking up from below, all he could see was a handful of rooftops peeking over the top.

The smoke was coming from several huge pyres that had been built down by the river, and now that the wind had shifted a bit, he knew what they were burning.

He kicked Ogre into a gallop.

More than a few heads turned toward Aspar as Ogre brought him up to the crowd, but he ignored the shouts demanding that he identify himself, swinging himself down instead and striding toward the fire.

It was difficult to count the corpses, heaped as they were, but he reckoned there were more than fifty. Two of the blazes were already so hot that white bone was beginning to pop and fall into the coals, but in the third he could see faces beginning to blister. His heart labored as he searched for Winna's sweet features, smoke stinging his eyes. The heat forced him to step back.

"Here," a burly fellow shouted. "Watch yourself. What are you doing?"

Aspar turned on him.

"How did these people die?" he demanded.

"They died because the saints hate us," the man replied angrily. "And I'll know who you are."

About six men had gathered behind the fellow. A couple of them had held pitchforks or long poles for working the fire, but other than that they didn't seem to be armed. They looked like tradesmen and farmers.

"I'm Aspar White," he grunted. "The king's holter."

"Holter? The only forest within six days of here is the Sarnwood, and it don't have a holter."

"I'm the holter of the King's Forest," Aspar informed him. "I'm looking for two strangers: a young woman with blond hair and a dark young man. They would've come in with two cowherds."

"Don't have much time to look for strangers," the man

said. "Seems like all we have time for these days is grief. And for all I know, you might be bringing us more of that grief."

"I mean you no harm," Aspar responded. "I only want to find my friends."

"You work for the king, then?" a third man put in. Aspar glanced at him from the corner of his eye, unwilling to take his gaze completely off the more threatening fellow. The new speaker was sunburned, with close-cropped hair, half gray and half black, and was missing an upper right tooth.

"The way I hear it, their aens't no king."

"True, but there's a queen," Aspar said. "And I'm her deputy, with full power to enforce her laws."

"A queen, eh?" the thin fellow said. "Well, we could use a good word with her. You see what's happening to us here."

"They don't care in Eslen what's become of us," the first man exploded. "You're being fools. They didn't send this man here to help us. He's just come for his friends, like he said. As far as he's concerned, the rest of us can *rot*."

"What's your name?" Aspar said, lowering his voice.

"Raud Achenson, if it's anything to you."

"I reckon you've got somebody on the pyre there."

"Mighing right I do. My wife. My father. My youngest boy."

"So you're angry. You'd like someone to blame. But I didn't put 'em there, you understand? And Grim hear me, I'll put *you* there if you say one more word."

Raud purpled, and his shoulders bunched.

"We're with you, Raud," said a fellow behind him.

That released the big man like a catapult, and he sprang at Aspar.

Aspar punched him in the throat, hard, and he went down.

Without stopping, Aspar leapt forward and caught the man who had cheered him on, grabbing him by the hair. He yanked out his dirk and put the tip under the man's chin.

"Now, why would you try to kill your friend?" he asked.

"Didn't—sorry," the man gasped. "Please—"

Aspar released him with a hard push that sent him tumbling. Raud was on the ground, gasping for air and getting little, but Aspar hadn't crushed his windpipe. He gave the rest of the crowd a hard look but didn't see anyone who looked like a taker.

"Now," he demanded, "what *happened* here?"

The gray-and-black-haired man studied his feet.

"You won't believe it," he said. "I saw it myself, and I don't."

"I maunt I'll try it, anyway."

"It was a thing like a snake, but so *big*. It crossed upstream. We reckon it poisoned the water. The greft sent his knights after it, but it killed most of 'em."

"I've seen it, too," Aspar said, "so I've no trouble believing you. Now, I'm going to ask you again, and this time someone answer me. Two strangers, a man and a woman, the woman with wheat-colored hair. They would have come with two children, cowherds named Aethlaud and Aohsli. Where would I find them?"

A woman of middle years cleared her throat at that. "They might be at the Billhook and Bail," she offered uncertainly.

"You there!"

The shout came from uphill, and Aspar turned to find a man riding down from the city gate. He was dressed in lord's plate and mounted on a black stallion with a white blaze.

"Yah?" he answered.

"You're Aspar White?"

"Yah."

"You'll want to talk to me, then."

The man reached down and clasped Aspar's hand, then introduced himself as Sir Peren, servant of the Greft of Faurstrem, whose seat was Haemeth. The holter mounted Ogre, and together they started up the hill.

"Your friends spoke of you," Peren said once the crowd was behind them. "Winna and Ehawk."

"You know them? Where are they?"

"I will not lie to you," Peren said. "I saw them last this morning. They were dying. They might be dead by now."

"Take me to them, then," Aspar said, knowing his voice was harsh, unable to do anything about it.

Peren glanced at him. "You've found it, then?" he asked. "The cure?"

Aspar looked downhill to the pyres. A whole town infected by the woorm's poison, and him with a bagful of the fruit.

"Is the greft infected?" he asked rather than answering directly.

"No, but his son led us against the waurm," Sir Peren replied. "He, too, lies on his deathbed." The man seemed nervous, Aspar thought.

Aspar relaxed his shoulders with a deep breath. They had been waiting for him. Either Ehawk or Winna had told someone he'd gone to find a cure, and word had gotten around.

Was he a prisoner? It was starting to feel that way. He probably could kill Peren and escape, but that meant Winna and Ehawk would surely die if they weren't already dead.

"I'll see my friends," he said. "Then we'll see about the greftson."

By the time they reached the tower, two more armed and armored men had joined Peren in escorting him. Once they passed the outer keep, a servant took Ogre, his only ally, and by the time they entered the bailey and came into the audience of the greft, he had seven guards following him.

The Greffy of Faurstrem wasn't a large or prosperous one, and the audience chamber reflected that fact in its modesty. An ancient throne of oak sat on a small stone dais, with a banner draped behind it depicting a hawk gripping a scepter and an arrow in its claws. The man on the throne was ancient, too, with a silver beard that nearly piled in his lap and rheumy gray eyes.

Peren dropped to his knee.

"Greft Ensil," he said. "This is Aspar White, the king's holter."

The old man shook, every part of him, as he raised his

head to regard his visitor. He stared at Aspar for a long, wasted moment before speaking.

"I thought I would never have a son," he said at last. "The saints seemed to be denying me. I was almost resigned to it, and then, when I was sixty, the saints made a miracle and gave me Emfrith. Emfrith, my lovely boy." He leaned forward, eyes blazing.

"Can you understand that, holter? Have you any children?"

"No," Aspar replied.

"No," Ensil repeated. "Then you cannot understand." He sat back and closed his eyes. "Three days ago he rode out against a thing I believed only existed in legend. He went out like a hero, and fell like one. He is dying. Can you save him?"

"I'm not a leic, my lord," Aspar said.

"Do not make *mock* of me," the old man shrilled. "The girl told us. You went to the Sarnwood to locate the cure for this poison. Did you find that cure?"

"Is she alive?" Aspar asked.

The men around Ensil looked suddenly uncomfortable.

"Is she alive?" Aspar reiterated in a louder voice.

Ensil shook his head.

"She died," he said. "As did the boy. There was nothing we could do."

And suddenly Aspar smelled autumn leaves, and he knew murder was about—but whether already happened or on the way, he could not know. His throat thickened and his eyes burned, but he stood straighter and made his face stone.

"I'll see her body, then," Aspar said. "I'll see it now."

Ensil sighed and signed with his hand. "Search him."

Aspar dropped his hand to his dirk. "Mark me, Greft Ensil. Maunt my words. I have the cure for your son, but it isn't a simple tonic or the like. It needs doing in a particular way, or the result is poison that will only kill him all the quicker.

"And here's the other thing. If Winna Rufoote is already dead, from whatever cause, then you won't have my help. If you try to force me, I reckon I'll fight and probably die, and I swear to you, so will your son. You cann? Now, I'm reckoning you say my friends are dead because you're afraid I only brought antidote enough for one or two. Trouble with that is, if they aren't really dead, you'll kill 'em soon so I don't know I've been tricked.

"But I know already, and I have enough cure for all three of them. The only thing will save your son is that girl drawing breath. So I'll see her body, dead or alive, sprootlic. *Now.*"

Ensil stared at him for another long moment as Aspar battled doubt. Had he guessed right? Or was she really dead? He couldn't believe the last, so he had to believe the first, even if it got him killed.

"Take him," Ensil muttered.

Aspar tensed for the battle, but then he saw the chamberlain bow and point left.

"This way," the man said.

Aspar didn't weep often, but when Winna's faint breath fogged the polished steel of his knife, a single salty droplet worked its way out of the corner of his eye.

They were in a sickroom improvised from a chapel. Ehawk was there, too, unconscious but breathing a little better, along with twenty or so others, many of whom were still awake enough to groan and wail.

Aspar retrieved the berries from his pouch and was about to start force-feeding them to Winna when he took pause.

He'd been right about the greft's intentions. He might get a few berries down Winna, but as soon as they understood that he'd lied about the complexity of the cure, they would probably confiscate the entire pouch.

"Where is the greftson?" Aspar demanded. "This would be better done all at once."

"He's in his own chambers."

"Bring him then, and quickly."

Then he knelt back down and stroked Winna's face, his heart making weird motions in its bone cage.

"Hold on, girl," he muttered. "Just a few more minutes."

He touched her neck but could find only the weakest pulsing there. If she died in the time it took them to bring the other fellow down . . .

"I'll need to work without eyes on me," he told the remaining men. "We'll need to improvise some sort of tent around their beds."

"Why?" the chamberlain asked.

Aspar tightened his gaze on the man. "You know of the Sarnwood witch, yah? You know how few come before her and live? And yet I did, and she made me a gift of one of her secrets. But I was forced to swear a geos that no eyes but mine would witness this cure. Now, do as I say, and do it sprootlic! Bring some wine and a small white cloth, too."

The chamberlain looked dubious, but he sent men off to bring the things Aspar had demanded. A few moments later several men bore a litter into the room on which lay a young man of perhaps nineteen winters. His lips were blue, and he looked quite dead.

"Sceat," Aspar said under his breath. If the greftson was dead, he wasn't walking out of there, and neither were Winna and Ehawk.

But then the boy coughed, and Aspar realized that much of the blue color came from some kind of paste that had been swabbed over him. Some local attempt at medicine, more than likely.

With poles and sheets, the greft's men quickly built a tent around the three bodies, placing a small brazier inside, along with the wine.

The instant the sheet was closed, Aspar began mumbling in the Sefry cant of his childhood, as Jesp had done when she pretended to do magic. He was amazed at how readily it came to him, considering how much distance he'd tried to put between himself and all that. Normally his survival depended on his senses, wits, and weapons. Today it depended on how well he remembered how to play the charlatan.

Breaking between singing and chanting, he crushed some berries and, as gently as he could, pushed five of them down

Winna's throat, following that with a little wine, then holding her mouth shut until she swallowed weakly. Then he moved to Ehawk and did the same thing. The greftson's eyes fluttered open as he began the process on him.

"Swallow," Aspar said.

Looking confused, the boy did so.

Raising his voice, Aspar ended the chant with a flourish.

He went back to Winna, who, he saw with leaden heart, seemed exactly the same. He fed her two more berries, then drew back the flap of the makeshift tent.

The greft had been carried in on a sort of armchair and sat regarding him with skeptical eyes.

"Well?" he growled.

"Now we wait," Aspar said truthfully.

"If he dies, so do you."

Aspar shrugged and settled onto the stool next to Winna. He glanced at Greft Ensil. "I know how it is to lose someone dear," he said. "I know how it is to be threatened with that loss. And I suppose I would let a stranger die if it meant saving someone I loved. I don't fault you for the sentiment or the lie. But you might have given me the benefit of the doubt."

The old man's face softened somewhat.

"You don't understand," he said. "You're too weak in years to understand. Honor and bravery are for the young. They have the constitution for it and no sense, no sense at all."

Aspar maunted that for a moment.

"I don't claim to know much about honor," he said finally. "Especially after the show I just put on."

"What do you mean?" Ensil asked.

Aspar produced the remaining Sarnwood fruits. "I'm tired of all this," he said. "I gave your boy and my friends more than the amount the witch said would make the cure. I've tried 'em myself, so I know they aren't poison. They got my horse better, too. Three berries each, that's what you're supposed to give 'em." He reached into the bag and pulled out a few. "I'm keeping these because after this I'll find that woorm and kill it, and I might need them. But in the meantime, there's plenty more here. Distribute 'em as you see fit."

"But the chanting? The song? The wine?"

Aspar ticked them off on his fingers.

"Fraud, deceit, and I was thirsty. But the berries are real." He tossed the bag to the chamberlain, who caught them as if they were eggs. "Now," he went on, "I've been riding for a few days without sleep. I'm going to try and get some. If you honorable fellows are goin' to slit my throat while I'm with Saint Soan, try and do it quietly."

Fingers on his face stroked him awake far more pleasantly than the kiss of a razor might have. At first he was afraid that it was only a dream, that he wasn't seeing Winna's half-lidded eyes looking back at him from the cot. But after glancing around at the situation, he managed to convince himself.

Winna's hand dropped loosely by her side.

"Weak," she murmured. Then her eyes focused on him again. "Glad you changed your mind," she whispered. "Glad to see you one more time." Tears streamed from the corners of her eyes.

"I didn't change my mind," he said. "I found the witch. She gave me what I asked for."

"No."

"Yes."

She closed her eyes and wheezed a few breaths.

"I don't feel well, Aspar," she said.

"You're better than you were," he assured her. "You were close on Saint Dun's gate when I got here. Now you're awake." He took her hand in his. "How in Grim's name did you end up in the castle?"

"Oh. The girl, Haudy, told someone; I'm a little hazy. They came and took us, asked a lot of questions about you." She closed her eyes. "I told them that if you came here, you wouldn't have it. I didn't think you would. I didn't think I would see you again."

"Well, here I am, and with the cure."

"Ehawk?"

He glanced at the boy, who was asleep but seemed to have better color. The greft was asleep, too, guarded by four knights, but to his surprise Aspar found the greftson looking at them.

"What is this?" the boy managed. "What's going on?"

"The story is you tried to fight a waurm," Aspar said.

"Auy," the young man replied. "That's right, and then . . ." His face screwed up in concentration. "I don't remember much after that."

"Emfrith! My sweet boy!"

The guards had shaken their lord awake and were helping the frail old man move toward his son.

"Atta!" Emfrith replied.

Aspar watched the two embrace.

"How do you feel?" the greft asked.

"Weak. Sick."

"You've been out of your head, unable even to recognize your own father."

After a moment, the greft drew himself up and faced Aspar, his eyes wet with tears.

"I regret . . ." He paused, as if struggling up a mountain under a heavy load. "I regret my treatment of you, master holter. I will not forget that you have done this. When you leave here, you shall have whatever I can give to help you on your way."

"Thank you," Aspar said. "Food and maybe some arrows will do. But I'll need them soon."

"How soon?"

"Midday, if it please you, Greft. I have a woorm to slay, and I'm in a hurry to get at it."

Winna's hand came back to his and gripped it. "Do you understand?" he asked her. "I'd stay with you or wait until you can ride—"

"No," she said. "No, that would be too long."

"That's my lady."

He bent to kiss her and found her weeping again.

"We won't grow old together, will we, Aspar?" she whispered. "We'll never have children, or a garden, or any of that."

"No," he murmured. "I don't think we will."

"But you love me?"

He pulled away a bit and wanted to lie, but he couldn't.

"Yah," he said. "More than I have words for."

"Then try and get killed later rather than sooner," she replied.

She was sleeping again a bell later, but her color had improved. The greftson was actually able to sit up, and Ensil was true to his word, providing him two pack mules replete with provisions and mountain clothing.

By the time the sun stood a bell after noon, the pyres of Haemeth were darkening the sky at his back.

CHAPTER TWO

GOATBACK

COMMENTS ON THE VIRGENYAN LEAST LOON

Uncommon in the world at large, this peculiar creature is found in isolated nesting places: little-used parlors, small garden nooks, and the most remote corners of libraries and monasteries.

When confronted or even noticed, they usually retreat to fortresses existing entirely in their imaginations. They feed on isolation. Peculiar among the animals, which tend to have clearly defined mating rituals, the Virgenyan Least Loon has instead a series of uncoordinated and spastic stances that, far from promoting the continuance of its kind, tend it more quickly toward extinction.

Its characteristic . . .

"STEPHEN," Pale said. "Are you there?"

"Yes," he said. "Sorry."

"Your eyes had gone glassy, and the way down is steep. Shall I take your hand again?"

"Ah, no, thank you. I think I can manage."

He concentrated now on the narrow trail. Earlier a cloud had come along and engulfed them, an odd experience for a boy from the low country. Now they were descending out of it into a small upland valley.

Roughly rectangular sheep pens came into view, built of piled stone. They attested to the local livelihood, as did the sheep themselves. A crooked line of smoke drifted up from the only obvious human habitation, a sod-roofed dwelling with a couple of small outbuildings.

"What's that smell?" Stephen asked, wrinkling his nose.

"Oh, you'd better get used to that," she said.

The shepherd was a young man with black hair, dark eyes, and long, lean limbs. He regarded Stephen with undisguised suspicion and Sister Pale with delight, clapping her in a tight hug and kissing her cheek. Stephen found he didn't care for that at all.

He liked it even less when they started speaking in a language quite unfamiliar to him. It wasn't the fractured dialect of Almannish he'd heard back in Demsted or likely any related language. He thought it was probably a Vhilatautan dialect, but he'd experienced those only as written languages, never spoken, and this was much changed from the millennia-old tongues he'd studied.

For the first time he found himself more annoyed than intrigued by an encounter with a speech unknown to him. What were they talking about, those two? Why was she laughing? And what was that peculiar, perhaps disdainful look the fellow was giving him?

After what seemed like far too much of that, the man finally offered Stephen his hand.

"I am Pernho," he said. "I help you and Zemlé. Can count on me. Ah, you going where?"

Stephen stole a glance at Pale—Zemlé? In their haste to escape it was a question they had never touched upon. He tried to keep his face neutral, but clearly he wasn't good at that sort of thing because she caught his suspicion immediately.

"I already know it's north," she said. "Everyone knows that. But now you have to choose: northeast, northwest, or whatever." She nodded toward Pernho. "If you trust me, you have to trust him."

"Yes, that's the problem, isn't it?" Stephen said.

Sister Pale shrugged and lifted her hands as a sign of surrender.

Stephen rolled his eyes.

"Clearly I have no choice," he continued. With Ehan and Henne, he might have found his way across this tumult of mountains, but without them it seemed impossible.

"I love a confident man," Sister Pale said wryly. "So where are we off to?"

"A mountain," Stephen said. "I don't know what it's called now. *'Velnoiragana'* was its name two thousand years ago. I think now it might be known as *'eslief vendve,'* or *'Slivendy.'* "

"Xal Slevendy," Pernho mused. "But we also call it *Ranhan,* 'The Horn.' That's not so far, as the eagle goes. But way is—" He frowned and made a twisting motion with his hands. *"Nhredhe.* No horses. You'll need kalboks."

"Kalboks?" Stephen asked.

"You asked about the smell," Sister Pale said. "You're about to find out what makes it."

Kalbok: As unlikely as any creature in a child's bestiary, the kalbok seems kindred to the sheep or goat, having the same lens-shaped horizontal pupils, back-curving horns, and general woolly appearance. It stands, however, at the shoulder the size of a small horse and is muscled like one, creating an oddly massive appearance that is, however, balanced on legs that seem by comparison rather flimsy.

The inhabitants of the Bairghs favor them over horses

for mountain routes, owing to their native nimbleness on rocks and steep trails. They will take a saddle or pack, although with a reluctance and lack of grace even a mule would find excessive. And it has one other inescapable, distinguishing trait.

Kalbok: A walking stench.

"I've never heard of people riding goats," Stephen muttered.

"I imagine there are many things you've never heard of," Pale suggested.

"I'm going to vomit again," Stephen said.

"They don't smell *that* bad," Sister Pale replied.

"I've no idea what you *would* consider foul-smelling, but I never want to meet it," Stephen said, fighting down his urge. "Doesn't your friend ever wash these things? Or at least comb the maggots out of their fur?"

"Wash a kalbok? What a strange idea," Sister Pale mused. "I can hardly wait for the next thing you'll think of to improve life for us simple mountain folk."

"Now that you mention it, I have some ideas for improving your roads," Stephen said.

In fact, his nausea was only by about half due to the scent of kalbok; the rest came from its gait across what even Aspar White couldn't possibly refer to as a road. Even calling it a trail was akin to confusing a mud hut with a palace. Their route dipped and turned along the lips of gorges and up promontories that seemed to be held in place only by the roots of straggling, half-dead junipers. Even the dogs took extra care in placing each step.

"Well," Sister Pale said, "be sure and submit your suggestions to Praifec Hespero when we see him again. As a sacritor, he has some sway in these matters."

"I will," Stephen said. "I'll distract him with a detailed proposition while his men are spiking us to trees." A sudden worry occurred. "Your friend. If Hespero is following us—"

"Pernho won't be there when they arrive. Don't worry about him."

"Good." He closed his eyes and instantly regretted it because it only made him dizzier. With a sigh, he opened them again.

"He called you something," he said then. "Zemlé."

"Zemlé, yes. It's my birth name."

"What does it mean?"

"It's our name for Saint Cer," she explained.

"And the tongue you were speaking?"

"Xalma, we call it."

"I should like to learn it."

"Why? It isn't widely spoken. If you want to get along in the mountains, better that you learn Meel."

"I can learn both," Stephen said, "if you'll teach me. It should help us pass the time."

"Very well. Which first?"

"Your language. Xalma."

"So. Then I know just how to start the lesson." She touched her hand to her breastbone. *"Nhen,"* she said. Then she pointed to him. *"Wir. Ash esme nhen, Ju esh wir. Pernho est wir. Ju be Pernho este abe wiré . . ."*

The lesson continued for the rest of the day as the kalboks climbed steadily higher, first through rocky pasture and then, as they crossed the snow line, into a dark evergreen forest.

Before evening the forest had given way to a desolate, ice-crusted heath where nothing grew at all, and Sister Pale's words came muffled through her scarf.

Stephen's paida and weather cloak were back in Demsted, and he was thankful for the ankle-length quilted robe and heavy felt jerkin Pernho had provided him. The cone-shaped hat he was less certain about—he felt he looked silly in it—but at least it kept his ears warm.

Clouds sat on them for most of the journey, but as the sun was setting, the air cleared, and Stephen peered awestruck at the giants of ice and snow marching off toward every horizon. He felt tiny and titan all at once and intensely grateful to be alive.

"What's wrong?" Pale asked, studying his face.

Stephen didn't understand the question until he realized that he was weeping.

"I suppose you're used to this," he said.

"Ah," she replied. "Used to it, yes. But it never loses its beauty."

"I don't see how it could."

"Look there," she said, pointing back. After a moment he thought he saw movement, like a line of black ants against the white.

"Horses?" he asked.

"Hespero. With some sixty riders, I should say."

"Will he catch us?"

"Not soon. He'll have to stop for nightfall, just like us. And he'll be much slower using horses." She clapped him on the back. "Speaking of which, we'd better make camp. It's going to get very, very cold tonight. Fortunately, I know a place."

The place she meant turned out to be a cave, snug, dry, and very small once the two of them, her dogs, and the kalboks were inside. Pale conjured up a small fire and used it to warm some salted meat Pernho had given them, and they had that with a beverage she called barleywine that tasted something like beer. It was pretty strong stuff, and it didn't take much before Stephen felt light-headed.

He found himself studying the woman's features, and to his embarrassment, she caught him at it.

"I, ah, should have told you before," Stephen said, "but I think you're beautiful."

Her expression didn't change. "Do you?"

"Yes."

"I'm the only woman for fifty leagues, and we're sleeping unchaperoned in a cave. Imagine how flattered I am when you shower me with compliments."

"I . . . no. You don't—" He stopped and rubbed his forehead. "Look, you must think I know something about women. I don't."

"You don't say."

Stephen frowned, opened his mouth, closed it. This was going nowhere. He wasn't even sure why he'd started it.

"How much farther do we have to go?" he asked instead.

"Two days, maybe three, depending on how much snow we find in the next pass. That's just to the mountain. Do you know where to go once we get there?"

He shook his head. "I'm not certain. Kauron went to a place called Hadivaisel. It might be a town."

"There's no town at Xal Slevendy," she said. "At least—" She broke off. " 'Adiwara' is a word for Sefry. The old people say there's a Sefry rewn there."

"That must be it, then," Stephen said.

"You have some idea how to find it?"

"None at all. Kauron said something about talking to an old Hadivar, but that supposes he'd already found the rewn, I guess. And that was a long time ago."

"You'll find it," she said firmly. "You're meant to."

"But if Hespero finds us first . . ."

"That will be a problem," she acknowledged. "So you'll have to find it quickly."

"Right," he said without a lot of hope.

He was starting to appreciate just how *big* mountains could be. And he remembered the exit from the rewn in the King's Forest. Four yards away, it had been invisible. It was going to be like searching for a raindrop in a river.

He pulled out the pages he'd copied, hoping to find a better translation. Pale watched him without comment.

Among the pages was the loose sheet he'd found; he'd nearly forgotten it. It was very old, the characters on it faded, but he recognized the same odd mixture of letters on the epistle he'd carried and understood with growing excitement that what he held was actually a key for translating it.

Of course, Hespero now had the epistle, but he ought to be able to recall—

Something suddenly shivered through him.

"What?" Pale said.

"There was something in the chapel," he said. "I haven't

really had time to think about it. But I swear I heard a voice. And my lamp; there was a face in it."

"In the lamp?"

"In the flame," he said.

She looked unsurprised. "Ghosts get lost in the mountains," she said. "The winds fetch them up into the high valleys, and they can't get out."

"If this was a ghost, it was an old one. It spoke a language a thousand years dead."

She hesitated then. "No one knows what happened to Kauron," she said. "Some say he never returned, that he vanished into the mountains. But some say he appeared in the chapel late one night, babbling like a man with fever, though his skin was cool. The priest who found him put him to bed, and the next morning there was no sign of him. The bed showed no trace of being slept in, and the priest was left wondering if he'd really seen him or merely had a vision or a dream."

"Have *you* ever felt anything there?"

"No," she admitted. "I've never heard anyone else report anything unusual, either. But you're different: a Revesturi and Kauron's heir. Maybe that's why he spoke to you."

"I don't know. Whoever—whatever—it was, it didn't seem nice or even helpful. I felt as if it was mocking me."

"Well, I've no idea, then," she said. "Maybe Kauron had enemies and you've attracted them, too. In the mountains, the past and the present aren't distant cousins. They're brother and sister."

Stephen nodded and refolded his notes.

"Well," he said, "I think I'll try and get some sleep."

"About that." She sighed. "I may have to give you one more chance, you know."

"What do you mean?"

"Because, as I said, it's going to get awfully cold tonight."

He opened his mouth to say something, but she closed it with a kiss that smelled pleasantly of barleywine. He kept his eyes open, wondering at how different a face looked from that close.

She nibbled around to his ear and down the side of his throat.

"I *really* don't know much about women," he apologized.

"So you said. Then it's time you had a lesson, I think. I can't give you the ultimate lesson; this time of month you might get me with child, and we don't want that. But there's no point in skipping to the back of the book, is there? I think some of the early chapters can be pretty entertaining."

Stephen didn't reply; anything he said was potentially the *wrong* thing.

Besides, he'd pretty much lost interest in talking.

CHAPTER THREE

A NEW VIEW OF HISTORY

IGNORING SIR LEAFTON'S protests, Anne hurried to the far end of the square, where the Craftsmen had been quickly building a redoubt, piling crates, planks, bricks, and stone between two buildings that together commanded most of the breadth between the two walls.

In the few bells they'd had, they'd done a creditable job, but it wasn't good enough. As Anne watched, a wave of armored men eight deep crashed into it, about half of them wielding pikes to keep the Craftsmen back as men with sword and shield pushed forward. Already they were spilling over the top. That quickly, Anne saw her plans crumbling.

It would be only seconds before their line was breached.

"Saints," Austra shrieked, echoing Anne's sentiments as one of her men fell, a spear driven through his mouth lapping out the back of his head like a monster's tongue.

"Archers!" Leafton bellowed, and suddenly a black hail

fell from the roofs and upper windows of the buildings. The charge faltered as shields raised to ward off fletchéd death, and the Craftsmen's line closed solid and surged back to the wall.

Anne experienced a brief flash of hope, but they were still terribly outnumbered. Should she go now, while she had the chance? Take Austra and Cazio into the tunnels? At least she would avoid capture, and Artwair's hands wouldn't be tied by threats to her life.

But the thought of leaving her men to die was intolerable.

The attackers re-formed their ranks and battered at the wall again. Many fell, but they kept pushing.

"Majesty," Leafton said, "I beg you. Move away from here. They will break through at any moment."

Anne shook his arm off and closed her eyes, feeling the ringing of steel and hoarse cries of pain vibrate through her, reaching through it and beneath her for the power she needed to boil blood and marrow. If she could summon the same sort of power she had had at Khrwbh Khrwkh, she might be able to turn the tide or at least give her men respite.

But at Khrwbh Khrwkh there had been something potent in the earth, a pocket of sickness she had been able to draw to the surface, like pus in a boil. Here she sensed something similar, but it was more distant and more subtle, and lurking behind it she could feel the demon, waiting for her to open the way. Thus, a part of her faltered.

But a sudden new tenor entered the sounds of fray, and she opened her eyes to see what had happened.

Her heart fell when she saw that the attackers had been re-inforced and were now nearly double their number, or so she · thought at first.

Then she realized that wasn't the case at all; the newcomers weren't armored, at least not most of them. They wore guild clothing and jessy, woolen plaid and workman's flenne. They carried clubs and pitchforks, fishing spears, hunting bows, knives, and even a few swords, and they were cutting into her attackers from the rear.

The Craftsmen all sang out at once and went slashing over

the wall. Blood ran like rainwater down the streets of Gobelin Court.

"The people of Eslen," Austra breathed.

Anne nodded. "I sent four men to spread the word. I thought I would test the theory that I have their support." She turned to her friend and smiled. "It appears that I do, at least some of them."

"And why shouldn't you?" Austra excitedly replied. "You're their queen!"

At sundown Anne stood at the window of Saint Ceasel's Tower on the Fastness. It was a beautiful afternoon; the sun's great belly was impaled on the distant towers of Thornrath, making a red mirror of the Ensae, which she could just make out between the great paps of Tom Woth and Tom Cast. She could see the Sleeve, already velvety with shadow, and far below that the vine-covered dwellings of the dead in Eslen-of-Shadows and farther out on the misty rinns. The wind was from the sea, and it smelled strong and good.

This was her home; these were the sights and smells of her childhood. And yet it was strange now. Until a year ago this frame she looked upon—Thornrath, the rinns—contained most of the world she knew. Oh, she'd been east as far as Loiyes, but she knew now that that was a small distance. Today, in her mind's far gaze she could see *beyond* the rinns to the hills and forest, across the strands and plains of Hornladh and Tero Gallé, to the South Lierish Sea, to the white hills and red roofs of Vitellio.

Every sight, every sound, every league traveled had made her something different, and home no longer fit the way it once had.

She turned her attention to the north, to the city. There was the palace, of course, the only thing that really stood above her now, and below was her little kingdom of Gobelin Court. Volunteers continued to arrive, and Leafton and the other Craftsmen were working quickly to make them useful. The redoubt was infinitely more secure than it had been during the first attack, and all the natural walls were now well manned.

Robert's men hadn't been idle, of course. She could see them all around, a few streets away from her perimeter, building their own camps, trying to cut off aid from the outside. She'd even seen a few small siege engines rumbling down the hill, but most of the streets approaching the quarter weren't wide enough for them.

"Do you think they'll attack again tonight?" she asked Leafton.

"I doubt it. Nor, I think, will they fight in the morning. A siege is what I imagine. He'll try and keep us contained here until we're out of supplies."

"Good," Anne said.

"Your pardon, Majesty."

"I have something to do tonight," she told him. "In the Sefry house. I will be unavailable all night, possibly into tomorrow. I am *not* to be disturbed, and I leave the defense of this place entirely to you."

"Of course, you must have your rest," Leafton said. "But in case of an emergency—"

"I won't be available," she asserted. "I'll take four men of your choosing to guard me, but other than that, do not send anyone into the house after me. Do you understand?"

"I don't understand, Majesty, no."

"What I meant was, 'Will you obey?'" Anne clarified.

"Of course, Majesty."

"Very good. Austra, Cazio—it's time we were going." She laid her hand on Leafton's arm. "You're a capable man," she said. "I trust you. Keep my men safe. Please."

"Yes, Majesty."

Anne wasn't sure what she'd thought the entrance to the Crepling passage would look like, but she'd imagined it would be hidden, an invisible wall panel of some sort, a rotating bookcase, a hatch beneath a rug.

It was, at least, located in the cold cellar of the building, behind racks of wine and hanging meats. But the entrance itself was just a little door set into the living rock into which the Sefry house was built. It was made of some sort of dark metal, with hinges and hasps of polished brass. Mother Uun produced a rather large key. She turned it in the lock, and the door opened almost noiselessly, revealing a descending stairway.

Anne allowed herself a wisp of a smile. Artwair and others in her command had assured her that the city and castle of Eslen were nearly impregnable, that its poellands and massive walls could frustrate nearly any army. Yet the city had fallen more than once. She tried to remember the stratagems by which her forefathers had won Eslen and dimly recalled the lesson as one to which she had paid a bit of attention.

Looking back on it, it seemed rather vague, the tale of that siege. There was lots of talk about bravery and bloody determination but not much detail about how William I had actually ended up in the Hall of Doves, with his sword driven into Thiuzwald Fram Reiksbaurg's liver.

How many times had it happened like this? A small group of women or Sefry invading the fortress through this passageway to work some sort of mischief, to open the lower gates that a larger force might enter? Mother Uun, it seemed to her, was the keeper of far too much power. The fate of a dynasty could hinge on her Sefry whims.

But any man who sought her aid wouldn't recall exactly what had happened, wouldn't know how he'd gotten into the castle, wouldn't remember how much power this lone Sefry wielded.

But Anne would remember. She *would* remember, and she would do something about it. When she was queen, there would be no walking into the castle unopposed.

With a sudden shock, Anne realized how intently Mother Uun was watching her. Could the Sefry read her thoughts?

"Well?" she asked.

"At the base of the stairs you will find the passage," the Sefry explained. "Take the right-hand way, and it will take you outside the city, to the rinns. Take the left-hand way, and you will find your way into the dungeons, and from there into the castle, if you so wish. If the lower way is filled with water, you will find the valves that drain them in a small chamber to the left, just before the point where the water reaches the ceiling. They will take time to open up, of course, on the order of half a day."

Anne nodded. If her vision was accurate, Sir Fail's fleet would arrive in two days. If Thornrath was in Artwair's hands by then, her uncle could confront the fleet and keep the outside gates open long enough for her to exit, then lead in a larger force.

She'd considered trying to take the palace with the men she had with her but didn't think there would be enough of them. There were hundreds of guards in the castle. The thirty men she had left wouldn't be enough to do more than tip her hand.

Either way, it was probably going to be difficult getting men to follow her through a gate they couldn't remember even while they were looking at it. But it could be done. Cazio had managed to follow her would-be assassin, after all. And her brother, Uncle Fail, and the Craftsmen had managed somehow to leave Eslen, led by Alis Berrye, if the rumors were true.

Yes, it could be done, and she had to take the first step: making certain the way was open.

"Take Cazio's hand, Austra," Anne said. "The rest of you, link hands as well. Keep them held until I tell you to let go. Do you understand?"

"Yes, Majesty."

"Very well. And now we go."

"Go where?" Cazio asked.

Cazio wondered if he'd gotten drunk without knowing it. He was aware of Austra's hand, of the stone beneath his feet, of Anne's face in lamplight, but he kept getting lost in the details.

He couldn't actually remember what he was doing or where they were. It was like walking through a terrible sort of dream. He kept thinking he was waking, only to discover that he'd only dreamed he was doing so.

He remembered going into the Sefry house and Anne talking about something or other with the old woman. He recalled that they'd gone down to the cold cellar, which seemed peculiar.

But that felt like a long time ago.

Maybe it *was* a dream, he decided. Or maybe he was drunk.

Maybe— He blinked. Anne was talking to someone again. Now she was shouting.

And now he was running. But why? He slowed to look around, but Austra tugged hard on his hand and screamed for him to keep going.

He heard unfamiliar laughter somewhere.

He tasted blood on his lips, which seemed especially odd.

CHAPTER FOUR

DEATH SONGS

NEIL FELT the death calm settle about him. His breathing evened, and he savored the salt air as he watched a sea eagle banking in a sky equally blue and gray. The wind gentled from the southwest, ruffling the soft new grass of the hillside like a million fingers combing verdant hair. All seemed still.

Closing his eyes, he murmured a snatch of song.

Mi, Etier meuf, eyoiz'etiern rem,
Crach-toi, frennz, mi viveut-toi dein . . .

"What's that, Sir Neil?"

He opened his eyes. The question had come from a man just about his age, a knight named Edhmon Archard, from the Greffy of Seaxeld. He had quick blue eyes, pink cheeks, and hair as white as thistledown. His armor was good plain stuff, and Neil couldn't see a dent on it.

Of course, his own armor was just as new. He'd found it in his tent the morning after Robert escaped, sent as a present by Elyoner Dare, who'd had his measurements taken "for clothes," or so she had claimed. Still, Neil had the impression that in Sir Edhmon's case, the man in the armor was as untested as the steel itself.

"It's a bit of a song," Neil explained. "A song my father taught me."

"What's it mean?"

Neil smiled.

" 'Me, my father, my fathers before. Croak, you ravens, I'll feed you soon.' "

"Not very cheery," Edhmon said.

"It's a death song," Neil said.

"You believe you're going to die?"

"Oh, I'm going to die; that one thing is certain," Neil said. "It's the when, where, and how I'm not so clear on. But my fah always said it was best to go into battle thinking of yourself as already dead."

"You can do that?"

Neil shrugged. "Not always. Sometimes I'm afraid, and sometimes the rage comes on me. But now and then the saints allow me the death calm, and I like that best."

Edhmon flushed a little. "This is my first battle," he admitted. "I hope I'm ready for it."

"You're ready for it," Neil said.

"I'm just so tired of waiting."

Even as he said that, he flinched as one of the ballistae behind them released with a booming twang, and a fifty-pound stone flung in a flat arc over their heads, smiting the outer bailey of Thornrath and sending a shatter of granite in every direction.

"You won't be waiting much longer," Neil assured him. "That wall's coming down within a bell. They're mustering their horse behind the waerd already."

"Why? Why not take them up into the wall? Why risk them against us?"

Neil considered his reply for a few minutes, hoping to find an answer that wouldn't frighten Edhmon too much.

"Thornrath has never been taken," he said at last. "From the sea, it's probably impossible. It's too thick, too tall, and ships are completely vulnerable to bombardment from above. Likewise, the cliffs of the cape aren't easily scaled from the seaside. A few defenders can keep any number of men from climbing up there, especially if the attackers are trying to bring up horses and siege engines. And without engines, they face the waerd, which can't be taken without them."

He pointed south down the spit of land that separated them from the wall, a ridge just ten kingsyards wide that plunged in cliffs to Foambreaker Bay on the right and the Ensae on the left. It went that way for forty kingsyards and then widened enough for the waerd, a wedge-shaped fortress with its sharp end pointed at them and gates hidden around behind it. It had three towers and stood separated from the great wall behind it by about ten yards.

"We can't just ride around the waerd, or they'd pelt us right off the cliffs with whatever they've got: stones, boiling oil, molten lead, all of that sort of thing. We'd never make it around to even give the gate a go. So we have to break the waerd from this side, and preferably from a distance. Out here we have a never-ending supply of missiles, though we don't have a flat wall to hit. More often than not, our stones just skip right off."

"I can see all of that," Sir Edhmon said. "But I still don't see what that's got to do with the cavalry."

"Well, when the wall comes down, we still have to cross this causeway and get through the breach before we can capture the castle. And we can only go a few at a time, about six or seven abreast. Then the horse will come to meet us before the ridge widens there.

"Meanwhile, they've been saving their missiles for when we come into their shorter range, about ten paces down the causeway. While their cavalry hold us, they'll keep launching rocks or whatnot into those of us who are queued up behind. And if they do it right, four or five of us will die for every one of them. Maybe more. If the knights stayed in the waerd, they wouldn't be much more use than any footman. Riding against us, they can do real damage.

"We'll lose some men to the engines while we're rushing the breach, but we'll get in, move our own artillery up, and start battering the gates of Thornrath itself. Before that happens, though, they might kill enough of us to make us think twice about the whole endeavor. At worst they will have cut our numbers greatly." He slapped the young knight on the shoulder. "Besides, they're knights. Knights *ride* into battle. How do you think they'd feel on the wall, throwing rocks at us?"

"But there must be an easier way in," Edhmon said.

"This *is* the easy way in," Neil said. "To get to this approach, an army invading Crotheny would have to either land fifty leagues north of here and fight their way past the sea fortresses or cross the border with Hansa and make their way through Newland, which as you've seen can be flooded. According to Duke Artwair, this is the first time Thornrath has had to be defended from land. The southern approach, I'm told, makes this look easy."

"But you make it sound so hopeless," Edhmon said. "We might as well be riding off a cliff, and those of us in front will surely die."

"Only if things go the way *they* want," Neil said, nodding at the waerd.

"How else can things go?"

"Our way. Our first charge hits them so hard, we cut right through their horse and plunge into the breach. If they don't hold us, they can't bombard us, at least not for long."

"But that would take a miracle, wouldn't it?"

Neil shook his head. "When I first saw Thornrath, I thought it must be the work of giants or demons. But it was built by men, men like us. It didn't take a miracle to build it; it won't take one to capture it. But it will take *men*. Do you understand?"

"That's it, Sir Neil. You tell 'im how it is!" Neil was startled by the shout and found that it was Sir Fell Hemmington who had spoken. "You hear that, lads? One charge or nothing!"

Suddenly, to Neil's utter surprise, the whole column took up that refrain.

"One charge or nothing!"

He'd been talking to Edhmon without realizing that anyone else had been listening. But he *was* the leader, wasn't he? He probably was supposed to have given some sort of speech, anyway.

The shouting doubled in fury as another stone struck the waerd and with a low rumble the wall finally collapsed, leaving a gap some five kingsyards in width. At the same moment, the enemy cavalry began to appear around either side of the fortification.

"Lances!" Neil shouted, couching his own long spear. All along the front rank, the others dropped level on both sides of him.

"One charge!" he shouted, spurring his mount, still feeling calm as the horse broke into a dead run.

The sea, as always, was beautiful.

CHAPTER FIVE

WITCHHORN

"WHAT'S THAT LOOK?" Zemlé asked from the back of her kalbok, a few kingsyards away. "It's not guilt starting to gnaw you, is it?"

Stephen glanced at her. In the buttery light of the morning sun her face was fresh and very young, and for an instant

Stephen imagined her as a little girl wandering the highland meadows, fussing at goats and combing through clover in search of a lucky one.

"Should I be?" Stephen asked. "Even if you consider what we did to be, ah—"

Her arched brows stopped him in the middle of his sophistry.

He scratched his chin and began again. "I never took a vow of chastity," he said, "and I'm not a follower of Saint Elspeth."

"But you were planning on being a Decmanian," she reminded him. "You *would* have taken the vow."

"Can I tell you a secret?" Stephen asked.

She smiled. "It wouldn't be the first one."

He felt his face go warm.

"Come on," she prompted.

"It was never my idea to enter the priesthood. It was my father who wanted that. Now, don't get me wrong; you know my interests. I could never have followed them without some attachment to z'Irbina, so I was willing. But I wasn't much looking forward to that vow of chastity. I suppose I comforted myself with the thought that I was likely to remain mostly chaste whether I took the vow or not."

"That's silly," she said. "You're not what I would call ugly. A little inept, perhaps . . ."

"Oh," Stephen said. "Sorry about that."

"But perfectly trainable," she finished. "A *tafleis anscrift-eis.*"

Now his ears were burning.

"Anyway," he went on, "I suppose I had vaguely hoped I might somehow move on to one of the less . . . *stringent* orders. And as things are, there's not much chance of me taking the Decmanian vows now. Or even of living much longer, really. We should have gotten up earlier."

"This pass is too dangerous without daylight," she replied. "We started as soon as made sense. As for the other, I'm sure you feel you could die happy right now. But I promise you, there's still plenty to live for."

"I don't doubt that," Stephen replied. "But Hespero is still back there, and then there's the woorm. Of course, we haven't seen it lately. Maybe it's given up the chase."

"I doubt that," Zemlé said.

"Why?"

"I told you—because the prophecy says it's the waurm will drive you to the Alq," she replied.

"But what if I'm not the one spoken of in the prophecy? Aren't we making a rather large assumption?"

"It followed you to d'Ef, and from d'Ef at least as far as the Then River. Why would you begin to doubt now that it's following you?"

"But why *would* it follow me?"

"Because you're the one who will find the Alq," she said, her voice hinting at exasperation.

"That's a *'catel turistat suus caudam'* argument," he objected.

"Yes," she agreed. "It goes round and round. Doesn't mean it's not true."

"Well, is it supposed to kill m—Kauron's heir?"

"I've already told you what I know," she said.

Stephen remembered the monster's glance as it found him from half a league away and shivered.

"Is it that bad?" she asked.

"I hope you don't ever have to find out, no matter what the prophecy says," Stephen replied.

"I'm kind of curious, actually. But set all that aside; you *did* have a look on your face. If it wasn't guilt, then what was it?"

"Oh. That."

Her eyes narrowed. "What do you mean, 'that'? Don't you dare tell me you don't want to talk about it."

"I—" He sighed. "I was wondering what would happen if we simply forgot this whole prophecy business and just went off into the mountains someplace. Maybe Hespero and the woorm would kill each other and everyone would forget the Alq."

Her brows leapt up. "Go off together? You and me? You mean, like husband and wife?"

"Ah, well, I suppose I did mean that, yes."

"That's all well and good, but I hardly know you, Stephen."

"But we—"

"Yes, didn't we? And I enjoyed it. I like you, but what have either of us to offer the other? I've no dowry. Do you think your family would take to me under those conditions?"

Stephen didn't have to think about that for long.

"No," he admitted.

"And without your family, what do you have to offer me? Love?"

"Maybe," he said cautiously.

"Maybe. That's exactly right. Maybe.

"You wouldn't be the first to confuse sex with love, Stephen. It's a silly confusion, too. Anyway, a day ago you were desperately in love with someone else. Can a few well-placed kisses change that so easily? If so, how can I trust in any constancy from you?"

"Now you're making fun of me," Stephen said.

"Yes, I am, and no, I'm not. Because if I didn't laugh at you, I might get angry, and neither of us needs that right now. If you want to run off into the mountains, you'll have to do it alone. I'll go on to the Witchhorn and try to find the Alq myself. Because even if the praifec and the waurm do destroy each other, there are others looking, and someone will find it eventually."

"How do you know all this?" Stephen asked.

"The *Book of Return*—"

"But you've never *seen* the book," Stephen snapped, cutting her off. "Everything you know is based on a thousand-year-old *rumor* about a book no one has seen except Hespero, if even that is true. So how do you know *any* of this is true?"

She started to answer, but he cut her off again.

"Have you ever read the *Lay of Walker*?"

"I've heard of it," she said. "It's about the Virgenyan warrior who fought off the demon fleet of Thiuzan Hraiw, isn't it?"

"Yes. But here's the thing: Historically, Walker lived a century or so before the start of the Warlock Wars, a hundred and fifty years before Thiuzan Hraiw even began to build his fleet.

"Chetter Walker fought off a fleet, all right, if you call ten ships a fleet. And they were from Ihnsgan, an ancient Iron Sea kingdom. But the epic, you see, was written down five hundred years later, *after* the chaos of the Warlock Wars, when Virgenya's new enemy was Hansa.

"Thiuzan Hraiw was from Hansa, and his name has a very typically Hanzish sound to it. So the bards—*sworn* as they are to keep the songs *exactly* the way they heard them on pain of being cursed by Saint Rosemary—nevertheless have Walker living in the wrong century, fighting the wrong enemy, with weapons that hadn't been invented yet. Oral tradition always promises it's kept history straight, and it *never does.* So what makes you think your ancestors kept their little saga faithfully?"

"Because," she replied stubbornly, "I *have* seen the actual book, or at least part of it, the part about *you.*"

That brought him up short. "Have you? And how did you manage that?"

She closed her eyes, and he saw her jaw tighten.

"I was Hespero's lover," she said.

That afternoon Zemlé pointed out the top of the Witchhorn. Stephen supposed he'd been envisioning something shaped like an ox horn, curving up into the sky, surrounded by storm clouds, lightning, and the distant black shapes of evil spirits whirling about its peak.

Instead, aside from being perhaps a bit taller than its neighbors, it was—to him, at least—indistinguishable from any other mountain in the Bairghs.

"We'll reach the base of it by tomorrow noon," she said.

He nodded but didn't answer.

"You haven't spoken since this morning," she said. "I'm beginning to feel annoyed. Surely you understood that you weren't my first lover."

"But *Hespero*?" he burst out. "Oh, I think you might have mentioned *that* before I followed you up here, before I put all my trust in you."

"Well, the point was rather to have you trust me," she pointed out.

"Right. And I did. Until now, anyway, when I have no choice."

"I'm not *proud* of it, Stephen, but the saints hate a liar. You asked, and I told you. It's more important that you believe the prophecy than think well of me."

"How old were you when this happened? Ten?"

"No," she said patiently. "I was twenty-five."

"You said he left your village years ago," Stephen snapped. "You can't be much older than twenty-five now."

"Flatterer. I'm exactly twenty-five, as of last week."

"You mean—"

"Since he returned, yes," she said.

"Saints, that's even worse!"

She glared at him from her kalbok across about three kingsyards of broken ground.

"If I were close enough," she said, "I would slap you. I did what I had to. I'm not a fool, you know. I had the same doubts about the prophecy as you. Now I don't."

"Did you enjoy it?" he asked.

"He was a good deal more experienced than *you*," she shot back.

"Ah. No *tafleis anscrifteis* there, eh?" he responded sarcastically.

Her face contorted, and she began a retort but then closed her eyes and took a few deep breaths. When she opened her eyes, she was more composed.

"This is my fault," she said at last, evenly. "I knew you were young and lacking experience. I should have known it would do this to you."

"Do what?"

"Make you stupid with jealousy. You're jealous of a man I slept with before I ever met you. Does that make any sense to you at all?"

"Well, it's just that—"

"Yes?" she asked patiently enough to make him feel once more that he was a little boy.

"—he's evil," he finished weakly.

"Is he?" she asked. "I don't know. Certainly he's our enemy in that he wants the same thing we do. But I haven't betrayed you to him; indeed, I betrayed him to you. So stop being such a boy and try to be a man for once. You don't need experience for that, just courage."

That night saw no reprise of the night before. Stephen lay awake for long bells, excruciatingly aware of Zemlé's every breath and movement. His mind moved downward toward sleep in fits, but a strong breath or turn of her body would snap him back.

She's awake. She's forgiven me . . .

But he wasn't sure he needed forgiveness. She'd slept with a *praifec*. Surely that was a sin even if Hespero was a Skaslos reincarnated. And just before—

He sighed. That wasn't the real problem, was it?

Hespero's touch was the shadow under his own. The touch of a man who knew how to please a woman.

He cycled through ever smaller orbits of remorse and anger until the stone floor parted like tissue and something pulled him through.

Suddenly he was sticky and wet, and his flesh and bone ached as from a high fever. Panic sent him grasping for something, anything, but he was in a void—not falling but floating, surrounded on all sides by terrors he could not see.

He tried to scream, but something clotted in his mouth.

He was on the verge of madness when a soothing voice murmured to him in words he didn't understand but which reassured him nevertheless. Then, gently, a band of color drew across his eyes, and his heart calmed.

His vision cleared, and he saw the Witchhorn, much as it

had looked in the light of sunset, albeit with more snow. He floated down toward it like a bird, over a valley, over a village, and then, with a touch of vertigo, up its slopes, along a winding trail, to a house in a tree. A face appeared, pale, copper-eyed, a Hadivar face, and he knew now that Zemlé was right, it just meant Sefry.

More words came, and still he couldn't understand them, but then he landed. He walked to the north side of the mountain, where moss ruled, to a stone face and through a clever door, and then he was in the rewn.

Beginning to understand. Joy filling his heart.

He woke to a gentle pat on his face and found Zemlé there, her eyebrows drawn in concern, her face—her lips—only a motion away.

But when she saw that he was awake, she straightened, and the look of apprehension vanished.

"Bad dreams?" she asked.

"Not exactly," he replied, and related his vision.

Zemlé didn't seem surprised.

"We'll eat," she said. "Then we'll go and hope we find this mythical town of yours."

He smiled and rubbed the sleep grit from his eyes, feeling much more rested than he ought to.

Choron, he wondered to the heavens, *have you become a saint? Is it you guiding me?*

The descent was considerably more trouble than it had been in his dream, and his confidence in the vision faded as they made their way down the broken slopes into a deep, resin-scented evergreen forest.

"Do you know where you're going?" Zemlé asked doubtfully.

For an instant he didn't understand her question, but then he understood that their roles had changed. Since entering the valley, she had been looking to him as the guide.

"I think so," he replied.

"Because there is a quicker way to the mountain."

He nodded. "Perhaps, but I want to see something."

A bell later, the signs began to appear. They were subtle at first: odd mounds in the forest floor, depressions that resembled dry streambeds but were too regular. Eventually he made out bits of wall, though rarely higher than the knee. He continued on foot, leading his mount, and between footfalls he had flashes of narrow, fanciful buildings and figures in bright clothing.

"Hadivaisel," he said, motioning all around him. "Or what's left of it."

"That's good, then?" she asked.

"Well, at least it means I *do* know where I'm going."

And so they pressed on, east toward the mountain, to the traces of the trail there. The tree house of his vision was gone, but he recognized the tree, though it was older and thicker. From there he began to lead them north and steadily higher, to Bezlaw, where the mountain's shadow never lifted and the moss grew thick and deep white forest pipes stood from rotting logs.

It was already nearing dusk when they reached the ancient shade line, and Zemlé suggested a halt. Stephen agreed, and they set about situating the animals.

The hounds wouldn't be situated, though; the hair bristled on the backs of their necks, and they growled constantly at the congealing darkness. Stephen's own hackles were up. His hearing had improved over the last few days, and he heard at least some of what the beasts heard.

And he didn't like it.

There were things coming on two feet, certain in the darkness.

And some were singing.

CHAPTER SIX

✤

THE SPOOR OF DEATH

DEATH TOLD Aspar where to go. Dead trees in the forest, dead grass and gorse and heather on the heath, dead fish in the rivers and streams it preferred.

Following death, he followed the woorm, and with each day its trail grew plainer, as if its poisonous nature was waxing as it went.

The Welph River was clogged with carcasses, its backwaters become abattoirs. Spring buds drooled noisome pus, and the only things growing with a semblance of health were the fresh heads of all-too-familiar black thorns.

Strangely, Aspar felt stronger every day. If the poison of the woorm was multiplying in power, so was the efficacy of the witch's cure. Ogre, too, seemed more filled with energy than he had been in years, as if he were a colt again. And each setting sun brought them closer to the beast—and Fend.

Beyond the Welph, Aspar no longer knew the names of places, and the mountains rose about him. The woorm preferred valleys, but on occasion it crossed low passes. Once it followed a stream beneath a mountain, and Aspar spent a day in the dark tracking it by torchlight. The second time it did that, he didn't follow it far, because the tunnel filled with water. Instead, cursing, he reentered the light and worked his way up the mountainside until he found a ridge that gave him a good view of the next valley. He promised the Raver a sacrifice if the thing didn't escape.

Straining his eyes in the dusk, he finally saw its head cut-

ting waves in a river two leagues away and began finding his
way down.

After that it was simple, and he was riding so close on its
trail that he found animals and birds that were still dying.

Of course, another big mountain loomed at the end of the
dale, and that could present problems if the monster found a
way under it, too. He planned to catch it before the mountain, though.

He hadn't by the next morning, but he knew he was close.
He knew it by the smell. He checked the arrow then as he did
every morning, doused the remaining embers of his fire, and
returned to the chase.

The valley gained altitude, filling with spruce, hemlock,
and burrwood. He rode on the southern side of it, at the base
of a cliff of tired yellow rock that rose some twenty yards,
above which he could make out what looked to be a trail
winding through rocky, shrubby ground. He was watching
the long line of the rock face, considering that if he could
find a way up there, he might gain a higher vantage. He
didn't see much hope of that, though. He had a feel for the
way land lay, and it didn't look as if the cliff was going to
offer a slope any time soon.

Above the cliff more mountains rose, sometimes visible,
sometimes hidden by the angle.

He thought he heard something and stopped to listen. It
came again, clearer: a human voice shouting.

A moment later he located its source. There was a line of
perhaps sixty horsemen on the upper path; maybe they had
just joined it from a trail he couldn't see. The cliff was about
thirty kingsyards high here, and they were a bit upslope from
the precipice. The shouting man was pointing down toward
him.

"Good eyes," Aspar murmured sourly.

The sun was behind them, so he couldn't make out their
faces, but the leader looked to be in some sort of Churchish
garb, which put Aspar on guard immediately. He noted that
three of them had bows drawn and ready.

"Hail, down there," the leader shouted. Aspar was startled

at how familiar his voice was, though he couldn't place it right away.

"Hail, up on the ridge," he responded loudly.

"I'd heard you were dead, Aspar White," the man returned. "I really believe it's no longer possible to trust anyone."

"Hespero?"

"You will call him 'your grace,'" the knight at Hespero's side demanded.

"Now, Sir Elden," Hespero replied, "this is my holter. Didn't you know that?" Judging from the volume, he had said it entirely for Aspar's benefit.

Aspar thought about playing along but quickly discarded the idea. He'd been alone in the forest for enough days to have lost any taste for dissembling.

"Not anymore, your grace!" he shouted. "I've seen enough of your work."

"That's fair," Hespero replied. "I've heard enough of yours. Fare you well, then, holter."

Aspar turned his head and made as if to ride away but kept his eyes up. He saw Sir Elden draw his bow.

"Yah, that's all the excuse I need," he muttered under his breath.

He'd been wondering if he even required that, but Hespero had solved that problem for him with a word too low to hear. He leapt off Ogre as the first shaft missed him by more than a yard. As he found the ground, he calmly took aim and put one in the archer, right up through the bottom of his chin. He slipped another arrow to string and sent it after Hespero, but another mounted man surged into the path of the shot, catching it in his armored side.

The remaining ready archers scrambled off their mounts, and he noticed at least six more stringing their bows. He fired again, then whirled at a crash into the underbrush. He found himself looking down his shaft at the first man he'd shot, who had fallen from the cliff and lay broken on a boulder at its base.

Aspar stepped that way and ducked under an overhang just as arrows appeared to sprout from the earth like red-topped wheat. He caught the dead man and dragged him in, giving his body a quick search, taking his arrows and provisions, then finding a bit more than he had bargained for. Because in the man's haversack was a horn—and not only that, a horn Aspar recognized, made of white bone and incised with strange figures.

It was the horn he'd found in the Mountains of the Hare, the horn Stephen had blown to summon the Briar King.

The horn they had given to Hespero for study.

Aspar put the horn back in its bag, looped it around his neck, took a deep breath, and bolted.

Most of the barrage missed him; one missile struck his cuirass and glanced away, and then he was well in cover of the trees, back on Ogre, and off at a gallop.

As it became clear he had outdistanced anyone who might be following, he slowed his pace and had time to wonder what it meant that Hespero was here. Coincidences happened, but he was sure this wasn't one.

He thought about it as he rode, still at a reasonably brisk pace, checking behind him every thirty beats or so at first, less often later. Coming down a cliff was easier than going up one, especially if one had rope, and he was betting Hespero's party had rope. Lowering horses down the cliff would take time, if they were able to manage it at all, so he should be able to keep his distance from any pursuers if he stayed away from the crags.

Of course, there was always the chance they knew the lay of the land better than he did. The cliff might become a gentle slope or sprout a ravine leading down. But there was nothing he could do about that.

Aspar wondered if Hespero was following the woorm, too, though given the direction he'd come from, that didn't make a lot of sense. Perhaps, instead, he was following what the woorm was after, which, if he could believe Fend, was Stephen.

So what was Stephen doing up here in the mountains? And why was everyone so interested?

That he couldn't know, but he guessed he would soon, because all the trails seemed to be converging. It ought to be interesting when they did, he reckoned.

The forest here wasn't dead yet, although the track he was following was probably a mortal wound. It was too bad, because he found himself liking the conifer-rich landscape. Aspar had been in evergreen forests before, but only in the heights of the Hare. He liked the novelty of finding one on relatively flat ground.

What were the forests of Vestrana and Nahzgave like? They were even farther north. He'd heard tales of vast cold swamps and great boreal trees that dug their roots into ground frozen for more than half the year. He would like to see such places. Why had he waited so long?

Maybe they weren't even there anymore. For all he knew, up north they'd been having greffyns and woorms and whatnot venoming the earth for years. He knew *where* they were coming from now, but he didn't know why or how. Maybe Stephen could reckon that out, if Stephen was still alive. Was it a sickness, a rot, something that happened in the world now and then? Were their seasons longer than centuries, spells of quickening and dying? Or was someone—or something—*doing* this?

Was Hespero behind it all? Was Fend? Surely there was someone he could kill to make it stop. Or maybe the Briar King was right. Maybe the sickness was humanity itself, and it was *everyone* that needed killing.

Well, that was all tinder and no spark, and he wasn't going to get the fire going just by thinking about it. He knew killing the woorm would put a stop to some of it, and maybe killing Hespero and Fend would help, too. He was certainly ready to give that a go.

Ogre picked his way over a collection of stones that looked suspiciously like a fallen wall, and Aspar noticed other such jumbles that weren't natural to the terrain. Men and women had lived here once, built houses. Now the forest fed on their bones.

It was the way of things: Nothing was constant. Trees

burned and produced meadow, meadows grew into thickets, and eventually the great trees came back and shaded out the grass and brush and smaller trees. Men made pastures and fields, used them for a few lifetimes, then the wood took them back. So it had always been until now. Now things had gone wrong.

He'd fix that or die. He saw no other choices.

Not much later he came to a broad clearing where he could make out the full loom of the mountain ahead. He realized he was already on its slopes, and from this angle he could see the woorm's trail as a narrow but obvious line wiggling up the peak.

He could even see the front end of the trail, though the distance was too great to discern the beast itself. It was headed to the north face.

He could also hear Hespero's men again, off to his right. Probably they were all on the same slope now, ridge and valley having evened out. He reckoned by the racket that they were probably almost a league away, though, and unless they had some shinecrafting, they'd have difficulty picking up his trail without backtracking along the cliff.

He patted Ogre's neck. "You ready to run, old boy?" he asked. "We need to beat 'em to it."

Ogre lifted his head eagerly, and together they hurled themselves at the mountain.

As Anne fled, Robert's taunting laugh echoed in her ears.

How had he escaped Sir Neil? How had he known where to ambush her or about the secret passages at all?

But Robert wasn't really a man anymore. She knew that. Probably he was like the Hansan knights and couldn't die.

Had he and Sir Neil fought? Had he killed her knight? Or had the armies of Hansa already arrived, crushing Artwair and her army?

She wouldn't think like that. She couldn't. All that mattered now was to escape him long enough to think, to find safety for her and her companions. One of her men had died already, too confused by the glamour of the passage to run when she had commanded it, speared in the back by one of Robert's soldiers. That left Anne five companions: three Craftsmen, Cazio, and Austra.

He'd been *waiting* for them with twenty men and a handful of his black-clad women to guide them.

Cazio, thank the saints, was still with her.

She tried to sweep away her fears and frustrations and concentrate. The passage should begin dividing up ahead, shouldn't it? She'd never been here before, but she *knew* the place, could feel where it was going. If she could get them into the castle, into the passages there, they might be able to hide.

In the meantime, her men in Gobelin Court would all die, because even if Artwair succeeded in taking Thornrath in time to let Grand-uncle Fail's fleet in, it would still take too long to win a siege now that her stupid little plan had begun to fall apart.

She felt helpless, but being dead or a captive would make her even more so.

"Hands!" she shouted. "Everyone keep holding hands!"

Anne searched back over her shoulder but saw no telltale lantern light behind them. Of course, the passage twisted and twined often enough that their pursuit needn't be far to remain unseen.

Austra, with her in the front, held their only working lamp, and it now showed them two possibilities.

"The right branch," she decided. They turned right, but after only sixteen paces they reached a dead end so freshly made that she could smell the mortar.

She hadn't foreseen *this*. In her mind's eye, the right passage wound its way through the outer wall of the castle and eventually, after a few more turnings, directly into her mother's old solar.

"He's blocked it up," she murmured bitterly. "Of course he would."

It was exactly what she had planned to do.

"The other one?" Austra asked hopefully.

"It goes under the castle, into the dungeons."

"That's better than being caught, isn't it?"

"Yes," Anne agreed. "And there are ways into the castle from the dungeon. Just pray he hasn't blocked this one off, as well."

Sounds of pursuit seemed near as they moved back into the left passage.

"Where are we going?" Cazio asked.

"Don't ask questions," Anne said. "It'll only make things worse."

"Worse," Cazio muttered. "It's already worse. At least let me fight."

"No. Not yet. I'll tell you when to fight."

Cazio didn't answer. He might have forgotten already that they'd been talking.

The tunnel branched again, but as she suspected, the one she wanted was blocked off, this time a lot less neatly; its ceiling had been collapsed. It looked as if it had been done in haste, but it was every bit as efficient.

"He can't know all of them," she told Austra. "He *can't*."

"What if he has a map of some sort? Maybe your mother or Erren had one."

"Maybe," Anne said. "If so, we're done for." She stopped, a little chill working up her spine.

"Did you hear that?" she asked Austra.

"I didn't hear anything," her friend replied.

But Anne heard it again, a distant whispering of her name. And she remembered.

"There *is* one passage," she murmured. "I saw the opening, but even I couldn't see where it went. There's a sort of fog there, and something else . . ."

"Something worse than Robert?"

An image flashed then, painfully bright, of the red-tressed demon. But that wasn't right. That wasn't who was whispering to her.

"You know what it is," she replied. They reached a small chamber with two passages leading out of it. Both were blocked.

"You mean *him*?" Austra hissed. "The last of the . . . ?" She didn't finish the thought. Her breath was coming hard.

"Yes."

Anne made her decision and reached for the place she knew instinctively was there, a small depression in the stone.

She found the catch and pressed it. Something inside clicked, and a portion of the wall eased open. Anne saw that the stone had been cut very thin and somehow fixed to a thick wooden panel.

"Quickly," she said to the others.

She ushered them through, stepped in, and pulled the door shut, listening for it to click into place. Then she turned to see what their situation was.

The six of them just managed to crouch on a small landing in a rough tunnel carved of living stone. After the landing the passage descended rather dramatically. If it hadn't been so narrow, going down it at anything but a fall probably would have been impossible; as it was, they were able to control their descent by bracing their hands against the walls. Austra handed the lantern back to Cazio, and Anne led, with the light coming from behind her, throwing her shadow down the strange warren. The air was thick with a burned sort of smell, but it wasn't hot; if anything, she had a chill.

"He's down there," she murmured.

"What does he want with you?" Austra wondered aloud.

"I've no idea," she said, "but it looks like we're going to find out."

"What if this is all part of Robert's trap?" Austra asked. "What if *he* sent that vision? He might be able to do that."

"He might," Anne conceded. "But I don't think he could fool me about who he is. And Robert is behind us. I can hear the Kept up ahead."

"But a Scaos . . ."

"Virgenya Dare made him our slave," Anne said firmly. "I'm the rightful queen, so he's my servant now. Do not fear him. Trust me."

"Yes," Austra said weakly.

Then she continued. "Remember how we used to play in the horz?"

"I remember," Anne said. She reached behind her for Austra's hand. "This is all happening because of that, somehow. Because we found the grave."

"Virgenya Dare's grave?"

"I was wrong about that," Anne said.

"You? Wrong?"

"It happens," Anne replied wryly. "Well, now, are we ready to meet a real live Scaos?"

"Yes." She didn't sound confident, though.

"Then off we go. Cazio, are you still all right there? And the rest of you?"

"Yes," Cazio replied, and their companions echoed the reply. "But who, by Ontro, are you talking about? And how did we get into this wretched tunnel?"

"What was that?" Anne asked.

"I said, 'How did we get into this tunnel?' "

"I think he knows where he is, and he's remembering it," Austra said.

"What do you mean, remembering it?" Cazio asked irritably. "I've never been here before. I don't even remember how I *got* here."

"This place must be older than the glamour," Anne said. "That's probably good."

"Glamour?" Cazio muttered. "What glamour? The last thing I remember is the Sefry house. Was a spell cast upon me?"

"It's the same with me!" one of Leafton's men, Cuelm MeqVorst, exclaimed.

"Yes," Anne replied. "A shinecrafting was done to you, but we're beyond it, and there isn't time to go into detail. We are being pursued by the usurper and his men."

"Let's fight them, then," Cazio said.

"No, there are too many," Anne said. "But those of you in the rear, keep watch. Be ready. If somehow they find the way into here, we *will* have to fight."

"They can only get to us one at a time," Cazio pointed out.

"True," Anne said. "You might be able to hold them off long enough for us to die of thirst."

"What do we do, then?" MeqVorst wanted to know. His voice was edged with panic.

"You follow me," she said firmly. "You may hear or see strange things, but unless there's an attack from behind, keep your hands still unless I say so. Do all of you understand?"

"Not entirely," Cazio said, and the other three men murmured agreement.

"Where are we going?"

"The only way left to us. Down."

The scorched odor became stronger, at times stifling, and Anne fancied she smelled mingled with it the acrid scent of fear coming from those behind her.

"I hear it now," Austra gasped. "Saints, he's in my head."

"We can't go farther," MeqVorst protested fearfully. "Men I can fight, but I'm not going to be food for some great bloody spider."

"It's not a spider," Anne said, wondering as she said it if that was true. After all, no one knew what the Skasloi looked like, at least not that she'd ever read or heard. They were known as demons of shadow whose true forms were hidden by darkness.

"Stay calm, all of you," she said. "He can't hurt you as long as you're with me."

"I . . . it feels . . . the voice . . ." The warrior's voice trailed off, and Anne thought she heard him weeping.

The murmurs grew louder but remained unintelligible until they finally reached level earth once again. Then they seemed to subside as they encountered yet another dead end.

Again Anne knew where the hidden entrance was. She found the latch, feeling as she did so a peculiar tingle.

The wall in front of them silently swung open, and lamplight poured from the tunnel into a low, round chamber.

Something shifted in the new light, something *wrong,* and she stifled a shriek. Austra didn't manage to, and her scream reverberated in the hollow depths.

Anne stood stiffly, heart pounding, vision swimming.

It was only after several slow, thundering pulses of her blood that she understood that she was looking not on some sort of monster but at a woman and a man. The man was horribly disfigured; his face had been cut, burned, and who knew what else. His filthy rags covered very little of his body. The woman's face was smudged and bloody. She wore men's clothing of a dark hue.

To her amazement, Anne recognized her.

"Lady Berrye?"

"Who's there?" Lady Berrye asked sluggishly. She sounded drunk. "Are you real?"

"I am."

Lady Berrye laughed and squeezed the man's shoulder. "It *says* it's real," she told him.

"Everything says it's real," the man gruffed with a strange accent. "But that's what we tell ourselves, walking in the graveyard, yes?"

"You were my father's mistress," Anne said. "You're hardly older than me."

"You see?" Lady Berrye said. "It's Anne Dare, William's youngest daughter."

"Yes," Anne said a bit angrily. "It is."

Lady Berrye frowned at that and swayed to her feet. Her expression grew trepidatious.

"Please," she whispered. "I can't, not again."

She came closer, and Anne saw how gaunt she was. She had always seemed cheerful, a woman just leaving girlhood, with cheeks ruddy and smooth. Now her skin lay close to her skull, and her bright blue eyes seemed black and feverish. She reached a trembling hand toward Anne. Her fingers were torn and dirty.

The man was also pushing himself up, muttering in a language Anne did not know.

The instant Berrye's fingers brushed Anne's face, she jerked them back to her mouth, as if she had burned them.

"Saints," she said. "She *is* real. Or more real than the others . . ."

Anne reached for the hand.

"I am real," she confirmed. "You see my maid, Austra. These others serve me, as well. Lady Berrye, how did you come here?"

"It has been so long." She closed her eyes. "My friend needs water," she said. "Do you have any?"

"You both need water," Anne said apologetically. "How long have you been down here?"

"I don't know," Lady Berrye replied. "I might be able to work it out. I think it was the third day of Prismen."

"Twice a nineday, then."

Cazio passed her his waterskin, and she handed it to Berrye. Alis quickly took it to the scarred man.

"Drink slowly," she said. "Carefully, or you will not hold it down."

He had a few sips, and then a fit of coughing wracked his body, causing him to fall. Berrye had a little, then knelt to give him a bit more. As she did, she began to speak, though her gaze stayed on the man.

"I am your mother's servant," she began.

"I doubt that very much," Anne replied.

"I am coven-trained, Your Majesty. Not from the Coven Saint Cer, but I am a sister nevertheless. My task was to be your father's mistress. But after his death, I sought out your mother."

"Why?"

"We needed each other. I know it is difficult for you to believe, but I have served her as well as I could. I came down into the dungeons to free a man named Leovigild Ackenzal."

"The composer. I've heard of him." She glanced at the mutilated man. "Is this . . . ?"

"No," Lady Berrye said. "Ackenzal would not come with me. Robert has hostage people he cares for, and he refused to risk their injury for his freedom. No, this is, so far as I can tell, Prince Cheiso of Safnia."

Anne gasped, feeling as if she had been slapped. "Lesbeth's fiancé?"

At the mention of her aunt's name, the man began to groan, then cry out incoherently.

"Hush," Lady Berrye said, stroking his head. "This is her niece. This is Anne."

The ravaged face turned up toward her, and for an instant Anne could see the handsome man he once had been. His eyes were dark, and worlds of pain poured from them.

"My love," he said. "Always my love."

"Robert accused him of kidnapping Lesbeth and giving her to the enemy. I thought he had been executed. I found him searching for a way out after I discovered that Robert had sealed off most of the passages." She looked suddenly a bit frantic. "Your uncle, you know—"

"Isn't human? I'm aware of that."

"Have you taken the throne from him? Is his reign ended?"

"No. He's searching for us even now. This was the only tunnel he hadn't blocked."

"I know. I hoped I could find a way out in the warrens around the Kept. Instead he has caught us here."

"You've met the Kept?"

"No. Your mother came to see him once, and I was with her. But Robert has the only key I know of. We could not gain entrance."

"Then we still cannot."

Lady Berrye shook her head. "You don't understand. The key is to the main entrance and takes you to the antechamber outside his cell. Outside, you understand? So that he sits within the walls of ancient magicks. So that he can be controlled. Anne, we are *in* his cell."

As she said it, the walls seemed to shift like vast coils, and Austra pinched the lamp out, plunging them into utter darkness.

"What?" Anne cried. "Austra?"

"He told me to—I wasn't—I couldn't—"

But then the voice was back, no longer whispering but shivering through the stone and into her bones.

"Your *Majesty*," it said in a mocking tone. Anne felt acrid breath on her face, and the darkness began a slow, terrible spin.

CHAPTER SEVEN

TRIEY

LEOFF SMILED at the little flourish of notes Mery added to the normally staid and melancholy *Triey for Saint Reusmier*.

She had permission to do so—the triey form encouraged extemporaneous elaboration—but where most musicians would have added a doleful grace note or two, Mery instead offered a wistful yet essentially joyful reiteration of an earlier theme. Since the piece was a meditation on memory and forgetfulness, it was perfect despite its novelty.

When she was done, she glanced up at him, as always, for approval.

"Well done, Mery," he said. "I'm amazed someone your age understands that composition so well."

"What do you mean?" she asked, scratching the side of her nose.

"It's about an old man thinking back to his youth," Leoff expanded. "Remembering happier times, but often imperfectly."

"Is that why the themes fragment?" she asked.

"Yes, and they're never quite put together completely, are they? The ear is never quite satisfied."

"That's why I like it," Mery said. "It's not too simple."

She shuffled the music on her stand.

"What's this?" she asked.

"That may be the second act of *Maersca*," he said. "Let me see."

Suddenly his heart felt cast in lead.

"Here," he said, trying to sound casual. "Give me that."

"What is it?" Mery asked, glancing at the page. "I don't understand. It's mostly shifting chords. Where's the melody line?"

"That's not for you," Leoff said with a good deal more force than he meant to.

"I'm sorry," Mery said, drawing her shoulders in.

He found that he was breathing hard. *Didn't I put that away?*

"Don't be. It's not your fault, Mery," he said. "I shouldn't have left it out. It's something I started, but I'm not going to finish it. Don't give it another thought."

She looked pale.

"Mery," he asked, "is anything wrong?"

She peered up at him with wide eyes.

"It's sick," she said. "The music—"

He knelt and clumsily took her hand with his maimed one. "Don't think about it, then," he said. "Don't try to hear it in your head, or it *will* make you sick. Do you understand?"

She nodded, but there were tears in her eyes.

"Why would you write something like that?" she asked plaintively.

"Because I thought I had to," he said. "But now I think maybe I don't. I really can't explain more than that. Do you understand?"

She nodded again.

"Now, why don't we play something happier."

"I wish you could play with me."

"Well," he said, "I can still sing. My voice was never extraordinary, but I can carry a tune."

She clapped her hands. "What shall it be, then?"

He fumbled through the music on his desk.

"Here we go," he said. "It's from the second act of *Maersca*. It's sort of an interlude, a comical side story to the main plot. The singer here is Droep, a young boy scheming to, ah, visit a girl at night."

"Like my mother used to visit the king?"

"Umm, well, I wouldn't know about that, Mery," Leoff temporized. "Anyway, it's nighttime, and he's under her window, pretending to be a sea prince from a very distant land. He tells her he speaks with the fish of the sea, and he explains how word of her beauty has come to him under the waves and across the world."

"I see it," Mery said. "The bream tells the crab, and the crab tells the bluefin."

"Exactly. And each has a little theme."

"Until we get to the porpoise, who tells the prince."

"Exactly. Then she asks what he looks like, and he tells her he is the fairest of all who live in his country, which is true, in a way, since he's made the country up."

"No," Mery said. "That's still a lie."

"But amusing, I think," Leoff said.

"The melody is, anyway."

"Ah, a critic already," Leoff said. "But to continue, she asks to see him, yet he swears that only by magic was he able to come to her, and if she gazes on his face, he must return home, never to come again. But if she should lie three nights with him *without* seeing his face, the spell will be broken."

"But then she'll know he lied," Mery said, puzzled.

"Yes, but he reckons that by then he will have managed to, well, ah, give her a kiss."

"That's a lot of trouble to go through for a kiss," Mery said dubiously.

"Yes," Leoff said, "it is. But that's how it is with boys his age. You wait until you're a little older, and you'll see exactly how much trouble the young men will go through to win your attentions. Although I suggest that if one should ever claim to be from some far-off land, one you've never heard of—"

"I should insist on seeing his face." Mery giggled.

"Exactly. So, are you ready to play?"

"Who shall sing the woman's part?"

"Can you?"

"It's too low for me."

"Well, then," Leoff said, "I shall sing falsetto."

"And the duet?"

"I'll improvise," Leoff replied. "Here, we'll skip the part where's he's introducing himself and get straight to the song."

"Very well," Mery said. She put her fingers to the keys and began. Under her influence, the accompaniment bounced even more boisterously than he'd imagined it might.

He cleared his throat as his cue arrived.

I have heard from the sea,
From the denizens of the sea,
Across a thousand leagues
The report has come to me
Of a lady so lovely
In such a far country
That I, the prince of Ferrowigh
Must hurry here to thee

You were bathing near the birm,
Admired by a bream
Who told his friend the crab
Who came scuttling by just then
And the crab told old bluefin
Who told a skate or ten
That I, the prince of Ferrowigh
Must come your heart to win . . .

For the first time in a long time it occurred to Leoff that he was *happy.* And more than that, optimistic. The terrors of the past months receded, and he felt as if good things actually might happen again.

He realized that he believed Ambria's promise of escape, had believed it from the moment she'd told him. But in a way, it didn't matter now.

"Well, aren't we all jolly?" a feminine voice interrupted. He jumped.

Areana was standing inside the doorway, watching them.

She hadn't spoken to him since the morning she had found him with Ambria.

"Areana!" Mery cried. "Won't you join us? We really need someone to sing the part of Taleath!"

"Do you?" she said skeptically, her gaze fixed on Leoff.

"Please," he said.

She just stood there.

"Come on," Leoff said. "You must have heard us. I know you want to sing it."

"Do you?" she asked coldly.

"*I* want you to sing it," he answered.

"I can start again," Mery said.

Areana sighed. "Very well. Start it again."

Mery grew tired a bell or so later and went to take a nap. Leoff feared that Areana would leave, as well, but instead she walked over to the window. After a moment's hesitation, Leoff joined her.

"There's something going on at the great wall, I think," Leoff said. "At Thornrath. There's been smoke for days."

She nodded but didn't seem to be looking at the wall or at anything else, for that matter.

"I thought you were very good singing Taleath's part," he attempted again, "although it's not the part I wrote for you."

"There will be no part for *me* in this travesty," she snapped. "I won't do it."

He lowered his voice. "I'm only working on it to keep Robert from hurting you or Mery," he said. "I've no intention of performing it."

"Really?" Her gaze met his and softened a little.

He nodded. "Really. I'm working on something quite different."

"Good," she said, looking back outside. He struggled to find some way to keep the conversation going, but no acceptable words offered themselves to his tongue.

"You've made me quite foolish, you know," she said, her voice sounding thick. "Quite foolish."

"I didn't mean to."

"That makes it worse. Why didn't you tell me about you and Lady Gramme? I should have guessed, I suppose. She was your patron, and she is beautiful, and skilled, and you get along famously with Mery."

"No," Leoff said. "I . . . there was nothing to tell until the other night. She came—I was unprepared . . ."

She laughed resentfully. "Oh, yes, and so was I. And there's no hiding I had the same idea. I thought I might ease your pain and I—" She began crying and gulped.

"Areana?"

"I was a virgin, you know. Not so fashionable in Eslen, but out in the poellands it's still something to be . . ." She waved her hands helplessly. "Anyway, that's gone. But I thought if I was with someone kind and gentle, someone who wouldn't try to hurt me, I might wash it away, what . . ."

She leaned her arm on the windowsill and buried her face in it. He watched her helplessly, then reached out and stroked her hair.

"I wish it hadn't happened," he said. "I never meant to hurt you."

"I know," she sobbed. "And I expect too much. Who would touch me now?"

"I'm touching you," he said. "Here, look at me."

She raised her tear-streaked face.

"I think you were right," he admitted, "about how I feel about you. But there's something you need to understand. What they did to me in the dungeons—it changed me. I don't just mean my body or my hands; it altered me inside. I'm sure you know what I'm talking about. For so long, for so very long, I've been able to see no better end for all of this than revenge. It's all I've really thought about. It's all I've been planning. In the dungeon, I met a man; well, I heard his voice, anyway. We spoke. He told me that in Safnia, where he's from, vengeance is considered an art, something to be done well and savored. It made sense to me, I have to say, to make Robert pay for the things he's done. The other music I've been working on—that's my revenge."

"What do you mean?"

He closed his eyes, knowing he ought not to tell her but plunging on anyway.

"There are more than eight modes," he said softly. "There are a few others so forbidden that they are spoken of only in whispers, even in the academies. You saw—you *felt*—the effect of music when it's properly composed. We not only were able to create and control emotion, we made it literally impossible for anyone to stop us until we were done.

"That was using mostly the modes we know, but what made that piece so very powerful was my rediscovery— Mery's rediscovery, really, come to that—of a very ancient forbidden mode. And now I've found another, one not used since the days of the Black Jester."

"What does it do?"

"It can do many things. But a properly structured piece, when performed, might kill anyone who heard it."

She frowned and searched his face with such a gaze that he knew she was looking for signs of madness.

"This is true?" she said finally.

"I haven't tested it, of course, but yes, I believe it is."

"If I hadn't been there, if I hadn't been part of the music in the Candlegrove, I don't imagine I would believe you," she said. "But as it is, I think you could do almost anything if you put your mind to it. So that's what you've been working on?"

"Yes. To kill Prince Robert."

"But that's—" Her eyes narrowed. "But you can't play."

"I know. That's been a problem all along. Robert can play, however. I had thought if I kept the mechanics of it simple enough, he might actually do it himself."

"But more likely Mery would play it."

"In which case I had thought to stuff her ears with wax," Leoff said. "You understand, I agree with you—I always did. I think he plans to kill all three of us. I hoped to give the two of you a chance, but if I couldn't . . ."

"You thought you'd take him with us."

"Yes."

"But what's changed?"

"I've stopped working on it," he said. "I shan't finish it."

"Why?"

"Because I have hope now," he said. "And even if that fails . . ."

"Hope?"

"For something better than revenge."

"What? Escape?"

"There is a possibility," he said. "A chance we might survive this and live out our lives in better circumstances. But if we can't—" He placed his ruined hand on her shoulder. "To make this music, this music of death, I have to surrender to the darkest parts of me. I can't afford to feel joy, hope, or love, or I can't write it.

"Yet today I realized I would prefer to die still capable of love than have my revenge. I would rather be able to tell Mery that I love her than slay all the evil princes in the world. And I would rather touch you as tenderly as I'm able, with these things that used to be hands, than bring such dread music into the world. Does that mean anything to you? Does it make sense?"

They were both crying now, quietly.

"It makes sense," she said. "It makes more sense than anything I've heard or thought lately. It makes you the man I fell in love with."

She took his hand and kissed it gently, once, twice, thrice.

"We're both injured," she said. "And I'm afraid. Very afraid. You say we might escape . . ."

"Yes," he began, but she put a finger to his lips.

"No," she said. "If it happens, it happens. I don't want to know any more. If I'm tortured, I will confess. I know that about myself now. I'm no brave lady from a romance."

"And I'm no knight," Leoff said. "But there are many ways to be brave."

She nodded, coming closer. "However much time we have," she said, "I would like to help you heal. And I'd like you to help me."

Leoff leaned down and touched his lips to hers, and they

stood for a long moment, locked in that very simple kiss.

She reached for the stays on her bodice. He stopped her.

"Healing is done slowly," he said gently. "A bit at a time."

"We may not have very much time," she pointed out.

"What's been done to you shouldn't happen to anyone," he said. "And it may be harder to get over it than you believe. I would like to make love to you, Areana, but only if it were the first of many times, and of many more things that a man and a woman might do together, *be* together. If we try this now and fail, I fear the consequences. So for the moment, believe we will live and give this time."

She pressed her head into his shoulder and put her arms around him, and together they watched the sunset.

"You have to go back to your room," Leoff told her a few bells later. They were quietly lying on his bed, her head nestled on his chest.

"I'd like to stay here," she said. "Couldn't we just sleep, actually sleep? I want to wake up with you."

He shook his head reluctantly. "Tonight is the night," he said. "Someone will come to your room. I'm not sure what will happen if you aren't there. Best we stick to the plan."

"Are you serious? You really think we might escape tonight?"

"I didn't want to believe it at first, either, but yes, I think the possibility is real."

"Very well," she said, untangling from him, standing, and smoothing her gown. Then she bent and gave him a long, lingering kiss. "Until I see you again," she said.

"Yes," he managed.

After she was gone, he didn't sleep but lay awake until he reckoned the midnight bell was about to toll. Then he dressed in a dark doublet and hose and a warm robe. He bundled up his music and, just as the bell began to peal, padded out of his room and down the stairs.

Despite his caution, there were no guards to slip past. The halls were empty, silent, and dark save for the candle he carried.

When he entered the long corridor that led to the entrance hall, he saw a light ahead, as diminutive as his own. As he drew nearer, he made out a dark red gown and quickened his steps, his heart racing double time, like an ensemble that had quite escaped the measure of its leader.

At the doorway he paused, puzzled. Ambria sat in a chair, waiting for him. She wasn't holding the candle; it flickered in a small sconce on a table near the chair. Her chin was on her chest, and he thought it odd that she had fallen asleep at such an anxious time.

But she wasn't asleep, of course. Every angle of her body was somehow wrong, and when he came close enough to see her face, it looked bruised and swollen, and her eyes seemed far too large.

"Ambria!" he gasped, and went down on his knee. He took her hand and found it cold.

"Leovigild Ackenzal, I presume," someone very near said.

Leoff was proud of himself; he didn't scream. He straightened, lifting his chin, determined to be brave.

"Yes," he whispered.

A man stepped from the shadows. He was massive, with a grizzled half-shaved face and hands the size of hams.

"Who are you?" Leoff asked.

The fellow grinned a horrible little grin that sent a profound shiver through the composer.

"You might call me Saint Dun," he said. "You might call me Death. Right now, you just consider yourself warned."

"You didn't have to kill her."

"Don't *have* to do nothin' in this life but die," he replied. "But I work for His Majesty, and this is what he asked me to do."

"He knew all along."

"His Majesty, he's busy. I haven't spoken to him lately. But I know him, and this is what he would have wanted. Lady Gramme didn't know about me, you see. I didn't figure in her plans." He stepped closer.

"But *you* know about me," he added softly. "And I reckon you need to know I can't be bribed or otherwise bought, like some here. Now His Majesty knows who his friends are, or he will when he returns to find 'em still alive. And as for you, I'll ask you to make a choice."

"No," Leoff said.

"Oh, yeah," the man replied. He gestured at Ambria's corpse. "That's the price *she* pays for this little attempt. Your price is to choose who dies next: Gramme's little brat or the landwaerden girl." He smiled and tousled Leoff's hair. "Don't worry. I'm not asking you to make a snap decision. I give you until noon tomorrow. I'll come up to your room."

"Don't do this," Leoff said softly. "This isn't decent."

"The world aens't decent," the killer replied. "Sure you ought to know that by now." He pointed with his chin. "Go on."

"Please."

"Go on."

Leoff returned to his room. He glanced at the bed where Ambria had lain, remembering her touch. He went to the window and gazed out at the moonless night, taking long, deep breaths.

Then he lit his candles, took out the unfinished music, pen, and ink, and began to write.

CHAPTER EIGHT

THE BATTLE OF THE WAERD

THIS WAS no joust, and there was no clever turning at the last moment to glance the blow. Not with horses galloping flank to flank, not when any deflection of spear by shield risked having it plunge into a battle-brother to the left or right. One might try to skip the blow upward with a last-instant tilt of the shield, but then one would lose sight of the target.

No, this was more like war galleys meeting at full oar, prow to prow. What was left was flinching and not flinching.

Neil didn't flinch; he met the shock of the killing point in the center of his shield, blowing out his breath as it happened to prevent it being knocked out of him.

His opponent, in contrast, panicked and shifted his shield so Neil's spear struck the curving edge. As the stun of contact went through him, Neil watched his weapon deflect and drive to the right, striking his foe's shield mate in the throat, shattering his neck into a bloody ruin and sending him hurtling back into the next rank.

The broken shaft of the first man's lance struck Neil's helm, turning his head half-around, and then the real jolt came as the full weight of horses, barding, armor, shields, and men slammed together. Horses went down, screaming and kicking. His own mount, a gelding named Winlauf, staggered but didn't fall, largely due to the press that surrounded them.

Neil clutched for the blade Artwair had given him, a good solid weapon he'd named Quichet, or Battlehound, for his father's sword. But before he could do that the head from a lance in the second rank of Thornrath's defenders slipped its slaughter-eager point through his shield and into the shoulder joint of his armor before the shaft shivered.

He felt as if he'd fallen naked through the icy surface of a midwinter mere; Battlehound came up in his hand, seeming to lift of its own accord. The horse of the man who had hit him was just tripping over the mount of the first man he'd met, which had gone down in the shock. The knight, still holding the broken spear shaft, was coming out of his stirrups, hurtling like a javelin toward Neil. Battlehound straightened Neil's arm and locked it, so that the flying man found the weapon's mortal-making point in his gorget.

The impact knocked Neil backward out of his stirrups, so

he flipped over his mount's haunches and down into the hooves of his next line.

Then there was blood and noise, and his body was seizing from the pain. Getting up was dark agony, and he wasn't sure how long it took him to do it.

When he did, he found the causeway mounded with men and horses, but his men still were surging forward. Overhead, flame and stone and feathered death were wracking the battle ground, but their charge was pushing through it.

Winlauf was dying, and only a few men on either side retained their steeds. This was the moment; if they were pushed back now, most of them would perish in the killing zones of the siege engines. Here they were inside all but arrow range, and the presence of the defenders' own men deterred that.

"One charge!" he howled, unable, really, to hear himself. Half his body felt like it was gone, but it wasn't the half that was carrying Battlehound.

As the very sky seemed to catch fire, Neil put everything that was in him to killing.

"What is that?" Stephen asked Zemlé.

She shook her head. "I don't know. Ghosts? Witches?"

"Do you know the language of the song?"

"No. It sounds a little like the Old Tongue. A few words sound familiar."

Stephen caught a shimmer, then, eyes reflecting fireglow. The dogs were barking and howling as if they had gone insane.

Whatever they were, they weren't slinders, as he first had feared. They were coming far too cautiously. He couldn't be certain, but judging by the behavior of the dogs, the intruders were actually circling the camp.

"Whoever you are," he cried, "we mean you no harm."

"I'm sure that's of great comfort to them," Zemlé said, "considering there are at least ten of them and we're basically unarmed."

"I can be pretty intimidating," Stephen said.

"Yes, well, at least you're not a blithering coward," she observed.

"I am, actually," he confided, though her assessment made him feel suddenly very warm. "But after a point you just get stunned and stay stunned. I don't have the sense to be scared anymore." He frowned. The song had ceased, but words were being exchanged, and then the sounds clicked into place.

"Qey thu menndhzi?" he shouted.

The wood fell suddenly silent.

"What was that?" Zemlé asked.

"What they're speaking, I think. A Vadhiian dialect. Kauron's language."

"Stephen!" Zemlé gasped. The dogs dropped to the ground, still snarling, but oddly cowed.

Someone had stepped into the clearing.

In the firelight, Stephen couldn't tell what color his eyes were, but they were large. His hair was as milk-white as his skin, and he was dressed in soft brown leathers.

"Sefry," he whispered.

"You're Hadivar," Zemlé said.

"You speak with old words," the Sefry said. "We are thinking you are the one."

"Who are you?"

The stranger studied the two of them for another moment or two, then tilted his head.

"My name is Adhrekh," he said.

"You speak the king's tongue," Stephen said.

"Some," Adhrekh said. "It has been a long time since I have used it."

More Sefry appeared at the edge of the firelight. All were armed with swords nearly as slim as the one Cazio carried. Most had bows, as well, and most of the arrows in those bows seemed to be pointed at him.

"My, ah, my name is Stephen Darige," he returned. "This is Sister Pale." He wasn't sure why he shied from the more familiar name he'd been using.

Adhrekh waved that away. "The khriim is here. You speak the tongue of the ancients. Tell me, what was his name?"

"His name? You mean Brother Kauron? Or Choron in your speech."

Adhrekh lifted his head, and his eyes flashed with triumph. The other Sefry plucked the arrows from their bows and returned them to their quivers.

"Well," Adhrekh mused. "So you have come, after all."

Stephen didn't quite know what to say to that, so he let it go by.

"Why did you abandon the village?" Stephen asked.

Adhrekh shrugged. "We vowed to live in the mountain, to keep guard there, and we have. It is our way."

"You live in the Alq?" Zemlé asked.

"That is our privilege, yes."

"And it was Brother Choron who asked you to guard it?"

"Until his return, yes," Adhrekh said. "Until now."

"You mean until the return of his heir," Zemlé corrected.

"As you wish," Adhrekh said. He moved his regard back to Stephen. "Would you like to see the Alq, pathikh?"

Stephen felt a chill, half excitement and half fear. 'Pathikh' meant something like lord, master, prince. Was Zemlé actually right? Was he really the heir to this ancient prophecy?

"Yes," he said. "But wait. You said the khriim was here. Do you mean the woorm?"

"Yes."

"You've seen it?"

"Yes."

"In the valley? Where?"

"No. Once you led it near enough, he was able to find his way. He's waiting for you in the Alq."

"Waiting for me?" Stephen said. "Maybe you don't understand. It's *dangerous*. It kills anything it touches, anything it comes near."

"He said he wouldn't understand," said another of the Sefry, this one a woman with startlingly blue eyes.

"I understand that if the woorm is in the mountain," Stephen said, "I'm not going there."

"No," Adhrekh said, his face melancholy. "I'm afraid you will, pathikh."

"Qexqaneh," Anne gasped, hoping she remembered the pronunciation correctly.

The thing in the darkness seemed to pause, then press against her face like a dog nuzzling its master. Shocked, she swatted at it, but there was nothing there, although the sensation persisted.

"Sweet Anne," the Kept snuffled. "Smell of woman, sweet sick smell of woman."

Anne tried to collect herself. "I am heir to the throne of Crotheny. I command you by your name, Qexqaneh."

"Yessss," the Kept purred. "Knowing what you want is not the same as having. I know your intention. Alis-smells-of-death knows better. She just told you."

"Is that so?" Anne asked. "Is it? I'm descended in a direct line from Virgenya Dare. Can you really defy me?"

Another pause followed, during which Anne gained confidence, trying not to reflect too closely on what she was doing.

"I called you here," the Kept murmured. She could feel the vastness of him contracting, drawing into himself.

"Yes, you did. Called me here, put a map in my head so I could find you, promised me you could help me against *her,* the demon in the tomb. So what do *you* want?"

He seemed to withdraw further, but she had the sudden feeling of a million tiny spiders nesting in her skull. She gagged, but when Austra reached for her, Anne pushed her away.

"What are you doing, Qexqaneh?" she demanded.

We can talk like this, and they cannot hear us. Agree. You don't want them to know. You don't.

Very well, Anne mouthed silently.

She felt as if she were whirling again, but this time it wasn't frightening; it was more like a dance. Then, as if she were opening her eyes, she was standing on a hillside bare of any human habitation. Her body felt as light as thistledown, so flimsy that she feared any breeze might carry her off.

All around her she saw the dark waters, the waters behind the world. But this time her perspective seemed reversed. Instead of perceiving the waters as flowing together—trickles building rinns, rinns pouring into broohs, broohs into streams, streams into the river—Anne descried the river as a great dark beast with a hundred fingers, and each of those fingers with a thousand fingers more, and each of those with a thousand, reaching and prying and poking into every man and woman, into every horse and ox, into each blade of grass, tickling, gesturing—waiting.

Into everything, that is, except the formless shade that stood before her.

"What is this place?" she demanded.

"Ynis, my flesh," he replied.

Before she could retort, she realized it was true. It was Ynis, in fact the very hill upon which Eslen stood. But there was no castle, no city, no work of Man or Sefry. Nothing to be seen.

"And these waters? I've seen them before. What are they?"

"Life and death. Memory and forgetfulness. The one drinks, the other gives back. Piss on the left, sweet water on the right."

"I'd like you to be more clear."

"I'd like to smell rain again."

"Are you he?" she asked. "The man who attacked me in the place of the Faiths? Was that you?"

"Interesting," Qexqaneh mused. "No. I cannot wander so far. Not like this, pretty one, disgusting thing."

"Who was it, then?"

"Not *who*," Qexqaneh replied. "Who *might* be. Who *will* be, probably."

"I don't understand."

"Aren't mad yet, are you?" he replied. "In time."

"That's not an answer."

"Good enough for the geos, milk cow," he replied.

"*Her,* then," Anne snapped. "The demon. What is she?"

"What was, what hopes to be again. Some called her the queen of demons."

"What does she want with me?"

"Like the other," Qexqaneh said. "She is not she. She is a place to sit, a hat to wear."

"A throne."

"Any word in your horrible language will do as well as the next."

"She wants me to become her, doesn't she? She wants to wear my skin. Is that what you're saying?"

The shadow laughed. "No. Just offers you a place to sit, the right to rule. She can hurt your enemies, but she cannot harm you."

"There are stories of women who take the form of others and steal their lives—"

"Stories," he interrupted. "Imagine instead those women finally came to understand what they really were all along. The people around them didn't understand the truth. There are things in you, Anne Dare, aren't there? Things no one understands? No one *can* understand."

"Just tell me how to fight her."

"Her true name is Iluumhuur. Use it and tell her to leave."

"It's that simple?"

"Is it simple? I don't know. Don't care. Neither should you, since you'll never live for it to matter. Your uncle's warriors block your every exit. You will die here, and I can only savor your soul as it leaves."

"Unless . . ." Anne said.

"Unless?" the Kept repeated mockingly.

"Don't take that tone," Anne said. "I have power, you know. I have killed. I might yet win my way through this. Perhaps *she* will help me."

"She might," he said. "I have no way of knowing. Call her true name and see."

Anne coughed out a sarcastic laugh. "I somehow find that an outstandingly bad idea despite your reassuring words.

No, you were going to offer me a way past my uncle's troops. Well, then, what is it?"

"I was just going to offer my assistance in defeating them," he purred.

"Ah. And that would involve . . ."

"Freeing me."

"Why didn't I think of that?" Anne mused. "Free the last of the demon race who enslaved humanity for a thousand generations. What a wonderful idea."

"You have kept me for far too long," he snarled. "My time is past. Let me go so that I may join my race in death."

"If death is what you want, then tell me how to kill you."

"I cannot be killed. The curse holds me here. Until the law of death is mended, I cannot die any more than your uncle can. Release me, and I shall mend the law of death."

"And die yourself?"

"I swear that if you release me, I will deliver you from this place. I will leave, and I will do all in my power to die."

Anne considered that for a long moment.

"You cannot lie to me."

"You know I cannot."

"Suppose I consider this," Anne said slowly. "How would I free you?"

The shadow seemed to waver for a moment.

"Place your foot on my neck," he snarled bitterly, "and say, 'Qexqaneh, I free you.' "

Anne's heart raced faster, and her belly seemed to fill with heat.

"I want to go back to my friends now," she told him.

"As you wish."

And with that she stood once more in darkness, with the earth tugging harder at her feet.

Aspar followed the woorm trail up a talus slope wiry with young trees to a great crack in the mountain, a natural cul-de-sac fifty kingsyards wide at the mouth and narrow toward the rear, where a great cascade of water plunged from far above. Predictably, the waterfall had dug a deep pool for it-

self, and just as predictably, the creature's trail vanished
into it.

The holter dismounted and walked the border of earth and
water, searching for any other sign of the beast but only confirming what he already knew: The beast was in the mountain now. Whether it had reached its destination or was just
passing through again, he could not know.

"Sceat," he muttered, taking a seat on a rock to think.

Was Fend still riding the woorm? The last time he'd spoken to anyone who saw it, they'd reported two people on its
back. If that was the case, then either the water passage was
short enough for the men to survive or the two had dismounted as they had in the Ef valley. If that was true, they
were waiting somewhere for the woorm to perform whatever
task it had here.

The third possibility was that Fend and his comrade had
drowned, but he didn't think that was particularly likely.

On the chance they had dismounted, he checked carefully
for traces but didn't see any sign of men on foot. Given the
fact that the earth here was covered in high moss, fern, and
horsetail, it would be nearly impossible to avoid leaving
some trace, even for Sefry.

That suggested that the woormriders had gone swimming
with the woorm, which in turn implied that he might be able
to follow. That belief was strengthened by the likelihood
that this was the entrance to yet another Halafolk rewn.
Sefry couldn't hold their breath any longer than humans, so
he ought to be able to make the swim, as he had done to enter
Rewn Aluth.

Of course, a short swim for the beast might be a long one
for him. Still, going after it was likely to be his only hope
now.

That meant that once again he and Ogre had to part.

Wasting no time, he unbuckled the stallion's saddle and
slid it off, along with the blanket. Then he removed the bri-
dle and hid it all beneath a small rock overhang. Ogre
watched him the entire time, seeming strangely attentive.

Aspar walked him back to the entrance of the rift, then

around the side of the mountain opposite the approach he expected Hespero and his men to take.

There he put his forehead against Ogre's skull and patted his mount's downy cheek.

"You've been a good friend," he said. "Saved my life more times than I can count. Either way this goes, you've earned your way through. If I don't come out, well, I maun y' can take care of yourself. If I make it, I'll find someplace quiet for you where y' can stud and eat. No more arrows or greffyn poison or what have you, yah?"

The bared bay tossed his head, as if shaking off Aspar's embrace, but the holter calmed him with another few strokes on his cheek.

"Just stay over here," he said. "I wouldn't have one of Hespero's men riding you. Don't suspect you would, either, and they'd probably kill you then, so just rest. I might well need one more fast ride out of you aer this is over."

Ogre stamped as he walked away, and Aspar cast one glance back and raised an admonishing finger.

"Lifst," he commanded.

Ogre whickered softly, but he obeyed and didn't follow.

Back at the pool, Aspar unstrung his bow and wrapped it in an oiled beaver skin, tying it taut. He put the sinew in a waxed bag and tightened that, as well. He wrapped up his arrows, especially *the* arrow, in otter skin and bundled it all to his bow. He checked to make certain he had his dirk and hand-ax, then sat by the pool, breathing deeply, getting himself ready for a long underwater swim.

At his eighth breath, bubbles appeared in the pool, and then the water suddenly began to rise. Aspar watched for a few heartbeats, rooted, but as he understood what was happening, he grabbed his things and darted through the trees to the cliff, where he started climbing as swiftly as he could.

The rock face wasn't all that difficult, and when the sudden flood slapped against the stone, he was already some four kingsyards up, well above it. But it wasn't the water he was worried about, so he continued, straining his limbs, practically vaulting from hold to hold.

He heard a low, dull whump, and a moment later a brief shower of water pelted him, though he was already as high as the tops of the lower trees.

Looking over his shoulder, he saw the woorm tower up, wreathed in poisonous vapors, eyes glowing like green moons beneath the shadow of the sky.

CHAPTER NINE

AN UNEXPECTED ALLY

OBSERVATIONS QUAINT & CURIOUS: THE VIRGENYAN
LEAST LOON, PART THE SECOND, THE PERENNIAL CAPTIVE
Some scholars in times past have wondered what need the
loon has for feet, legs, or indeed limbs of any sort. They
cite as the source of their confusion the fact that the creature spends the vast majority of its time in captivity, carried hither and yon by its keepers. What they fail to see is
the humorous side of the VLL's natural history, to wit,
that though it is often a helpless captive, its nature is to be
dissatisfied with such humiliation.
Its legs, therefore, exist for the sole purpose of allowing it
to walk from one detention to the next . . .

DESPITE THE STEW of anger, fear, and frustration that
seethed in Stephen, he had to admit that the Sefry were better hosts than the slinders.

Yes, he and Zemlé were captives in the sense that they
weren't given any choice about where they were going.
However, the Sefry handled them gently—royally, even—

bearing them on small chairs set atop wooden poles and con-
straining them with numbers rather than violence.

Their path wound deeper into the shadow forest, through
fernlike trees and dense vines that drew closer, narrower,
darker, until with a start Stephen realized that they had
passed into the living stone of the mountain itself without
his noticing the transition.

There the journey became more harrowing, and he wished
they'd been allowed to walk as the cortege proceeded down
a steep, narrow stair. On the left was stone, and to the right
there was nothing but a distance their lanterns did not pene-
trate. Even the rewn had not seemed so vast. Stephen wondered if the mountain was entirely hollow, a brittle shell
filled with darkness.

But no, not just darkness; something tugged lightly at the
hairs of his arm and neck, and the faintest musical hum vi-
brated from the stone itself. There was power here, sedos
power such as was only hinted at by the faneway he had
walked and the others he had known. Even in Dunmrogh, at
Khrwbh Khrwkh, where Anne Dare had unleashed the dor-
mant might of an ancient fane, he hadn't sensed this sort of
subtle puissance.

Thankfully, the seemingly bottomless pit finally showed
its foundation, and the Sefry took them through a more man-
ageable cavern. It was still grand but low enough that he
could make out the glittering stone teeth depending from its
ceiling.

"It's beautiful," Zemlé murmured, pointing at a column
that glowed as if polished in the lamplight. "I've never seen
stone take such forms. Or is it stone at all?"

"I've read of such things," Stephen said, "and seen them
elsewhere. Presson Manteo called the ones that hang 'drip-
pers' and the ones that point up 'drops.' He thinks they are
formed pretty much as icicles are."

"I see the resemblance," Zemlé allowed, "but how can
stone *drip*?"

"Stone has both a liquid and a solid essence," Stephen explained. "The solid essence is predominant, but under special conditions, beneath the earth, it can become liquid. It is possibly how these caverns were formed. The stone liquefied and flowed away, leaving only space behind it."

"Do you believe that?"

"I don't know," Stephen said. "At the moment, I'm a lot more interested in why we're being held captive."

"You're not captives," Adhrekh said again. "You are our honored guests."

"Wonderful," Stephen said. "Then thank you for the hospitality, and would you please take us back now?"

"You have traveled a great distance, through many hardships, pathikh," Adhrekh said. "How can we allow you to leave without achieving what you came for?"

"I did not come to find the bloody *woorm,*" Stephen snapped, loudly enough that his voice echoed through the cavern. "I could have met *him* back at d'Ef if I'd wanted."

"Yes," another voice said drily. "You could have. Might have saved us all a lot of trouble, at that." The voice was somehow familiar.

As Stephen followed the sound, they came to a stop, and his bearers carefully settled the palanquins onto the floor. The stone here looked handworked, and he smelled water.

His gaze fastened on a familiar face, and his heart went jagged in his chest.

"Fend," he said.

The Sefry smiled. "I'm flattered you remember me," he said. "Our last meeting was a hectic one, wasn't it? What with all the arrows and swords, greffyns and Briar Kings. There wasn't really much time for a proper introduction."

"You know him?" Zemlé asked.

"In a way," Stephen said flatly. "I know that he's a murdering villain, without honor, compassion, or any other admirable quality."

Fend's single eye widened. "How could *you* know that? Can you pretend to hear my thoughts? You wouldn't be relying entirely on Aspar's opinion of me, would you?"

"No," Stephen said. "I've Winna's opinion, as well. She was your prisoner, you may remember. And I saw with my own eyes what happened in the grove near Cal Azroth. And I saw the bodies of the princesses you murdered there."

Fend shrugged lightly. "I've done things that would seem regrettable, I agree. But I do not regret them because I understand why I did them. When you also understand, I believe you will think better of me.

"I hope so, because I am in your service." He nodded to Adhrekh. "Thank, you, sir, for your hospitality and your help in finding this place."

The other Sefry shrugged. "We are only its keepers," he replied.

Stephen had been so focused on Fend's evil face that he hadn't noticed at first what he was wearing. It was armor of an exceedingly baroque and antique sort, plate and chain chased in a metal that resembled brass. It was the breastplate that really drew Stephen's attention, depicting as it did a bearded human head adorned with horns. He'd seen a nearly identical engraving when he'd been at d'Ef, searching for clues to the nature of the Briar King. He'd thought at first that it was supposed to represent the king, who was usually depicted with horns. But the caption of the engraving had called it something quite different.

He realized with a chill that without really knowing it, he had taken several steps toward Fend. He stepped back quickly.

"Could you repeat that last bit?" Stephen asked. "About how you serve *me* now?"

"That's how it is," Fend said. "I've been trying to find you for months, to offer you my services."

"You've been following me to find this mountain," Stephen said. "Don't let him fool you, Adhrekh. He hasn't come here for any good purpose."

"Only *you* could find the mountain," Fend replied. "And it's probably true that if I had managed to catch up with you earlier, I would have had a difficult time at best convincing you to come here. But this is where you were supposed to be, just as I was fated to accompany you and now to serve you. It really won't be so confusing once you understand things."

He stepped forward, drawing a nasty-looking dagger from his belt. Stephen flinched, but Fend offered it to him hilt first, then knelt at his feet.

"It was better this way," he said. "I am here; I've found the secret mountain and the armor of my station. Now I offer you my life."

Stephen took the blade, wrapped in a miasma of absolute disbelief. Fend was evil; there was no doubt about that. What was he playing at here?

Aspar wouldn't hesitate, would he? He'd plunge the knife straight in and try to figure out what the Sefry was up to later. And he owed Aspar so much, owed him *at least* the death of this man . . .

But he wasn't Aspar, and even Aspar might not be able to strike down someone kneeling in front of him. Stephen liked to think even Aspar couldn't do that.

So he dropped the knife on the ground.

"Explain this to me," he said, gesturing first at Fend, then at the rest of the party. "Any of you. Tell me what is happening."

"You are Kauron's heir," Zemlé said.

Startled, he whirled on her. "Did you know, then? Were you part of this trap?"

Her eyes widened in hurt. "No. I mean, I didn't know the particulars. I knew that you were Kauron's heir. I don't know this man, Stephen. I've never met any of these people."

Studying the group more closely, Stephen noticed another figure, standing beyond Fend. To his surprise, he realized it was a human in the robes of a monk.

"You!" he shouted. "Who are you?"

The man stepped forward.

"My name is Brother Ashern," he said, bowing. "I am also at your service."

"Are you Hierovasi or Revesturi?"

"I am neither," he said. "I am pledged to the saint of the mountain. That appears to be you, Stephen Darige."

"You're all mad, aren't you?"

"No," Fend replied, "not mad. Determined, yes. And unfortunately, there isn't time enough for the sort of discussion that will clear things up entirely. Praifec Hespero and his men are nearly here. It would be a mistake to let them enter the mountain. Even on the slopes, Hespero might be able to draw on the power of the seven fanes. If he enters the mountain, even the woorm might not be able to stop him."

"Yet if Brother Stephen had time to walk the faneway—" Brother Ashern began, but Fend shook his head.

"That would take days. Hespero is approaching. I've seen him. Isn't that right, Stephen?"

"He's been following us," Stephen admitted. He looked sharply at Fend. "But you and he were allies."

"I once worked with him," Fend admitted. "It was necessary to reach this present point. But our interests no longer coincide. He wants what is yours by right. *You* wended the horn that woke the Briar King. *You* found this place."

"But I don't even know what this place is!"

"Don't you?" Fend asked. "Don't you know who your first predecessor was? The first of your kind to come here?"

"Choron?"

"Choron? No, he was merely returning something to its proper place. It was Virgenya Dare found this place, Stephen. This is where she walked the faneway. This is where she discovered the magicks that destroyed the Skasloi. Would you give that kind of power to Hespero?"

"No," Stephen said, his head whirling, "but I wouldn't give it to you, either."

"I'm not asking for it, you half-wit," Fend snarled. "I'm only asking you take it for yourself."

"Why?"

"Because it's the only *way*," Fend replied. "The only way to save our world."

"I still don't understand what you expect me to do."

"I am at your command," Fend replied. "The woorm is at

your command. These warriors are at your command. Simply *tell us* what to do."

"You expect me to believe all this?" Stephen snapped, his frustration reaching a boil. "I was brought here against my will. Now you claim you'll follow my orders? It doesn't make sense!"

"We had to bring you here," Adhrekh said. "I'm sorry we had to use coercion to get this far, but we cannot force you any farther. You are Choron's heir. If you want to leave, leave. But if you do, this other one will take your place."

"Are you saying you would obey Hespero?"

"It's the geos of this place," Fend said. "If you do not take up the scepter, someone else will. And when they do, we must follow them. You must decide."

"If I agree, and if I tell you to destroy Hespero and his forces?"

"We will try," Fend replied. "I think we will win. But as I said, his power waxes. Unlike you, he has dreamed of this place for decades."

Stephen glanced at Zemlé, then turned his gaze to Adhrekh.

"I want to be alone with Sister Pale for a moment," he said.

"Don't take too long," Fend warned. "A decision delayed may be a decision denied."

"There's something really wrong here," he told Zemlé once they were alone.

"It's certainly confusing," she admitted.

"Confusing? No, it's more than that. It's madness. Do you know who Fend *is*? The things he's done? Whatever else I know or don't know about this situation, I know Fend can't be trusted."

"That may be so, but if they're right about Hespero, maybe we should worry about the Sefry later."

"You mean I should do what they're asking? Order them to attack Hespero? I— No, this makes no sense. If Fend is eager for me to do something, that's an excellent sign that I shouldn't do it. Besides, Fend and Adhrekh seemed agreed on the matter of the praifec. Fend's been riding the woorm, so I assume he has some control over it. Adhrekh and his people have been acting pretty freely. So why do they need *me* to tell them to do what they already want to do?"

"They said something about a geos—"

"Yes," Stephen said, "I know. Yet it sounds *wrong.*"

"Maybe . . ." Zemlé began, then shook her head.

"What?" he said.

"You're already—"

"What?"

She let out a long breath.

"It's what you were saying, days ago. About how you keep getting off your path. You've been living for other people, Stephen. Even the way you talk about Aspar—you were his companion, never his equal. Could you—just consider this—could you possibly be *afraid* of the power you're being offered? Could it be you don't trust it because you *can't,* because if you're in command, you'll have no one to blame but yourself if things go wrong?"

"That's not fair," Stephen said.

"Maybe it isn't," Zemlé said. "I haven't known you that long. But I think, ah, I think I know some things about you. I think maybe I see some things about you far more clearly than you see them yourself."

She reached out and gripped his hands in hers.

"Think, Stephen. Even if Fend is lying, even if Virgenya Dare was never here, still, what secrets might this place hold? What might you learn? I can *feel* the power here, so I know you must, as well. This is what you came for, and all you have to do is submit to *leading.*"

He closed his eyes.

Zemlé was certainly right about the terror he felt at the idea of taking command. How could he send anyone to fight and die? And yet what if his other uncertainties were, as she said, merely his way of trying to justify inaction?

After all, Fend and Adhrekh weren't saying anything terribly different from what Fratrex Pell had said. Maybe it was true. Maybe he *was* the one who was supposed to do this.

He just hadn't ever believed it. He had supposed all along that he would find Virgenya Dare's journal and translate it, and if he found something of use, he would do what he had always done: take it to someone else, someone who would know how to use the information.

And yet, how had that worked out? Desmond Spendlove had used his translations to commit abominable acts. He had given Praifec Hespero the benefits of his research, yet more people had died horribly as a result. Now Hespero was coming to get *him*.

Maybe it really was time he stopped being the source of someone else's power. Maybe it was time he took charge.

Zemlé was right. When the threat posed by Hespero had passed, then he would have the leisure to come to a full understanding of his situation. Then he could consider how to deal with Fend.

He took Zemlé by the shoulders and kissed her. She stiffened, and at first he thought she would push him away, but then she loosened up, returning his gesture with enthusiasm.

"Thank you," he said.

He found the others waiting for him, more or less as he'd left them.

"If you're serious about this," Stephen said, "then let it be done. Stop Praifec Hespero—no matter what, don't let him enter the mountain. Take him captive if you can, but do what you must."

"Now, that's the way it's done," Fend said. He bowed. "As you command, pathikh, so it shall be accomplished."

Stephen felt his teeth clench, and he waited, fearing that he had unlocked some secret curse, walked straight into a trap. But nothing happened except that all the other Sefry bowed, too, which was certainly strange enough in its own way.

"Where is the woorm?" Stephen asked.

Fend smiled and made a long, low whistle, and behind him the waters parted. Two great green lamps rose above them all. A faint, appreciative murmur went up among the Sefry, who were clearly collectively insane.

Stephen stumbled back, trying to shield Zemlé with his body.

"Th-the poison!" he stammered.

"Has no effect, here," Adhrekh assured him. "The sedos power in the mountain creates it harmless. And we have proof against it once we are outside."

Stephen couldn't tear his gaze off the thing, but after a long moment he realized they were still waiting for him to say something.

"Fine," he said. "There's the woorm. Where are your warriors? How many do you have?"

"There are twelve," Adhrekh said.

That, finally, was enough to make Stephen look away from the monster to see if the fellow was joking.

"Twelve? But there are more than twelve of you here now."

"Yes. But most of the Aitivar are forbidden to fight. Twelve will have to be enough. And we have the khriim with us, as well as the khruvkhuryu."

"The what?" Stephen began, but he was too late. They were already in motion. Fend sang out again, and the great head dipped down so he and Ashern could mount. Adhrekh and eleven other warriors set off at a jog toward the far end of the cavern.

Suddenly Stephen was full of doubt again. Someone was plucking at his sleeve, and he turned to see who it was. It was a Sefry he hadn't noticed before, one so ancient that even in torchlight Stephen fancied he could see the bones through his skin.

"Pardon, pathikh," the man wisped, "but do you wish to watch? There is a higher vantage."

"Yes," Stephen said. "I think I'd like that a great deal."

He followed the Sefry, growing uneasier by the moment.

He felt like the man in the old story about the Damned Saint who was trapped in a bottle. The man got one wish, and then the saint would kill him. There were only two things he could not wish for: to be spared—or for the saint to die.

CHAPTER TEN

✝

THE SHIPS

"ANNE?"

She found Austra shaking her gently.

"I'm fine," Anne told her friend.

"What happened? You were talking to—it—and then you went still as a statue."

"Nothing," she lied. "I'll tell you later. For the moment, I need you all to stay here and stay still. I have to do something else and must not be disturbed."

"Very well, Anne."

"Anne?" Alis whispered weakly.

"Yes, Lady Berrye?"

"Do not trust him."

"Oh, I don't," Anne replied.

Then she settled on the floor, cross-legged. She closed her eyes and imagined she was at the Coven Saint Cer, in the womb of Mefitis. She focused on an invented middle distance and tried to picture a light there, slowing her breathing until it was deep and steady, until she could feel the slow pulse of the tide beneath Ynis and the deeper, secret motions of the earth.

Until she was calm and quiet.

As the light flickered into being, she had a moment when she felt as if she were spreading out, as if the stone and water of Ynis and Newland were becoming her flesh and blood. The Kept ached like a pustule, as did the thing in Eslen-of-Shadows, but that rushed suddenly away as the darkness shattered and she found herself in a forest clearing. Although the sun stood at noon in a brilliant clear sky, she cast no shadow, and she knew that this time she had finally come to the right place.

"Faiths!" she called.

For a moment she thought they might not appear, but then they stepped into the clearing: four women, masked and gowned as if for a costume ball, as similar and as dissimilar as sisters.

The first, on Anne's right, wore a dress of deepest green and a sneering golden mask. Her hair fell in amber braids almost to her feet. Next to her stood a brunette in a mask of bone and a rust-red dress. The third Faith was as pale as the moon, with silver locks. Her gown and disguise were black. The final woman wore a white mask and a white dress, and her hair was darker than coal.

"You've all changed," Anne noticed.

"As have the seasons, the winds, and you, my dear," the first Faith said.

"Where have you been?" Anne asked. "I've tried to find you before."

"This sort of visiting has become more difficult," the bone-masked Faith said. "The thrones are appearing."

"Yes, the thrones," Anne said. "One of you once told me that you couldn't see the future. You said that you were like chirgeons, that you could feel the sickness of the world and sense what was needed to make it well."

"That's true," the black-gowned Faith replied.

"Very well," Anne said. "What do you feel now? I'm asking for your advice."

"This is a dangerous time for us to give you advice," the green-gowned woman replied, spreading her hands. Her sleeves fell back, and Anne noticed something she hadn't seen in any of her earlier encounters with the Faiths.

"What is that?" she asked.

The woman dropped her hands, but Anne stepped forward.

"It's all right," the white-clad sister said. "She had to know sometime."

Anne caught at the Faith's hand and felt an odd tingle of contact, as if she held something very slippery. But the arm came up obediently so she could see the mark tattooed there: a black crescent moon.

"I was attacked by a man wearing this mark," she said. "A follower of yours, perhaps?"

The Faith turned to her sister. "You explain," she said, "if you're so certain she should know."

A wry smile appeared below the black mask.

"Anne, I don't think you appreciate how important it is for you to take the throne: the literal throne of Eslen and the eldritch one that is beginning to appear. We have tried to explain to you, but at every turn you have jeopardized yourself by giving in to selfish desires."

"I wanted to save my friends from certain death. How is that selfish?"

"You know how, yet you refuse to admit it. Your friends do not *matter,* Anne. The fate of the world does not rest with them. After everything you've experienced, Anne, you are still spoiled, still the girl who fought to keep her saddle in a place where she had no use for it simply because it was *hers.* A little girl who will not share her toys, much less give them up.

"You almost ruined everything at Dunmrogh. For right or wrong, we decided you should be parted from your friends so you could see things more clearly. Yes, we have followers—"

"And bloody wonderful ones, too," Anne snapped. "One of them tried to rape me."

"Not one of ours," the honey-haired faith said. Her voice, too, was honeyed. "Someone our servants hired without knowing enough about him. In any event—"

"In any event, you proved to me that I can't trust you. I never really believed I could, but now I know for certain. You have my thanks for that."

"Anne—"

"Yet I'll give you one more chance. Do you understand my predicament? Can you see that much?"

"Yes," the palest Faith answered.

"Well, then, if you're so interested in my being queen, can you show me a way out of this that doesn't involve freeing the Kept?"

"You can't free him, Anne."

"Really? And why is that, pray the saints?"

"It would be very bad."

"That's not an explanation."

"He is a *Skaslos,* Anne."

"Yes, and he's promised to mend the law of death and die. Is there something wrong with that?"

"Yes."

"Then what is it?"

But they didn't answer.

"Very well," Anne said. "If you won't help me, I'll do what I must."

The golden-haired Faith stepped forward.

"Wait. The woman Alis. The two of you can escape."

"Indeed? How?"

"She has walked the faneway of Spetura. If you augment her power with your own, you can pass through your enemies unseen."

"That's the best you can do? What about my friends?"

The women glanced at one another.

"Right," Anne said. "They don't matter." She turned away.

"Farewell," she said.

"Anne—"

"Farewell!"

With that, the glade shattered like colored glass, and the darkness returned.

"Well," the Kept said. "You've compared the wares. Are you ready to deal?"

"Can you lift the glamour on the passage? The one that makes them unknowable to men?"

"Once I'm free, yes. But only once I'm free."

"Swear it."

"I swear it."

"Swear that once free, you will do as you've promised: mend the law of death and then die."

"I swear it by all that I am, by all that I ever was."

"Then place your neck at my feet."

There was a long pause, and then something heavy struck the floor near her. She raised her right foot and brought it down on something large, cold, and rough.

"Anne, what are you doing?" Alis asked in the blackness. She sounded frantic.

"Qexqaneh," Anne said, lifting her voice. "I free you!"

"No!" Alis shrieked.

But of course, by then it was too late.

Their mounted foes were all dead, and now the remaining defenders of the outer waerd were swarming to protect the gap opened by Artwair's ballistae. The hole was almost near enough for Neil to touch when something struck his shoulder from above so hard that it drove him to his knees.

Neil looked up dully at a man standing over him, lifting his sword to deliver the deathblow. Neil cut clumsily at the fellow's knees. His weapon was too blunted from slaughter to slice through the metal joint, but the bones within snapped from the impact just as the strike from above glanced hard from Neil's helm.

Head ringing, he rose grimly to his feet, put the tip of Battlehound on the man's throat, and leaned.

He had no idea how long they had been fighting, but the early culling had been done. He and the eight men he had left standing were pitted against perhaps twenty warriors with sword and shield and perhaps another five defenders on the wall who had the proper angle to shoot at them. Reinforcements trying to reach them across the causeway were still being ground up by concentrated missile fire from the waerd's engines.

He dropped down among the bodies and held his shield

over his head, trying to catch his breath. The defenders were being smart and conservative, staying in the gap rather than rushing out of it.

Neil glanced around at his men. Most were doing as he was, trying for a rest despite the rain of death from above.

He reached to feel his shoulder, found an arrow jutting there, and broke it off. That sent a sharp, almost sweet jag of pain through his battle-numbed body.

He glanced at the young knight Sir Edhmon, who crouched only a kingsyard away. The lad was bloody head to toe, but he still had two arms and two legs. He didn't look frightened anymore. In fact, he didn't look much of anything except tired.

But when he glanced at Neil, he tried to grin. Then his expression changed, and his eyes focused elsewhere.

For a moment Neil feared a wound had caught up with him, for those who died often saw the Tier de Sem as they left the world.

But Edhmon wasn't looking beyond the mortal sky; he was staring over Neil's shoulder, off to sea.

Neil followed his gaze as a fresh rain of arrows fell. He was greeted by a wondrous sight.

Sails, hundreds of them. And though the distance was great, it was not too great to see the swan banner of Liery flying on the leading wave steeds.

Neil closed his eyes and lowered his head, praying to Saint Lier to give him the strength he needed. Then he lifted his eyes and felt a sort of thunder enter his voice.

"All right, lads," he cried, swearing he heard not his own voice but his father's exhorting the clan to battle at Hrungrete. "There's Sir Fail and the fleet that'll put the usurper to his heels if we do our jobs. If we don't, those proud ships will be shattered, and their crews will go down to the draugs, because I know Fail well enough to tell you he'll try to get through, no matter the odds, whether Thornrath is in Bloody Robert's hands or no.

"It's not far we've got to go. We're eight against twenty. That's hardly more than two apiece. Saint Neuden loves odds like that. We're all going to die lads, today or some other. The only question is, will you die with your sword rusting in a sheath or swinging in your hand?"

With that he rose, bellowing the raven war cry of the MeqVrens, and the other seven leapt up with him, some shouting, some praying aloud to the battle saints. Sir Edhmon was silent, but his face held a grim joy that Neil recognized as his own.

They marshaled shoulder to shoulder and charged up the slope.

There was no great shock of contact this time; the shields bumped together, and the defenders pushed back, cutting over their rims. Neil waited for the blow, and when it hit the edge of his battle board, he hooked his sword arm up and over the weapon. Edhmon saw that and cut the arm Neil held thus trapped, half severing it.

"Hold the line steady!" Neil shouted. The warrior in him wanted to surge over the fallen man, deeper into the defenders, but with numbers against them, that would be foolish. Their line was their only defense.

One of the largest men Neil had ever seen pushed into the enemy force from behind. He was a head and a half taller than the rest of them, with a wild yellow mane and tattoos that marked him as a Weihand. He carried a sword longer than some men were tall, wielding it with both hands.

As Neil watched helplessly, the giant reached over his own men, grabbed Sir Call by the plume of his helmet, and yanked him through the shield wall, where the Weihand's comrades hacked him to pieces.

With a roar of impotent rage, Neil slammed his shield into the man in front of him and beat at his head once, twice, thrice. The third time the shield dropped, and Battlehound slammed into his helm so hard that blood sprayed from his nose.

He pointed his sword at the giant and raised his voice above the din.

"*Weihander! Thein athei was goth at mein piken!*" he roared.

The result was remarkable: The giant's face, already red, went perfectly livid. He charged toward Neil, disrupting the shield line he was supposed to be defending.

"What did you say?" Sir Edhmon shouted, panting heavily.

"I'll tell you when you're old enough," Neil shot back. "But saints forgive me for insulting a woman I've never met."

Before the Weihander could reach him, a new man filled the line in front of him and let his shield drop a little, perhaps as a ruse. Neil jerked his own shield up and then quickly chopped back down so that the pointed bottom of the board caught on the top of his foe's guard and brought him down on one knee. Neil then clubbed the back of his head with Battlehound's hilt.

Howling, the warrior charged into him, and they both went sliding down the rocky slope made by the fall of the waerd wall. Neil hit him again but couldn't get the leverage he needed for a lethal blow; his arms and legs felt as if they'd been poured of lead.

He dropped his sword and felt for the dagger at his waist. He found it but discovered his foe had had the same idea a moment earlier as he felt the point of a dirk scrabble against his breastplate. Cursing, he fought his weapon free, but the moment had been enough; his breath went cold as steel slid through the joint on his side and between his ribs.

Choking back his scream, Neil plunged his knife under the back lip of the man's helmet and into the base of his skull. His foe made a sound like a short laugh, jerked, then stopped moving.

Grunting, Neil pushed the limp corpse off him and tried to stand, but he hadn't managed that when the giant reached him. He got his shield up in time to catch a blow from the fellow's huge sword. It struck like thunder, and something in the shield cracked.

The giant cocked his weapon for another try, and Neil straightened and struck him under the chin with what remained of his shield. The Weihand stumbled back and fell.

Unfortunately, so did Neil.

Gasping, he threw off the board and retrieved Battle-hound. A few kingsyards away, the Weihand rose to meet him.

Neil glanced back at the gap and saw Edhmon and four others still standing; the waerd defenders seemed to have all fallen. Sir Edhmon was starting down the slope toward the giant.

"No!" Neil shouted. "Stay together; find the siege engines. They'll be lightly guarded. Stay together; make sure you get at least one of them! Then move on."

The Weihand glanced at Edhmon and the others, then grinned fiercely at Neil.

"What's your name?" he asked the giant.

His enemy paused. "Slautwulf Thvairheison."

"Slautwulf, I apologize twice. Once for what I said about your mother, the second for killing you."

"Just the first will do," Slautwulf said, hefting his sword. "Silly bugger. You can hardly lift your weapon."

Neil pressed his left hand over the hole in his side, but he knew there wasn't any point; he couldn't stop the blood.

Slautwulf charged then, his greatsword arcing out to cut Neil in half. Neil intended to outdistance the blow by a hairs-breadth, then rush in during the backswing, but he stumbled in the retreat, almost losing his footing entirely. The stroke missed by a decent margin, though, and the Weihand came again.

This time Neil narrowly avoided the stroke, then charged in as he'd planned. Slautwulf, however, anticipated that. Rather than trying to swing the blade again when he didn't have time, he brought the hilt down on Neil's helm. Neil let his legs go and collapsed, bending with the blow as much as he could, tumbling forward and thrusting Battlehound up-ward with all his might. He lay on his back with Slautwulf's surprised face peering down at him.

"I only have to lift it once," Neil pointed out.

"Jah," Slautwulf managed, spitting blood as the greatsword dropped from his hands. The warrior hadn't any armor beneath his battle skirt or undergarments, for that matter. Battlehound had pierced straight up through his groin, pelvis, intestines, and lungs.

Neil managed to roll away before the giant toppled. They lay there for a moment, staring at each other.

"Never worry," Neil rasped in the Weihand's tongue. "Saint Vothen loves you. I see his valkirja coming for you already."

Slautwulf tried to nod. "I'll see you in Valrohsn, then."

"Not just yet," Neil said. He put his fist into the ground and began to push himself up.

But an arrow knocked him back down, and all the wind out of him.

I'll just lie here a moment, he thought, *gather up my strength.* He closed his eyes, listening to his ragged breath.

The ships, he remembered, and he wanted to see them again.

His eyes felt as if they had been sewn shut, but after what seemed like an unimaginable effort, he managed to open them, only to find himself still facing Slautwulf. Sucking a deep, painful breath, he managed to turn his head to face the sea.

Another arrow thumped into his breastplate.

Right, he thought. *Stupid. Now they know you're still alive.*

But he didn't have to move anymore. He could see the ships, the Lierish ships. Had he saved them? If Edhmon and the others managed to take down even one of the siege engines, Artwair could risk another charge, and enough would get through to take the waerd. With the elevation of the waerd to provide cover, they could take down the Thornrath gate in a day. They didn't even have to occupy the whole wall, just enough of it to allow ships to enter through one of the great arches.

If . . .

His vision blurred until the sails and sea began to melt together. He tried to blink it away, but that only smudged things more. Gradually his vision focused once more, but instead of the sea he now saw a face, high-cheekboned, strong, pale as milk, with eyes so blue that they seemed blind. At first he thought it was the valkirja he'd lied to Slautwulf about seeing.

But then he knew who it was.

"Swanmway," he murmured.

Brinna, she seemed to say. *Remember? My real name is Brinna.*

He remembered kissing her.

He knew he ought to be thinking about Fastia, but as the light faded, it was only Brinna's face he could hold in his mind.

CHAPTER ELEVEN

FREE

STEPHEN SHIVERED as he stepped onto the ledge. His vision plummeted through empty space for what seemed the better part of a league before it reached trees and stone. It couldn't *really* be that far, because he could make out the figures of the praifec and his men approaching a sort of cul-de-sac in the mountain.

Still, he gripped Zemlé's hand more tightly.

"I think I'll be sick if I stay out here," he said.

"You've stone beneath your feet," she answered. "Just remember that. You won't fall."

"If a strong wind comes—"

"Not very likely," she assured him.

"Look there," said Ione, the ancient Sefry who had led them to this high aerie. He pointed, flinching as his hand came in contact with the light. Fend and his warriors wouldn't have any such worry; the westering sun had already filled the valley below with shadow.

Stephen leaned a little farther and saw what the old man was pointing at: a pool of deep blue water. And as if on cue, the woorm—khriim?—suddenly erupted from it.

"Saints," Stephen prayed, "let me have done the right thing."

Aspar froze for an instant, then grabbed for the pack on his back, cursing his luck. Naturally he would have his best shot at the thing when his bow was unstrung.

He fumbled out the watertight bag and pried at its fastening, but the wax made it tough to get the knot open, especially when he found himself glancing up at the woorm every few heartbeats. It grasped at the trees with its short forelimbs, dragging its tail from the pool, rearing almost as high as Aspar sat. A perfect target . . .

He heard the whir of an arrow and knew suddenly that the woorm wasn't the only easy target. He heard it skip off the stone behind him. That meant the only place it could have come from was . . .

There.

Fend and his companion were in the monster's saddle, and the companion was taking aim at Aspar again. Cursing, he levered himself up just as a red-fletched missile struck his boot. He didn't feel any pain, but the impact and his reaction sent him tumbling toward the edge. He threw his arms out to catch himself . . .

. . . and watched his bow, the string, and the black arrow fall toward the forest floor.

"Ah, sceat," he snarled.

He spent exactly one heartbeat deciding what to do next. Then he leapt for the nearest treetop, some five kingsyards below him.

The presence of the Kept seemed to uncoil all about her, stretching vaster with each instant, and her bones hummed as if a saw were cutting through them.

Free.

The word struck her as if the Kept had somehow cast it into a lead ingot and hurled it at her. Her breath voided her lungs in a single painful gasp, and her heart felt as if it were liquid with terror. Confidence, command, certainty—all were swept aside, and she was a mouse in an open field, watching the hawk descend.

Free.

There was no joy in the word. No elation, no relief. It was the most vicious sound Anne had ever heard. Tears exploded from her eyes, and she trembled uncontrollably. She had doomed them all, ruined everything . . .

Freeeee.

Something cracked like thunder, so loud that her shriek was lost in it.

And then . . . nothing.

He was gone.

It took what seemed a very long time to regain control of herself and her emotions. She heard the others weeping and knew she wasn't alone, but that did nothing to ease the humiliation.

Finally, after an age, Austra had the presence of mind to relight the lamp.

Their eyes confirmed that the chamber was empty. It was much larger than she had imagined.

"What have you done?" Alis asked weakly. "Dear saints, what have you done?"

"W-what I thought was best," Anne managed. "I had to do something."

"I don't understand any of this," Cazio said.

Anne started to try to explain, but her breath caught, and she suddenly felt like crying again.

"Wait," she said. "Wait a moment, and I'll try—"

Something suddenly hammered on the other side of the secret door.

"We're found!" Austra gasped.

Cazio came to his feet and drew his weapon. He looked shaky, but it gave Anne heart. Screwing up her resolve, she determined to be strong.

"The Kept promised to kill Robert's men," she said.

"I'm thinking he lied to you about that," Alis replied.

"We'll see," Anne replied.

"Someone give me a weapon," Prince Cheiso said weakly but with determination. "I need a weapon."

Cazio caught Anne's eye, and she nodded. He proffered the Safnian a dagger. He glanced at the other three men, remembering vaguely there once had been four of them. What had happened to the fourth?

But after the soul bending he'd just experienced, nothing would surprise him.

"What are your names?" he asked the warriors.

"Sir Ansgar," one of them said. Cazio could just make out a small beard. "These are my bondsmen, Preston Viccars and Cuelm MeqVorst."

"The passage is narrow," Cazio said. "We'll take turns. I'm first; work out the rest of the order among you."

"I pledged an oath to Sir Leafton that I would face her foes first," Ansgar replied. "I hope you will allow me to honor that oath."

Cazio started to object, but Ansgar, after all, was wearing armor. He was probably more suited, so to speak, to the situation.

"I yield the priority," he said. "But please do not kill them all. Leave some for me."

The man nodded, and Cazio stepped back, hoping his head would clear a bit more. At least their foe hadn't made it through a few moments earlier, when they were all still weak. Maybe Robert's men had been affected, as well.

He'd have to ask Anne exactly what had happened once this was over.

"Maybe they *won't* make it through—" Austra began, but suddenly a wand of flickering light appeared in the stone, carving through it. An instant later, not only was the hidden doorway gone, so was a large lump of the passage.

"Saints," Anne breathed. "He's got a feysword."

And indeed, Robert Dare stepped through the gap. Sir

Ansgar started forward but paused when the usurper held up his hand.

"Wait a moment," he said.

"Majesty?" Ansgar asked, glancing at Anne.

"Do as he says," Anne said. "What do you want, Robert?"

Robert was shaking his head.

"Amazing. He's gone, isn't he? You let him go."

"I did."

"Why? What could he possibly have promised you? But I can guess, can't I? He told you he would help you defeat me. And yet here I stand, unvanquished."

"We haven't begun fighting yet," Cazio said.

"Did someone ask you to speak?" Robert snapped. "I've no idea who you are, but I'm certain neither Her Majesty nor I gave you leave to speak. Stab me if you wish, but please don't sully my language with that ridiculous accent."

"Cazio has my leave to speak," Anne snapped, "and you do not, unless it is to beg forgiveness for your treachery."

"*My* treachery? Dear Anne, you've just loosed the last Skasloi upon the world. Do you know how long he's been planning this? He was the one who taught your mother to curse me, who made me what I have become and broke the law of death. You have fallen into his design and betrayed our entire race. Your treachery outshines mine as the sun does, ah, some small star."

"You left me no choice," Anne replied.

"Oh, well, if that's the case— No, *wait,* you had at least two other choices. You might have told him no and surrendered to me. Or you might have fought me and died."

"Or we could fight you and live," Cazio said.

"*You* are becoming annoying," Robert said, poking the shining blade toward him. "Surrender, Anne, and all of you will live, I promise you."

Cazio would never know what Anne might have said to that, because Cheiso suddenly rushed forward, howling in anguish, and launched himself at Robert.

The usurper raised his eldritch weapon, but not quickly enough. Cheiso plunged his borrowed dagger into the prince's chest. Robert promptly thumped him on the head with the hilt of his weapon, but the momentary truce had ended, and the flood had come.

Robert's men surged into the chamber. Cazio leapt toward the prince, but Ansgar was already there, swinging a blow that might have decapitated Robert had he not ducked it, then thrust his feysword into Ansgar's belly. The weapon went through him as if he were butter, and Robert carved up and out his shoulder, splitting the knight's upper body into two pieces.

"Now you," Robert said, turning toward Cazio.

But it wasn't the first time Cazio had faced a man who couldn't die or, for that matter, a sword he couldn't parry. As Robert cocked for the cut, he lunged long and stop-hit the prince in the wrist. Robert snarled and slashed at Acredo's blade, but Cazio disengaged and stabbed him in the wrist a second time. Then, avoiding the next, even wilder blow, Cazio made a draw-cut to the top of Robert's hand.

"Not much of a swordsman, are you?" he said, grinning, bouncing on the balls of his feet. "Even with a sword like that."

Robert rushed him then, but again Cazio avoided the beat at his blade and sidestepped the charge as one might a bull, leaving his blade in a high line for Robert to run into. The usurper did, the blade taking him in the forehead so that his skull stopped and his feet went flying out from under him. Cazio had the great pleasure of seeing the bastard land flat on his back.

"Zo dessrator, nip zo chiado," he pointed out.

He had to say it quickly, however, for Robert's men—and women—were swarming all around. He placed himself as best he could in front of Anne, engaging two, then three, and finally and impossibly four. He saw Preston and Cuelm fall, and then it was just he, standing between the three women and the mob.

Worse, he saw Robert in the background, dabbing a cloth at his pierced head.

"Kill them all," he heard Robert shout. "I've lost all patience with this business."

* * *

Aspar threw his arms around the trunk of the fir and gritted his teeth as his body stripped the topmost branches. The scent of resin exploded in his nostrils as the treetop bent earthward under his weight, and for a moment he felt like the jungen who once had ridden saplings to the ground for fun.

This one wasn't going all the way to the ground, though, so he let go before it could snap him back up. That left him falling another five kingsyards into shallow water that was still draining off from the woorm's eruption.

He was lucky. The water didn't hide a boulder or a stump, but it still felt as if a palm the size of a boy had slapped him with all its might.

The pain galvanized him rather than slowing him down, and he managed to slosh to his feet and take stock of the situation.

Aspar couldn't see the woorm just now, but he could hear it crashing through the forest. He spun and ran toward the base of the cliff, hoping against hope that he would find his bow and the precious arrow. But though the water was receding, it left in its wake a jumbled mess of sticks, leaves, and needles. It could take him a bell—or ten—to find his gear.

He still didn't see the woorm, but he drew his dirk and, reaching for his ax, encountered the horn where he'd tucked it in his belt. He plucked it out, staring at it for a moment.

Why not? He didn't have much to lose at this point.

He raised the horn to his lips, took the deepest breath he could manage, and blew a shrill high note that he remembered very well from a day not long gone. Even after he ran out of breath, the peal hung in the air, reluctant to fade.

But fade it did, and the woorm was still coming.

He'd reached the cliff now, and fortune favored him a bit; his bowstave was caught in the lowest branches of an everic. But he didn't see the arrow anyplace, and the woorm—

—was suddenly turning away from him, moving out of the canyon.

But *something* was still coming, something man-sized and moving far too quickly for a man.

"Sceat," he groaned. "Not a another one of these bloody—"

But then the monk was on him, his sword a barely visible gleam in the dusk.

Stephen stiffened as the high clear note of a horn sounded in the evening air.

Zemlé noticed. "What is it?"

"I recognize that horn," he said. "That's the Briar King's horn. The one I blew, the one that summoned him."

"What does it mean?"

"I don't know," Stephen replied absently.

Below, the khriim had been doing unusual things. Instead of moving straight toward the praifec and his men, it had gone off through the trees, in the direction of the cliffside. Just after the horn blew, however, it resumed its course, moving toward the approaching war band.

Stephen felt a tingle as a line of eight horsemen formed and charged the creature. He wondered if they stood a chance. A knight, a horse, armor, and barding at a dead gallop all concentrated on the steel tip of a lance was a formidable force.

He saw the Sefry warriors now, as well: twelve small figures approaching the praifec's men at a trot. He caught an actinic glitter and realized that they had feyswords, like the knight he and his companions had fought in Dunmrogh.

The riders broke against the khriim like waves against a rock, except that a broken wave flowed back out to sea. The horsemen and their horses lay where they fell.

So much for that.

Stephen felt something move across his skin, and all the hairs on his arm stood up. He wasn't cold, but he shivered.

"The horn . . ." he murmured.

"What's that?" Zemlé gasped. She pointed, and Stephen saw a dark cloud approaching, or so it appeared to be at first glance.

But it wasn't a cloud; rather, it was a collection of thousands of smaller things, flying close together.

"Birds," he said.

They were of all sorts—corbies, martins, swans, hawks, curlews—and all were crying or singing, making whatever noise they made and raising the strangest cacophony Stephen had ever heard. When they reached the valley, they began spiraling down into the forest, forming an avian tornado.

The forest itself was behaving in an equally peculiar manner. An acre of it was moving; the trees were bending toward one another, knitting their limbs together. Stephen was reminded of the effect of the dreodh song on the tree they'd fled the slinders into, but if it was the same magic, it was far stronger.

"Saints," Zemlé breathed.

"I don't think the saints have much to do with this," Stephen murmured as he watched the birds descend into the quickening forest and vanish as if swallowed.

A shape was forming now, a shape Stephen recognized, albeit larger than he had ever seen it before, maybe thirty kingsyards high.

Moments later, antlers spreading from his head, the Briar King tore his roots from the earth and began to stride purposefully toward the khriim.

Aspar waited until the last second and hurled his ax. The monk tried to turn, but that was the thing about moving fast: it made it harder to change direction. His attempt only spoiled the cut meant to take Aspar's head off. It soughed over the holter's head instead as the attacker hurled past.

Aspar turned to find the fellow already coming back, but he was delighted to see that his ax had found its mark and savaged the man's weapon arm, the right one. The sword lay discarded on the waterlogged moss, and blood was pumping from his biceps.

He was a little slower, but not much. His left fist arced out in a blur; Aspar felt as if he were moving underwater as the knuckles connected with his chin. He smelled blood, and his head rang like a bell as he stumbled back.

The next blow dug into his flank and broke ribs.

With an inarticulate cry, Aspar threw his left arm around the man, stabbing at the monk's kidney with his dirk, but the blade never made contact. Instead the fellow twisted oddly, and Aspar found himself somehow hurled into a tree.

His vision flashed black and red, but he knew he couldn't stop moving, so he rolled to the side and tried to get to his feet, spitting out fragments of his teeth. He grabbed a sapling and used it to pull himself up.

It was only when he tried to put weight on his leg that he realized it was broken.

"Well, sceat," he said.

The man retrieved his sword and was returning with it gripped in his left hand.

"My name is Ashern," he said. "Brother Ashern. I'd like you to know there's nothing personal in this. You fought well."

Aspar lifted his dirk and shouted, hoping it would drown out the approaching hoofbeats, but Ashern heard them in the last instant and turned. Aspar launched himself, and everything went red.

Ogre reared from a full gallop, his hooves striking down at the monk. Brother Ashern's swing cut right through the lower part of the great beast's neck, and the churchman continued turning, deftly blocking Aspar's desperate knife thrust.

Then Ogre's hoof, still descending, hit him in the back of the head and crushed his skull.

Aspar fell, and Ogre collapsed just next to him, blood pumping from his neck in great gouts. Gasping, Aspar crawled over, thinking he might somehow close the bay's wound, but when he saw it, he knew it was no use. Instead he cradled the stallion's head in one arm and stroked his muzzle. Ogre seemed more puzzled than anything.

"Old boy." Aspar sighed. "You never could stay out of a fight, could you?"

Red foam blew from Ogre's nose as if he were trying to whinny an answer.

"Thank you, old friend," Aspar said. "You rest now, yah? Just rest."

He continued stroking Ogre until his breath stopped and his terrible eyes went dull.

And for a while after.

When Aspar finally lifted his head again, he saw, four kingsyards away, the case of the black arrow.

Nodding grimly to himself, he strung his bow and crawled until he found a branch the right size and shape to use as a crutch. His leg was pulsing with awful pain now, but he ignored it as best he could. He retrieved the arrow and began hobbling toward the sounds of combat.

CHAPTER TWELVE

ENTIRELY SWORD

CAZIO LUNGED deep, driving Acredo through a swordsman's eye. A blade cut at him from the right, but with his rapier busy killing, the only thing he had to deflect it with was his left arm. He got lucky and caught the flat, but the pain was terrific.

Withdrawing Acredo's bloody tip, he parried another blow, retreating all the while, wondering how much farther back the chamber went. Robert's men were taking advantage of the space to spread out, forcing Cazio to retreat more quickly or be surrounded. He reckoned he would kill one, maybe two more of them before one of their cleavers cut off enough of him to end the fight. After that, he wasn't sure what he was going to do.

No. He couldn't let them have Austra or Anne. He couldn't think that way.

He deepened and slowed his breathing, willed the muscles he wasn't using to relax.

Z'Acatto had spoken once or twice of something called *chiado sivo*, or "entirely sword," a state of oneness that a true dessrator could enter in which he might accomplish fantastic things. There had been times when Cazio had felt he was *almost* in that state. He had to let go of winning and losing, of life and death, of fear, and become nothing but motion.

Parry, attack, parry, disengage, breathe, feel the sword as part of his arm, his spine, his heart, his mind . . .

They can't hurt me, he thought. *There's nothing here to hurt, just a sword.*

And for a long, beautiful moment he had it. Perfection. Every move correct, every motion the best. Two more men went down, then another two, and he wasn't retreating anymore. He controlled the rhythm, the footwork, the floor itself.

For a moment. But recognizing that moment, he lost the detachment he needed to prolong it, and his assault faltered as two men arrived to replace every one he put down. He retreated again, ever more desperate as Robert's forces began to encircle him.

He realized he'd lost track of the women and hoped against hope that his instant of *chiado sivo* had given them a chance to escape.

Even you might have been proud of me, z'Acatto, he thought as the corner of his eye warned him of a new fighter, flanking him.

No, not flanking him, flanking Robert's men.

And not just one man but a *horde*.

The newcomers were unarmored but fighting with long, wicked knives and firing short, powerful-looking bows. Cazio's antagonists were all down within a few heartbeats, leaving him gasping, still on guard, wondering if he would be next. Just because they were Robert's enemies, that didn't make them Anne's friends.

But those who were closest merely smiled at him, nodded,

and finished their butchery. He reckoned there were at least fifty of them.

He also realized belatedly that they weren't human but Sefry.

The folk of Gobelin Court had finally weighed in on a side, it seemed.

Aspar paused, gaping, wondering how long it had been since anyone had witnessed anything remotely like what he was seeing. He'd thought he was numb, but now he understood he wasn't so much numb as insane.

He could see them because they had flattened the forest for half a league in every direction. The Briar King was a hulking mass roughly sembling human shape, albeit with the antlers of a buck, but all and all he was less human in appearance than he had been before.

The apparition was locked in combat with the woorm, which coiled about him like a blacksnake around a mouse. The king, in turn, had both titanic hands gripped about the monster's neck.

As Aspar watched, a stream of green venom spewed from the great serpent's mouth, not just vapor but a viscous liquor that spattered upon the forest lord and began to smoke, burning great holes in him. The stuff of the king shifted to fill those gaps.

He didn't see Fend. The saddle was empty, and a quick scan of the forest showed nothing, though a little farther off a battle was raging between the praifec's men and some other force. He couldn't make out much of that.

A rush of pain and fever from his leg reminded Aspar that he might lose consciousness at any time. If he had anything to do here, he'd better do it now.

And he certainly had something to do. He wasn't going to think about it anymore; there was no riddle here.

He knew which side he was on.

He carefully opened the case and brought forth the black arrow. Its head glittered like the heart of a lightning stroke.

The praifec had said the arrow could be used seven times.

It had been used five times already when Aspar had received it. He'd shot it once to kill an utin and save Winna's life.

That left one.

He set the shaft to his string and sighted, feeling the wind, watching the curl of vapors around the combatants, willing his shaking muscles to quell so his mind could tell them what to do.

One deep breath, two, three, and then he felt the shot and released the string. He watched the flash of light grow tiny and vanish at the base of the woorm's skull.

Aspar caught himself holding his breath.

He didn't have long to wait. The woorm shrilled an awful stone-shattering scream, and its body twisted as it arched back, vomiting venom. The Briar King grabbed it by the tail and unwound it and hurled it into the forest. Part of the king's arm tore loose and went with the monster, and he staggered as great chunks of his body sloughed away. He gripped a tree to steady himself but continued to melt.

"Grim," Aspar muttered, and closed his eyes. He sank down next to the spruce he'd used for support, watching the great coils of the woorm heave up into sight and subside behind the trees. With each heartbeat the sounds of its thrashing diminished.

He couldn't see the Briar King anymore at all.

Exhaustion flooded through him, and relief. That, at least, was done.

He knew he ought to try to set the bone in his leg, but he'd have to rest first. He drew out his water flask and had a drink. His food was back with Ogre's tack, but he didn't have much of an appetite, anyway. Still, he probably needed to eat . . .

His head snapped up, and he realized he'd dozed off.

The Briar King was watching him.

He was only about twice the size of a man now, and his face was almost human, albeit covered in light brown fur. His leaf-green eyes were alert, and Aspar thought he saw the faintest of smiles on the forest lord's lips.

"I guess I did the right thing, yah?" Aspar said.

He had never heard the Briar King speak, and he didn't now. But the creature stepped closer, and suddenly Aspar felt bathed in life. He smelled oak, apple blossoms, the salt of the sea, the musk of a rutting elk. He felt larger, as if the land were his skin and the trees were the hairs upon it, and it filled him with a joy he had never quite known, except perhaps when he was young, running through the forest naked, climbing oaks for the sheer love of them.

"I never knew—" he began.

And with the suddenness of a bone snapping, it all ended. The bliss went out of him like blood from a severed vein as the Briar King's eyes grew wide and his mouth opened in a soundless scream.

There, on his breast, something glittered like the heart of a lightning bolt . . .

The king locked eyes with him, and Aspar felt something prickle through his body. Then the form that stood before him simply fell apart, collapsing into a pile of leaves and dead birds.

Aspar's chest heaved as he tried to draw a breath, but the scent of autumn choked him, and he clapped his hands to his ears, trying to shut out the deep keening that shuddered through the earth and trees as with a single voice the wild things of the world understood that their sovereign was gone.

Like lightning flashing before him, he saw forests crumbling into dust, great grassy plains putrefying, leagues of bones bleaching beneath a demon sun.

"No," he gasped, finally managing to breathe.

"Oh, I think yes," a familiar voice countered.

A few kingsyards behind where the Briar King had stood was Fend, with a bow in one hand and an evil grin on his lips. He was dressed in weird armor, but the helm was off. His mouth was smeared with dark blood, and he had a light in his eyes that was crazy even for him.

Aspar fumbled for his dirk; he didn't have his ax or any more arrows.

"Well," Fend said, "that's that. You killed my woorm, but

that's not all bad. You know what happens when you drink the fresh blood of a woorm?"

"Why don't you tell me, you piece of sceat."

"Come, Aspar," Fend said. "Don't be so angry. I'm grateful to you. I was *supposed* to drink the blood, you know. The problem was how to get to it once the beast had served its purpose. And you solved that problem rather neatly. Even better, you gave me the one thing I needed to slay His Majesty Stickerweed."

"No," Aspar said. "The arrow could only be used seven times."

Fend waved a finger.

"Tsk. It's not like you to believe in the phay stories, Aspar. Who told you it could only be used seven times? Our old friend the praifec? Tell me, if someone could make a weapon this strong, why would they limit its use?"

He walked over to the pile of rot that was all that remained of the Briar King and lifted the arrow out.

"No," he said. "This will be useful for some time to come, I think. You still have the case, I imagine. Ah, there it is."

"Yah. Come and get it."

"Killed Ashern, did you? These Mamres monks are always a little too confident in their speed and strength. Makes them forget that skill—and in your case simple hardheadedness—can go quite a long way."

He fitted the arrow to his string.

"I shouldn't think this will hurt much, considering," Fend said. "That's fine with me. You took my eye, but I consider the debt paid now. I'm sorry you can't die fighting, but it would take too long for you to heal, and you'd continue to be a nuisance. But I can let you stand, if you'd like, so you can die on your feet at least."

Aspar stared at him for a moment, then propped his makeshift crutch under his arm and pushed himself painfully up.

"Just tell me one thing," he said, "before you kill me. Why Qerla?"

Fend grinned. "Really? Not 'Why kill the Briar King' or

even 'What's this all about'? You're still on the Qerla thing?
But that was so long ago."

"That's it. That's all I want to know."

"I didn't want to kill her, you know," Fend said. "She was
a friend of mine once. But I thought—*we* thought—she was
going to tell you."

"Tell me what?"

"The big Sefry secret, you dolt."

"What the sceat are you talking about?"

Fend laughed. "Living with us all those years, and you
never guessed? I suppose that's fair. Even some of the Sefry
don't know."

"Don't know *what*?"

"What we *are*," Fend said. "We're Skasloi, Aspar. We're
what remains of the Skasloi."

"But—"

"Ah, no, sorry. I've answered your question. That's all you
get."

He raised the bow, and Aspar tensed himself for one last
try. The dirk wasn't balanced for throwing, but—

Did he hear hoofbeats? He had a sudden image of Ogre
come back from the dead and nearly laughed.

Fend's eyes narrowed, then widened in shock as an arrow
struck his breastplate, followed quickly by another in the
knee joint. Aspar turned to find there was indeed a horse
thundering up behind him, but it wasn't Ogre; it was a dappled gray he'd never seen before.

The rider he recognized by her pale skin, black bangs, and
almond violet eyes. She had a bow and shot it again, this
time at Fend's head. But he twisted aside, and the arrow
missed. The horse thuttered to a stop, and she leapt off,
slinging her bow on her shoulder.

"Come on," she commanded. "Mount."

"Fend—"

"No, look," she said. "There's more. Get on!"

She had to swing the broken leg over for him; the pain was
so acute, he nearly fainted. But he saw what she meant: Sev-

eral armored figures were coming to Fend's aid. Fend himself was rising, fitting the deadly arrow to his string.

Leshya whirled her mount, and they were running. Aspar meant to take her bow and have a parting shot at Fend, but a hard bounce struck pain through him like a sledgehammer, and he sank away from the world.

Anne blinked in astonishment as the Sefry went down on their knees before her.

"I thought Mother Uun said that Sefry wouldn't fight," Austra said.

Anne nodded and squeezed her friend's hand.

"Which one of you leads?" she asked.

A black-eyed fellow with pale yellow hair and silvery mail dipped his head.

"I am captain of this troop, Your Majesty."

"What is your name, sir?"

"Cauth Versial, Highness," he replied.

"Rise, Cauth Versial," Anne said.

He did so.

"Did Mother Uun send you?" she asked at last.

"She told us what the Kept promised you."

"But that was only moments ago," Anne protested. "How could she know? How could you arrive so quickly?"

"We were waiting, Majesty. Mother Uun foresaw this possibility."

"I don't understand," Anne said. "Mother Uun said she was one of his guardians; she helped keep him imprisoned. Why should he go to her?"

"These are very ancient matters, Your Majesty," Cauth said, "and I do not understand them completely. Only that it was part of our geos that if he were ever freed, he could command us in one thing."

"And he commanded you to save my life."

"To protect you and serve you, Majesty."

"Then your service isn't over?"

"No, Majesty. It is not. Not until you release us or we die."

"How many of you are there?"

"One hundred fifty, Majesty."

"A hundred and— Do you know a way into the castle from here?"

"Yes, Majesty," he said, pointing. She turned and saw that she had practically backed against a massive metal portal.

"He's right," Alis said. "Prince Robert may have filled in every other passage, but he would not cut himself off from the Kept. Yet a key is needed."

Even as she said it, the door opened soundlessly, revealing an ancient Sefry so frail and thin that Anne was almost afraid that he was another sort of walking dead. His eyes stared blankly into nothing.

"Majesty," the old man said. "You have come at last. Welcome."

Alis made a sputtering sound. "You had your tongue cut out," she said. "And your eardrums burst."

The aged Sefry smiled. "I healed."

"You don't seem very upset that your charge has escaped," Anne said.

"It was fated," the Keeper replied. "I felt him go and came here."

"Command us, Majesty," Cauth said.

Anne took a deep breath. "Do you think you have enough men to take the castle from within?"

"With the element of surprise, I should think so."

"Very well. Cazio, you're with me. Austra, take ten of these Sefry for a bodyguard. The Kept said he lifted the glamour on the passages. Let's find out. Find Sir Leafton. Have him drain the lower passages and send runners out to bring reinforcements from the army. The rest of you, come with me. No, wait. My uncle Robert was with these men. Find him first and bring him to me."

But Robert, unremarkably, was nowhere to be found.

CHAPTER THIRTEEN

✣

MURIELE'S WATCH

WITH ALIS gone, Muriele felt blind to the outside world. She had her two windows, of course, and occasionally the guards would let something drop when they thought she was out of earshot, but she rarely trusted that, since anything she "overheard" from them might be part of one of Robert's games.

But something *was* happening outside, of that she was certain. Through her southern-facing window, she could see a good bit of the city, and for days something had been happening near the Fastness, in or near the Sefry quarter. Fires were burning, and she had glimpses of armored men and siege engines moving along the streets leading there.

Was it a revolt of some sort? Or had Robert become even more distempered and decided for some reason to slaughter the Sefry?

There was a third possibility, but it was one she hardly dared think about. The Crepling passage was supposed to have an outlet in Gobelin Court. Had Sir Fail returned? But no, he wouldn't be able to remember the passage. Unless Alis—

But Alis was dead. Wasn't she?

On that question hung Muriele's most slender hope. But locked in a tower as she was, she had plenty of time to entertain even the most forlorn possibilities.

The girl's last words had been in Lierish, Muriele's native tongue. *I sleep. I sleep. I'll find you.*

Alis was coven-trained and well versed in the virtues of a

thousand venoms. Might she somehow have only appeared to be dead?

No. That was an inane hope.

She conjured other scenarios. Perhaps Praifec Hespero had come to the conclusion that the Sefry were heretics in need of hanging and the Sefry weren't surrendering quietly. *That* certainly made sense.

Perhaps something had gone wrong with Robert's Hansan alliance and Hansa had somehow managed to gain a foothold in Eslen.

But no, that wasn't likely at all. Her marriage gown had been fitted, and the other preparations for her wedding seemed to be moving along smoothly.

Her east-facing window, while providing a marvelous view of the confluence of the Dew and Warlock rivers, did not tell her much at all. She very much wished she could see west toward Thornrath or north to the King's Poel. If there was a battle, that was where it would be.

She entertained herself as best she could and waited for something to happen, because everything was out of her hands now.

She found she liked that in a way. The only thing that really grieved her was that she didn't know what had become of Anne. The shade of Erren had assured her that her youngest daughter was still alive, but that had been months ago now. Had Neil MeqVren found her?

Even if he had, he wouldn't—*couldn't*—bring her here. So it was best to pretend that Anne was safe, protected, anonymous in some far country.

On what she reckoned to be the fifteenth day of Etramen, Muriele awoke to the clash of arms. Sometimes the wind would carry the sounds of steel from the city and the voices of men shouting. But this seemed nearer, perhaps in the inner keep itself.

She went to her window and craned her neck to look down, but since the Wolfcoat Tower was set in the southern wall of the keep, she had very little view of the inner courtyard. She could hear better with her head in the air, however, and she was more certain than ever that there was fighting below.

A movement farther toward the horizon caught her attention. Beyond the walls of the city she could see a bit of Eslen-of-Shadows, the necropolis where her ancestors slept, and beyond that the muddy, shallow southern channel of the Warlock. At first she wondered if a flock of swans had settled on the rinns, but then the perspective of distance worked itself out, and she saw that they were boats: galleys and canal boats, mostly. But she couldn't see any standards or sign that let her recognize their origin.

When the guard brought her meal, he looked frightened.

"What is it?" she asked him. "What's happening?"

"It's nothing, Queen Mother," he said.

"It's been quite a while since you called me that," she observed.

"Auy," he replied. He started to say something else but shook his head and closed the door.

A brief moment later it opened again. It was the same fellow.

"Don't eat it," he said, his voice pitched very low. "His Majesty said if ever . . . just don't eat it, please, Your Highness."

He closed and locked the door again. She set the food aside.

Time passed, and the tumult quieted, then renewed itself farther down, in the outer keep. She had a very thin view of the Honot Yard before the great gate of the outer keep, and she made out sun glinting off armor there, along with dark streams of arrows. Shouts of valor and shrieks of agony filled the air at times, and she prayed to the saints that no one she loved was dying.

It was nearly dark when she heard the ring of steel in the tower itself. She composed herself in her armchair and waited, with no idea what to expect, thinking that at least it was *something*, something Robert hadn't planned. Even if that meant they were invaded by slaughtering hordes of

Weihands, that was better than whatever her brother-in-law would think of next.

She winced as the fighting came to her door and a piteous howl cut through the heavy beams and stone walls. She heard the familiar scrape of a key in the lock.

The door swung wide, and the bloody body of the guard who'd warned her not to eat the food flopped onto the threshold. He blinked at her and tried to speak, but his mouth was pouring blood.

Just behind him came a man she did not recognize. He had a distinctly southern look to him, enhanced by the weapon he carried, the sort she had known Vitellians to wield. His dark regard picked quickly through the spare chamber and returned to focus on her.

"You are alone?" he asked.

"I am. Who are you?"

Before he could answer, another face appeared behind him.

In the first few heartbeats, all Muriele saw was the regal bearing and stern gaze. Saint Fendve the War Witch incarnate.

It was only as the woman lifted off her helm that Muriele recognized her daughter. Her skin was dark and weather-changed, and her hair fell only as far as her throat. She wore men's clothes and even a small breastplate, and one cheek bore an angry-looking bruise. She looked wonderful and terrible, and Muriele could only wonder what had eaten her daughter and taken her shape.

"Leave us for a moment, Cazio," Anne said quietly to the man.

The swordsman nodded and vanished back through the doorway.

When he was gone, Anne's features softened, and she rushed forward, meeting Muriele halfway as she rose.

"Mother," she managed to choke out, and then she dissolved into tears as they wrapped their arms around each other. Muriele felt strange, almost too stunned to react.

"I'm sorry," Anne gasped. "Those things I said to you. I was afraid they would be the last." She broke into deeper sobs, and months of isolation suddenly distilled in Muriele. Endless days of suppressed hope collapsed.

"Anne." She sighed. "It's you. It's you."

And then she was crying with her daughter, and there was too much to say, and not enough. But there would be time, wouldn't there?

Against all odds, they had time.

Leoff wiped tears from his eyes and tried to compose himself; it was nearly noon.

So much depended on such little things. Did Robert's executioner have any mercy in him at all? Probably not, and in that case, his night's work was in vain. Even if Ambria's murderer took a small pity on him, so many other things had to go right. He had to slip the wax into Mery's ears unseen and not have her protest or wonder aloud why he had done it. He had to be allowed to stand near Areana so he could cover *her* ears at the crucial moment.

Even if he managed all of that, he wasn't sure it would work. Some sound would enter their heads regardless of how well he prepared. It might be too much.

It suddenly occurred to him that if he could find a needle, he *might* be able to pierce Areana's eardrums in time.

But it was beyond thinking about now, for he heard boots thumping in the hall.

A moment later his door opened, and even the poor plan he had arranged fell into disarray.

For there stood Robert Dare.

The prince smiled and drifted into the room, glancing around it with a sort of mock interest. For a single, beautiful moment, Leoff thought the usurper had countermanded the executioner, but then Mery and Areana were escorted in by the killer, four guards, and Lord Respell.

"Well," Robert said, shuffling through the papers on Leoff's desk, "you do seem to have been busy."

"Yes, Your Majesty."

Robert looked surprised. "Oh, it's Majesty now, is it? What brings that on?" He glanced over at Mery and Areana.

"Oh, right," he said, tapping his head with his index finger.

"Please, Your Majesty."

"Oh, please yourself, you simpering dog," Robert snapped. "I am in no mood to grant clemency. Noose is my man. How would he feel if I gave him authority to make decisions and just snatched it away from him, eh? Well, that's not how you breed loyalty, is it?"

"Let it be just me instead," Leoff said.

"No," Robert said. "You've work to do for me, remember? Unless you've finished."

"I have done a great deal, but I am not finished yet," Leoff said. "And I still need helpers."

"You will have to make do with half the staff," Robert said. "But here, before you make your little decision, why not perform some small piece of this for me. I'm told the three of you make very pretty music together. Wouldn't you like to do that one more time?"

Leoff blinked. "Of course, Sire. And perhaps if it pleases you—"

"If it pleases me, then I shall take no *further* steps in disciplining you," Robert snapped.

Leoff nodded, trying to make his face into a mask.

"Very well," he said. "Mery, Areana, come here, please."

They came. Mery seemed puzzled but not particularly concerned. Areana was white and trembling.

"Leoff," she whispered.

Leoff pulled up the piece. "Let me add a few quick notes," he said. "I think Your Majesty will enjoy this best if you'll just give me a few seconds to confer—"

"Yes, yes, go ahead." Robert sighed. He walked over to the window and peered out, his brow furrowed.

"They'll be here soon," Lord Respell said uneasily.

"Shut up," Robert said. "Or I shall have Noose remove your tongue."

Leoff wondered what the exchange was about, but he couldn't spend any time on it. Instead his mind was racing furiously through the darkling chords.

"Mery," he whispered. "You must play this with expression. You won't like it, but you must. Do you understand?"

"Yes, Leoff," she replied primly.

"Areana, you'll sing this top line. Use the words from *Sa Luth af Erpoel.*" He dropped his voice even lower. "Here—this is *very* important."

He penciled in new notes on the last three measures. "You must both hum these beneath your breath. *Ontro Vobo,* yes?"

Areana's eyes widened, and he saw her swallow hard, but she nodded.

"All right, then," he said. "Shall we? Mery, if you would begin."

"Yes, go on," Robert said. He didn't turn from the window.

Mery placed her fingers on the keyboard, stretching to complete the awkward chord, and pressed. The notes throbbed in the air, a little menacing but mostly intriguing, illicit, the thrill of doing something a bit wicked made sound.

Mery's hands grew more sure, and Areana joined, singing words that had absolutely nothing to do with the music but that rang out with a stark sensuality that stirred sudden shameful desire in Leoff, so that as he added his own voice, he found himself helplessly imagining the things he would do to her, the ways he could bring pleasure and pain to her lithe body.

The song was a death spell, but it had to be built. Playing the last chord wouldn't do anything unless the listener had been drawn to the edge of the precipice.

Until now, the mode had been a modified form of the sixth mode, but now Mery took them with a frantic run of notes into the seventh, and lust subtly became madness. He heard Robert laugh out loud, and a look around the room at open mouths or tight grins told Leoff that they were all insane with him.

Even Areana's eyes sparkled feverishly, and Mery was gasping for breath as it all quickened into a lumbering whervel and then softened, shifting into the mode for which Leoff had no name, spreading out into broad chords.

The world seemed to sag underfoot, but Areana's voice was black joy. Fear was gone, and all that remained was the longing for night's infinite embrace, for the touch of decay, that most patient, inevitable, and thorough lover. He felt his bones straining to slough free of his flesh and then rot like tissue.

The end was coming, but he no longer wanted to sing the extra notes. Why should he? What could be better than this? An end to pain and striving . . . rest forever . . .

Distantly, he felt a hand grip his, and Areana leaned close, no longer singing. But she hummed in his ear.

He drew a painful, horrible breath and realized he hadn't been breathing. Shaking his head, he took up the hastily written counterpoint, though it seemed to cut through his brain like an ax. He doubled over, still humming, trying to cover his ears, but his hands were like stones, falling to the floor, and black spots filled his vision. His heart beat weirdly, stopped for a long moment, then thumped as if it would explode.

He found his face was pressed against the stone. Areana had collapsed beside him, and in a fevered panic he reached for her, fearing her dead. But no, she was breathing.

"Mery."

The girl was slumped at the hammarharp, eyes open and blank, spittle on her chin. Her fingers were still on the keys, jerking madly but not pressing to produce sound.

Everyone else in the room lay on the floor, unmoving.

Except for Robert, who still stood gazing out the window, stroking his beard.

Forcing his legs to work, Leoff crawled to Mery and pulled her down into his arms. Areana was trying to sit up, and Leoff drew the three of them together, where they huddled, trembling.

Mery had started a sort of hiccupping, and Leoff tried to stroke her hair with the club of his hand.

"I'm sorry," he murmured. "I'm sorry, Mery."

"Well," Robert said, turning at last. "Very pretty, just as you promised." He strode over to the man he'd called Noose, who lay facedown in a pool of his own vomit. He kicked him in the ribs, hard. Then he knelt, touched his hand to the assassin's neck, and moved on to Lord Respell, who had fallen against the wall in a sitting position. Respell's eyes were still open, frozen in a look of adoration. Robert drew a knife and cut the arteries in Respell's neck. A bit of blood drooled out, but it was clear no heart was pumping.

"Very good," Robert murmured, "All quite dead. Very good." He strode over to the hammarharp, took the score, and began rolling it up.

"This was just what I wanted," he said. "I commend you on a job well done."

"You knew?"

"I thought that old book might be useful," Robert confided with an awful false joviality. "Not to me, but I had it in mind that you might be able to unravel its secrets, if properly motivated."

"You're horrible," Areana managed to croak.

"Horrible?" Robert sniffed. "Is that the best you can do?"

He slipped the manuscrift into an oiled leather scroll case.

Leoff thought he heard a faint commotion coming from the door. Groaning, he forced himself to his feet and scooped up Mery.

"Run," he wheezed.

"Oh, come now," Robert began, but Leoff was concentrating on fighting the vertigo, on staying balanced on his legs. Areana was right behind him.

They broke out into the hall and stumbled toward the stairs.

"This is really annoying," Robert called from behind.

Leoff tripped on the stair, but Areana caught him. His lungs hurt, he needed to stop, but he couldn't, wouldn't . . .

Why hadn't Robert died? Had he plugged his ears? Leoff hadn't noticed anything.

He watched his feet as if they weren't part of him because they didn't *feel* like they were. He knew they were moving too slowly, as in a Black Mary. He remembered Robert's dagger, wet with blood, couldn't look back for fear of seeing it cut Areana's beautiful, soft throat . . .

Then suddenly they were face-to-face with men in armor.

"No!" Areana cried, and lurched forward, but the men caught her—and then Leoff and Mery—in strong arms.

It was then that Leoff noticed the woman who was with them, the same woman who had come to free him from his cell.

"You are safe," she said. "Robert is still up there?"

"Yes," he gasped.

"With how many men?"

"It's just him."

She nodded, then spoke to one of the soldiers.

"Take them back to Eslen. Make them comfortable and see that a leic tends them immediately. Her Majesty will want the best for them."

In a daze, no longer able to resist even if he wanted to, Leoff allowed himself to be carried outside to where many more men and several wains waited.

On the wagon, he let his muscles unfurl and lay back in the warm sun. Mery had begun to cry, which he hoped was a good sign.

"I never gave up hope," Areana told him. "I remembered what you said."

"You saved us," Leoff replied. "You saved me."

They rested against each other, with Mery between them. The sun on Leoff's skin felt clean and real, a thing apart from horror.

Except . . .

"I've given Robert something terrible," he murmured. "An awful weapon."

"You'll fix it," Mery whispered, sounding tired but firm.

"Mery? Are you all right?"

"You'll fix it," she repeated. Then she fell asleep.

It was silly, the faith of a six-year-old, but it made Leoff feel better. And long before they reached Eslen, he'd joined Mery in slumber.

EPILOGUE

BEST WORK

NEIL AWOKE to clatter and fuss. He was in an airy chamber, lying on good linen, and he felt terrible.

A glance around showed him that he was surrounded by the wounded. He tried to sit up and then thought better of it. Instead he lay there, trying to piece together his memories.

The battle for the waerd; he remembered that pretty well, but everything after was spotty. He thought he'd been on a boat at one point and had heard a familiar voice. Then he remembered leafless trees covered in black ravens, but that might have been a dream.

And then—*certainly* this was a dream—a very long run down a dark tunnel, crowded with people; some he knew, some he didn't. Of those he knew, some were dead, some still living.

He found he'd closed his eyes again and opened them to see a young lady in a wimple offering him water. He took it, amazed at how good it tasted. The sunlight coming through the window reminded him of pollen, of being very young, lying in the clover watching the bees work, before he had ever lifted a war board or seen a man die.

"What's happened?" he asked the woman.

"What do you mean?" she replied.

"Is this Eslen?"

"Yes," she said. "You're in the Liexguildhouse. You're very lucky. Saint Dun had you, but he let you return to us."

She beamed at him, then lifted a finger.

"A moment. I've been asked to report when you're awake."

She scurried off before he could ask another question.

But only moments later, a shadow fell across him and drew his eyes up.

"Your Majesty," he murmured, trying again to rise.

"Don't," she said. "Don't stir. I've been waiting for you to wake, and I'd hate to kill you with my presence. Oh, and you might as well get used to calling me Queen Mother."

"As you wish, Queen Mother," he replied. "You look well."

"You've looked better," Muriele allowed. "But I'm told you really ought to be dead. If the Church still held any sway in this city, you might be tried for shinecraft."

Neil blinked. She had meant it as a joke, of course, but he suddenly recalled his vision of Brinna's face. Brinna, who had saved his life once, somehow had used a part of her own life to do it. Could she have done it again, from afar? Did he owe her his life again?

"Sir Neil?" Muriele asked.

He shook his head.

"Nothing," he replied. "A wild fancy." His eyes felt tired, but he forced them open.

"You've no idea how happy I am you're alive," Neil told her.

"I'm very pleased myself," the queen mother replied. "And extremely pleased with you, my friend. You brought my daughter back to me. And you brought her back as a queen. I cannot think how to thank you."

"No thanks—"

"Of course," Muriele replied. "But you must let me do *something* for you."

"You can tell me what happened," he said. "I don't remember much after the waerd."

She smiled. "I missed most of it myself, but I've been awake to ask questions. After you fell, Artwair took the waerd with few additional losses and, having done that, managed to break the Thornrath gate in a matter of bells. Sir Fail brought his fleet in, and the wind was with them.

"While all of that was going on, however, my reckless daughter invaded the inner keep through the dungeons, with a relative handful of Sefry. Robert's forces were thin in the castle, however, either marshaling to fight Artwair and Fail on the King's Poel or dealing with the insurrection in Gobelin Court. So Anne and her Sefry took the inner keep without much trouble.

"The fight in the outer keep was bloodier, but Anne had reinforcements from Artwair by then."

"Wait," Neil said. "I'm sorry, Highness, but I think I missed part of your story. Anne went into the castle with Robert's permission, but it was a trap. How did she get Sefry troops? Or reinforcements?"

"That's a much longer story, and it needs to be told in private," Muriele said. "Suffice it to say that when the men on the outer Fastness understood they were being attacked from both sides—and that the monarch they were fighting for had apparently vanished—things ended without the horror of bloodshed we might have had."

"That's a mercy," Neil said, remembering the piles of bodies around him at Thornrath. He knew what she meant, of course.

"Anne is queen, then?" he added.

"Regent. She must be confirmed by the Comven, but that seems fairly certain, since Robert's cronies have been set to their heels or are imprisoned, awaiting trial."

"So all is well," Neil said.

"Well enough," she replied. "At least until Robert returns with the armies of Hansa and the Church."

"You think that likely?" Neil asked.

"Very likely, indeed. But that is, as they say, a worry for another day. Mend up, Sir Neil. We've use for you yet."

                              *   *   *

Aspar bit hard into the aspen branch Leshya had placed in
his mouth as she popped the bone in his leg into its proper
place. The agony actually left spots in his eyes, as if he'd
tried to look into the sun.

"That's the worst of it," she promised as she began to tie
the splint. Beneath her broad-brimmed hat she looked drawn
and pale, even for a Sefry.

"You shouldn't have left Dunmrogh for another month,"
he said. "Your wounds—"

"I'm fine," she said. "And if I'd stayed any longer, you'd
be dead now."

"Yah," Aspar said. "About that—"

"No thanks are necessary."

"Not what I meant."

"I know," she said, inspecting her splinting. Then she
looked at him. "I left Dunmrogh as soon as I could stand,"
she explained.

"Why?"

She seemed to consider for a moment.

"I thought you would need my help."

"Really?"

"Yes."

"That's all? That's it? You were full of holes, Leshya,
deep ones, and that needs time. What if you had died?"

"Then I'd be dead," she said cheerfully. "But I get feelings. I hear things on the wind, and sometimes I see things
that haven't happened yet. And I saw you, facing off against
the khriim, and reckoned you might need my help."

"The what?"

"The sedhmhar. The big thing you killed."

He frowned. "You *saw* me?"

"Through a teardrop. Up on the cliff, trying to get your
bow strung."

He shook his head skeptically. "You could never have
tracked me here that fast, not unless you left a day after I did,
and I know you couldn't have gotten up that soon. You were
almost dead."

"I didn't track you," she said. "I recognized the place and came straight here."

"You recognized the place," he said in utter disbelief.

"The mountain, Aspar. It has a Halafolk rewn in it: the first, the eldest of the rewns. I was born here. So yes, I recognized it. Once I was here, it wasn't that hard to find you, not with you calling attention to yourself the way you were."

He digested that for a moment. "And you came just to help me?"

"Yes. Witness—now we're leaving, and quickly."

"Why? They're your folk."

She chuckled. "Oh, no. Not anymore. Not for a long time. They'll kill us if they catch us, both of us, I promise you."

"Fend—"

"Not one of mine, I swear."

"I know that. I know where Fend is from. But he told me something just as he was about to kill me."

"That being?"

"That the Sefry are Skasloi."

She was reaching for her knife and froze in midmotion. Then she laughed again, picked up the knife, and slid it into a scabbard.

"I always wondered if you knew that," she said. "I thought you might, having been raised by us."

"No," Aspar said. "*That* I would have remembered."

"I should think so."

"But how?"

"Well, I'm not *that* old, my friend. I wasn't *there*. They say we changed our form somehow, to be more like you. To fit in."

"But the Skasloi were all killed."

"The great ones. The princes. And most of the rest of us. But a few changed, posed as slaves, and so survived."

She caught his gaze and held it. "We aren't *them*, Aspar. The Skasloi who enslaved your ancestors are dead."

"Really? And it never occurred to any of you that you might like to have things the way they were before?"

"I suppose some feel that way," she said.

"Fend, for instance? Your folk back in the mountain?"

"It's complicated," she temporized. "Sefry are no more simple than humans and not much more united."

"Don't put me off," he said.

"I'm not," she replied. "But we should start moving again. We'll have to be a lot farther from here before I start to feel safe."

"But you'll tell me as we ride?"

She nodded. "Plenty of time. It's going to be a long ride."

"Good, then." He reached for his crutch, and she stooped to help him, but he warned her back with his palm.

"I can do it," he said.

And after a bit of grimacing, he did, though he needed her help to mount.

He felt stupid sitting behind her, wrapping his arms around her waist. Like a kindling.

"We need more horses," he said.

"I've some ideas about that," she told him.

She nudged the horse into motion.

"He came to you," she said softly. "The Briar King."

"Yah."

"And what? What did he do?"

Aspar paused a moment. "You didn't see?"

"No. I saw him go to you through a gap in the trees, but I was riding fast. By the time I found you again, he was gone, and Fend was there."

"He's dead, Leshya."

Her spine stiffened.

"I thought I felt something," she murmured. "I'd hoped . . ."

"Fend shot him with the same arrow I used to kill the woorm."

"Oh, no."

"What does that mean?"

"I'm not sure," she said. "But it isn't good. It isn't good at all."

He looked around him at the trees, remembering the visions of desolation that had been the Briar King's parting cry.

"Maybe you'd better tell me what you know about that, too," he muttered.

She agreed with a curt nod of her head. Her shoulders were trembling, and Aspar wondered if she was crying.

Stephen looked up and smiled as Zemlé entered the scriftorium.

"Couldn't wait, could you?" she asked. "We've only been here two days."

"But look at this place," Stephen said. "It's magnificent!"

He nearly wept as he said it. The great room around them was fantastically huge, brimming with thousands of scrifti.

"You know what I found?" he asked her, knowing he was gushing, unable to feel silly about it. "The original *Amena Tirson*. Pheon's *Treatise on Signatures,* of which no copy has been seen in four hundred years!"

"Virgenya Dare's journal?"

"No, I haven't found that yet," he said. "But I will in time, have no fear. There is so much here."

"There's more," Zemlé said. "While you've been with your books, I've been exploring. There's a whole city out there, Stephen, and I don't think all of it was built by the Aitivar. Some of it looks older, so old that they have those stone drips and drops you were talking about on them."

"I'll see all of that," Stephen promised. "You'll show me."

"And there's the faneway they keep talking about."

"Yes, that," Stephen mused. "They seem altogether too eager for me to walk that. I'll want to research a bit before I do it. The faneway Virgenya Dare walked? We'll see."

"You don't trust them?"

"I don't know," Stephen said. "I wish I really understood what happened on the mountain the other day."

"I thought you said Hespero summoned the Briar King."

"I suppose he did," Stephen said. "I gave him the horn, months ago. And he did make short work of the khriim, which is, I suppose, why the praifec summoned him. Still, it seems a little odd. I thought Hespero wanted the Briar King destroyed. He sent us out to do just that."

"Maybe he hoped they would kill each other," she suggested. "And maybe they did. The Briar King shrank rather quickly after the khriim fell."

"Maybe," Stephen allowed.

"We're just fortunate that Fend and the twelve were able to break Hespero's forces."

"I'd be happier if they'd captured him in the bargain," Stephen said. "He can always come back."

"If he dares, I'm sure you'll be ready for him."

Stephen nodded, scratching his head. "So they tell me." Then he fell silent.

"Is something the matter?" she asked.

"You remember what you were saying about the traditions from the *Book of Return*? You called the woorm 'khirme,' almost the same as the Aitivar word for it, khriim."

"Sure."

"But you also mentioned another foe, Khraukare: the Blood Knight. You said he's supposed to be my enemy."

"That's what the legend says," Zemlé agreed.

"Well, the day we got here the Aitivar said they'd found the khriim and the khruvkhuryu. They meant Fend. 'Khruvkhuryu' and 'khraukare' are also cognate. Both mean 'Blood Knight.' But Fend claims to be my ally."

She looked troubled but shrugged. "You're the one who pointed out how untrustworthy the legends can be," she said. "Maybe we just had it wrong."

"Yet there's more," Stephen continued. "When I saw Fend's armor, I was reminded of an engraving I once found in a book and of the caption beneath it. It said, 'He drinks the blood of the serpent, and rises the tide of woe, the servant of Old Night, the Woorm-Blood Warrior.' "

"I don't understand."

"I think Fend *wanted* the khriim to die so he could taste its blood and *become* the Blood Knight."

"But how could he have known the praifec would summon the Briar King?"

"He admitted that Hespero was once an ally. Maybe he still is. Maybe this whole business was some sort of performance for my benefit. All I know is, something still isn't right."

Zemlé caught his arm.

"I've spoiled your mood," she said. "You were so happy when I came in."

He smiled and grabbed her around the waist. "I'm still happy," he said. "Look, whatever Fend is up to, he's pretending to be my ally, and for the moment, that's more or less the same as *being* one. I have everything I need here to figure out what's really going on, and I *will*. You were right, Zemlé. It's time I took matters into my own hands." He pulled her closer. "Specifically, it's time I take *you* in my hands . . ."

"You've certainly grown bolder, sir," she murmured.

"I'm in a library." Stephen laughed. "It's where I do all my best work."

ACKNOWLEDGMENTS

Thanks to my early readers: my mother, Nancy Ridout Landrum; my wife, Lanelle Keyes; and my friend Nancy Vega. Many thanks to Steve Saffel for seeing this book from conception through the editing process, and for his friendship and moral support. Thanks to Betsy Mitchell, Jim Minz, Fleetwood Robbins, and Nancy Delia for taking up the task of production under difficult circumstances. Thanks to Eric Lowenkron, copy editor. Thanks to Dave Stevenson for the snazzy cover design and Stephen Youll for another cool piece of cover art.

Special thanks to Shawn Speakman for his continuing support, and for creating and maintaining my website.

Thanks to Terry and Judine Brooks for wonderful company and conversation touring *The Charnel Prince*—I appreciate you letting me tag along, guys.

Thanks to "Debbie" Wan Yu Lin, Kim Tatalick, and Meredith Sutton for keeping Archer happy and distracted long enough for me to get some work done.

And another thanks, Nell, for everything.

Read on for a sneak preview of *The Born Queen*,
the next chapter in Greg Keyes's
thrilling epic
THE KINGDOMS OF THORN AND BONE,
from Del Rey Books.

HARRIOT

A SHRIEK OF PAIN lifted into the pearl-coloured sky and hung on the wind above Tarnshead like a seabird. Roger Harriot didn't turn; he'd heard plenty of screams this morning, and would hear more than a few more before the day was done. Instead he focused his regard on the landscape, which the west tower of Fiderech castle afforded an expansive view of. The head itself was off to the west, presently on his left hand, stacks of white stone jutting up through emerald grass, standing high enough to obscure the sea beyond, although as it slouched north toward town the gray-green waves became visible. Along that slope he could make out wind-gnarled trees, their branches all reaching the same direction as if to snatch some unseen prize from the air. From those twisty boughs hung strange fruit. He wondered if he would be able to tell what they were if he did not already know.

Probably.

"Not everyone has the stomach for torture," A voice assured him. He recognized it as belonging to Sacritor Praecum, whose attish this was.

"I find it dreary," Roger replied, letting his gaze drift across the village with its neat little houses, gardens, and ropewalk. Masts of ships stood behind the roofs.

"Dreary?"

"And tedious, and unproductive," he added. "I doubt very much it accomplishes anything."

"Many have confessed and turned back to the true path," Praecum objected.

"I'm more than familiar with torture," Roger told him. "Under the iron, men will confess to things they have not done." He turned a wan smile toward the sacritor. "Indeed, I've found that the sins admitted by the victim usually come from the guilty hearts of their interrogators."

"Now see here . . ." the sacritor began, but Roger waved him off.

"I'm not accusing you of anything," he said. "It's a general observation."

"I can't believe a knight of the Church could have such views. You seem, almost, to question the resacaratum itself."

"Not at all," Roger replied. "The cancer of heresy infects every city, town, village, and household. Evil walks abroad in daylight and does not bother to wear disguise. No, this world must be made pure again, as it was in the days of the Sacaratum."

"Then—"

"My comment was about torture. It doesn't work. The confessions it yields are untrustworthy and the epiphanies it brings are insincere."

"Then how would you have us proceed?"

Roger pointed toward the headland. "Most of these you question will end there, swinging by their necks."

"The unrepentant, yes."

"Best skip straight to the hanging. The 'repentant' are liars, and those innocents we execute will be rewarded by the saints in the cities of the dead."

He could feel the sacritor stiffen. "Have you come to replace me? Are the superiors not pleased with our work?"

"No," Roger said. "My opinions are my own, and not popular. The patiri—like you—enjoy torture and it will continue. My task here is of another nature."

He turned his gaze to the southeast, where a pale road vanished into forested hills.

"Out of curiosity," Roger asked, "how many have you hung?"

"Thirty-one," Praecum replied. "And besides these behind us, twenty-six more await proving. And there will be more, I think."

"So many heretics from such a small village."

"The countryside is worse. Nearly every farm-and-woodwife practices shinecraft of some sort. Under your method, I should kill everyone in the attish."

"Once an arm has gangrene," Roger said, "you cannot cure it in spots. It must be cut off."

He turned to regard the whimpering man behind him. Roger had first seen him as a strong, stocky fellow with ruddy windburnt cheeks and challenging blue eyes. Now he was something of a sack, and his gaze pleaded only for that dark boat ride at the border of the world. He was tied to a wooden pillar set in a socket in the stone of the tower, his arms chained above him. Six other pillars held as many more prisoners, stripped and waiting their turn in the spring breeze.

"Why do you do your work up here, rather than in the dungeons?" Roger wondered.

The sacritor straightened a little and firmed his chin. "Because I believe there *is* a point to this. In the dungeons they contemplate their sins and yearn for sunlight until they wonder if they really remember what it looked like. Then I bring them here, where they can see the beauty of the world—the sea, the sun, the grass—"

"And the fate that awaits them," Harriot said, glancing at the gallows trees.

"That, too," Praecum admitted. "I want them to learn to love the saints again, to return to them in their hearts."

"You filthy whoreson," the man on the pillar sobbed. "You vicious little sceat. What you did to my poor little Maola . . ." he shuddered off into sobs.

"Your wife was a shinecrafter," Praecum said.

"She was never," the man croaked. "She was never."

"She admitted to tying Hynthia knots for sailors," he shot back.

"Saint Hynthia," the victim sighed. His energy seemed to be ebbing as quickly as he had found it.

"There is no Saint Hynthia," the sacritor said.

Roger tried to bite back a laugh, then thought better of it and let it go.

The sacritor nodded in satisfaction. "You see?" He said. "This is Roger Harriot, Knight of the Church, an educated man."

"Indeed," Roger said. "I'm educated enough to—on occasion—consult the *Tafles Nomens,* one of the three books available in every attish."

"The *Tafles Nomens*?"

"The largest volume in your library. The one on the lectern in the corner with the thick coat of dust on it."

"I fail to see—"

"Hynthia is one of the forty-eight aspects of Saint Sefrus," Roger said. "An obscure one, I'll grant you. But I seem to recall that one ties knots to her."

Praecum opened his mouth in protest, closed it, then opened it again.

"Saint Sefrus is male," he finally said.

Roger wagged a finger at him. "You're guessing that, based on the Vitellian ending. You've no idea who Saint Sefrus was, do you?"

"I . . . there are a lot of saints."

"Yes. Thousands. Which is why I should wonder that you didn't bother to check the book to see if Hynthia was a saint before you started accusing her followers as shinecrafters."

"She gave sailors knots and told them to untie them if they needed wind," Praecum said, desperately. "That reeks of shinecraft."

Roger cleared his throat. "And Ghial," he quoted, "the queen, said to Saint Merinero, 'Take you this linen strand and bind a knot in the name of Sephrus, and when you are becalmed, release the wind by untying it'."

He smiled. "That's from the *Sacred Annals of Saint Merinero.* Was he a heretic?"

The sacritor pursed his lips and fidgeted. "I read the Life of Merinero," he said. "I don't remember that."

"The Life of Merinero is a paragraph in the *Sahtii Bivii*," Roger said. "The *Annals* is a book of seven hundred pages."

"Well, then I can hardly be expected—"

"Tell me. I've noticed you've a chapel for Mannad, Lir, and Netuno. How many sailors make their offerings there before going out to sea?"

"Few to none," Praecum exploded. "They prefer their sea-witches. For twenty years they've spurned—" he broke off, his face red, his eyes bugged half from their sockets.

"Truth?" Roger asked mildly.

"I have done what I thought best. What the saints wished of me."

"So you have," Roger replied. "And that clearly is neither here nor there as concerns the truth."

"Then you have come to—to . . ." His eyes were watery, and he was trembling.

Roger rolled his eyes. "I don't care about you, or this poor bastard's wife, or whether every person you've hanged was innocent. The fact that you're an ignorant butcher *is* the reason I'm here, but not for any of the reasons you fear."

"Then why, for pity's sake?"

"Wait, and I promise you will see."

A bell later, his promise was kept.

They came from the south, as Harriot reckoned. There were around half a hundred of them, most in the dark orange tabards of the Royal Light Horse, riding boldly out of the forest and up to the gates of the castle. As they drew nearer he saw that ten of them wore the full lord's plate of knights. There was a single unarmored fellow appareled in the Vitellian manner, complete with broad-brimmed hat. Next to him was the most singular of the riders, a slight figure in a breastplate with short red hair. At first he thought the person a page or squire, but then—to his delight—he realized who it actually was.

I was right, he thought, trying not to feel smug.

"It appears Queen Anne herself has come to pay you a visit," he told the sacritor.

"Heresy," the sacritor muttered. "There is no Queen Anne."

"The Comven crowned her," Harriot pointed out.

"The Church does not recognize her authority," Praecum countered.

"I'll enjoy you telling her that," Harriot replied. "You and your fifteen men."

"Up there," a clear, feminine voice shouted. "Is one of you the sacritor of this attish?"

"I am," Praecum replied.

From his vantage, Harriot couldn't make out much about her features, but even so he felt a wintry chill, and her eyes seemed somehow darker.

"M-Majesty," the sacritor added. "If you wait but a moment, I can offer you the humble hospitality of my poor attish."

"No," the woman replied. "Wait where you are. Send someone down to show us the way up."

Praecum nodded at one of his men, then began rubbing his hands nervously.

"That was a quick change of mind," Harriot observed.

"As you said, we're outnumbered."

"Not if the saints are on our side," Harriot replied.

"Do you mock me?"

"Not at all."

The sacritor shook his head. "What can she want here?"

"You haven't heard about Plinse, Nurthwys, and Saehaem?"

"Towns in Newland. What about them?"

"You've really no better ear for news than that?"

"I have been quite occupied here, sir."

"So it appears."

"What do you mean?"

Harriot heard clattering on the stairs.

"I think you'll find out in a moment," he remarked. "Here they come."

Harriot had never met Anne Dare, but he knew quite a bit about her. She was seventeen, the middle daughter of the late William II. Reports by Praifec Hespero and others described her as selfish and willful, intelligent but uninterested in using her intelligence, least of all for politics, for which she had no inclination whatsoever. She had vanished from sight around a year ago, only to turn up at the Coven Saint Cer, where she was being trained in the arts of the Dark Lady.

Now it seemed she took a great deal of interest in politics. Perhaps it was the slaughter of her sisters and father that spurred it, or the numerous attempts on her own life. Perhaps it was something the sisters of Saint Cer had done to her.

Whatever the case, this was not the girl he had read about.

He hadn't expected freckles, although he knew she was fair-skinned and red-haired and those things usually went together. Her nose was large and arched enough that if it were a bit bigger, one might call it a beak, but somehow it fit pleasantly below her sea-green eyes, and though she wasn't classically beautiful like her mother, there was an appeal about her.

She focused her gaze on Praecum. She didn't say anything, but the young man at her side placed his hand on the hilt of his rapier.

"Her Majesty, Anne I of Crotheny," he said.

Praecum hesitated, then went down on his knee, followed by his men. Harriot followed suit.

"Rise," Anne said. Her gaze wandered over the tortured souls on the rooftop.

"Release these people," she said. "See that they are treated."

Several of her men broke away from her group and began to do that.

"Majesty—"

"Sacritor," Anne said. "These people are my subjects. Mine. My subjects are not detained, tortured, or murdered without my consent. I do not remember you asking my consent."

"Majesty, my instructions come from z'Irbina and Fratrex Prismo, as you must know."

"Z'Irbina is in Vitellia," she replied. "This is Hornladh, in the empire of Crotheny, and I am its empress."

"Surely, Majesty, the holy Church is above temporal rulers."

"Not in Crotheny," he said. "Not according to my father, not according to me."

The sacritor lowered his head. "I am a servant of the Church, Majesty."

"That's immaterial to me. You are accused of torture, murder, and treason. We will try you tomorrow."

"As you tried the sacritors of Plinse, Nurthwys, and Saehaem?"

Her gaze switched to him, and he felt a chill. There was still something of a girl in there, but there was something else, too, something very dangerous.

"Who are you?" she demanded.

"Sir Roger Harriot," he replied. "Knight of the Church, in service to his grace Supernnirus Abullo."

"I see. Sent by z'Irbina to aid in this butchery?"

"No, Majesty," he replied. "That's not my business here."

"What is your business, then?"

"I and forty-nine other knights of the Church were sent to aid His Majesty Robert in keeping the peace."

"Yes," Anne said. "I remember now. We were wondering what happened to you."

"We got word that things had changed Eslen."

"And so they did," Anne replied. "The usurper is fled, and I have taken the throne my father meant me to have." She smiled thinly. "Did you think you would be unwelcome?"

"That occurred to my liege," Harriot admitted.

"Have your companions returned to z'Irbina, then?"

"No, Majesty. We have been waiting."

"For what?"

"For you."

Her eyebrows lifted, but she didn't say anything.

"You're an unusual queen," Harriot went on. "You personally led the invasion of Eslen castle. Since taking the crown, you have managed a number of these visits to interfere with the resacaratum. We thought that, given your pattern, our friend Praecum here would eventually prove irresistible."

"Well, you were right about that," Anne said. "So this was all a trap, then."

"Yes, Majesty. And now you are surrounded. I urge you to surrender to my custody, and I promise you will not be harmed."

"Not until I've been convicted of shinecraft, you mean?"

"That I cannot speak to."

Praecum had regained a little colour. "You were serious, sire Harriot! The saints are with us. Forty-nine knights—"

"Each with a guard of ten, all mounted," Harriot finished.

"That makes—" Praecum's lips moved silently. "Five hundred."

"Yes," Harriot replied.

Anne smiled. "How convenient that I brought two thousand, then."

Harriot all but felt the heart stop in his chest.

"Majesty?"

"This was indeed a trap, Sir Harriot," she said. Something tightened around her eyes, and then she reached forward so the heel of her hand came against his forehead.

He felt the bones in his skin go suddenly heavy and febrile. He fell to his knees, but she did not release the contact. His skin felt everywhere stung, his lungs seemed full of flies. And in his head . . .

He saw Abullo's host in their camp, waiting for the morning, some sleeping, some on watch. He seemed to be one of the watchmen, suddenly crushed down by this same black torpor, and he watched, uncaring, as nimble shadows slipped into the camp, slitting the throats of the sleeping and waking alike. Some woke and managed to fight, but it wasn't long before all five hundred were dead. The eyes he watched through dimmed, and he felt himself dragged along as if by a swift river, and screamed . . .

He came back to the sunlight gasping, watching the distant corpses swinging from their branches. His breeches were wet.

He looked up at the queen, and her smile broadened into a terrible thing.

"Now about your surrender," she began.

Harriot summoned a dogged reserve of will. "Do you understand what you've done?" He gasped. "The full wrath of the Church will fall on you now. There will be holy war."

"Let z'Irbina come," she replied. "I have seen enough of their work. Let them come, and receive the justice they deserve."

Harriot steadied his breath and felt his fever fade. "That's bold talk," he said. "How is the Hansan fleet?"

"Encamped along the coast, as you must know," Anne replied.

"And you truly believe you can fight Hansa and the holy Church?"

Her gaze intensified, and he flinched. It took all he had in him not to cower.

"What do you think?" she asked, softly.

I think you are mad, he silently opined, but he could not say it.

She nodded, as if she heard him anyway. "I've a mind to let you return to z'Irbina," she said. "So you can tell them what was done and said here. And let me add this; from this moment, all servants of the Church in z'Irbina shall either renounce their allegiance to that corrupt institution or leave our borders within the nineday. Beyond that time, any churchman—regardless of rank—will be arrested, imprisoned, and tried for treason against the empire. Is this clear enough for you to repeat, Sir Roger?"

"Very clear, Majesty," he husked.

"Very well. Go. As you've pointed out, I've other things to attend to now."

They let him keep his horse and arms. He went to the camp, and found the bodies where they had fallen, most still in their blankets. The field was thick with ravens, and the clouds threatened rain.

Roger sat there for a few moments as the earth seemed to tilt. He didn't know if Anne really understood what would happen now; even he couldn't imagine the full scope of the slaughter that was now inevitable. The five hundred who had died here weren't even a start.